The
Secret
Country

The Secret Country

FRANK O'NEILL

CROWN PUBLISHERS, INC.   NEW YORK

Author's Note: This is a work of fiction. Except for historical personages, none of the characters is intended to represent any real person, living or dead. These imagined characters do, however, live in a real world. License has been taken with the organizational structure of the CIA and the KGB in Germany, but the governmental restrictions placed on the citizens of the East German state at this date, in particular the fortified frontier, are to the best of my knowledge accurately represented. To my knowledge there is no known weapon like PSYCHIC, but if the lives of real people were to be affected by such a device, it would not be a unique event.

Published by Crown Publishers, Inc., 225 Park Avenue South, New York, New York 10003 and represented in Canada by the Canadian MANDA Group

CROWN is a trademark of Crown Publishers, Inc.

Manufactured in the United States of America

Library of Congress Cataloging-in-Publication Data

O'Neill, Frank.
    The secret country.

    I. Title.
PS3563.N495S4   1988   813'.54   87-16175
ISBN: 0-517-56728-8

Book design by June Marie Bennett

10 9 8 7 6 5 4 3 2 1

First Edition

*To Andrew Winser
with thanks long overdue.*

The
Secret
Country

Prologue

The wind gust destroyed the map. The two days of rain had made it as slimy as rotten wood and as soft as oatmeal. He had taught his stiffened fingers to cradle it as he drew it from a pocket, to touch it gently as a wound. Kneeling in the ditch now, he had checked the roads and the watchtowers around the border village, Palingen, whose pale lights he could see against the tossing pinewood. The forest, he knew already, extended a kilometer and a half to the frontier near Lübeck. He raised the map to fold it. He was a city boy; he did not listen to the gathering shriek of the pines. A blast from the Baltic flung itself upon him, rattled the leaves on the ditch bank by his chin. The map billowed, split, whipped, disintegrated. He looked unbelievingly between his hands. He saw only the wet, flat fields, the driving rain, the howling forests, and—barely perceptible, like a sickly dawn—the floodlights of the new frontier behind.

He stayed shocked and still. The death of the map seemed to him a last deprivation, a final loneliness. It did what his sodden clothes, his beginning fever, his hunger, the lead in his limbs, his weary terror so far had not. He had gone through the rain, the land, the danger, with the tottering inexorability of a failing clockwork mouse. Now he threw the scraps from his hands and stuck his head toward the frontier and shouted into the black wind, "Bastards! Murderers!" And then with more conviction and repeated into hysteria, "Thieves! Thieves! Thieves! Thieves!"

Only his head and shoulders stuck up out of the ditch. The shoulders were small and sharp and moved fiercely with each shout. His fever made it sound like a dry barking.

He had been hiding for four days now. For two days he had been without a plan. He had intended to cross on Monday night, much farther south, south of Hamburg, where West Germany juts into East Germany near the town of Lüchow. He had known so little. "The frontier has been fortified," he had read, like everybody else, together with the supporting drivel about "fascist infiltration" and "national defense." He could barely remember what he had thought it would be like. Some sentry boxes, barbed wire of sorts, barriers on the roads, some police, some dogs. It was for the dogs that he had brought the knife. The fully sealed frontier, after all, was only a year old.

1

So that at his first sight of it he had recoiled, thinking that he had blundered into some special place. He turned north. He had to walk. His passport was not valid in the frontier regions; he was afraid of the bus or train. He walked on the flat Mecklenburg farm roads where the gray sky lowered on his head. He felt as though fingers from it could pluck him from the road. He walked north twenty kilometers. He had the map, a treasure as precious and forbidden as a gun.

But the frontier was always the same. Exclusion zone, a fence, five kilometers of patrolled country, trip wires, guard towers, floodlights, a military road, a sloping parapet, a rearing fence of heavy wire. Beyond that, he could not see. And—at first most frightening of all—between the parapet and the military road lay a fifty-meter strip of raw, bare earth. It lay across the land, passive and blandly murderous. Mines. He could not face it. It lay to the north and the south. He turned north.

Tuesday, at dawn, he ate the last of his food. His legs were caked with mud. His clothes were torn. They would be looking for him. He did not dare go to a village or a farm.

On Tuesday morning it began to rain. It did not stop. It was a cold October. In a few hours now it would be Wednesday's dawn.

He crawled out of the ditch. He set off toward the wood.

All Wednesday, he lay in a hole. He had found it in the pinewood at first light. He had begun to cough. It sounded explosive, but the wind must have kept it from the patrols. His hole smelled of earth and sickness. He had not dared come out of it in daylight. Inside his wet clothes, he ached with thirst. His eyes wept. He had no strength. He was not thinking well. Trickles of rainwater ran from time to time down his ribs; he shuddered and his lungs stabbed him. Farther north, the frontier became a river, then an estuary, then the October sea. His body turned to ice at the thought.

He could not turn south again. Here was his last chance to cross by land.

Night came.

He had never been so close. Ten meters to the edge of the forest, twenty to the inner fence. He could see the clods of plowed earth on the mine strip. When the patrol truck with the searchlight on its roof drove by he could see the rain on the driver's slicker. For the first time, he could see the West. Through the four-meter-high chain-link fence, through the dead illumination of the strip, he could see small, swift, vagrant lights; a Western road, Western lives in motion like thoughts in the night. And in between, the lights of the border shone steadily, north and south, fifteen hundred kilometers. The trucks rolled on their appointed beats. The searchlights turned. The watchtowers in their hundreds were duly manned. The fifty thousand border troopers kept their watches and reliefs. Behind him, the People's Police, with reports and radios and dogs and cars, swept the roads and towns. The State prospered.

He looked at it with hatred as dry as cinders. With hatred he could harden his will to bone. With hatred he could chance the mines, whose impacted anger he now felt as like his own. He felt the blade of the knife by his leg.

He had once been a Party member. The Party had been his life. Marxist-Leninism had been his faith, literally from his mother's knee. East Germany behind him, the frontier at his face, had both been his. He had been a guardian of the State until, two years ago, at Party headquarters, he had refused to falsify a report. His name was Oswolt Krel and he was twenty-three.

At two in the morning, he crawled out.

Corporal Dieter Benecken liked to ride his machine at night. Then he felt himself flying alone down a ribbon of light, the frontier. The watchtowers passed like distant harbors. The motorcycle growled and thumped on the communication road between the two fences and gave a feel of motion headlong and precise. The fields and forests were black except for the edge where the frontier light spilled over—there, a shadowland.

He was a good soldier of the Border Troops. He was proud of his service.

He was riding dispatch tonight. There was a report of the disappearance of a former Party member, one Oswolt Krel, young but with past access to Party files, whose escape would be particularly undesirable. It had taken a day to find and reproduce an up-to-date photograph. The copies had just arrived from Berlin. Corporal Benecken was urgently distributing them along forty kilometers of frontier.

He rode watchful but rapt by speed, buffeted by the near-gale, his eyes mainly on the rough surface of the lighted road with only a sidelong watch into the gloom. But suddenly, topping a rise, he saw a movement: a panicked scurrying below and ahead of him from the inner fence, through the shadows, back into the wood.

This was not unusual. Badgers, foxes, bucks would sometimes run against the fence. Corporal Benecken had taught himself this:

in the night, terrified animals look like blocks or shadows; terrified men look like spiders.

He thought this was a man.

He twisted the throttle; the machine reared and leaped. He reached the place; he braked so that it spun. He cut the engine; at once he was a man alone in front of a night wood in a wind.

For a second he still sat. Two-way radios were bulky; dispatch bikes carried none. By standing order, unless the target could be shot at once, he should ride to the watchtower a kilometer and a half away, report, and let the search be raised.

The man had just entered the wood. In five minutes he could be deep within it. Conditions were difficult for dogs. The frontier was not everywhere as impassable as could be wished. Escapes happened.

The man could be he whose photographs Corporal Benecken was carrying. His arrest could make Corporal Benecken a sergeant. Corporal Benecken had an automatic rifle. Party types were never dangerous.

But he had not counted on the step from the light into the wood. He looked once behind him for reassurance to the high, straight fences. His foot stumbled. Wet branches brushed his face. Smells of fungus replaced the tang of gasoline. He waited for his eyes to adjust. Boughs and brambles caught the pale light of the frontier and writhed back into blackness ahead. He listened. The wind surrounded him. He had his rifle raised now, its muzzle searching blindly. His footing was unsure. He crept forward. The dark came in behind him. He touched the flashlight on his belt.

All at once he froze. He felt certain that a man was very close. His hand clutched at the curtain of wind around him. His hand searched for the flashlight and sprang back to the rifle. The human presence turned thick with menace, stayed thin as air. His back crawled. Though Corporal Benecken was neither a coward nor inept, he felt foolish and afraid.

And then he saw a quick shaking of the undergrowth at the limit of his sight. The impression of a moving body separate from the trees.

Now he was a soldier. His left foot flowed forward, his weight steadied, he was in marksman's form. The good Kalashnikov settled of itself, with its smooth stock and grip banishing the wood. He felt the fugitive's back within his sights. He fired; on automatic, the rifle pressed his shoulder. The clean smell of cordite wiped away the wet leaves. He saw something stop, pitch forward. He lowered the rifle. He heard faintly a sobbing breath. Then nothing. Nothing moved.

He lowered the rifle. He smiled seriously at his success. *Not so bad*, he thought. Flashlight in hand, he moved forward.

His aim had been good. The flashlight led him through the thicket to his prize. He stood over it, cursing: a fine dead doe.

He looked suddenly behind him.

Oswolt Krel lay behind the dune. Rain had given way to a cold, high wind. The stars were clear. He tried to bury himself in the sand. He was shaking with fever. He hardly knew whether he was burrowing into the dune or being convulsed with trembling.

But he had used the knife. A little north of the forest he had come upon a farmhouse. A chained dog barked at him. He ran back into the wood. But he saw that the dog's bark brought no one and that the dog had a bowl of food. His stomach churned. He crept toward the house. He walked toward the dog. He saw the dog's wet mouth lunge at him on the chain and then its eyes turn suddenly afraid. He ran the knife through its chest, straight out through its quarters. He pushed it aside. He wiped the knife. He scooped the swill in the bowl into his mouth. More than sustaining him, it had redeemed his cowardice with the guard.

Not cowardice, quite. The truth was worse. He had stood close to the man's shoulder, smelled the sweat in his uniform, seen the fear in his hands. The knife was raised. The man could never have brought his rifle around in time. He could have killed him silently and escaped. More, he could have used his clothes, his gun, his machine, something; he could have improved his plan.

But he had watched his face. Sober, mastering fear, alive with duty. His own age. A servant of the State, a guardian of the country, a frugal country of forests and farms and schools and cities, of the socialist hope believed in and worked for, of small rewards and brave dreams; his own, all but twenty meters of it behind him now, the only country he had ever known. His heart had suddenly gone out in kinship. It rose above the horrible betrayal to the years of his happy duty, his belief. To kill this soldier would be to kill himself.

And the soldier, his other self, had coldly raised his rifle to shatter his back. And had smiled.

He followed when the guard went to the murdered doe. No purpose now; the burst would have been heard. He wanted only to destroy. But the man had turned. He was on his guard. He had the rifle. Oswolt Krel was no guerrilla. He faded into the wood.

*   *   *

So the week of torture had finally brought him here: the north, the sea, the Baltic beach, the end.

No directions. The coast, river, marsh, sea, mingled and twisted. Even his memory of the map had split now. The dunes stretched in front and behind. West? North? There was a village. He did not dare go to find its name.

But he had a pole star. Set off, as by black velvet, by the sea, a town in the distance glittered. He had seen nothing like it. It was not the frugal yellow light of cities he had known but a light like fireworks, like festivals, like crystal; light for the rich. It was the West.

Maybe it was Travemünde. He didn't know. It didn't matter. The beach seemed to lead him straight toward it.

He knew his brain was sick, his thoughts worth little. His stomach was suddenly touched with the fear that this was an illusion—no town, no lights. He guessed it wasn't. He could see no frontier. How that could be he could not imagine.

But he could still walk. He pulled himself out of the sand. Ragged clouds flew across the stars. The wind was scouring the sky. For shelter, as well as concealment, he kept behind the dune line. From patches of black weed he scuttled across sand. From time to time, the magic city reappeared.

And closer. The beach led to it like a silver street. He began to know that, crawling for two days in the confusion of marshes and beaches and lagoons, he had slipped through a hole in the frontier. He was beyond rejoicing, but a thought repeated like a dry cough in his brain: *I have succeeded.* He quickened his pace.

And so the realization, when it came, was more than he could take in. The beach curved slightly and when he had rounded half the curve, the city of light seemed to have a spill of harsher light below it. And then, he saw straight across the beach, two hundred meters away, like the recurring horror of a dream, the unchanging frontier still before him.

The shock of it pulled him to the beach. Without its background of forest or field, the frontier was grotesque beyond belief: the towers, and wires and fences frozen in floodlight on the empty beach, the sand castle of an evil child. A truck was parked in front of it.

He came to his senses and ran. He was deep in the exclusion zone, in full view of at least one tower—and there might be others, black against the black sky. He ran toward the dunes. He seemed not yet to have been seen.

The soldier, rifle slung, standing against a dune, had his back to him in the stance of urination. Oswolt Krel swerved. He had almost put a hillock between the soldier and himself when the soldier turned.

The order, then, that he had heard for a week in his mind with dread. *"Halt! Stehen bleiben! Parole!"* Halt! Freeze! Password!

It sounded like an order to a ghost. Oswolt Krel thought, *I must look like hell.* He choked back a crazy laugh.

The soldier moved toward him and unslung his rifle. An *Aufklärer*, a frontier reconnaissance scout, his uniform separating from the dune as he approached. His face firming, but still uncertain, curious, not entirely hard.

Oswolt Krel sank onto the sand. He looked up toward the *Aufklärer*. He babbled, "Almost drowned. Fishing boat. Freezing. Help me."

The *Aufklärer* stood above him. His hand was still on the rifle, but forgotten there. He looked down at the derelict on the sand, concerned, but still with authority. He said, "There is no fishing allowed here. Where did you come from?"

And Krel, with every muscle that remained to him, rose up, the knife blade first, into the soldier's belly, ripping upward, the handle straining in his grip. The breastbone almost knocked it from his hand. He sawed against it.

The soldier never screamed. His breath came in a shocked moan. But his hand tightened on the rifle. The Kalashnikov fired; its magazine sprayed the dunes before the *Aufklärer* dropped it. He sagged against Krel.

Krel drew the knife out of the breast and held back the soldier's head so that his throat was white above the army collar and brought the blade against it. The knife went through to bone. He dropped the soldier.

He had a moment of great peace. He was released. His old life was behind him. His anger flowed out with the soldier's blood; the debt was paid. The ties were cut with the soldier's veins; no doubt now that he would be free or die. He looked down at the crumpled body in the widening stain at his feet. He felt as much gratitude as he had ever felt.

The frontier was alive. The rifle burst had been heard. Krel heard an engine start. From the watchtower an arm of light punched forward, probed. He heard a siren gather to a shriek.

No hope in the dunes. The police would surround the district. None behind. The police in the village would be out already. On the beach he would be like an ant on paper.

He didn't choose. He simply ran, dodging the arm of light. He saw the headlights of a truck separate from the frontier. The wind had whipped snowy tracings on the chop, but the sea was deep in a bay here. No breakers.

The water dragged at his feet, and at his thighs. It rose to his waist and cut him like a knife. The city of light shone so close across the water that he could see movement in its streets. It laid a crystal path for him on the sea. A searchbeam circled and stabbed. He heard shots. He threw himself flat, swimming. His lungs caught fire. He gasped.

He must have been in a current. He saw the light skip, miss him. He faintly heard shouting, a curse. He swallowed brine.

He was alone. No voice. No light. The sea crawled and hissed. When he swallowed water he struggled. The sea slapped his face to and fro. He still swam, but sluggishly, as though the cold were a net about his limbs.

The current carried him, but he did not know it.

He was flooded with warmth. He remembered the cold vaguely. He did not want to think about it. He took a long breath mixed with brine.

A perfect whiteness was beside him. It didn't go away. Finally he looked at it. *How odd,* he thought. *A swan.*

He drifted farther.

His back dragged on sand. The chop broke over him, thumped his shoulders. The wind brought the cold again. A breaker buried his head. He crawled away from it. The waves still broke against his feet.

The man whose house was nearest liked Travemünde out of season and liked the beach at night. He was slightly drunk; he had been watching, in a soulful way, a white swan swimming in the surf. He thought Krel was dead, but he was a sensible man and when he had called the police he ran back with blankets. He was accustomed himself to hunting waterfowl; he knew how fast cold water kills. They nearly lost Oswolt Krel in the hospital in spite of this—pneumonia such as one seldom saw. But Travemünde, a desirable resort, had good facilities.

Oswolt Krel was the only successful escaper to come to Travemünde in that first year of the Berlin Wall and the additionally fortified frontier. On the other hand, he was fifth in the province of Schleswig-Holstein and fifty-eighth in all West Germany. It was not really difficult yet.

1

MAY 1984

Giovanni Sidgewick Stears, Boston Florentine and known since Choate as "Wop" among Wasps, sat in the massive comforts of the Drei Löwen, the inn of Lüderbach, half a kilometer from the West German frontier and eight kilometers from Creuzburg in the East. He had paced outside while the darkness fell, admired the red-roofed farmhouses and the village church, stood on the bridge while the wake of the willows turned silver in the darkening stream. The two hillocks between Lüderbach and the East melted into the night.

And then a strip of light, like a fluorescent snake, sprang up across the valley. From the Baltic to Bavaria, the East German frontier had turned its floodlights on and the border fence stood out black on the ridge before them. Wop Stears said quietly into the East, "Good luck," and suppressed it immediately as too hackneyed to hold good fortune. He turned back to the inn. He was cold. He was hungry and knew in advance that he would barely be able to swallow his food. It was a little after eight and he had time to kill. Captain August Herter of the East German army, defector and messenger to the CIA if he lived, would not try to cross for six more hours, and until then there was nothing left for Wop Stears to do.

═══

Captain August Herter had arrived in the area just across the frontier the day before. He had come most of the way from East Berlin by train and the last twenty kilometers on foot, much of it in hiding, and by night. The part by train had been just as memorable.

He had been seeing his country for the last time—quite certainly for his last time as a free man. He knew that he was a traitor to his fellow passengers, a commissioned officer attempting a defection to the West, but the thought was entirely abstract. He had looked around him slowly: at an old woman who smelled of camphor, at a clerk with angry short gray hair, at a young mechanic with a chapped red face and a bag of sweat-soiled soccer clothes. They were faces of three in the morning at railroad stations, eroded by anger and anxiety and fatigue. He could admire their endurance, admire their small acts of kindness among themselves, but their anger took away the light and it was beyond his strength or skill to give it back himself. He could not regret them.

The roadbed was rotten. His country staggered past. Now between Erfurt and Gotha, heading west. Through a little town, a muddy main street across the track, a pale girl wrestling a baby carriage through the doorway of a streaked brick house, paper blowing in the street. A dirty, unloved, unloving place, but he saw it now without anger and with pity, and even the bright new factory banner—*The Workers of the Thuringian State Carburetor Plant Ceaselessly Agitate for Peace*—struck him as more pathetic than insane.

The sharp diesel smoke of the East hung outside the window and stained the view. It crept in to mingle with bodies and tobacco. The train was full. That was good. On a route ending so near the Western frontier, papers would be inspected during the trip. August Herter had no real doubt about the false passport or the false employment record in the frontier region that the general had provided, but rushed Vopos—the Volkspolizei, the People's Police— would be the less likely to look closely or to remember him precisely later.

Since cadet school, August Herter had imagined the day of battle. He had imagined well, and reality was not entirely a surprise. His stomach was tight, his head was clear, and his veins were full of an alien electricity. This would in one respect be like the battle he had foreseen. Trained as an infantry officer in the nuclear age, he had always expected one desperate action in which he might very well die. He had not expected to be alone. He suddenly laughed to himself, which caused the old woman knitting beside him to look up malevolently; it had never occurred to him that he would feel much as he had felt five minutes before he had his first girl.

But still his chest had tightened as the Vopos came, though both were almost boys and as threatening as string beans. The old woman gave her passport with a tick of annoyance, like a nasty aunt, and the rest with boredom. The Vopo looked at his twice. Just inside August Herter's eyes was a full proposal from General Sucher of East German State Security, the Staatssicherheitsdienst, to the American CIA: a skullful of sirens, beatings, and arrests. The Vopo gave his passport back. General Sucher had even warned him, "It is hard for an officer to look like a mechanic. You may stand out a little. Do not react."

10

He had left the train at Gotha. Eisenach, twenty kilometers on, was the frontier, too obvious for him, and there were only villages in between. A blackened steam engine smoked on a siding; patches of its soot had settled on the crimson plastic flowers around Karl Marx's granite neck. Herter hoisted his small rucksack. Walking down the platform he thought, *From now on there are only enemies.*

He set off through the border country of Thuringia and Hesse, the loveliest and most innocent of German lands. His way lay through hills of apple trees and pine and villages of red roofs and timbered brick. Until Creuzburg, he could be a hiker. The exclusion zone began there, beyond the Werra River. He crossed that at night by the railroad bridge, reaching cover near the frontier by dawn.

Herter was a professional judge of terrain. For concealed movement, this terrain was tolerable, not good. A small, rural valley between hills rising to four hundred meters on either side. The frontier cut straight across the valley and, to the south of it, rose slightly up the flank of the ridge. He counted three guard towers, only one close by. The hills were wooded. That was good. He lay now in pines on the northern ridge. A company of violets flowered on a mossy rock and the green of the apple trees below him would have done for a girl's summer dress. He would stay there through the day. The woods were separated by open fields and the weather was clear. That was not good at all. But this crossing place had not been selected for terrain. The general's anonymous helpers in the West had found out that the mine strip in this small area was unmined and the Border Troops unit somewhat understrength. Very few others could have found this out. It was his margin. He would have to deal with the fence, the patrols, and the self-firing devices himself.

The landmarks were easy. Due west were two hillocks, one with a monument, and between them, the Western village of Lüderbach. Twenty degrees south, where the flank of the valley began to climb, was the Americans' forward observation post. Their flag, suddenly not the enemy's, rose from the top of a ridge in the pines. Ten degrees south of there, where the land before the frontier became steep and brushy, was his crossing point. A line between his present cover and that point would take him across fields, but the night and his clothes would be dark. The danger would be the fences—trip wires, perhaps sensors. But he was not an infantry officer for nothing. The distance was a thousand meters. He could move slowly. He could crawl.

All this was as the Westerners had said in the letter passed to him at the agreed place and moment among the Sunday crowd on the Alexanderplatz in East Berlin. He had touched it like a snake, pocketed it like a death warrant. He could have been arrested then and there. But no. The girl had looked like a Western tourist. No doubt that was how they did it. Brave of her, too. He could have been a trap. The accuracy of their information heartened him.

For the letter had promised also a diversion a kilometer south of his crossing. He had at first paid little attention. In his professional experience, such plans rarely worked. That was still his opinion. But as he studied the frontier, he had come to know that his life depended on the chance that it would work after all.

To move through hostile country and to control fear were both elements of his chosen profession.

He had never seen the frontier. He knew the procedure, at regimental level, for breaking out from it into the West, but he had never seen it and had not known quite what it looked like, though its elements had been recently explained to him.

What shocked him was the village in a cage.

A village beside the river, half-timbered, red-roofed, shaded by apple trees, with meadows sloping to a copse of willows by the stream where the goosegirl met the prince.

The whole, the church, the barns, the rooster, and the rat, surrounded by a four-meter fence of barbed wire with searchlights at the corners and guards at the gate. A half kilometer away, across green fields, was the frontier. It was as though right here, literally under Western eyes, his government had unmasked and chosen to treat its people openly as convicts rather than to risk a plowman's escape or to evacuate a few kilometers of land. He had run across the phrase "security of frontier settlements." He had never imagined what it meant.

The fields were farmed but the steeple roof had fallen, old oil barrels littered the green, there were no flowers, and, though the day was cold, the chimneys gave no smoke.

An old woman bent alone over a spinach patch. A man, questioned by the guard, drove a cart of manure through the gate. A carpenter morosely hammered the scaffold for a sagging wall. Later in the day, a youth and a girl walked slowly hand in hand to the barbed-wire gate. They looked through it and walked back again.

Easily in sight on the next swelling hill were the tractors of the Western farms. He saw a farm wife and her children walk out to the field to take their father lunch.

A village where Germans kept Germans like beasts in a zoo was the family's daily view, and August Herter's government did not care. Why should it care? The country was this village, enlarged.

Captain Herter, twenty-four years old, trained for battle, whose heroes were Rommel and von Moltke, remembered the pride with which he had sworn to defend this country, and, lying in the birdsong and balsam of the pinewood, he wept. His love for his general and his gratitude for being allowed to redeem his honor by his general's side overwhelmed him. It amazed him, like a miracle of nature, that honor had been vouchsafed him from a senior general in the heart of the Staatssicherheitsdienst, the SSD, the secret police, the prime force in the degradation of his country.

He got out a little Bible, blew breadcrumbs from its binding, and then read the Ninety-second Psalm. There was a lot in the Bible that he hadn't read yet, but he had read this before.

He studied the tactical situation.

———

Giovanni Stears studied it also, though like a playwright sitting in the back row of the stalls. He was cautiously satisfied. The piece so far held together. The actors seemed all right.

Nice place. Brick inn on the village green, paneling much in evidence in the dining room, even a fire for the May night in a hearth with someone's coat of arms on it. A plump waitress carried tankards and plates and dewy bottles. Looking pleased, the landlord, no stout host but a young man with a neat red beard, stood by the kitchen door, which let out a steam of gravy. The place was full.

Which pleased Stears too. His volunteer German ally sat at another table, sharing it in the German manner with a family of strangers and talking to them: father with gold spectacles on a round face, a succulent blond wife, and a really rather appealing little girl. Nobody would associate that table with the silent American gazing around the room. A zither player dressed as a local peasant played, of all things, "Amazing Grace." This was a vacation region.

Surprising how precisely one could read the words in faces. Yes, the father was quite right, he had recognized his table companion correctly. Stears's ally was the great photojournalist Heinrich Bessel. African famines, Cambodian wars, Nicaraguan Indians, one of

Khomeini's political jails: always the voice and lens of liberal humanity and sense.

Specifically, the sense to realize from such assorted horrors that the CIA might often be on the side of light and not the side of truncheons. Bessel did not appear to have that much sense; he had a libertarian beard and the scrawny, defiant body of the reflexive Left—but appearances, thank God, could deceive.

As could the CIA. As could Stears. The leading part in abetting Herter's crossing would be taken neither by Stears, who knew what Herter's mission was, nor by Bessel, who might have guessed. The leading role tonight would be taken by Dr. Oswolt Krel, the great professor of constitutional law at Munich, who was also the leader of a tried, discreet, apolitical escape-help ring; and who was most of all the German neutralist who publicly decried the CIA as the exact equivalent of the KGB. Dr. Krel thought that the refugee was a pacifist of private conscience and would not have touched the matter had he known otherwise.

Dr. Krel was not in the dining room. Dr. Krel, with his helpers, was in the chilly woods outside. This, underlining the deception, made Stears feel both guilty and triumphant about it. It was not easy to judge Dr. Krel and be sure one had it right. Oswolt Krel's escape as a young man twenty-odd years before had been marked by a courage even above the usual and an ethical nobility second to none. His brilliance as scholar and German stylist was not in doubt. His escape-help ring had become the most self-effacing, the most effective, and quite possibly the bravest of them all. Krel's insistence that it was for persons of private conscience only—which had almost come to mean for nobody who had publicly preferred Jefferson to Stalin—struck Stears as ethically snobbish and often vilely cruel; Krel's dogmatic "neutralism" struck him as sanctimonious and puerile. Stears respected Krel and was pleased to have hoodwinked him.

There was an exhilaration in it—to be unquestionably, superbly on the side of right and yet above the truth and beside the law. How better to bring in Dr. Krel and his network than the cause of a regular officer of the East German Nationale Volksarmee, the NVA, defecting for neutralism, for conscience, for humanity? Who better to bring in Dr. Krel than Heinrich Bessel, one of the consciences of the German press? Krel could hardly refuse. Especially since reputations are fragile and Bessel was closer to editors than Oswolt Krel.

At Bessel's table, the father shook Bessel's hand, delighted. What an unexpected pleasure to meet a famous man! The blond wife

14

warmly smiled. The little girl thought it was fun. A nice family, thought Stears from across the room, really.

The waitress leaned over. A telephone message for Herr Bessel. Might he be excused? Of course. Perhaps they are sending you to Afghanistan! said the father. Stears quickly looked away.

The waitress brought Stears's plate. Hare with wild mushrooms and *Spätzle*, which was what the kitchen steam had smelled of. Good, if you took away the pineapple slice and jam. Stears too, though less merrily, shared his table. A heavy man with violent bristles and a silent woman.

The man said suddenly, "American army?"

"No," said Stears. "I am just on holiday."

"I was at Stalingrad. It was worse fighting than anything you Americans had to do. Americans could not have done it." He nodded wisely. He was drunk.

"Terrible," said Stears.

Bessel came back from the telephone.

"After we finished the horses we ate the skin. We were glad of it."

Bessel headed for the men's room.

"When the skin was gone—"

Wop said, "Excuse me," and stood up. It was not polite.

In the lavatory, Bessel said, "They expect him to come over a little after three tonight. There will be no moon. They have something planned to give him a little extra time, but they won't talk about it. They are very close-mouthed, which is good, I suppose. I am to meet them on the road outside this village at four."

He went on soberly, a man to whom the world's horrors were daily work. "They also say that he may have a better chance than most but that they can promise nothing. It is more and more difficult."

Stears nodded. The men's room was cold and white.

He said, "We can only hope. I'm grateful. We're grateful. It won't be forgotten."

He finished his dinner without tasting it and amid silent, looming comment on his discourtesy from across the table. He went out to his car. Two guests, Bessel and himself, getting up in the middle of the night might be noticeable. He put on a sheepskin coat and sat in the car. The night would be long and cold. From time to time he got up and walked around the square. On the hill above him were the faint lights of the U.S. Army post, where there were weapons and skills and communications and men, all to be unyieldingly and utterly denied to the lonely man on the fence until he was already secure.

Meanwhile, Stears himself sat restive and idle and safe. This was not good, for he was prey then to the spirits of the night, like spiteful moths, that crowded around him whenever his belief in the personal valor of his work for the CIA wavered. The CIA was the exorcist of Stears's dishonor. He had been born of an expatriate Bostonian father—who had described himself to anyone who would listen as a refugee from Beacon Hill and banking—and the wayward daughter of a Tuscan count. Wop's youth had been poisoned by a wartime spent in Vichy France and then by years all but in hiding in neutral Switzerland. His father had exchanged a youthful reputation as Yale's best budding poet for a questionably fashionable prewar fascism, exercised on a dwindling private income in Europe's nicer cities. This had been followed by much less fashionable wartime follies that had landed him just short, in the victors' eyes, of legal treason. To the puzzled, then pleading, eyes of his small son it had made him the target of averted glances, cutting voices; a creature of anxious smiles, moist eyes, and eager handshakes.

There was worse. While Stears's American father had even to Cambridge eyes elaborately unmanned himself, his Italian mother's uncle, the Marchese Ferrara-Ugolino, had with singular tactlessness become an authentic Allied hero, a partisan, and a thrice-wounded captain of the anti-German resistance. Stears grew up with a paternity and an Americanism that became as nagging as an amputated leg. It had chased him from a prosperous career in his familiar exile, Switzerland, giving financial advice to Arabs, into freelance work for the CIA, thence into a poisonous tangle of real and deadly treasons in the regrettable North African kingdom of Berbia, and finally into the career CIA itself. The exorcism worked, but creakily.

Though the CIA was his exorcist he still resisted embroidering the flat reality of his work for it, but tonight the circumstances conspired. He had visions of his mother's prodigious uncle, his later boyhood's friend and terror; he saw him in sheepskin too, in the night hills, looking down on an Umbrian village and the line of German trucks. In counterpoint, and automatically, he saw his parents in their frivolous and fatal cowardice: the Paris café photographs of them among Dalí and Dada and Gertrude and Ford; his

16

pretty, silly mother, his witty father, the château and houseparties in Bordeaux while the rest of the world fought; and then the fading apartments, the friendships refused, the hateful letters, the exile that ended in death.

He shook it off more than once. What he was doing tonight was tinsel bravery: the danger was not his. Still, it was for honor of sorts, and redemption.

———

Shaking with exhaustion and bathed in sweat, August Herter lay in the brush. His back still felt the searchlight sweep across it in the open field.

Twelve centimeters from his face, a trip wire glinted between roots a handbreadth from the ground. He had seen it. He would avoid this one, though he did not yet have the strength. He imagined others around him. A spiderweb. He told himself, *Stop it. You are trained for this.*

0208. The diversion was planned for 0312.

The frontier towered over him. The brush slope rose another forty meters. But he could see it plain.

It was bathed in a cold, low light, like the hands of an alarm clock. That surprised him, but it was obvious when he thought about it. The searing light he had expected, so near to an American observation post, would mask the activities of the enemy on the other side.

The frontier was its own world, a broad and various landscape compressed into sixty infernal meters.

Access road. Mine strip. Vehicle trap. Main fence. All formerly just names, a scheme. All now here.

The vehicle trap frightened him, though he did not know why. It was the last element before the fence, a concrete ditch the farther side of which rose to form a low parapet. His muscles rehearsed it: take off hard and land with his arms well over the parapet and his toes with purchase on the concrete. It would not be difficult. But the concrete was as white as bone, and the trap looked like a mouth.

Between the brush and the access road, the grass was short. He would cross that on his belly as he had crossed a kilometer already.

But he could not crawl on the mine strip. His Westerners could be wrong. It would be a quick death, but he could not press his face against that smooth and deadly earth. Beyond the grass, he would abandon stealth.

And so now he raised his eyes, above the trip wire, as he had not let himself before, to the final fence.

And there they were.

Against the fence were three tiers of flattened metal boxes the size of a large book. The tiers were staggered; they formed a diamond pattern. From each box, connecting it to the next on its tier, ran three wires.

The boxes were clean and shiny. He had thought they would be black.

They were bombs. Called SM-70s, they were one of the developments of his country in the last decade, permitting both a more peaceful frontier, fewer defections among the Border Troops, and a reduced population in the prisons. There were fifty-four thousand of them along the frontier.

If one of the wires was touched, the neighboring SM-70s would go off in a simultaneous blast of shrapnel.

He had been shown how to disconnect them. There was indeed a way. He would test it while climbing the fence, in the light—and his back to the rifles if he should be seen.

He was not a suicide. The desperate action sometimes worked. Men have assaulted machine-gun nests with hand grenades and lived. He could be over the fence, he thought, in three minutes. If the diversion bought him the first of those unseen, it might well take more than two for the guards to get in range. Almost no shoulder weapon is accurate beyond three hundred meters.

0240. He waited. He dreaded moving. It occurred to him that he could regain his cover and make his way back to Berlin before the end of his leave. He would be a major one day, and a colonel. He saw himself as a colonel with one romance safe in his memory.

He saw the village in a cage.

———

At two in the morning, by the car at the edge of the wood, Dr. Ursula Hecht had looked at her watch. Her nerves were such that her stomach hurt. She chided herself. She was an anesthesiologist. Every day, she held the lives of patients in her hands more closely than she held the escape of this poor East German. But only at these times, when she was part of Dr. Krel's tiny, trusted band, did her nerves turn cold. It was not time to enter the wood. She made herself sit and breathe slowly.

This worked, and with it came a warmth of fellowship and love for her comrades. What an army! Carl Ringenhauer, high school mathematics teacher, with a neck like an old chicken and frayed cuffs. Emil Leuven, the one rich man of them, a carpet manufacturer with soft eyes and fine gray hair, who got out of his beautiful Mercedes with diffidence. Herself, whom Emil had held in his arms for half an hour on a dreadful night when a girl drowned on a lungful of blood on the mine strip while the guards closed in. Manfred Stolz, the apothecary. Very few, no one young, and no one a hero. So said Dr. Krel, her Oswolt.

Dr. Krel half turned in his seat and patted her hand. They were in Emil's car. It was cold. The rich lingering of cigars seemed odd. He said, "We do what we can, Ursula, and so does he. That is all we can do."

She said, "I know."

"And this one has a better chance than most."

"I know."

He took his hand away. She would have liked to hold it and would have done so still if they had been alone as she would have done once in company. At these times the extremity of his emotion and the rigor of the self-control with which he bridled it united in the remoteness of a star. The eyes in the thin, unmoving face looked sideways at the green figures of the clock, communing with time, with fate, with his own terrible memory.

She had shared that memory for twenty years: Krel's escape in the first year of the fortified frontier and the Berlin Wall; his exhaustion, cold, and sickness; his casting up on the beach of Travemünde opposite the East German shore; his refusal to take the life of an East German guard. She had learned the crevices of Krel's history through Oswolt's nightmares, which, sharing Oswolt Krel's pillow long ago, she had shared as well.

And shared his tension still through the brief nostalgia of his hand: the suppression of an anger that he found degrading and would not admit.

But he said calmly to Ringenhauer and Stolz, "Do not flaunt the flashlights. Keep your voices down. If you are obvious they may not believe. This has been done to them before. Don't worry. They'll see. They'll hear."

Both nodded.

"When you fire the charge, your part is done. Come back through the wood at once. At once, do you hear? They have shot through the fence before. You will see the car lights start forward through the wood. That is all we can do. It will certainly look like something. Perhaps it will be enough."

He turned to herself and Emil. "You know the crossing point precisely?"

"Yes," said Emil.

"This one will not get lost. Well, you know your jobs. Ursula, let us hope that yours will not be needed. Poor Ursula," he said. "I think it takes more out of you than out of the refugees." He patted her cheek. Her body smiled.

She shook her head quickly and slid out of the car. Her medical bag was in her hand. Her eyes were already used to the dark. She followed Emil toward the East, toward the frontier, into the wood.

There was so little they could do on these nights of fate.

She would not hear the diversion but the response to it. So would the refugee.

She sat against a tree, two or three meters back into the wood. Emil sat beside her. The end of the wood was the legal frontier, indicated by small striped posts. The fortified frontier was fifty meters back. The intervening countryside of East Germany was cleared of brush and clearly signposted for the visitor. *"Achtung Minen! Lebensgefahr!"*

It was psychologically very hard to convey to the refugees that the frontier and its horrors were not the end, that fifty meters more of deadly danger lay before them, and that the guards not only might shoot into the zone beyond the fence, but were under orders to.

Somewhere, opposite them in the brush, beyond the perverted light, was the refugee. She tried to imagine him.

She saw a searchlight spring out and swing.

0313. The guards in the watchtower had seen the lights in the woods to the south.

Urgent voices barely heard. An engine in the night. A light detached itself from the tower and moved fast. A motorcycle.

Come now! she thought into the night.

Emil's hand gripped hers. She heard, too, and froze. A lower, heavier engine coming closer from the north, beyond the brow of the hill. If the refugee did not hear it and moved now he would be in its path. And she saw a movement in the brush. And a blush of light over the hill.

But the refugee saw it too. The movement stopped.

A patrol truck, pick and shovel on its door, machine gun on its roof, lumbered past, whining in low gear. It left behind the sour smell of Eastern diesel. She thought, in the alien terms that she had learned, *A concentration of forces at the diversion zone. Good!*

And now he came. A man rose suddenly in the dead light. She could not see his face. He stood still for a heartbeat and looked around him.

Quickly! she thought.

He ran across the bare earth. She held her breath. She saw again the mangled body of the girl, blood bubbling at the mouth, and heard the nervous voices of the guards and the taut ones of the officers. Only a year ago. But it was true. No mines this time. He leaped the vehicle trap. No hesitation now. His courage raised her heart.

But now the horror. He was at the fence. She suddenly heard his breathing. It brought him as close as if his head were in her lap.

He cut the first three wires. She passionately watched his hands. She saw that he knew: the wires had to be cut as delicately as a vein. If they were pulled or twitched he would die.

He began to climb. He reached the cutters to the next wires. A bomb was by his face.

An explosion thudded to the south. This was the charge set off by Ringenhauer and Stolz to simulate a mine. His hand jerked in shock. *My God, they didn't think of that!* She shut her eyes.

But his hand had missed the wire. He cut again. Engines moved on farther to the south. She felt a moment of triumph that the legion of brutes beyond should dance to her friends' music.

More sounds now, behind and above her. That would be the Americans. She almost smiled. Her friends were waking up all Europe.

A trick of light now let her see his face. Young and rapt. She pressed it to her heart.

The searchbeam struck her in the face. The refugee, straight in front of her, was suddenly pitch-black, crucified against the fence in a searing light. She saw his blank hand cut again. He climbed. Engines bellowed to the south. A siren sounded from the tower, but that, she knew, was superfluous. Trucks had radios.

He had perhaps two minutes. His head was now level with the top of the fence and his hand was poised at the first of the top tier of wires. She found herself on her feet about to call out to him, but Emil stifled her mouth. He was right. Concealment was now unnecessary, but the refugee's concentration should not be jarred. There was still a live bomb on either side of him. She heard the truck change gear.

She saw the wires fall loose. One, two, and three.

And then she shouted, "Quickly, quickly! Jump from where you are! They will still kill you unless you get to us!"

She knew the peril in what she said, for she was telling him to run over mined land. But in truth the cleared strip was not heavily mined. It was necessary to keep it cut, and that had to be made easy and quick; Border Troops sent beyond the fence routinely defected. The truck and its gun were the danger.

She saw him look for her. His feet moved quickly up. When he was almost at the top, his head turned, toward the rise down the frontier. She saw herself that the brush at the top of the rise was touched with advancing light.

Emil beside her said, "The gun's on top of the truck. They'll see him any minute."

———

The sergeant said to Wop Stears, "He'd better move his ass. He better had. They got a gun on that thing."

Stears touched the sergeant's arm for silence. The arm was muscular and tense. The sergeant was a young Southerner with smooth cheeks and a solemn, guileless mouth. The medical corpsman beside him nodded agreement. Stears and the men were inside the wood, in darkness, watching through the boughs and brambles. Stears saw his defector, erect above the fence, stand like an emblem. Or a target.

The escaper's movements were now unsure. The top of the fence was round, quite innocent-looking, not spiked, but extremely difficult to get over without losing footing. He struggled with it, then threw himself across it and seemed to hang for a moment by a half-caught foot. He could not jump. He fell.

"Way to go!" said the sergeant. He murmured to himself, "Boy, I love to see that."

Ursula let out her breath. It was not such a great drop and he had time now even if he lay for half a minute, winded.

Until she heard his breath. It was a man struggling not to cry out. And saw him try to rise. He pitched forward and this time did cry out. She saw his left leg drag bent behind him.

The headlights of the truck shone over the hill.

And Time folded its arms. The refugee began to move again. He could not stand. He doubled himself up, moaned, straightened himself, cried out, doubled himself up, one meter. The truck was fully over the hill. A soldier, rocking with its motion, stood by the gun. Push, and the driver pointed ahead to the footprints in the mine strip. Moan, and the truck braked. Push, and the gunner pointed to the severed wires. Twenty meters to go. She could see his eyes. She could see the saliva on his mouth.

The gunner pointed to him. It was a difficult shot. A stanchion of the fence was in the way. He spoke urgently down to the driver. The gears clanged.

Emil put his arms around her. She saw again at once the broken girl and knew that she could not endure to see such a thing again. She pushed Emil's arms away.

The young man was a bare ten meters from her. She ran down the slope. She was not entirely reckless. To risk shooting a citizen of the West beyond the fence would at least require an officer's instruction, if only on the radio. She saw the refugee push harder, stretch out his hand.

The world turned red. The ground stamped on her. A terrible pain replaced her legs. Her brain was black but she opened her eyes. She was not near the refugee. She was on her back. There was a dense smell of earth and cordite. She felt herself flow out through her thighs. She saw Emil stand rigid, open-mouthed by the wood. She tried to call to him. She knew by now, a mine.

Stears saw a flash under the woman and she cartwheeled and landed like a rag doll while earth rattled down upon her. He stared, appalled. A black flow began around her skirt. He heard the sergeant say, "Shit!" and felt him move toward the wood's edge. He followed. The woman moved her head.

Stears caught suddenly at the sergeant's arm. "You can't," he said. "Stop."

The sergeant turned on him. "You want me to let her lay there?"

The woman seemed to try to look around her.

"It's an act of war, for Christ's sake," said Stears. "That's East Germany."

The sergeant pulled away and ran out into the open ground. Stears grabbed him from behind and, wrestling with all his strength, pulled courage, decency, and pity back into the wood.

Ursula saw the refugee bleeding from his face. *My God*, she thought, *I have killed him*. But Emil was now able to reach out and grasp his hand and pull him to the border posts. Emil was not alone. Other men had come out of the woods around him. She looked for her Oswolt but he was not there, and she felt the first breath of desolation on her. One man began to move toward her, and another shouted at him, grabbed his arm. The last thought of her life was surprise that he shouted in American.

"You bastard!" said the sergeant. He shook himself free from Stears, swung at him, then stopped and shook his head. His face was as crumpled up as a tearful boy's. "I guess you don't like it either," he said.

"I don't," said Stears. He thought, Not "bastard," Just "control."

"She saved him," said the sergeant. "They would have killed him. Those cocksuckers would have killed him right there."

"He's in bad shape anyway," said Stears. He motioned to the corpsman. "Let's get on it."

2

In the afternoon sun the chalet smelled sweetly of wood and creaked like a boat at anchor. The smell of medicine was sharp and new. Up from the village came the voice of the railroad announcer and the bell of the church clock. Three o'clock and the Munich train. Wop Stears went to the balcony and looked down at the baroque church, white and gold, the railroad station, the gabled hotel, the guests in boots and loden. Reit im Winkl, a safe and pretty place. The peaks of the Bavarian Alps were still grandly snowed, but in the valley the grass was tender. The air was cold for shirtsleeves.

He heard quick, light footsteps above. The nurse was moving. The patient must be awake. He climbed the stairs and went in without knocking. Until his chief, Brindle Woods, arrived from London, he was the master of the house.

August Herter's face, the soldier's tan lying over shock and pain, looked like ivory. He lay in the deep lassitude of the first return of strength. Under the covers, his leg was thick and propped. The eyes were large and deep as a stag's, and, for the first time, intelligent.

A tape recorder, patient as the nurse, turned in a pine closet, quiet as a mouse. Delirium had not been wasted.

Herter's injuries had been extensive but not extremely threatening, given the presence of an army ambulance a kilometer away. A compound fracture, an artery severed by debris, lacerations, and severe shock. An extemporized but unarguable excuse to have his man whisked by U.S. Army ambulance to the U.S. Army hospital at Fulda, bypassing for the moment the German civil frontier authority, the Bundesgrenzschutz. After twenty-four hours, the medical imperatives had shrunk to antibiotics, morphine, and nursing.

Stears had done well; Brindle Woods had said so. Brindle Woods, from London, had spun his finest web over both the Germans and the army. So that Stears and his man came to photogenic Bavaria, as planned, though in an unmarked ambulance.

Wop stood in the door, silently. There is a moment when the underlying character of an agent relationship—suspicion, coercion, symbiosis, or respect—is set, and this, while the stretchers and the sirens and the morphine began to fade away into the alpine air, was the time. So he looked at Herter as gently as at a sick child, as if to say, "Begin as you wish, you have paid already." The time for hard debriefing would come later, with Woods.

And Herter looked back as at the first inhabitant encountered on a new planet.

So Stears entered the first note on the fresh white page within him: *This one has not been in the secret country for long.*

Herter, on the bed, said, "Who was she?"

"A volunteer. A private person. A doctor. It was never expected that she would do what she did. I am told that they make a promise not to."

"And she is dead?"

"Yes."

"You did not send her?"

"If she had known of me, she would not have been there. Nor if she had known what you were."

Herter moved his eyes away, to the window, to the pasture across the valley. He said quietly, "Then is she the last of their murders or the first of yours?"

Stears said, "She will not be their last."

But he had mistimed it. Herter was still weaker than he had thought. This question must have roamed through the corridors of his delirium, and after it Herter's attention faded. Stears left the room. He stood in the sitting room on the well-worn rug, looking at the bookshelves: children's books, novels by Günter Grass—the most modern name on those shelves—memoirs of alpinists in Gothic type, dog-eared, the covers stained. A family's collection, but not his and possibly not anyone's. Parched for innocence or gladness, he looked through the children's books. He had slept the night before.

The door closed again. The nurse's footsteps came down the stairs. She was American, a tall, dark-haired, long-faced girl quite in place parking a bicycle outside a Slavic languages class at Vassar. She was a Company nurse with clearance.

He smiled at her. She looked back with severe gray eyes. She was first a nurse.

She said, "He's still in a lot of pain, you know. He's still in shock. He was moved before he should have been, and the morphine's been cut too low. He's not a tape recorder." A voice, too, of Vassar.

He nodded, accepting the accusation. "We can't risk his memory. He's got to be carrying a lot in his head, and some if it must be urgent. I can't have him drugged to the gills. It's better that he hurts than that it's wasted. Speaking of tape recorders, will there be anything on it?"

"No. Not a word. He groaned a little in his sleep. Incidentally, I tried him for English. No reaction."

"Good," he said. "I thought so." And then, "Keep it running, though. You never know."

She said, "Leave him alone tonight. If I can give him a good night's sleep, he'll be more use to you tomorrow."

"Yes. I had thought of that."

She smiled at him suddenly. He had entered acceptability.

"He's kind of a nice kid, you know. For once."

He nodded.

Brindle Woods arrived with the evening swallows and the evening chill. He came from Munich in a rented Mercedes with no driver, little luggage, and a bottle of malt Scotch. He looked exhilarated; this was a hard-edge operation. He looked good-humored; he had spent the day in Munich. He wore a smoke-green loden coat.

Woods looked at Stears in the chalet door. He said, "Is something wrong?"

"No," said Stears.

If he looked startled it was only at the coat, and at that only in the sense that a man who kept a suit of armor propped up in the hall could still unbalance you by wearing it to dinner. The coat hung as a fixture in Brindle Woods's London office. Never once had he been crass enough to wear it. But it hung by the London herringbone to suggest that Brindle Woods, old German hand, could walk at will out into the Cold War, into Wiesbaden, under the Airlift in the leaden sky, into the Gehlen compound with the Theatinerkirche on the skyline, indistinguishable from the rehabilitated native population if it ignored the Zippo lighter, the button-down collar, and the Harvard tie. It also helped him forget that the coyer sensibilities of the Bundesrepublik had caused him to be moved from his Munich apartment of twenty years to an operating base in London.

Seeing the loden on, if not in, the flesh, Stears knew that he was seeing his chief for the first time through his chief's own eyes.

Brindle Woods said, "As a matter of fact, quite a lot is wrong. Bonn is not pleased. Bonn is not pleased at all."

"I handled it with kid gloves. I did not step out of line. This was a misfortune."

Woods said, "The Pentagon is not pleased. The Pentagon is very furious."

Stears shrugged. "The very least we've got them is a genuine NVA officer. He must be some use."

"The German papers are full of tiny insinuations. American army ambulances. The emigrant has not been seen by immigration authorities. Rapid arrival of American unit at the scene of the outrage. They do say 'outrage,' mind you. 'Another example of DDR brutality.' They're not sure what's up. Nobody's actually accusing us. Dr. Krel's nose is out of joint, I think."

"The ambassador . . ."

"Wants your gizzard, on the whole."

"So what do I do?"

"Make it worthwhile. This is normal." He smiled at Stears. "Your operation's getting more complicated than I'd expected. It doesn't worry me. You can handle it."

He said it with satisfaction, as though scoring off enemies not present. Brindle Woods was chief of GERMINATE. GERMINATE, a sort of urchin within the Company alternately suckled and abandoned by orthodoxy, took care of operations that implicitly denied the legitimacy of the East German government, or looked blearily toward reunification, or were blatantly provocative or undermining of the Deutsche Demokratische Republik, the former Soviet Zone, East Germany. Not the real rough stuff, most of it, not really, but Bonn had come to feel that GERMINATE bordered on surliness, insensitivity at least, and spoiled the high tone of discourse between the Bundesrepublik and its best debtor. So GERMINATE had been moved to Margaret Thatcher's London and Woods was randomly inclined to be touchy.

Woods said, "Let us not forget the details. We seem to be going operational. Have you assigned a code name?"

"Two possibilities," said Stears. "If it's a G for normal-status German operations, then the next sequence is GRU. I don't like GRUESOME, so let's do GRUFF. If we go for a special E status, then it's down to ELA. That would be ELAND."

Woods said, "He'll be an E if he's anything. But you're a day out of date. ELA's gone. We're at ELB."

"ELBE," said Stears.

Woods said, "You can't use a straight geographical name as a code. It has to be a compound. You know that."

"ELBEMAN," said Stears.

"ELBEMAN," said Woods. "Yes, ELBEMAN. I like that. I have never liked grotesque code names. I spent nine months with GASP once. That was in the early days."

"At least it's nonreferenced," said Stears. "Couldn't possibly have anything to do with him."

"Exactly. ELBEMAN."

They sat in the parlor after supper. Stears had cooked. The nurse had eaten with them and gone back upstairs. A chalet party with a girl. They were on the edge between work and company. The Scotch was in heavy round glasses with trout flies or setters. L. L. Bean comes to Berchtesgaden.

"What's he like?" said Woods.

"An officer. A real one. Green Beret. Marines. The best. How in hell did anyone in the secret police get hold of him? People like that don't sleaze around with the SSD."

Woods went to the bookshelf and, with a quick frown, exchanged the places of two books and scanned the shelves. He had found the supper things without looking. *So this has been home*, thought Stears.

Woods said, "That is a significant point. What about the woman?"

"I thought Krel taught them better."

"Stop it," said Woods. "You're not that tough."

"It was the worst thing I have ever seen. She had to do it. It was an ordinary piece of ground. It had grass on it. It had leaves. Even I could see his face. She must have seen his eyes. They would have killed him in front of us. It was terrible not to help him. And it was absolutely perverted not to help her. I watched her die. I stopped an American sergeant from going to her. I stopped him. Perverted. Dachau stuff. We were only following our orders." He said the last in German.

"For reasons that you know."

Stears raised his glass and said with mock worldliness, "Yes. But you asked." He added, "This has begun badly. We had no right to involve a woman like that. Especially with lies. Even if she died by accident."

"The soldier offers his flesh. We offer our innocence. Everyone admires the soldier, but wounded bodies are a degradation too. They lessen the world. The point is what it pays for."

Stears looked at him, the slight, bright-eyed mandarin, and thought, *That would be very good, but he's said it before.*

Brindle Woods lightly shrugged away his own profundity.

Stears said, in mock cockney, "It's girls like us what keeps your daughters safe."

Brindle Woods shrugged less gracefully.

Brindle Woods said sharply, "Does he know I'm here?"

"He's not deaf. He's knows someone is."

"I'd recommend we build a little tension," said Woods. "The truth is, he'll be bursting to talk. We'll wait until late morning."

"I figured we'd work together?"

"Definitely. You lead. You develop. You're handling him anyway. I am the adversary. Maybe he's holding out. Maybe he's a dangle. But not obvious. Not so a virgin would pick it up. Then, if he counters . . ."

"Yes," said Stears. "Then I've got a flashlight I can shine in his face and you can pull his toenails out."

Brindle Woods looked at him without amusement.

Stears said, "It would seem rather obvious that he has risked his life to give us something. Do we treat him like three A.M. in the squad room?"

Brindle Woods rose and stood by the fire. He looked down at Stears.

"1951," he said. "We had infiltrated agents into the USSR. Stalin's USSR. Some were old Vlasov men. Some were émigrés. They were very brave. They got in on foot, by parachute, sometimes on freighters. I was the last Westerner that some of them spoke to. I was young and they were true heroes."

He looked at Stears in silence. A cube of ice popped and split in a glass.

"They died, kicked to death in the Lubyanka. They died of cold and disease and starvation in the camps. One drowned with his head and shoulders pushed into a cesspool. That one was a doctor. I was learning Russian in those days and he used to read Pushkin to me. Pushkin and Mandelstam. I found out what happened to him five years ago.

"The whole operation had been penetrated, you see, right from the beginning. That bastard Philby was part of it. But there were people who came in from the East as well. One of them was a good clean young Red Army officer, defecting. So don't talk to me like that, Stears. You haven't earned it."

"I apologize. I should not have. I am sorry."

"I believe you. Try it my way."

He said it cordially. For Brindle Woods did not ignore his fortune in having acquired a new number two who was not an innocent, whose suits were English and whose French was French, who knew the difference between a Bellon oyster and an Arcachon, and yet who had not had to be disabused of any illusions about the might of the Opposition or the meagerness of the home support. Stears was unusual in the Company: not only—rare in itself—a former part-time agent who had become an officer and professional but— almost unheard of—one who had done so after a notable and even lurid personal achievement in the Company's service. Giovanni Stears, to whom an overlord of the National Intelligence Advisory Board had confessed his treason just before blowing his brains out, had somewhat the same reputation in the more settled enclaves of the Company as a priest with a particularly sulfurous success with bell and candle might have at an ecclesiastical sherry party on a cathedral lawn.

Which was heartening for Woods, who had the manners of a bishop and the temperament of a heretic. As heartening as his personal knowledge of Stears himself, of his excellent background, of his pitiful father, of his sundered youth and the consequent certainty that of all officers of the CIA Stears was the least likely to draw back.

3

There was time before the first lecture, Dr. Krel's, for Renate Segla to stop at her own apartment for coffee, for order, for lipstick, for a toothbrush of her own; but to go straight from Dieter's door into the day made her feel skimpy and skillful and rash, so she dawdled on the way instead. On this June morning on the Marienplatz, the main square of Munich, the window boxes on the city hall were in first bloom, and the gray, Gothic pile, a steel engraving in the cold and snow, cascaded geranium scarlet and green. She stood and looked, still happy, more than a year after her escape, to be given pleasure by a street. She hadn't been hungry enough to eat Dieter's stale cereal from a murky bowl, but she smelled rolls and coffee behind her from the Peterhof and she had some at the outside window, standing up.

The university was up the Theatinerstrasse, past the palace, past the shops, past the gorgeous golden church. She hated Dieter's room, not because it was uncomfortable but because a clogged drain, a dirty mirror, reminded her of Over There, but she had resisted hurting his feelings about it because she loved the walk to school. She had yet to see a street more elegant than this, and by now there were shops where she had bought something for herself and she felt a citizen of it; she couldn't imagine the price of the lobsters in Boettner's window but she had splurged on a scarf at Münchner Chic. Beside the church, she stopped at the entrance of an arcade, between a furrier and a grocery. The grocer's girls, in snowy smocks, were setting up the window: pyramids of big crimson peppers, oranges with bright green leaves, crowns of lamb on silver trays. There was an astonishing amount of it she could afford, but that wasn't the point, any more than the opposite was the point in the fantasy land of furs when she turned around. The point was that it was theater, grace, joy, no less the tied bouquets of parsley than the cascades of red fox like rich girls' suntan or of dark mink like chocolate, like sex. "Bourgeois materialism," croaked a voice from a dirty corner, but she didn't even listen to it now, for it wasn't only vicious, it was dumb. Things could speak the joy of order and generosity and care. She had known they could when she was daily robbed and bullied Over There; she had known it could be the day the secret police came and she knew that her love, her life, her Konrad was gone forever; she had known they could when she heard the footsteps of the *Aufklärer* in the wood and dared not lift her head to see if the dogs were with them; she had known they could when she saw the fence itself. She had been right. To walk from accustomed love down an outpouring street to a university where she could ask or be anything she chose was worth all the pain and fear that, at nineteen, she could imagine.

She was a minor celebrity. By the University Station of the subway, where the students streamed up onto the street, she was greeted by faces she hardly knew. Outside of her few close friends, outside of one treasured luncheon with the great Dr. Krel, outside of nightmares from which Dieter soothed her, she never spoke of her escape; but she disdained also, as though a fugitive, to hide it. The greetings were to an event, she had decided, even to a sort of circus trick a little excessive for good taste, not particularly to her. She did not quite fit in. Inge, her good friend, had thought about it and gravely nodded over a bottle of wine. "Of course you don't," she said. "You're German. You're the only one left." And then, shifting into a frightful American accent, "Here on the campus of good old Munich U." So in a cotton sundress which she had enjoyed buying too much to have it anything but as smart as it could be she jostled her way through the T-shirts with eco-slogans on the braless bosom, ragged jeans, and jagged haircuts, Renate the blond German girl, eyes down, movements quietly purposeful as a pointer's, and apologizing to anyone she pushed.

Dr. Krel spoke from a dais. The benches in the hall were as packed as subway seats, and Renate's writing ledge bore a grubby little sticker for the Turd Alley Tape Theater, but Dr. Krel stood between the high Tuscan windows in a pool of vaulted space. She settled back as best she could, ignoring, beside her right ear, a tawny beard that sheltered pimples in its clearings. Of all men who had taken her by the hand, who knew her name, Dr. Krel came closest to a hero. "You've got a crush on him!" Inge said. "He's old enough to be your father."

"Well, maybe I have," Renate said. "Why shouldn't I?"

He was at least an academic superstar. He taught with passion. With her other teachers erudition seemed like consignments of stationery; with Dr. Krel, like dangerous surgery in the nick of time. The austere, magnetic face swung between enthusiasm and disdain; disdain for the comfortable fat of a body politic, its cozy compromises, the arm of custom on its yielding waist; enthusiasm for the architectural beauty that the scalpel bared, the hard white bone of juristic logic, the flayed constitutional muscles of the state. His German was wonderful. The bright vowels flashed like blades. The glottal stops had the tolerances of a watch. His sentences were perfect as snowflakes, intricate, precise, and gone.

At least Renate thought so, and she was not alone. But for her there was much more. She knew tantalizingly, vaguely, but surely of his great work in helping the escape of people like herself. She had asked to join it on their only personal meeting. "Too soon," he had said. "You are still a convalescent who must not go out in the cold." And then, with a look the hardness of which she respected utterly, "Besides, I would have to be very sure that you are what you say."

There was more besides that. She was closer, in many ways, to the remote Dr. Krel than to Dieter, who usually shared her bed, or to Inge, who constantly borrowed her clothes.

Because she and Dr. Krel had known fear and crossed it. Because they were brave. Because they knew it. She could never say it. She could barely think it. But it was true. Dieter had held her shivering and sweat-soaked body at four in the morning when she woke from nightmare, and she very nearly loved him for it, but he did not understand. Dr. Krel had taken her hand dryly and would never call her *du*, but she would not even have had to tell him. The terror in the wood, death spread-eagled on the wire, was the nightmare but not the courage. There came a point when, if you had come that far, you went on because you could not go back. The courage was to go to that moment, guessing that it would be there—for the frontier was older than she was, and one knew, at least vaguely, what it was like—rather than to bow to the tolerable gray days one by one in the safety of everything you knew. She had and Dr. Krel had, fact. And would anybody on her bench? She couldn't sense it and she doubted it. She had once thought Dieter, but, no, he wouldn't, and it didn't really matter anyway. No other man in her life would ever be Konrad, and that was certainly not their fault. Inge, maybe.

Her notes grew in front of her. She was a careful student. Some habits of Over There died hard; she even sat up straight. Dr. Krel spoke today of the essential division of the Anglo-Saxon peoples effected by the theoretically separated judicaries and executive of the American system and the integrated authority of the British. The first drew his greater ire, because it was ineluctably compromised from the beginning. The British was consistent in viable practice, though superficially encrusted with dubious precedent. Note in passing that the Eastern system, in which power attaches solely to an ideological premise and is used without reservation in its extension, is the most consistent of all, though repellent. She wrote it down. She loved Western paper, so white and smooth, and bright blue ink. Her notes made an abstract and pleasing pattern.

She had an hour before her next lecture. She had formed the habit of walking over to the Alte Pinakothek, the great art gallery of royal Bavaria, for a cup of coffee in the cafeteria. It was quieter than the students' Mensa, and she could look at one painting afterward, which was like having a cake with no calories. But she had to hurry and she was near the front of the hall. As soon as Dr. Krel dismissed them she stood up and was even pushing past the tawny beard when she heard his voice:

"Miss Segla!"

She quickly turned and saw the doctor motion for her to wait. When the crowd thinned he came toward her as she politely hurried down. He held his hand out formally, but the eye was warmer than the face, and she took his hand with enthusiasm.

"Renate, if I may."

She all but curtsied, her hand still in his. He relinquished it.

"I feel that we should talk together once more. Would you be free to lunch with me tomorrow?"

She treated it as a royal command and said, "Yes, doctor. Of course."

He smiled. "Close by here, then. The Bistro Terrine. In the courtyard between Amalienstrasse and Türkenstrasse. Do you know it?"

"I know where it is, doctor." It was expensive, but there was a post-hippie dress shop by it which Inge liked.

"Good, then. At one."

He walked away, putting into his first stride the ghost of a graceful bow.

He was much younger here than on the dais. She had forgotten that. From a public distance one saw the mouth, and there, and in the chin, an autocratic, dismissing impatience seemed to have set like glass. To go above that to the eyes, close up, was almost a shock, for they were quick and intense. When they looked straight at you they were not so much dominating as defiant. But there was another expression that surprised her more. When she arrived, he was sitting at the table, his face set, his eyes down, askance. She was close to him before he saw her. She had almost stopped first, alarmed. It was as though he saw a snake forming out of air beside him.

It passed at once. He rose and smiled. He took her hand.

"I am so glad that you could come, Renate." He used her name delicately, as though as a privilege. He was entirely still the grand professor, and also host, and man.

He called the waitress. Renate said, a little flustered, "A glass of white wine, please."

But Dr. Krel waved that away and said, "Two dry sherries. Chilled." And then to Renate, "You can have your white wine anywhere. You should take advantage of being here."

She didn't like the sherry much, but she enjoyed drinking it.

She had never been in a place like this. It was evidently very French, for there were posters of Mistinquett everywhere that there wasn't a mirror, and everything in sight was labeled—*Fromage, Urinoir, Cave, Le Bar*—without a word of German anywhere. On the mirror behind the bar, two swans in frosted glass intertwined their necks, looking left and right. The chairs were wicker and the tablecloths were check. But the customers and waitresses did seem to be German, after all. The customers were rich and young; she had seen that leather jacket in a shop and it was sixteen hundred marks. She guessed what their own table looked like: a great man and his new young mistress. She did not mind that at all.

Because it put off the reality. She had guessed immediately why he summoned her. Her time had come: to join, to save others, to put herself on the line. Now she was trusted.

She was honored and thrilled. She was also reluctant. And so she was ashamed.

For her life was whole and here. She had gambled the blood of her veins to get it. It was made up of things absolutely real: her apartment, conversation without fear, her meticulous lecture notes, weekend mornings in bed with Dieter, the pleasure of the shops. She was as careful and respectful of these things as a housewife of her shopping bag. She had come to feel that their concreteness was their virtue and that all ideology whatsoever, all engagement in abstract and lineless battles, carried a taint from Over There, where there was nothing else. Heroism was not life any more than having surgery was health. Konrad, her first love Over There, had been a hero, and he was not beside her on Sunday mornings but in the camps or dead. His friends were heroes and their lives were lived, if

36

they still had them, in little circles of fear and fruitlessness. She herself had been brave enough for anybody on the fence, and there was less grace in any of it than in a day in the woods with friends. She wanted to get on with her life. And that was selfish, piggish.

Dr. Krel said, "I have been watching you from a distance, Renate. I would say that you are doing well."

She nodded. She said, "Yes," quietly.

"You do not miss Berlin? Even East Berlin?"

"No, doctor. Actually, we lived, you know, in Potsdam. I only went to school in Berlin the last years."

"So you are doing well. I am glad. It is not always so. By no means always. It is a terribly sad thing. Hope is so high, so much is risked. And then nothing comes together. There is only disappointment and then bitterness."

She said, with a dismissal that she was at once ashamed of, "Then they let themselves get infected."

"But Renate Segla has no regrets?"

I deserved that, she thought. But she said, "No regrets, doctor, no. That is not to say no sorrows."

She was embarrassed, and she dropped her eye to the menu, which was in French and which she could not read.

"And your sorrows, what are they?"

She would have answered any question of Dr. Krel's, for she gave him a sovereign right. But if she had not seen his eye, which was dank with foreboding or doubt, she would have had to drag it out of herself.

"I am lonely, I suppose. This is a different country and I have no home to go back to. But everyone has sorrows. I will make this my home. It is just a matter of a little time." She smiled. "And one feels a little foreign in Bavaria. Our accent is so strong to them. One of my best friends calls me 'Ik.' "

" 'Ik?' " he said. "Oh, the Berlin *ich.* Well, they have no right. They talk like peasants." He dismissed it.

He said seriously, "You have a boyfriend, I think?"

And she smiled to keep it as light as she could. "Oh, yes. He is very nice."

It seemed that he was in some private way pleased at her tone, and she wondered, *Is that what this is? Does he really want a mistress?*

He said, "You are very lucky, of course. You have your fellowship. You had a good education in the East. And you are extremely beautiful."

"The fellowship makes a very great difference." She blushed. "And thank you."

She was supported modestly but quite adequately by a conservative American-German foundation that she actually knew very little about. It was indeed lucky. She was not extremely beautiful; she was pretty. She was slightly glad when the waitress came.

He ordered for her, tactfully, by suggestion.

He changed the subject completely. He said, "You spoke of some letting themselves be infected. What did you mean?"

"It was not a fair thing to say, doctor, but what I meant was this: the ones that cannot live with decent happiness in the West have let some of the lies of the East get inside them and are liars themselves."

"Not quite fair, no. But intelligent. Unfortunately it is also true in another way. Some of the most dangerous agents of the SSD are escapers whose lives have failed. Maybe more dangerous than the ones the SSD sends itself."

"I have heard that, doctor," she said. "Of course, it is terrible."

"That is why we have to be so careful. Especially in helping others. The damage done by not knowing can be irreparable."

She nodded. He was profoundly silent. *So here we go,* she thought.

But they didn't. He said, as though the other had been a topic of passing interest, "Are you enjoying your courses?"

She said, surprised, "Yes, doctor. Especially yours. It is inspiring."

Which sounded a bit wooden, but then she had poised herself as secret agent, prospective mistress, secret agent again, and now schoolgirl all within three minutes, and it was getting rather exhausting. But then she saw the doubt or sorrow in his eyes and thought, *He cannot ask me. It is for me to volunteer.*

She dropped her voice and said, "Doctor, I want to join your organization more than anything else. It is the most important thing I can do. I know that."

It might not quite be true, but she felt she had to say it.

She felt the weight lift off him. He said, "You will, Renate. You will. But I have to know you first. I trust you now, but I do not know you. There are many ways to serve, some very difficult and very urgent. We will not talk of this any more for now."

Though at the time she was overwhelmed by his forthrightness about himself, what they talked about was principally her.

"I was lucky as usual, doctor. It was less bad than I had thought. I took a train to Plauen. I was not dressed as a hiker or any nonsense like that. I dressed as a local working girl. I hid in the woods. I saw the guards but they did not see me. I crossed at night. I had heard there were no SM-70s there. How? A friend at Humboldt had told me. He had tried, but there were exercises in the area and he had to turn back. Nobody shot at me. Maybe I stepped on a mine and it didn't work. Who knows? I cut my hand badly on the top of the fence. I still have the scar a little. That was all that happened. Of course, I was terrified. I dream of it still. But in the end it seemed odd that all of life could change because I climbed a fence."

"Yes, Renate, you were very lucky."

He told her of his own crossing, the sickness, the terror, disaster finally almost certain.

"No, Renate, that was fundamental. That was decided in advance. I could never have gained my own freedom by killing another human being, another German. What freedom would that have been? The freedom to be like them. In such a case I would have let myself be taken, or have died. There is freedom also in the camps and in death."

She shivered with awe. It was like having lunch with Solzhenitsyn. As for herself, she would cheerfully have murdered the whole border command if it had been possible and needed.

And he was not self-righteous. He watched her face and smiled. "You think that's stupid," he said, "and you may well be right. But, Renate, for each of us there are trusts that cannot be violated. Mine was a little abstract, perhaps. But would you have betrayed your friend who told you about the frontier?"

"Of course not," she said. And then bleakly, for a chill she had forgotten about had touched her back, "I would have tried very hard not to."

"And he knew that too."

"Yes," she said. "He did." Which vanquished the chill.

"And you were not lovers?"

"Rudi Schreider? Oh, no. Nothing like that." She paused and considered and then went on. "I shall tell you. He was the friend of a man I truly loved. And still do, though I shall never see him again. He disappeared." She looked at him to be sure he understood. "A little after his conscription. He was older than I. I was really still a kid. He was a serious man and he had serious friends. A year after he disappeared, I could stand it no longer Over There and I went to one of them and he helped me. That's how it happened. So, you see, I trusted him."

"Trust is a wonderful thing," said Dr. Krel, and she nodded, for she had lived by it. "But I knew nothing about this. Tell me about this man. I may have known of him."

"I would rather not," she said. And found that her mouth had shut in a hard, straight line. She did not like that, for the worst infection of Over There was the addiction to distrust as distinct from its wary use, just as the one glowing gift of Over There was to learn sometimes to trust with your life.

So she said, feeling that she owed him as much as she could give, "Not because of my own feelings. I loved him. He was twenty when he vanished, more than two years ago. His people were officials. He could easily have become an officer, but he thought our army was an enemy force. He was going to work inside it. I was sixteen when we met. He was the first man I slept with. I do not mind saying any of that at all. But no more, please. He may still be alive. Even my escape may have hurt him. I do not want to identify him. Even to you, please, doctor."

He said, almost under his breath, "Then the authorities knew of you together?"

"They knew he had a 'little girl.' " She grimaced in distaste. "They came to see me one day. That was when I knew he would not come back. Two of them. Both middle-aged in scuffed leather coats. I didn't rank anything very grand. I don't think they expected much from me, and because I was more than they thought I was able to seem even less. I played a tarty little schoolgirl with a pouty mouth and bedroom eyes. Then a scared little bitch who wished she could tell them more. It wasn't difficult. Konrad had coached me. I could see one of the policemen rather fancied me, so I played up to that too. I kept looking at him. What I was seeing was myself cutting into him with a knife, a different place each time. There wouldn't have been much he could have done by the time he left."

"Dear God," said Krel.

And at that she finally did blush. "I'm sorry," she said. "I shouldn't have said that. I'm not like you. I'm not a noble person at all. I wouldn't know how."

"Oh, but you are," he said. "You are like my own friends there."

He told her of his own two friends of twenty-five years ago.

"They were better than I," he said. "To stay behind and work is much braver." He said that very simply. "To have helped them in their work is a privilege, though it shames me sometimes that mine is the point of the triangle that is in no danger."

He had let her see there a glimpse of the depths he could not yet talk about. She did not press. She saw that he respected her equally when, talking of Konrad's friends, she still held back all but the roughest outline of their portraits. She almost forgot the difference between Dr. Krel and herself in age and fame, for he weighed her every word and answered as though only his fullest thought would do. It came to her suddenly that her funny invention of herself as his sleek young mistress grossly undervalued what he was really freely offering her.

And he was the nicest host.

"Actually, Renate, those are *cèpes*. A *cèpe* is a mushroom the size of a soup plate that comes from France, but I have never had them with mussels except here."

"They're wonderful," she said. And then, because he had reverted to another subject, "No, my boyfriend now is not the man I will marry. The other, Over There, is part of that, but not entirely, for I shall not see him again. When I first came here I was very lonely and Dieter was very sweet to me. I am fond of him, but I think that after school he will go back to Hamburg and I doubt that I will go with him. Dieter is going to America this summer and I am not going with him. Of course, I don't have the money, but I could have found it if it mattered badly to me."

Of himself, he said quietly, "I suppose I was too busy, Renate, and this is not a thing to be proud of. There was a woman once. I knew her until she died and she was always my friend, but what was between us passed. I should not have let it do so."

So that by the time he ordered apricots with walnuts and liqueur her awe for her princely Dr. Krel was even greater than it had been when she had venerated him on the dais. But under the awe was now the beginning of a friendship that the awe made precious.

At the end he took her hand again and said, "Renate, I do most truly thank you. We shall meet again quite shortly."

She protested, "Doctor, it is I who thank you," but he smiled and walked away.

She was rather full, slightly drunk, and reeling with privilege.

41

4

In the morning the pain was still strong in Herter's legs and back, but it was a pain inside him now, not one on which he floated, and there was room left over for hunger and the alpine sun. His nurse brought him breakfast. Her name was Jacki and her German was too good for a foreign nurse. She was certainly part of the security staff. But he watched her lean over him with the first return of sexual pleasure and smiled with a second pleasure, for he knew enough of casualties to know that he now was mending. She caught it, and fluffed his pillow with pleased, severe encouragement.

In the SSD, in all the secret organs of his past, there had been an undisguisable odor of treachery and decay, like the smell of roaches around a drain. It was not in this girl. That gave him hope for his new world. The man he had seen clearly for the first time the afternoon before had puzzled him. Not cruelty, he thought, and not dishonesty, but irony, which he distrusted as the outer garment of excuse. Since last night there had been a new voice, clearly the chief. His debriefing would now begin. His purpose welled up in him.

By late morning, it had become wearily obvious to him that he was being played with, that his nerves were being strung. So when, near noon, he heard their steps in concert on the stairs he felt for them the same stale contempt as for the regimental security spies. He saw the smile on the first man's face and said, "Why did you wait?" And then, "It is what the Stasis do, tricks like that." He used the contemptuous abbreviation for the SSD men.

The second man, the chief, was silent in the background. He was small and prosperous and bright-eyed, like a guileful squirrel.

The other said, "For practical purposes you are now a citizen of the Bundesrepublik. We are in Reit im Winkl, a town in Upper Bavaria. That is to say, we are in your country. You are not a fugitive and we have no authority over you whatsoever. If you wish to, you can leave now."

Herter looked at him in disbelief, then at the bed, then smiled.

"Not just now," he said.

"Yes. That really wasn't planned for. Do you have a question about your condition?"

"The nurse has told me that the leg will probably heal without a limp. There is other damage that must be kept free from infection and strain. I can perhaps walk a little on crutches in three or four days. That is very lucky for me. Is it the truth?"

"That's it," said Stears.

Herter said quietly, "And it was bought with innocent blood. The mine would have killed me if it had not killed her. Is that not true? It is a terrible responsibility."

Stears nodded. "Yes," he said. And then, "We know nothing about you."

Herter looked Stears leisurely, full in the face. It might be rude but he had to know him.

"Yes," he said again. "But don't play tricks." He drew a deeper breath and began, "I am Captain August Friedrich Herter of the First Motorized Rifle Division, stationed outside Berlin." He stopped and quietly said. "I was."

"That is not the name on your passport."

"Indeed not."

Stears said, "Since your principal communicated directly with my colleague, whose name he evidently knows, we have decided to forgo cover names. You can take that as an earnest of good faith. It's not a common one. I am Giovanni Stears and my colleague is Mr. Woods. You know who we work for."

Herter nodded at them both. He said, though it sounded stiff, "I owe you thanks."

The one named Stears ignored it. He said, "Your passport was a genuine passport document made up with genuine stamps. It passed ultraviolet examination. Very difficult to arrange in a false name. Arranged by whom?"

"I cannot tell you that."

The other moved impatiently in the back of the room.

"Then he might as well go home," said Woods.

Stears said nothing. Silence pointed at the bed.

Herter said, "Not the name. I am not able to."

Stears shrugged and said, "What units of the Border Troops did you encounter?"

Surprised, Herter said, "Frontier Command South. Their district begins just north of there. Second regiment. I didn't notice the battalion."

"And NVA or Soviet troops in the frontier region?"

"Some units of the Fourth Motorized. Routine movements. I saw a small convoy of Soviet tanks on carriers. First Guards Tank Army."

"T-62s?"

"No. All the Guards units have T-80s now."

"We cannot get very far if we do not know who sent you."

Herter nodded slowly. "Yes," he said. "I should have expected that. A quick switch. And you are the friend and he is the enemy. I know all that. I was interrogated before I was recruited. Many times. And finally by the man who sent me. Do you understand? That should interest you very much."

Woods said, "It does. It could also be an SSD legend. Or KGB even better. Your crossing gives you credibility, but not complete, not complete at all. The mine could have been an accident. They've been known to blow themselves up. And a cynic would say they waited a long time to shoot. Sooner or later our service will have to decide what you are. If you want to be believed, you will have to earn it. I suggest that you stop behaving like an insulted virgin."

"I was sent by a general of the State Security Service attached to the National People's Army."

"Better," said Woods. "His purpose?"

"He wishes to work for you."

Stears sensed a gathering of will, as of an uncertain skier preparing to let go, and he said very mildly, "In what way would he wish to do this?"

He was right. There was a silence. Then Herter said, "He will destroy the confidence of the Russians in the loyalty of our army. He will contrive evidence that army intelligence has been freely passed to the West. He will confuse the SSD's security surveillance of the army. In this way, he will make it impossible for the Warsaw Pact to have sufficient confidence in our army to use it in a forward role. That is his principal aim."

He stopped. The railroad announcer's voice rose clear and disembodied and small. The Munich train would leave from platform three. Passengers for Salzburg and Innsbruck should change at Bad Tolz. All three listened to it, gratefully.

Brindle Woods said dryly, "Nice of him."

Herter raised himself on the pillow and looked past Stears direct to Brindle Woods. He said, "He can. He will. You do not know him." He sought Woods's eye, which did not leave the window, but the pain was strong and he lay back, wincing.

Stears said, "What did you say his name was?"

Herter opened his mouth, then quickly shook his head and looked at Stears accusingly. He looked trapped, muddled, and at bay. *Good*, thought Stears, *but easy now*.

Stears shrugged and smiled. He said, "You are right. We do not know him. But it can wait."

Herter breathed more deeply.

Stears said, "Because we are not interested in comedians."

Herter jerked his head and looked again at the courteous, smooth face above his pillow, and heard the light, drawing-room voice. *So this is how they kick you in the West,* he thought. He remembered General Sucher's eyes, how they had bored into him in the interrogation room, eyes that had brought him nearer to breaking than anything before until they had unimaginably filled with a rare gray light, a light of dawn on the glacier, and the general had said quietly, *That is enough. I am with you. Will you go for me to the West?*

Herter now looked straight into the safe and pleasant eyes above him and said, "My general is not the comedian."

But the American did not flinch. In the same tone, he said, "Then tell us how he will work."

So he began.

"The SSD is an organ of the KGB, and the Democratic Republic is an organ of the Soviet Union, and the NVA is an organ of the Red Army. Men like you will have read our constitution and you know that this is literally true. The first task of every unit of our state is to strip Germany of all loyalty to herself. It is worse than with Russia. Their government—"

He saw a shadow of weariness fall across both faces, and he interrupted himself sharply. "I know that you are both very wise and that it is tiresome for you to listen to what is only the everyday truth. But I risked my life to be able to speak. This will not hurt you very much."

The one by the bed, Stears, bowed his head and said, "You are right. I am sorry."

"The Russian government betrays its people, but in its own bad way it serves its nation. We do not have even that. Our government is like a man who spies on his wife to see that she is loyal to her pimp. This is no secret, and only government hacks pretend it is not true.

"With us everything is inside out. Our army supports our enemies and defends us from our friends. Everyone knows this."

Stears said quietly, "The DDR is not Poland. Your government has some support."

"Yes," said Herter. "Germans tend to believe. I did for many years. But Germans are also not stupid. Many, many know that what I say is true."

Stears nodded. Brindle Woods raptly surveyed the far side of the valley.

"Now this army, the NVA, is needed absolutely by both the Russians and the government, but for different reasons. For the government, it is the only guarantee that the Russians will not use East Germany as a bargaining chip with the West. For the Russians it is the only satellite army that is fully disciplined and trained enough to commit suicide for their sake. In a war, I and my men would die to drag more people into the Russian prison."

Brindle Woods said, "Excuse me, but who is this talking? Is this musings from the mess or an intelligence proposal?"

"It is what I tried to understand for four years and what my general made clear to me. Can you understand what it is like for me to lie here defenseless and say it in safety? But I will not waste more of your time with it. This is what my general's proposal stands on.

"Except for its officers, the NVA is wholly conscript. Every young man serves. Every young man. They have not found a way to take out their brains while they do so. Every kind of belief that exists in the country exists also in the army. The officers are all Party men. So they, of course, all love the government. I am in the Party, if they have not yet rubbed out my name. So is my general.

"So the army is never trusted. There is a second army within it. The SSD has its own army, officers and men, who tunnel through the real army like a tapeworm. Nobody knows who they are. They have secret ranks. But this invisible army is always more real than the army that may actually fight and die. The sergeant who has saluted you for two years, perhaps one day he snaps his fingers and—poof!—he has been a colonel all that time and now he arrests you. It is like magic. And maybe the recruit the sergeant-colonel is shouting at is a private-general. Now I am joking, I suppose. But who knows? Then there are the open Stasis who wear army uniform but do not obey the army."

Stears said, "In short, the Administration 2000 unit of SSD. Fair enough."

"Yes. But this secret army is not trusted, either. Some may get in the habit of being soldiers. Some look out only for themselves. So another part of the SSD, which these magic soldiers have no access to, recruits young men before conscription and when they are conscripted they spy on the secret soldiers, especially the officers. At the end they get Party jobs.

"At the very top of the SSD, these two sewers of spying and lies and fantasies and malice flow together and form Truth as our government perceives it about the men who may die for it one day.

"But all of this is simply child's play," went on Herter, "for it is all Germans so far, and Germans do not even matter in all this. Only Russians matter. And the Russians do not trust the SSD at all. Therefore, there are some in the SSD who only pretend to be SSD pretending to be soldiers—and perhaps they only pretend to be Germans or even human beings; they are really KGB. It is they from whom the Russians find their own truth. Of course, they are spied on in turn, both by SSD and by others in the KGB, and all these circles begin all over again in the KGB. This is how it is discovered whether Lieutenant Schmidt will order Private Müller to kill himself assaulting a West German machine-gun nest to help the Russians rob more Germans and whether Private Müller will obey. It is safer than asking them. This is how my army's loyalty is assured."

Brindle Woods said, "Thank you for the lesson. What exactly might your general's role be in all this? Chief of Satire?"

Herter hesitated. "I cannot tell you exactly," he said.

Woods said, "Ah." He said it to a cow across the valley.

"Because it would lead you too easily to him."

Stears caught it, the well-disposed man at the end of his patience. "We cannot deal with the Man in the Moon," he said.

Herter said carefully, "He is in a position to know what material the SSD is providing the KGB and what action the KGB is requiring the SSD to take."

Brindle Woods's eyes abruptly returned. Herter saw it, and the tension in his neck eased. He moved the blanket from his chest. The sun came straight into the room how. The scent of warmed pine mixed with antiseptic was strong and cloying.

Brindle Woods said, "What is his motive? And what is yours? Money?"

"No. Do you think I would have risked my life for that? Do you not know what my general risks?"

But Woods had not spoken harshly.

"Why not?" he said. "It's the usual motive. For good things and bad. And excuse me, but your man seems to specialize in betrayal."

"I can no longer serve a government that exists to imprison and divide my people. It is the same with the general."

Woods said, "Then what does he want? A round of applause? What do you want?"

"When it is time for him to come to the West, and he will be the judge of that time, he will require your help in crossing. Provision must be made for him to end his years here in dignity. But he does not want a gift, he wants to work. I will work with him."

Tell them that, General Sucher had said. *It is true and it is also within their horizon of belief so long as they assume that it is a dressing for other things. There are only a few motives they find reliable. They call them "MICE"—mäuser. It stands for Money, Ideology, Compromise, Exposure. So there must be money too, though not crudely. They are secret men too.*

Woods said, "So he'll cross. What does he do first? Go on. I interrupted you."

"That itself is important. It is the climax. The defection of the KGB's hand in the most secret heart of its only strong satellite would be terrifying for them in any case. The Russians believe nothing that they see by daylight, only what is brought to them out of the shadows. What if all their secret files are wrong? What if the NVA is full of their enemies, known to each other and organized? They will easily believe this. It is almost impossible for Russians to believe that people do not hate them. They are like a man who has big, fierce dogs and beats them every day. Has he cowed them? Or if one day he stumbles . . . ? There is a name he told me to say to you: Ogorodnik." He looked at Woods.

Woods said, "I take his point. Though he wasn't quite in the same position."

"But in fact he can do much more. There is a hunt going on now in the army for people who might possibly revolt if they were forced into war. Religious and pacifist elements especially. I do not know why; perhaps these elements really are increasing, but the government's response is extreme. I was questioned myself, repeatedly, and merely for going to church—which is not illegal—and refusing to spy for them there. There is no doubt that the KGB has pushed the SSD toward this. It is not so much a campaign of persecution, at least not yet, as it is one of discovery. Of course, they are hunting German nationalists and democrats too, but they are always doing that.

"Anyway, the KGB's preoccupation with this is specific, and my general is one of their fists. All over the army, men, and many officers, are being pulled into interrogations. Since the KGB trusts nothing, even the Stasi, most of this is outside the SSD's normal channels. The records are irregular. Most of these men are returned to their posts. Consequently, there are few people in Germany who know more about real dissent in the NVA than my general. That is how he found me.

"The NVA already has one invisible, magic army inside it, and maybe two. Suppose there were another? Suppose that when my general found a strong, brave man, who had resisted every attempt to corrupt him, he only pretended to break him but really recruited him and sent him back? That is really what he did with me, though I am not especially strong or brave. Of course, it is very dangerous and one day there will be a mistake. But my general knows this."

He saw doubt on both faces thickening into dismissal, and he said, "He is not speaking of a secret army that will suddenly rise up and drive out the Russians or anything like that. That is completely impossible, of course."

Stears nodded, relieved.

"He is not even thinking of an army of real sabotage, though a little could perhaps be done in that direction. He is thinking of its appearance. Of its appearance in the secret world to the secret eyes of the Russians. The men he recruits will do very little, but his own defection will make it seem much more. They will wonder how their most trusted fist has fled to the West with everything he knows—and for how long has he been their enemy? And then all sorts of small things will happen. This secret manual—and with us everything is secret—is unaccounted for. Where has it gone? The wrong oil is used in a regiment of tanks and all the engines are ruined. Who made the switch? A battle plan is published in the Western press. What is happening? It is as though something secret has stirred. So run for the secret security reports. But wait! They were handled near the very top by the worst traitor of them all. And if he was, who else is? Perhaps the German army is riddled from top to bottom with dissent. And even worse—perhaps you, the CIA, now know this and they do not.

"This is the worst nightmare the Russians have: that they will put the German army out in front, where it belongs, to be killed, and it will join the other German army with the Americans and turn on them. They are obsessed by this. Already they distrust the Polish army and the Czech, but they do not fear the Poles and the Czechs. They fear the Germans. I said my general could make them so distrust the German army that they could never use it. This is the truth. He can."

He paused. He looked at both men. The one with the accent, Stears, seemed captured, without pretense. He found the other man more difficult. He decided later what it was: a jeweler picking up a stone that was beautifully colored and probably glass. This one, with the perfect German, said, "Has he sent us something for hostage?"

August Herter said, "A hostage? I do not understand. There is I."

Brindle Woods said, but not unpleasantly, "But you're worth so little, aren't you? That was not what I meant. We would be interested in specific information that your general, or his masters, could never afford to give us simply in order to make us believe in him. That would interest us very much. Especially if we could authenticate it."

Herter said, "The general has good access to standard military intelligence. Exercises, interaction between German and Soviet units, weapons evaluations. He can send this, but as it becomes available. It would expose him to seek it out. The same applies to operations against your own agents. This is a separate and highly specialized department, but he is normally informed of matters that concern the army directly."

Be careful here, General Sucher had said. *They will find out who I am in the end but they must not do so too quickly.*

"Valuable," said Brindle Woods. "Admirable. Tempting. And very vague. Suppose very little 'becomes available'? Your man has excused himself in advance."

Herter said, "There is one specific matter of great importance to your service. It is in West Berlin."

"And you were told to speak of it? If all else failed?"

"Yes, I was told to speak of it. I am a messenger."

Woods said, "Or appetizer. Or bait. The German words have the same ending. *Vorspeise. Lockspeise.*"

Herter shook his head. "No," he said. "Messenger."

The general had said, *Do not expect to be a hero to them. Especially in the beginning.*

Woods said, "And what is this matter? Insofar as you know?"

"If the KGB knew for sure what it was they would be much happier. It is thought to be a program for receiving and analyzing the internal electronic pulses of an enemy aircraft so that ground defense can predict what the pilot intends as soon as he has touched the controls. It is an American program, of course. There appears to be a mass of equipment assembled for it in West Berlin—West Berlin is in the middle of Warsaw Pact airspace, you see. We think the project is code-named PSYCHIC. It is an army project, apparently, not air force. Anyway, that is what the KGB thinks it is. You, of course, will know whether they are right or not. It is a high priority for the KGB. Perhaps for our DDR service too."

"Is that what he is telling us?" said Woods. "What one of our own projects is? Perhaps he could tell us where the White House is."

50

"No," said Herter. "He is telling you that this project is in jeopardy and that one of your own scientists in it is working for the KGB."

"Which scientist?" said Woods.

"That he does not know."

"Oh dear," said Woods.

"But he knows how he is paid."

Stears, in a voice eager to believe, said, "Does he know exactly? That can be a great help."

It was transparent, but Herter was trying hard enough that he looked at Stears with gratitude and said, "I think so. It is paid in Swiss money from Switzerland. Apparently the KGB keeps money there. It is three thousand francs a month and it goes from Switzerland to a bank in West Berlin. But it is not paid to the man who will receive it. It is paid to someone else." He looked hopefully at Stears.

Stears said, "Would you possibly know what day it is sent?"

"No," said Herter, "I do not know that."

Stears gravely nodded. Brindle Woods said helpfully, "The KGB just tipped him off about that, did they? Thought he might be interested? Chatting in the corridor?"

"He saw a memorandum," said Herter. "It was passed quickly when he was being briefed. There was a pencil note on it."

"Three thousand francs," said Stears. "I take it he could find out more."

"About PSYCHIC, yes. Not about the payments. That, you understand, is not his field. It would be . . ."

"Of course," said Stears. "What does this agent do? What kind of information? How is he placed?"

"It is computers. PSYCHIC depends upon computers. That much my general knows. Yours are better than ours. Evidently this man works with them. The point is that if the Soviets know how this weapon works they can mislead it and if you are not expecting that it could be bad for you."

Stears said, "How will your general communicate as a rule? Has this been considered?"

"You must decide. He will not use any contact of your agency who has been used before. He suggests someone put in place specifically for this operation alone or . . ." He stopped, uncertain. "I have forgotten the word he used. Someone who has been there, but . . ."

"A sleeper."

"Yes, that was it. He thinks it should come out through the diplomatic bag."

"Given the impressive volume," said Woods.

"Perhaps so." He was not sure whether that was mocking.

Woods rose. "That is enough for now, though we have barely begun. We have an idea of what you want. There is a great deal more."

He walked toward the door, not looking back. The other, Stears, got up more slowly and stood beside the bed.

He said, "You should have rest. You should have thanks. I am sorry."

Herter did not reply. He had no idea whether the man meant it or whether it was his role.

August Herter lay in the clean bed in the bright pine room feeling the sunshine flow into his body while his spirit turned from elation to fatigue. His life was torn up; its roots were lying in the open air for these Americans to poke at. It occurred to him suddenly that he would probably never again see a single person that he had known until two days ago, except for General Sucher—and he was by no means sure of that.

General Sucher was back there in the dark wood, with the wolves.

He remembered his interrogations. He had been through many. The first ones had been only "chats." He was a good officer. His party record was unblemished. There was just the little problem that he was being seen at the Lutheran church. Quite within his rights, of course, but was something wrong? Or just curiosity, perhaps—nothing wrong with that. Perhaps.

In fact, this was almost true. He was not a deeply religious man. The church was an agreeable respite from a world the corners of which seemed to him increasingly caked with corruption, like a dirty butcher's shop.

Then would he furnish a little information on the private soldiers who were seen there too? Simply his duty as a Party member, wasn't it? Engage them in conversation? Flatter them a little? Find out what they were thinking?

No.

Now he was summoned frequently, at odd times of day. The tone was first wheedling, then injured, then bullying. He was called to his colonel's office. A corporal in his own company, present at the meeting and smiling insolently, stated that he had seen Herter "meeting suspicious persons"—a complete pack of lies. The Political Officer wrote it all down. His colonel looked ashamed.

His assignments were changed. Certain of his own men began to treat him with barely veiled derision. His colonel no longer looked him in the eye. His room was searched. He continued to refuse.

He was summoned to Berlin, to Normannenstrasse, the great orange cube of the SSD's supreme headquarters. He would be seen to by a general.

General Sucher had the power of the secret world, but not its air. While the others squeezed and prodded, General Sucher cut like a knife. This time there was no pretense. The constitution would avail him nothing. In that building, the law did not exist. He had a choice: take an active, secret part in the surveillance of churchgoers or be charged on fabricated evidence, court-martialed, and jailed. The choice was here and now. He would leave the office either to collaborate or under arrest.

He had refused. It had amazed him. He had refused, as he realized only later, as a Prussian officer.

And when the general had looked at him and said, "I am with you. Will you go for me to the West?" he had answered at once, "Yes," knowing simultaneously that he must have misheard, that he was mad to fall for the trick, and that there was no trick at all.

The persecution was stopped. He was cooperating.

He had had three more meetings with General Sucher. They were grueling sessions of instruction to which he had been summoned arbitrarily, at odd times, like a cowed collaborator called to his task. Once he had walked with General Sucher along the embankment of the Spree, where East Berlin retains a small, sad memory of its old grace. Beside General Sucher, beside the Spree, he felt fully for the first time what had been done to his country. He had carried away honor, devotion, and joy.

And now he had obeyed orders. He had turned a man who had risked his life on his judgment of a stranger into a comprehensible and cautious traitor preparing his nest.

Brindle Woods walked among the crocuses in the meadow below the house. The house was wood. Voices carried through it. It would not be proved that Herter spoke no English. He said to Stears, "This general is cagey as hell. And I don't like this anonymous business."

Stears said, "He'd have to be. The Company may not look so secure from where he stands. It's a hell of a plan."

"Yes. We can't refuse it unless we can show he's a plant. It may not be as much as his errand boy says it is, but it's interesting. Very, very interesting."

"Could he do it?"

"I'm not sure, Stears. Some of it might work. The boy's style's a little purple, but most of what he says is true. The bastards *are* paranoid. It's a good lever to work with, and this might be a good time. This fellow could give the Warsaw Pack a scare, at least, if he's what he says he is and he's on the level. That's not quite what worries me."

An early blue butterfly fluttered in front of them, small and brilliant as an electric spark.

Stears said, "Yes. Most of it can never be authenticated, can it? Not even when the general defects, if he does defect. So suppose he does defect. Maybe with special effects even, like Herter. Now we then assume that the SSD is all screwed up and so forth and maybe they even act as though they are. So we think that we've to a good extent neutralized the East German army. But really we haven't. It's all a sham. He's their man. The bluff of the century. Nasty shock and all that."

Brindle Woods looked him full in the face.

"Yes," he said. "Well done, Stears. Well done."

"But I don't believe a word of it. Herter's for real. I swear it."

Brindle Woods now ignored him. He said, "The two flows of intelligence that we could authenticate to some extent are operations against our agents and operational military intelligence, both of which he's fighting shy of already. So he baits the hook with this PSYCHIC. Which, by the by, is fascinating. I'd only picked up whispers of it until now—it's a Pentagon thing and they're holding it close to their chests. I thought PSYCHIC might be something like that. I hope the Comrades have it right. Embarrassing otherwise."

"He gave us an agent," said Stears. "This computer man."

"Bugger all, he did. He gave us the taste of one. We'll look and look and never find him and we'll tell ourselves we're out of luck. It's one of the basic methods of a dangle—promise something mouth-watering that only a professional could know. And then a lot that you can't check."

"He gave us a lead to the payments."

"Exactly," said Woods. "A piddling little check somewhere in Switzerland. Bugger all. You were a banker of some sort. You know that."

"Never that," said Stears. "But something like it. In Switzerland, if you recollect. Where that money comes from. Suppose I found it. Suppose he's really given us a way to find one of our people peddling computer secrets, that would change things, wouldn't it? The Comrades love computers. They wouldn't joke around with them, I should think."

"It would help," said Woods. "How would you find it?"

"We have an ace up the sleeve there, don't we?"

"Do we?" said Woods.

"A Hungarian ace."

"Do we?" said Woods.

Stears said, "Brindle, I don't know much about this, so stop me if I'm off the track, but the Company has a hidden source in Hungarian intelligence who has given us some good down-to-earth stuff about KGB routine financial transaction routes abroad."

"Go on," said Brindle Woods.

"I have this in digest form only," said Stears. "The KGB is using the Swiss banking system but it is not using the Swiss banks, not the big three, because they are getting too pious. They are using small foreign banks in Switzerland. There's not much provably illegal going on—but the Swiss government would not like having to take notice of it, and there could be trouble with bank charters if they did. These little banks are not the Swiss Bank Society and the Crédit Suisse—they're not God almighty. Therefore there's vulnerability somewhere."

"Go on," said Brindle Woods.

"These were exactly the little banks I used to know when I advised Arabs on how to keep their money. I know my way around them. If I can be steered so that I know which, or at worst which of two, banks would be handling a payment of this sort and a few likely names for the account it comes out of, I think I could do something. Even outside of Company channels altogether."

"Very nice," said Woods. "Well done. Forget it."

"Why?"

"You have this report in digested form, don't you? You don't know which banks the Comrades use. You don't know these account names. You hardly know anything about it."

"I just said so, Brindle."

"That is so you cannot do any of the clever things you just suggested. If you did, the KGB would be alerted and our Hungarian friend would be chopped up small and done with paprika. He's sacred. He is not to be put at risk for anything as vaporous as ELBEMAN."

"I would move very delicately," said Stears.

"No doubt," said Woods, dismissing it. "There's something else. Privates defect. Lieutenants defect. Herter may be on the level. Generals don't defect. His motive's too pat anyway."

"Refuse him? We can't. He claims to be a general of the SSD with KGB access and he's willing to stay in place. That's a Penkovsky by itself." The tip of the spire of the village church came into view as they walked from behind a fold of the meadow, and Stears addressed the rest to it. "It's peculiar to think that authenticating an asset of that rank is not worth using material the Company already has. Just a little banking information."

"Have you ever noticed," said Woods, "that the smaller alpine butterflies become the more brilliant their colors are?"

"Yes," said Stears.

"He knows we can't refuse him. But Penkovsky was never anonymous. We knew who we had and where he was. With this one, the only thing we can judge him by is regular military intelligence. It's valuable, and we can check it to some degree. We'll need lots of it. And PSYCHIC. If it's useful enough that they wouldn't use it for bait, we can begin to trust him. You can use your Geneva contacts without risking material that leads straight back to a long-term agent in place. It's just a matter of a little skill. No fun playing with the net down." Woods's voice took on the genial firmness of one making hard decisions for someone else. "As for the military material, he'll have to push for it. If he's in it for pay, we'll make it worthwhile. If he's in it for conscience, he may do it anyway."

"That's not what he wants to do," said Stears.

"That's not the point." Brindle Woods stepped around a crocus. "It should be. It just isn't."

Which somehow we endure, thought Stears.

He said, "This man's an agent in place too. If I start stamping around all over Switzerland and then we arrest the man he's given us in Berlin, that might not be the best thing. If I have what I ask for, I can go in quietly as a mouse. It's my old identity, Brindle— financial adviser to funny Arabs. Wouldn't even raise an eyebrow."

"No doubt," said Woods. Brindle Woods rubbed his foot vigorously on the grass and added, "It's not the cows they should put bells on, it's what they leave behind." He looked at Stears severely. "I have no intention of suggesting the release of the Hungarian material to a relatively inexperienced officer under my command. The chances for mishap are too great."

"Very well," said Stears.

Woods looked at him. "Quite so," he said. Woods's face took on the reflection of martyrdom to come but not yet uncomfortably close. "If only the CIA were the sole player in this field I could be sure that my decision would stick. I am gravely concerned, Stears. When the Defense Intelligence Agency comes to hear that their PSYCHIC has been compromised, they will very probably demand counteraction. If they back me into a corner, I could be forced to suggest that giving you such access is the only speedy method known to me of providing any. That could happen as early as next week."

"That would be a terrible thing, Brindle," said Stears.

"A terrible thing for the DIA if it went wrong. It would have been so much wiser for them to have shared PSYCHIC with the CIA from the beginning." Woods looked again at the offending shoe and forgave it. "If you had access to the Hungarian material, how would you use it in the ELBEMAN operation? Perhaps you would write me a proposal. In case my hand is forced, I mean."

5

Dr. Oswolt Krel closed his lecture. The white bones of federalism hung conceptually beside him in two differentiated skeletons, the Bundesrepublik and the United States. He dissolved them with his hand.

"Ladies and gentlemen," he said to his students, "you are excused."

He stood rigid at the lectern. His students slouched from their benches. The airy Tuscan hall crept with bodies; the air stirred with stalenesses of flesh, unlaundered linen, unpruned life. Putrefaction of the West, he thought reflexively—just as the gracious edifice of the law he taught was in truth the tenement of hirelings shielding swindlers and thugs. He watched his students drain from the room and felt bracing contempt. *It is the generation*, he thought, not for the first time, *where the corruption inside has reached the skin.* Today he added, *Not Renate Segla, but she did not begin here. That is why so much can be asked of her. If she is needed. Perhaps she will not be needed.* Four days had passed since her lunch with him. He stood still. There was one door. He waited for the hall to empty before he descended the dais.

He stood outside in the square of the university. The first summer weather was moving in over the Bavarian Alps. The air was warm and soft and a still dove-grayness hung over Munich. From the triumphal arch to the palace, the Italianate facades of Ludwigstrasse looked as gentle and distant as an engraving. Oswolt Krel looked down the street and up at the sky. His appointment was outdoors, but it would not rain for some time yet.

He set off toward the palace and the golden cupolas of the Theatinerkirche. To his right, the treetops on the hill of the Englischer Garten celebrated in the first fresh greens of summer; the beech leaves sparkled in the sun. He turned his face from them; their woodpaths had been where he and Ursula Hecht, then medical student, had courted; in a thicket there he had first rapturously claimed her breast. He fastened his mind upon her torn and dumpy body bleeding on the ground, the Americans scuttling back into the wood. She had liked the Englischer Garten even in the wrong seasons; she had liked their footprints in the frost around the lake. A foolish liking, affecting nothing. Concentrate on the

58

deceiving foreigners skulking in a German wood, using German faith for alien ends. It did not matter what Ursula had loved, frost or hot chocolate or Oswolt Krel. His emotion must not be merely private.

He walked briskly, as much from habit as for punctuality. He believed in walking. From here, the skyline was ringed by Munich mansions, cream and gold, with a frieze of spires behind them. He saw it still with lingering affection; twenty-two years ago it had been a coast on his voyage to joy: Munich's pastry richness to the eye, the unconstrained university, the exhilaration of free thought, a summer that the winters of Berlin made almost tropical. The chill of his soul, of his anger, of his nightmare casting-up on the beach at Travemünde had thawed as the last effects of his pneumonia had healed.

He was very great. A chisel mind and a driving will had been graced for a brief, essential time by gratitude and delight. Joy had served its purpose. His mind could in any case have drilled; as it happened, it had soared. He had seen the West with excited love and love through a newly emerged and fragile sensuality. His early essays, *Ethics, Law, and Property, Ethics of the Concrete, Conscience and the Public Imperative,* contained within their titles and scholarly apparatus intimations of Ursula's hips snuggling closer in the morning, Ursula pouring wine on picnics in the Oberbayern by an old car (their joint extravagance) that smelled of gasoline and rubber, and the silver drops on Ursula's upturned cloth collar as they walked to the Opera in the autumn fog. Which is only to say that they apprehended law and society as a subservient framework for human energy and heart.

Which had made them a public hit. The tone of his essays was rigorous and humane; it was—one could say it again without swallowing or looking quickly sideways—*German.* They floated free from the university into the weekly press. One hyperventilating reviewer discovered in them the union of Mommsen with Heine, picturesque as that might be. Krel became the darling of thoughtful Germans. Within twelve years of the beach of Travemünde, a Krel article in *Die Zeit* would bring the weekend to halt from Blankenese to Schwabing. The time was right. The skull in the lightning bolts had finally crumbled, Ulbricht had fenced himself into Prussia like a junkyard dog. There was briefly a taste for the heroic in West Germany, and Oswolt Krel, the thinker, the essayist, the escaper himself, rumored to be the daring helper of others like him, acquired a discreet cult.

West Germany was also getting rich. Oswolt Krel and Ursula, who was almost a doctor now, had started dining out and reading menus of clever new dishes between long new silences.

Oswolt Krel now looked again toward the trees of the Englischer Garten, torn between a sudden sense of loss become finally irrecoverable and a long-nursed vexation. But he had walked too far already. The trees, like Ursula's long-suffering passion, were behind him. He was almost at his destination.

He turned into the Hofgarten, beside the palace. He looked down the rows of café tables under the dim light of the arcade. The clouds were spreading from the Alps and there was a purple bruise on the sky behind the Isar. But he saw his friend at the usual table and nodded his head in greeting.

Heinrich Nadermann said, "My poor Oswolt, I am sincerely sorry. Ursula Hecht was a generous woman. These things are above politics." He rose to greet Krel with gentle gravity. He was a gray-haired man, mild of face, in a dark suit cut with a more urbane flourish than Dr. Krel's.

Oswolt Krel deflected pity with a twist of his head. "I am deeply angry, Heinrich," he said. He sat down and drew his chair closer to the café table. Its feet dragged in the gravel.

Nadermann considered. "It is not an uncommon reaction, Oswolt. Not an unhealthy one. Better for you than guilt."

Krel looked at him in challenge but only said, "I was tricked. I was cheated."

Nadermann opened his eyes quickly, very wide, and said, "How was that?" It could have been drolly meant, or not.

"The refugee was presented to me as a pacifist, a neutralist. He was presented by a man of conscience, almost a colleague. I had no reason to doubt his principles."

"In your terms," murmured Nadermann. "Who was this? As a matter of interest."

"Heinrich Bessel.

"Ah, Bessel," said Nadermann. "The journalist. More my colleague than yours, really."

Krel waved it away, provoked. "Ursula was killed. Killed horribly. You know that." He looked fiercely at Nadermann. "As you know by what means and that your country shares responsibility for them."

Nadermann lowered sad eyes. "A Soviet journalist does not make foreign policy, Oswolt, any more than a German professor does.

The necessity for that frontier is an obscenity—on that we have long agreed. My own people were German once, so how else should I feel? But that frontier is hardly a secret. One can stay away from it. It does not chase people."

"I know all that," said Krel. "She died horribly. I was not near her when she died. I ran through the wood when I heard the mine. I was too late. She was dead. But I was not too late for everything. Americans were there. American soldiers. . . ."

"The waiter," murmured Nadermann. "Careful." Krel stopped, confused. The waiter approached his shoulder.

"Coffee, with cream," said Nadermann.

"Yes. Yes," said Krel.

The waiter leaned over Krel, retrieved a dirty ashtray and a waiting tip. Krel recoiled. The waiter slowly wiped the table. Then withdrew.

"Americans," said Krel. "They had been hiding in the wood like thieves. They knew all about this pacifist, this neutralist. They were waiting for him. They surrounded him and carried him away."

"He was wounded, I think," said Nadermann.

"A bad leg. Yes, a wound."

"The Americans have an occupation garrison near there, do they not? The soldiers would have heard the mine. No doubt they had an ambulance. They would be disposed to help such emigrants."

"Soldiers perhaps," said Krel. "But there was a civilian with them. With the soldiers, giving orders. I did not see him, but he was there. What does that suggest?"

"Surely not the dreaded CIA?"

"You do not believe me," said Krel.

"That is not so at all, Oswolt. I only want to be sure that you believe yourself. Yes, a mysterious civilian, American soldiers, very likely CIA. Very likely you were tricked. Bessel does seem to be very fond of the Americans. I wonder if he knows who this man was. He must at least know who sent him."

Krel went on unchecked.

"There was something worse. When the mine went off the Americans all came running out of the wood. But when they saw that it was only some woman, some German woman they had not paid for, lying there in what agony we can only guess, they all ran back again. They only wanted their goods. Ursula was not put on their ambulance. Only their spy."

"That is very terrible," said Nadermann. "There are things I could say. You both knew about those mines. You were assisting

61

in a criminal act. There is a sense in which you have been tricked by the CIA each time you helped an illegal emigrant across the frontier. You claim to despise the Bundesrepublik's dependence on America, but you refuse to do anything positive about it—you restrict yourself to helping unauthorized emigration from an ally of my own country. But these are large subjects. We have discussed all this many times and agreed to differ. I am not the Politburo. I am genuinely your friend. It gives me no pleasure that the death of a woman dear to you has brought you closer to my views."

He paused as a couple made advances toward the next table, then moved a little farther on. Lunchtime approached. A smell of baked chicken thickened from a cheap restaurant, the Wienerwald, at the end of the arcade.

Oswolt Krel drew in breath to speak, but Nadermann said, "Why did you telephone me, Oswolt? You could have taken my personal sympathy for granted. Why did you need just now to see the bureau chief of Tass?"

"I was used," said Krel. "I was tricked. Do you think the CIA arranges to bring out an East German officer because he is unhappy? Because he writes a pleading letter?"

Nadermann minutely shook his head.

"No," said Krel. "The CIA does that because the man is part of one of the plots that foreigners play against each other on German soil."

Heinrich Nadermann looked at him with the quizzical, droll eye welcomed without misgivings at cocktail parties from Blankenese to Hampstead Heath. *Surely you and I are too intelligent to talk of gulags and Afghanistans,* it said. *That is for Ronald Reagan and the servants.* "That is a reasonable conclusion for a professor and a journalist," he said. "How nice. Our coffee."

The waiter set down the tray, stuck the bill underneath its corner, and moved to take the cups from it. Krel waved him away.

"It is known that I hate such things," he said. "It is known that I dedicate myself to all people whatsoever of free conscience, East or West, and to the intellectual maturation of a Germany that is owned by no one. That is why I help certain people through the frontier, not because I am some vulgar guerrilla for Mr. Reagan."

"You could hardly be that, Oswolt," said Nadermann. "You are not a vulgar man. Though some of your friends have been a little crudely ideological. Even poor Ursula."

"She was a brave and generous woman."

"I said it myself. I will say it always. You are right to be angry about her death. I will do anything I can to help." He paused, touched his lips to the frothed cream on the coffee, and dabbed them with a napkin. "Hot," he said. "Anything a foreign journalist can do. You have still not told me why you called me."

"The CIA tricked me into assisting a plot of theirs, violated every principle I stand for, and killed a woman I had loved. Help me destroy their plot."

Nadermann sat back and observed the filling tables and the formal garden beyond the arcade.

"We shall go for a walk now," he said.

Not the first walk.

Just at the beginning of his academic fame, just as his delight in Ursula was changing from a young man's urge to a ripening delight, he had become conscious of a growing unease, like an itch, like a tic. Among the thickening abundance of West Germany, he felt diminished. Waste, formless by definition, revolted him. On Saturday mornings, Ursula liked to shop for vegetables outdoors at the Viktualienmarkt. The first summer, he had loved the glossy aubergines, the flaming oranges, the dill in its feathery bunches after the turnips and brown apples of the East. But Ursula stuffed it all, essential or not, into her bag. He began to see past the pretty stalls in the market to the drunks lying with their heads on beer tables among broken pretzels, to the traffic wedged in the streets. He became frequently invaded by a thin, precise anger. He would carry the shopping bag home in silence, up the three flights of stairs to the cement landing of their apartment house, drop it on the floor, and go to his room to work and sulk. Sooner or later—that evening when she was standing in front of the burner with the frying pan, sitting alone afterward while Oswolt finished his work—Ursula would begin to cry in loneliness and puzzlement. He would be guilty, furious, and grieved. It was beyond him to explain that she herself, her generosity, her flesh, her unhidden desire for him, was the model of the slatternly abundance that weighed on him.

The world followed his own dark mood. In 1968, the West collapsed. America went berserk. France unraveled. Germany became richer and more vulgar by the day. The terrorists began. Oswolt Krel became haunted by doubt of his own vision. Constitutionally unable to accept his own actions as fortuitous or trivial, he could see his escape only as an epic of justice or as a crass betrayal. He became deeply depressed, irrationally bitter. Ursula, less dependent now, buoyed by her own patients, accepted him with delight as her nocturnal one. She was patient. She let him talk endlessly, even in querulous monologue, on the sofa, at supper, in bed. He needed her warmth and presence; she coaxed this into an unwonted frequency of affection. He was sometimes angrily grateful. She was glad. She didn't have much of him, but what there was to have, she had.

In 1972, he published a paper critical of the "obsession with bourgeois rights in Western legal systems." It was not a radical paper for its time but it was a surprise, coming from Dr. Krel.

A week later he was as usual in the state library. A gentleman reading there walked past his chair to the shelves. He dropped a note on Krel's book. "There is always a way back," it read.

He did not see the man for a month. He was waiting to cross Sonnenstrasse, clogged with six lines of traffic, shimmering with fumes. The man was suddenly beside him. He said, "It can cloy like chocolate in the end, can't it?"

He accepted then and there an invitation to an excellent lunch. He learned that the man was Soviet and German both, a Volga German. His name was Heinrich Nadermann. He worked for Tass. When Krel asked who else he worked for, he shrugged and smiled.

There followed a courtship of several months conducted over lunches on the Theatinerstrasse, on walks in the Englischer Garten (any erotic memories in those glades had been buried by Ursula's nightly domesticity), during intermissions at the Opera, all in the sites of the old, formal Germany while the students rioted, and scatological posters sprouted on the walls, and Paris stank of tear gas and Düsseldorf of exhaust and the Mercedes-Benzes reproduced like cockroaches.

And Nadermann talked. "Let's be honest, the West was wonderful once. Not only its buildings. Its law. Its life. But it's over. Gone forever. It took poison and killed itself in the war, and something quite different took its place. Haven't you noticed? You deserted us to join the bacteria feeding on a corpse. It was a pity for you. How were you to know?"

And Krel responded. "I can respect a faith in Marxism-Leninism. But I cannot admire a backward and stifled bureaucracy like the Soviet Union."

"Who asked you to?" said Nadermann. "Is aping the United States or the Soviet Union the best a German can do? That is why Germany is crucified. That obscene frontier you crawled over does not exist because East Germany is a little Russia, it exists because West Germany is a little Kansas."

64

"Perhaps both," said Krel.

"That is already an improvement," said Nadermann. "At all events it was enough to make the humanitarian Oswolt Krel slit a fellow German's belly on the beach. Yes, of course I know about that. Perhaps it is better that nobody else does, though."

Heinrich Nadermann became bureau chief of Tass in Bonn. He was known as a Soviet liberal, an expert on Euro-Communism. He was pinned on Willy Brandt's *Ostpolitik* like a medal. He was seen everywhere that counted. Krel was almost flattered that he was seen frequently with him.

They went to the Alte Pinakothek, the art museum. They were in the rooms hung with the German masters. By Dürer's *Portrait of the Apostles*, Nadermann said, "Let us at least be clear as to what this congeries called the postwar West—that is to say, America—has produced. The West cannot even make what it supposedly admires. Most of it is confessedly garbage. You want to eat synthetic candy while a woman prostitutes herself to a pervert on a movie screen? Well, go ahead, but let's not get serious about it. Are you going to tell me about Andy Warhol? That's your art now. Who can paint majesty now, as Dürer could? And the things the West can make—the toasters, the Mercedes-Benzes. They're useful, they're comfortable. I have them too. Do you want to make a philosophy out of them? My dear professor, this West is insulting you."

And so forth.

Nadermann reconnoitered, gambled, and won. What he said to Krel was not original, not profound, less than half true. But it was said well and it lodged inside Krel and grew: the image of a cleansed and gracious force, interchangeably Germany or himself, set free from the distant and not very interesting shabbiness of the East and the engrossing, pullulating, itching vulgarity of the West. Krel's essays underwent a change. They celebrated not an existing West but a hypothetical middle ground, largely opposed to it.

Which was an attractive way for Nadermann to help implement the directive from the Politburo to Moscow Center to every KGB man in the West: *The enduring priority is to detach the United States politically, ideologically, and culturally from its Atlantic allies.*

Krel's prestige fattened. He was found to have matured. The brave escaper, the cartographer of the liberties of the West, discovered the high moral plateau of neutralism and made it a place of pilgrimage. A discriminating neutralism: grant that the East is rapacious and despotic, do not blink at the frontier troops with their machine guns across your land, but answer them with innocence and suffering. Answer them as fellow Germans. Do not deny that the border guards also are hung on the two arms of the German cross—the arrogance of the United States and the fears of Russia. Do not fight them; heal them. The bravest soldier is the draft resister. The escaper who escapes with violence has not escaped. Every weapon defiles what it defends.

And so forth.

Could one deny in Munich that Dr. Krel—who still helped refugees across the frontier—owned the right to say it?

Could one deny in Moscow that Heinrich Nadermann of Tass deserved his successive promotions within the KGB?

Now Nadermann took Krel's arm. They walked between the rose bushes.

Nadermann said gently, "For many years I have asked you humbly for proofs of friendship. There is so much you could have told us. I never asked you to betray your student poets and your pacifist recruits and your young girls with a crush on Walesa. We agreed to differ there. But you had their confidence and many of them had leads to very different people—people within the armed services, people within the authorities, people who would not jibe at all at playing the CIA's games. People who did in fact play the CIA's games. You always rebuffed me. So you have no claim upon me, Oswolt. And we are certainly not in the business of private revenge."

He looked Krel mildly in the face.

Krel said, "You might profit by this too."

"Perhaps," said Nadermann, "though it does not help us all that much just to know that a junior officer has defected with CIA assistance. But there is the matter of your motive. Anger and grief are poignant, but they do not always last. Suppose you changed your mind."

"It is not only Ursula," said Krel. "It is not only the insult to myself. It is the insult to Germany. They pick us up and play with us. One of our own, this journalist of conscience, this noble Bessel, thinks nothing of cheating me for his American friend in the CIA. The CIA thinks it irreproachable to twist me into an action it knows very well I despise. They must be taught that such arrogance and treachery will be revenged, that Germans are not their lapdogs. They must feel us bite. I see Ursula's death, it is true.

66

I see it every night. But that is personal. You need not rely on it."

Nadermann said, "We rely on what a person can give us. We find one thing infallible, Oswolt. When a person truly wants a stronger connection with us, he is willing to give what he would not have given before. So far you have not even offered to try to find out who this American behind Bessel is, though I have hinted at it twice. I would have thought that would be important to you."

"Of course I shall do that," said Krel. He spoke with eager accord. "You are quite right. You will see."

"I use it only as an example," said Nadermann. "It is not very much. It may even be safer if you do not try—Bessel's contacts should not be so hard to find. There are more important things. Do you know something about this officer you have not told me?"

Krel unfastened a trailing cane of rose bush from his sleeve. The roses trembled. The bruise beyond the Isar had spread across the sky and a damp wind had rolled down from the Alps. Krel looked neither at the thorn he pulled nor at the sky but askance at a space in the air beside him.

"No," he said. Nadermann mildly shrugged. Krel raised his eyes from the pit of air and said, "But I think I have a means to know, a source. Perhaps someone available to me and me alone and of great value."

"Do you, now?" said Nadermann. "Tell me."

But Krel looked once again into the judgment beside him and said intensely and as though against dogmatic argument, "She is a person to be valued. Not to be wasted. Not to be used and thrown away. You must remember that."

"We are not bogeymen," said Nadermann. "Besides, this is your idea, not mine."

Krel walked fast again. He had a second appointment, for lunch, made previously. Not only had he little time, but lightning played over the Amersee and the gold Theatinerkirche was as though lit from within against the purple sky. He might escape the rain, but not by much. He was glad to hurry.

He walked wrapped in his new burden. He felt that he had broken out from moral railings that had confined him for years and was now exposed courageously and perilously on the cliff. Like all true courage, it was born of need, not of whim. It was needful for the Americans to learn the bitterest lesson. It was needful for the name of Oswolt Krel to be purged and justified. No doubt at all.

And, beyond that, a fading complaint demanded answer. Ursula Hecht had given him her love, her warmth, her life, and he had returned querulousness, self-absorbtion, cold. He had impoverished a life that should have been as rich as roses. He did not quite blame himself, for in his life he had met other and extraordinary demands, but neither did he disguise it or ignore it. Poor Ursula at the last, butchered for a trick, hideously dead! It was a burden of conscience he did not care to carry. If he had chilled her life, he could at least prove his anger at her death.

He was on Weinstrasse now. It was crowded with street musicians, from blues to Bach, with knots of young people around them. He pushed through T-shirts and jeans, students and tourists. He tested himself; he put Renate's face among them, saw her in her own young life, saw her given over to the workings of the KGB, accused himself of cruelty and treachery toward her. He rejected it at once. History takes what and whom she needs. The vague, the weak, the pimple-faced were useless to her. Those who could serve her must. He picked his conscience and found it clean. He had extracted, had he not, from Nadermann the promise that her jeopardy would be limited, her task not without an end. He had waited to offer her until there was no choice. The sacrifice he would impose upon Renate was in scale with the grandeur of his aims. Deep within himself, he found the half-formed thought that the more living the sacrifice, the better.

He stopped, affrighted. A tongue of lightning lashed over the Frauenkirche; an instant later the thunder cracked high-pitched and close. The air smelled of the storm.

Into it fell big drops of warm rain, the first jubilant rain of the year. It fell on the flower stalls and the street musicians and the ice-cream wagons. It was refreshing and clean and nobody tried urgently to shelter from it. It fell delightfully on the T-shirts of the girls.

Oswolt Krel just got to the restaurant dry. His company was there already: two priests from the Dutch peace movement. He rehearsed quickly the moral imperatives of neutralism. The tablecloths were white. Both the priests wore black.

6

Late that May, when spring performed even more unreliably in London than in Munich, Marie-Sophie Stears had stood on the stairs of her house on Aldford Street in London and considered her four suitcases in the hall below. They were from Hermès, made of pale pigskin and corded down the middle with a surcingle fastened by a horseshoe buckle. They stood on the white-and-black marble floor that Marie-Sophie had had done when the Stearses bought the house last year, right up against the mural after Piranese that had been done last month. Hercules was in it, and he could have perched his bulging haunches on the Hermès, had he chosen to sit down.

Marie-Sophie, at this moment, wore only bedroom slippers and smelled sweetly and still rather damply of soap. She held a small tube in her hand. She called abstractedly, "Giovanni!"

Stears looked out of the bedroom, through the bathroom's trail of steam that set off after Marie-Sophie but gave up halfway. What with her hand now on the banister and herself half-turned toward him, she would have made a particularly attractive poster but he forbore to comment, even with his eyes. Erotic suggestion when she was organizing things made her hand bat down on the air, something between distantly patting a head and slapping a wrist.

"Yes," he said.

"Couldn't we go skiing from Geneva?" she said.

"No," said sober Wop. "We'll be there three days and I'll be busy all the time. Anyway, it's nearly June."

"We used to ski in May when we lived there," she said. "Zermatt's not very far from there. They always have snow in May."

He gave up his pretense of rectitude, sat down on a seat by the stairs, and looked all up and down her with pleasure. "Sophe," he said, "sweetheart, why exactly do you need to ask that this instant?"

All of this was in French. Eighteen months of marriage and a year of London had scarcely improved her English.

She blushed, perfunctorily. "Because I have just thought that if we have any chance of going skiing," she said, "I shall have to take this sun cream and it will have to be put in the suitcases that are already packed. It happens to be a very special one and it is not easy to get."

"You don't even use sun cream," he said.

"I do now," she said. "It is what England has done to me."

And, now that he thought of it, the gold of her body, which had never altered much between January and July, had never developed the outline of suntan that blond women carry like a reproductive diagram any month after June, was several shades paler than he had ever known it. He had always assumed that her color came solely of her Moroccan blood, a constitution no doubt impervious to sun. He suddenly supposed it had required maintenance.

"Poor kid," he said. "Is it that bad?"

"Yes it is," she said. "So do let's go skiing."

She turned and retraced engagingly her trail of steam.

"It's not very likely," he said, but mainly to himself.

The plan had been that he would merely pause in London—to dry the blood of Lüderbach from his hands, to analyze those misgivings born at Reit im Winkl not already analyzed with Brindle Woods on the flight from Munich—simply to regroup before pursuing the shadowy traitor in Berlin through the Swiss banks. In the end, he had paused nearly two weeks. The DIA, it seemed, had browsed contently around Brindle Woods's trap before finally falling into it. At length, Stears was called to a meeting in an office steeped in melancholy and Balkan tobacco, filled with bric-a-brac of a vaguely Hapsburg mode. Here, introduced by Brindle Woods, he had elaborated his Geneva intentions to a gloomy Magyar with eyebrows like snowdrifts. "Does this young man know," the Hungarian had said, "that he will carry the fate not only of a brave man but of the friend of my youth?" And Brindle Woods, bowed down by gloom, replied, "He knows it well. Understand, though, that this was not my choice. My hand was forced by the military." The Magyar wheezed foreboding.

But Stears had not been able to keep Geneva from Marie-Sophie, nor that his business there was, as he lightly dusted it, "banking." "Darling," she had said, "that's just like the old days, and I'm coming with you, like it or not. You can abandon me all day if you have to."

So what had begun as a manhunt had acquired supplementary overtones of a small vacation and even, by now, of a honeymoon. It was to begin that evening, it seemed. As the CIA swallowed him, Stears had become accustomed to pretty suppers resentfully delayed, to whisky and sandwiches on a silver tray shared with Marie-Sophie on the sofa, to a wife in a dressing gown mournfully

70

sipping consommé, to one in bed perfunctorily acknowledging his presence as he turned out the light, to one grimly muttering as he found the bed in the dark. He had married at forty; he had been both flattered by her jealousy and bewildered by the change from the simple courtesies of weekend cohabitation.

But tonight had been back to flowers, candles, Sèvres plates, and Baccarat. Marie-Sophie, after settling her baggage, was back to smiles and touches. They were in the sitting room upstairs after dinner. The windows were still open for a unseasonably mild night; the wine bars of South Audley Street around the corner let out sudden hiccups of footsteps and loud voices. Marie-Sophie wore a long, loose green-and-blue Moroccan dress that floated around her. She lay against him on the sofa. His hands were on her tummy—like a bird inside its feathers she was much smaller than her dress. Never once before their marriage, and not at all soon afterward, had his almost French Marie-Sophie worn anything associated with the land of her birth. It touched him that she did so now, for he recognized it as a gesture of intimacy and trust far beyond anything of flesh.

"It will be funny to stay at a hotel in Geneva," she said. He nodded. She went on, "Do you know, in all those years I was never once upstairs at the Richemond."

"I should certainly hope not," he said. "What would you have been doing there?"

She smiled but said quietly, "I wonder what you will be doing there."

"Don't wonder," he said. "It makes no difference."

"Everything to do with you makes a difference," she said.

There was no edge to it, but he felt a wave of tightness roll across her belly as she said it. He moved his arms closer into her breast and touched her forehead with his chin. She smelled of Femme de Rochas. He said reasonably and accurately, "You never knew much about what I did. In Geneva you knew I talked to Arabs about their money but you didn't know who my clients were."

"I know," she said. But the tightness came back and stayed and spread to the top of her thighs. "What, Sophe?" he said.

She twisted in his arms and looked up at him and said, "You were in the same room then. You couldn't understand that, it's just a phrase I've made up for myself. You did the things people do, then. You had lunches and made money. Why should I have wanted to know exactly? Now I think there is a place where you can go and do anything, anything at all, and it will not matter what because it is not only secret, nobody is even allowed to ask. It's worse this time, since you went to Germany. It's almost like a smell. I can't imagine what you did there, and it would scare me to know. That's why I wanted to go to Geneva with you, because it would be our old life again. But it won't. God knows what you're there for."

"I'll leave the cloak and garrote at home," he said. It sounded both flippant and wooden.

"Damn," she said. "This is the last thing I wanted to talk about tonight." She lay back against him and put his hands back on her soft middle, but she weighed more now, the bird in its feathers replaced by a deliberate woman. "I know these things are done," she said. "I know the world is not simple. My father was close enough to the king in Morocco for me to hear a great deal I did not care to know more about. I'm not a little girl to say, 'Oh, horrid!' And you turned out to be a sort of part-time spy back then anyway, so what's the difference?"

"Quite," he said.

"Quite a lot, actually. No, don't let go of me. I'm not angry. That isn't the point at all."

She had it right, he thought, *pretty much.* He lay awake at an hour when the cars on Park Lane were single and swift. Marie-Sophie had gone to sleep abruptly within his rightful territory in bed, but he put off extraditing her until later. At Lüderbach he had taken a step far deeper into Brindle Woods's secret country than he had before. It was a shabby place; but he understood better now its seduction of the bad or foolish into staying there forever to play round after round of infantile and enthralling games. It offered ravishing liberties; even more, it offered intoxicating moments when one had a juggler's certainty that the center was oneself.

And so it was now. He had the name of a bank, the Antwerp Oriental Commercial Bank of Geneva, and three accounts with their numbers: Spondex S.A., Utrecht Sisal Brokerage, and Pieter Klaus Weinstein Associates. The bank inhabited the half-world of fringe banking, among accounts and deals that would seem rash and vaguely deplorable were they for the relief of orphan children. He knew it well. The accounts were the kind that wear respectable names in the way that the headwaiter of an expensive brothel nightclub wears a discreet smile. Dreary stuff, all of it; the stuff of business lunches that leave behind an indigestion unrelated to the food.

But not when delivered by Brindle Woods and the field director of the Hungarian desk. Not when the names came from a miniature camera slipped from a pocket in the directors' room of the State Bank of Hungary. Not when they hold a Hungarian patriot's life and liberty at one end and the identity of an American traitor at the other. When it was dressed up like that in glittering perfidy, one had to look close to see that it was the same shabby stuff as ever.

But the secret country existed, and it was not the preserve of swindlers. People, ELBEMAN, lived there because they had no choice. To say "A plague on both your houses" was not clever but craven. One could only go there and prevail and keep the memory of one's purpose as bright as one could.

And so, lying with the nipple of a warm, real breast touching his arm as Marie-Sophie slept, he rehearsed his hunt for a faceless quarry down the alleys of equivocal banks. He was brightly awake. He rehearsed it well.

Marie-Sophie had been right. Being in Geneva was more like their old life than he would have guessed. They arrived in the morning, separately engaged for lunch. He walked Marie-Sophie down to the lake and left her with a hug under a plane tree by a bed of pansies, newly watered. Geneva was cool—there had even been late snow in the mountains—and her fur jacket was soft and supple on her waist. He walked down the Quai to the bar at Les Bergues, where sherry, salted almonds, and the Paris paper appeared in front of him, just as though they had not been out of practice for a year. "One always comes back to Geneva, Mr. Stears," the barman said. *Whenever one wants money,* thought Stears, *even someone else's.*

He waited for Baruchi. Baruchi did not have far to come; they were lunching on his side of the river. As the Lake of Geneva funnels into the Rhône it splits Geneva into grave banks and naughty banks, Rolexes and cuckoo clocks. The division does not extend to restaurants—some of the most august are on the naughty shore; thus Yves-Paul Baruchi was spared the walk across the bridge to lunch required of the respectable. Which spared him much exertion, for he ate at the most expensive places every day.

Stears looked across the bridge over the top of the *Figaro*. Marie-Sophie's back would be approaching the farther side on its way to lunch with a girlfriend. A swirl of yellow and pink in the Jardin Anglais suggested tulips. The peak of the Mont Blanc was distant, cold, and clear. He had sat here two or three times a week in his former life; anybody noticing that Giovanni Stears, the investment counselor to Arabs, was back would think only of continuity, picking up the threads. He bit an almond thoughtfully in half. It would not be bad to pick up the threads. It would not be bad to be about to have a lunch at which nothing was risked but money. It would not be bad to whisk Marie-Sophie to Zermatt on Friday. It would not be bad to look from his old office down at the lake all summer and consider a blue-and-teak sailboat with snowy sails.

"You are waiting for someone, Monsieur Stears?" the barman said. He poured more sherry.

"Indeed. For Monsieur Baruchi," said Stears.

"Ah," said the barman, placing in one small sound discretion, amusement, commiseration, and the confederation of the upright against all rogues—a bravura performance, worth his tips.

The plan depended upon Stears getting confidences about some of the Antwerp Oriental Commercial Bank's accounts using precisely the contacts and excuses of a player in the Arab game. The old Stears was nicely placed for it—foxy enough to trade for secrets, upright enough to pay and not misuse them. This was a traffic far away from the KGB's and the CIA's; it would take great bad luck for the KGB's alarms to ring.

But in trading for such things, Stears would be undertaking to repay in a currency he no longer held. The world that deals in private Arab funds is small. If all went well, he would have barred himself from his old life forever.

Baruchi said, "And how is London, my friend?"

"A change," said Stears. "A wider field. Their new banking laws help."

"One hears the Arabs are selling their houses there," Baruchi said. "When I got your call I was worried. I said, 'Stears went all the way to London and now he must come home. We must pray he is not too late.' It worries me." He looked Stears intently in the face, as though fearing to see a dear friend's ill health, fearing to see strain.

Stears sighed. "I am too late," he said. "Geneva is the world center for Gulf Arab finance. It would be hard to get back one's place here. And the Gulf game is over. It is my hope that the field in London has just begun." *Nice feint and riposte*, he thought. *Remember you're fencing with a master. If he doesn't buy this the game's off.*

"The Gulf game is over?" murmured Baruchi. "I am privileged to hear from an acknowledged expert."

"My business depended on new fortunes. Where are the new Gulf fortunes with oil at fourteen dollars? All the Gulf has is debts and Palestinians. I would have ten times the competition now and a quarter the business."

Baruchi pursed his lips as though tasting wine and seemed to find it untainted. "And London? A great city, but I do not have time to go there. It is so sad." He looked sad. His gentle, lined face was weary on its neck over the dove-gray lapel.

And was not lying. Baruchi, to visit London, would have to have twelve years, counting eight off the sentence for good behavior. Even in 1947, young Yves-Paul Baruchi must have had charm. Stears, in his new life, had read the file. It seemed the Jewish would-be emigrants to Palestine could not believe their luck to find a Christian Lebanese young gentleman from Paris so ready and able to charter them a ship. Pity it sank. Pity the torpedo hole from two years earlier had only been patched with plywood. But then Baruchi had bought it from a scrapyard, hadn't he? No, not exactly; he had never paid for it at all.

"London has a different sort of Arab," said Stears. "More strictly a different sort of Muslim. Iranian, Pakistani, African, Philippine. Even Afghans."

"The hungry ones," said Baruchi. "The angry ones. The cruel. Dear, dear—I fear it makes for a far less pleasant lunch. I find that people so often expect me to discuss ruffians and criminals. I do not like it. I do not know how they expect me to talk about such things."

"The headwaiter has asparagus," said Stears. "The barman told me it has just arrived."

"A compensation of sorts. My friend, I found your phone call a little mysterious. Now I think I understand. *Bang bang!* That sort of business?" He crooked his finger around an imaginary trigger. "You have fallen to that?"

"No," said Stears.

"Nor have I," said Baruchi. Which, Stears knew, was really and truly only eight tenths a lie. "Then what are we talking about?"

"I am developing a line on a Pakistani connection. I am willing to share it. The profit is concessions that will be sold very cheap and become very valuable." He dropped his voice. "It is not an arms deal, but my principals expect their money man to have trustworthy connections in that field and be able to use them if necessary. I don't have that. You do."

Baruchi murmured, "Afghans." Then said, "With most men, I would now get up and leave the table. You have a very serious reputation, Mr. Stears. I am talking to that reputation now. Why me? I hate to say it, but we are not very good friends."

The waiter brought white asparagus arranged as a pale lily with a center of béarnaise.

"I am an American citizen," said Stears. "People forget that. I have assets in the States. I fall under all kinds of laws governing American business abroad. In my new field, I need a partner who does not. In this matter—and perhaps in others."

"A good reason," said Baruchi. "A problem one does encounter. A very general one, of course. I must still ask, 'Why me?' If it is not rude."

The wine waiter brought a nice Bordeaux. Stears tasted it and nodded. *Here goes,* he thought. *Roll the dice.*

"I have some rivals," he said. "I do not know their resources, and that is bad. But I have found certain accounts they operate and where they keep them. It is at the Antwerp Oriental. I have a dozen numbers of accounts—some, no doubt, will reveal very little, others more. You do a great deal of business with Antwerp Oriental. They must value you. If information about those accounts fell into my hands it would be of inestimable importance to me."

"I should leave the table now," said Baruchi. "You have made an implication that I find abominable. On the other hand that is a Château Gloria of 1976, a Bordeaux that deserves much respect. It is a cruel choice."

"It needs time to breathe before you taste it," said Stears. "It is a choice you should not rush."

He walked down to the lake again two days later, straight in line with the Jet d'Eau, the towering plume of motor-driven water on the other side. A gathering spring squall carrying scents of lake and woodland ruffled the skirts of spray and spread a rainbow over them. The Jet d'Eau was Stears's first childhood memory of Geneva, and he had taken pleasure in it ever since. At the Quai he turned the opposite way from Les Bergues, under the plane trees. Stears walked to his second meeting with Baruchi. There were ice-cream stalls and little boat basins at first, but after turning the corner toward the United Nations the Quai became more deserted. It was clearly about to rain, but probably not seriously. He was to meet Baruchi opposite the British consulate.

This meeting would be the payoff or the rejection, and Stears was not sure which. At all events he would go home tomorrow.

Marie-Sophie would not have a skiing trip, knew it by now, and had taken it with reasonable grace considering that the higher mountains had new, late powder from just such weather as this. The rain began to patter on the plane trees, whose young leaves gave a sudden toss.

Baruchi was late. Baruchi had stopped to buy a two-franc plastic umbrella, which, over today's chalk-stripe suit, gave him the appearance of a species of elegant but toxic fungus. He came as close to Stears as he could without sharing the umbrella.

"It is in order," Baruchi said, as though of a benign universe.

"Excellent," said Stears. "I had confidence."

"Arrangements at the Antwerp Oriental were possible. Certain papers will fall into your hands."

"Ah," said Stears. "And they will be?"

"Very ordinary documents. The housekeeping of a bank. Activity sheets on the accounts you asked for. When there are regular payments into an account also at Antwerp Oriental that account name will be given. As you well know, when payments go to another bank there is usually only a number."

"I am aware of that," said Stears.

"Understand that you get no more," said Baruchi. "No follow-up. No 'Exactly what is this or that?' I have thought a great deal about this. It is my conclusion that I am being led up some garden path, though I honestly do not know which. I have decided to ignore it. You have an exceptional reputation, Mr. Stears. These were my thoughts: 'Maybe Mr. Stears has told me something that is not quite accurate but in that case he will return me something one day of even greater value, for he is a gentleman of honor.' That is a wonderful reputation."

"You are very flattering," said Stears.

"Oh dear," said Baruchi. "I do hope not." They took five steps in silence.

Baruchi said briskly, "One stipulation. The documents are turned over to you outside of Switzerland."

"A nuisance," said Stears. "A waste of time."

"No, no," said Baruchi, and quickened his pace as though oppressed by the proximity of the lion and unicorn across the street. "A matter of honesty. You are getting simple documents. They are brought to you by a bank employee. He is no thief, he has legitimate access to these papers—they are nothing of actual value. Perhaps it is careless of him to have them in his jacket when he leaves the bank. But hardly criminal—they are not negotiable, are they?"

"Yes, yes," said Stears. "I understand."

But Baruchi was launched. "Only consider, Mr. Stears. There is a moment when this innocence could turn ugly. Suppose the bank employee gives these papers to a man like you. Now that, in Swiss banking law, would be a crime. It would be crime even if the bank itself chose not to prosecute."

"Yes," said Stears.

"In which you would share," said Baruchi, looking at him without favor. "Even Switzerland has prisons."

"Understood," said Stears.

Baruchi smiled at the beauty of it all. "But it is only a crime in Switzerland. In France it is not a crime at all. Surely you would not sink to felony when you have only to cross the border to stay an upright man?"

"In Italy also," said Stears, "it is no crime."

"In Italy also," said Baruchi, dismissing it. "So you will take delivery in Annemasse across the border."

"In Cervinia, rather," said Stears.

"Cervinia?" said Baruchi. "In the mountains? The Italian skiing resort? That is rather peculiar."

"Not at all," said Stears. "Just across the glacier from Zermatt. One can ski between the two. Give your man a little sun and exercise. There's hardly even a frontier post. But it's absolutely Italy."

"No doubt," said Baruchi. "But I had arranged Annemasse, just across the French border here. Much closer."

"Much closer," said Stears. He leaned suddenly toward Baruchi, whose umbrella shied into a plane tree, and spoke toward Baruchi's chest. "And much closer for certain eyes as well. There have been"—he dropped his voice—"*situations* in Annemasse. The Swiss are not fools. I have heard things." He touched his finger to his nose. "Enough. To be half wise is the greatest folly. Safer in Cervinia. There is a restaurant, the Aosta e Savoia. It is popular with skiers and easy to find. There on Saturday at one o'clock. There will be a lady with me for appearances. Your man will signal to me discreetly. I will take them in the men's room."

"Cervinia," said Baruchi irritably. "Very well."

"Cervinia," said Stears. And thought, *Sophe will have to have a whole new skiing outfit, boots to bonnet. Hers is all in London. I think I'll buy it for her after this. What a nice surprise it will be.* He had always enjoyed shopping for her.

"Good day then," said Baruchi. His umbrella had revealed its cheap materials by splitting against the plane tree. His old face was now wet with bright spring rain, like Stears's, though only on one side.

Marie-Sophie said, "What a stupid idea that was, skiing over to Cervinia. It was a sheet of ice on top, and slush down here. My ankles hurt. It was lovely on the Swiss side."

"I couldn't have known that," said Wop.

The restaurant they were in smelled of baking lasagna and German cigars. There were small puddles on the floor from ski boots, but the tablecloths were clean and white.

"Yes you could," she said. "Hardly anybody else was doing it, and anyway it's a southern exposure in May. You should have thought." But she spoke without rancor and went on, "Look at that terrific antipasto. I'm going to have three plates of it and nothing else."

"Switzerland has snow," said Wop. "Italy has antipasto. That is how the world works." He put his hand on hers. "We can go straight up the cable car to Testa Grigia after lunch and ski the Swiss slopes. It's not late." He had bought her a fur-trimmed cap which sat beside her like an urbane little animal. Her golden skin did not flush, but, coming in from the cold, it looked as though a current were running under it. He had bought her a peach-colored sweater, and he watched it emerge as she pushed the ski jacket off her shoulders.

"Does that man know you or something?" said Marie-Sophie.

"No," said Stears. "Which man?"

"That silly young man. He keeps wiggling his hand at us. He looks as though he rented his skiing clothes. He looks like a clerk."

"Oh, him," said Stears, screwing up his eyes."He does look familiar. I think he worked in my old building. I think he worked in the bank." He returned a greeting, loftily, and got the waiter by serendipity.

"The signora will have a great deal of antipasto," he said. "I shall have the cappelletti and the pigeon. Also some more wine."

Marie-Sophie finished her second glass and started on her third. "Did he have epilepsy then?" she said.

"The waiter?" said Wop.

"No," she said. She squeezed Wop's hand. "The silly man. This is very nice. Except my ankles."

"Your ankles were always fine," he said.

In the cable car, Marie-Sophie said, "That man, that funny man, when you got up and went to do pipi he followed you."

"I saw him," said Stears.

Marie-Sophie drew tracings on the iced window with her fingertip. The crystals melted at her touch.

"Did he want to tell you a filthy story or something?"

The dew froze again behind her nail, leaving little sharp pellets on the window.

"If he did, he forgot it," said Stears.

"What a pity," she said. But she looked at him askance.

He could not sleep. The street was well lighted and their bedroom was too close to it. It was too close also to two American drunks arguing with urgent and monotonous voices. Marie-Sophie seemed as usual to sleep soundly. Not only was their room too near the street, it also had twin beds and was just within earshot of the bass section of the Tyrolean band downstairs—all the result of late reservations even at a good hotel.

The bank papers was still in his skiing jacket. They were so because he had no privacy to open them; Marie-Sophie had been just perceptibly more present, quicker in her bath, coming back suddenly for a stocking, then usual—all very likely unconscious in her or even imagined in him. But they were still unopened; he had no idea whether they were worth anything at all. He felt not only curious but uneasy; that they should hang there stuffed into ski clothes carried an impression of casualness that had worried him since his first lunch with Baruchi into recklessness or even flippancy.

He got up. He opened the closet quietly and turned the jacket on its hanger. The envelope had bent to the shape of his waist. It was thick, the record of a dozen accounts—nine of them quite random and simply to blur any possible trail. He crossed the room, silent on the carpet, and sat on the window cushions. He opened the envelope with the tip of his finger. Down here in the village the snow was from a fresh late fall; light streamed in from the street and he could easily read.

He read for an hour, dropping the sheets silently onto the cushion one by one. As soon as he began, excitement or foreboding left him; pleasure in his ability remained, warm and dry. He had made his place in the world with appraisal like this. He had done it very well.

And did again. For it could easily have been missed. In none of the three accounts, all a.k.a. State Bank of Hungary, a.k.a. KGB, was there any monthly entry of two thousand dollars. But in Pieter Klaus Weinstein there was a repetition like the variations of a fugue. Every month, between the fifteenth and the twentieth and inserted at random between other transactions, were two small payments to a particular account. The payments were never the same.

But the sum of them was. And it was two thousand dollars.

And the name of the payee account was Mays. The name was simple and not easy to confuse. It was one of eighteen names with access to PSYCHIC in Berlin.

He smiled down at the paper and sat there for some time feeling sleep begin to rise within him. Now that it had happened he felt a satisfaction that his old life had joined his new, connected by ingenuity, cemented by an abstract trophy. It seemed a good augury. He looked out into the street and back into the eyes of Marie-Sophie.

He held them a long time and then he shrugged. He did not think that she had just opened them. Her hand came up from under the covers and motioned him to sit beside her. He did so, squeezing her covered knees aside.

She said, "Is that what you came for?"

He nodded.

"That was Cervinia?"

"Yes," he said.

"Will I ever know what it is?"

"No."

"Did you like me coming with you or was I just part of the act?"

"You know the answer to that," he said. "I'm very glad you came. And I didn't need you for that part of it anyway."

She nodded and looked out the window, beyond which the moon had come to rest between two peaks. She said slowly, "I have an uncle in Morocco whom I am very fond of," she said. "He's more old-fashioned than Daddy, he stays on his estates, and I used to go there as a child. He keeps hawks—it's the normal thing at home. One day I was out walking and I saw him standing alone in a field, so I ran up to him. He was out with a hawk—that was usual—and he was stroking it very gently, the way you would a young dog, and he was smiling down at the ground. When I got there, I saw what he was smiling at. It was a rabbit with blood all over its neck where the hawk had ripped its throat out. It had struggled a few feet on its stomach and you could see the mark in the soil. When I saw you sitting on the window smiling you looked rather like my uncle. That's all."

He stroked her hand and said, "No rabbit. No blood. That's the whole point."

"Yes," she said. "My uncle was a nice man too."

7

Two weeks after their lunch, Dr. Krel summoned Renate again. Would she come to his house the next evening? The note was delivered to her apartment. She had not known that he had the address.

The great Dr. Krel lived close by, but this was not surprising. The neighborhood of Schwabing, around the university, extends to both the somewhat grand and also the entirely bohemian from a center given over to shops for handmade pottery and posters for baby seals. New Porsches lived on her own plain Kaulbachstrasse.

Dr. Krel's house was as grand as Schwabing got. It had a balcony and gable picked out in gold and green. She went through a dark little garden and up steps. A manservant in a white coat answered the bell.

She was received in the library. Dr. Krel was alone. She smiled, but she smiled tensely, and she knew it; their lunch had left a faint queasiness which digestion had not quite removed, for the queasiness came not from the amount she had eaten but from the amount she had said. She had not dressed to be pretty.

But she felt at once guilty for her reserve. Dr. Krel seemed tired and sad. He smiled at though seeing a trusted comrade in a dark hour.

He said, "I am glad to see you again, Renate, though what we must talk about may not make you glad at all. No, sit here. This is not an interview. You are a friend, not a student."

So she sat in the leather armchair looking through the french window onto the trees and meadows of the Englischer Garten while the swallows wheeled through the evening air and the pagoda on the hill brushed the skyline with fantasy. The manservant came back with sherry on a tray. Renate took hers clumsily. She had never been served like that. Dr. Krel waited until the servant had closed the door behind him.

"You spoke the other day of infection," he said. "I have begun to fear a plague that may destroy us all."

She said, "A plague?"

"A bacillus sent among us, then. A few weeks ago, I was asked to assist in a border crossing. The request came from a notable man, a journalist of irreproachable honor, who would not divulge his own sources. This did not disturb me, given this man and his profession. After consideration, I agreed. The refugee was stated to be an officer of the NVA, defecting in the cause of neutralism. I could not easily refuse. His name was Herter. Captain August Herter, though the name on his papers, of course, was different. His unit was stationed outside East Berlin.

"My friends found a place where a crossing would have some chance of success, especially for a professional soldier. Instructions were passed by tourists, very courageous tourists, in East Berlin. A distraction was arranged at the frontier—you see, Renate, now that I trust you, I will tell you anything.

"It ended in tragedy. A horrible, horrible tragedy. The officer, though very badly hurt, was brought over alive. But one of my own friends, a woman as dear to me as anyone in the world, was killed."

She quietly said, "I read something about that. She was a doctor."

He nodded. A thought came to her, but she wondered whether she should speak it. She said anyway, "At lunch you told me about . . . a friend. Was that . . . was she . . ."

"Yes," he said.

She saw the disturbance in his eyes and the strength of his control. She wanted to take his hand. She felt much closer to him, as though he had stepped down from his dais into the fierce, shared griefs of youth. "I'm so sorry," she said.

"We all know that such may happen," he said. "We choose to do it. But I have learned, or I deeply suspect, something else. This officer was not as he was presented. I was used. I was lied to. Behind this was the CIA. My friend died for the CIA."

She didn't quite know how to take that, though it was clearly an offense. She said, "At least I suppose they were—"

But he quickly cut her off and said, "I know that they think themselves to be honorable men, and in certain contexts I could agree. But I stand for the pity and majesty of the human soul, not for the war machine of the Americans, whatever its aim. It was foul to trick me."

Well, that she could understand. "Yes, doctor," she said. "It was."

He had stood up now. The face had the energy that it had on the dais, but now of distress.

"Renate, that is perhaps the least of it. There is nothing more blind than a conspirator. The CIA thought that it used me. I

84

believe that it itself was used. I believe that that officer, who now knows a great deal of how we work and what we can do, and is trusted totally by the Americans, is a plant of the SSD. That, and more, is the bacillus."

She said, "How do you know this?"

"His escape seemed permitted. I have begun to have an instinct for such things and I would find it hard to explain. But there is one definite thing. At the end, the border troopers had him in their gunsights. They held their fire."

"But he was hurt."

"A mistake. A mine. It was my own friend who stepped on it. There are also other matters that I really cannot tell you of."

"But you are sure?"

"No, Renate, I am not sure. That is what is worst."

She had the feeling that something quite remote from her was growing larger and larger in the middle of the room and pushing her against the wall. She asked, "Why are you telling me this?"

"You know as well as anyone that the DDR is a small country and that the circles of dissent and humanity within it are quite intertwined. I also hardly need to spell out to you that, under Andropov, the Soviet Empire feels itself to be in danger and is hardening its shell. The plight of the Soviet dissidents grows ever more terrible. Poland we need not discuss. In Czechoslovakia, the church is assaulted. The DDR is the gladiator of the Warsaw Pact, and dissent there is growing stronger and more complex. Do you think it will be tolerated? Do you? I am asking you."

She shook her head.

"The key to dissent in the DDR is here, in the Bundesrepublik. You yourself told me at lunch, almost without being asked, the name of the boy who helped you find your way over the frontier. So be it—I am Oswolt Krel. Suppose I were a handsome young officer who had fled the NVA itself? Do you begin to understand, Renate?"

She said, "But you do not know that any of this is true. You said so. This soldier may be everything he seems."

"Yes," said Krel. "If so, I am doing an unforgivable injustice to a brave young man. There would be only one way to be sure. If we knew who his friends and comrades in the East were, and what he truly hoped to achieve, and—best of all—who was guiding him, and none of this from his mouth only, then we could clasp his hand in friendship. Or, if I am right, shout to all Germany that a snake is in its midst.

"Do not forget that they will act with discipline. If I am right, Herter will not be the only one. Reprisals will not be immediate. There will be nothing alarming. In time they will have a complete map of dissent within the DDR. Then they will move fast. They have used false refugees many times, from Günter Guillaume on, to insinuate agents into the West, but never, to my knowledge, for this particular purpose. Its time has come."

Dr. Krel went on. She found his voice insistent and numbing, both at once. "The remedy is not with the CIA, not even with the BND. Those are forces of war. Tyranny can only be countered by innocence. This new lie must be unmasked not by other liars but by those who have risked everything for truth. Just as their agents can prey on innocence here, so can forewarned innocence prey on them. Renate, I am asking you a great and terrible thing. Find out with whom this officer, this Herter, is associated. Find out who are his friends. Find out what sort of man he is. Will you consider doing this?"

She said, "Is he in Munich? Even if he is, his friends here will know no more of him than I do. He would be good at concealing his purpose. I do not understand."

He said, "I do not mean in Munich, Renate. I do not mean in the West. I mean in the place he comes from. In Berlin. In the East. You must go back."

She was miles from the room, hearing this. She wondered what the girl would say. The girl said nothing. Her heart was shaking her chest.

Dr. Krel leaned over her. "There is no way to ask this that would not be terrible. There are things that speech was not meant for. Yes, there is much that I can promise. Every resource we have will be yours. You will have documents. They will be believed. You will have an identity. A room will be arranged for you in a way that will not raise questions. Maybe even a job, though that is harder. There will be a Bundesrepublik passport when you leave. All this we can do and have done before. It is my belief that you will survive and that you will do as much against them as any single human being could do. All of this is true, and I can barely say it to you."

She said, "I have no way to do this. I am not the right person. I am sorry." So that was what the girl would say.

"You are exactly the right person. For you the first step would be simple. You would find your Konrad's friends."

"I don't know where they are," she said. And then felt herself become cold and hard, as she had when she first saw the fence. "How do you know his name?" she said.

"Because you told me. You were talking of your interview with the police. You said it was not difficult. You said, 'Konrad had coached me.' That was obviously your lover."

She did not protest. She went straight to that conversation in her head and listened to it over and a second and third time to be sure. She looked at him as though sheathing a knife. "All right," she said. So that was the queasiness.

Dr. Krel said, "I have no right to expect such sacrifice and courage. I know that very well." She heard it with amazement and sickness, for in his voice it had been decided and agreed and she no longer trusted her own tongue.

But she was suddenly with herself again and she said, "That is not all. Whether I could find Konrad's friends is neither here nor there. That is not it."

She could not go further and she sat, crumpled, looking into her lap. It came to her slowly. "It would not be worth it. I am worth more than that. I am not supposed to say that. It is probably a terrible thing to say. But I have a life that I am leading in the best way I can, and it has a value. I think it has a value even not only to me. I am real and it is real. This man who may and may not be some spy, the government over there that may have some plan, this information that I will maybe bring, it is all less important than one life lived properly, even if that life is only mine. I would have helped you help people. Of course I would. But I will not throw myself away for a strategy."

He said, "Everything you say is right. After all, you are free. Why should what has in fact been achieved in one life be sacrificed to what might be achieved in others?"

"That is not what I meant."

"No. Words are wonderful." He turned away.

"I would help people to have what I have. I would have to."

"But not to prevent it from becoming impossible that they should. The distinction is quite valid."

"No," she said. And he looked back at her, for now she had spoken almost in a wail.

"Not that. Not people at all. Do you know what would happen to me?"

She had not meant to say the last.

He looked infinitely sad. "Yes, Renate. I do. But it is all people, Renate. The rest is only an aid to thought. Or it is foolishness. I cannot let you make your decision on a false premise. They will use every resource to cut off escape as completely as Russia has. Emigration must be the gift of the government, solely. They will be quite largely successful. There will be more death, more prisons. People like this Rudi of yours will be found."

She felt as though she had been sick, sweaty and trembly and weak. She sat in silence, squeezing her hands for words that they did not contain.

Dr. Krel's tone changed and became brisk and helpful. "Let me ask you one simple, practical question. May I?" he said.

She neither nodded nor spoke.

"May I?"

She nodded.

"If you made contact with Konrad's friends, would they trust you?"

She said, "Maybe. I guess. I don't know."

"But they were used to you together. They knew you."

"They knew I was his girl. They didn't pay much attention to me. I was a kid. I told you that."

"But this one, Rudi Schreider, he helped you later without hesitation?"

"No," she said. "He thought I would be killed. But he did help. Rudi was sweet. He helped people." And drew amazingly amusing portraits on beer mats with a pen. She had forgotten that.

"And since then you have escaped and now returned at risk for an urgent purpose. That makes you rather different, doesn't it? Hardly a kid."

"Right," she said. "Probably a traitor. That's what they'd think." She wished she hadn't said that, for it was advancing into the reality of it, which was the last place she wanted to be.

"No. You are working for Oswolt Krel." He said it reprovingly. "There will be ways to confirm that."

She shrugged.

"And your Konrad disappeared after his conscription, and you told me yourself that he intended to work within the military. So there are contacts of some kind within the NVA. Can you seriously tell me that there is a private person in the West, an innocent person who is not a government spy, better suited to do this than you?"

She raised her eyes now. "I cannot answer that," she said. And then raised her shoulders and fought for mastery of her voice, for it was clear to her that she had somehow crossed through the door into agreement and though it hadn't quite shut behind her she had very little time left to get out.

Dr. Krel looked out the window. He said, as though gently saying the obvious to the bereaved, "This Herter will be so much like the man who trapped your Konrad. A brave young officer, secretly a dissident. Receiving confidences, for it is shameful not to trust a comrade like that. And even more secretly, of course, a Stasi spy. So much alike. Perhaps one could hardly tell the difference. But that is one thing that should not influence you."

And so, straightened, she felt that a fist had struck her in the chest. She sat a long time while sickness turned to cold inside her.

She said, "Do I have to say now?"

"No, you should not. You must think about it. Besides, you would not leave tomorrow morning. There are arrangements to be made for your safety. There are things to teach you. This university term ends in three weeks. It is probably safer if you stay until its end; you could not go much before then anyway. But tell no one. Talk to no one. It could only endanger you if you say yes."

She got up. He said gently, "These decisions are easier if they are not quite immediate. You will find you grow accustomed to your choice."

She barely said goodbye. She got to the door before the servant in the white coat.

She stayed out late, alone. She went to a movie the title of which she didn't catch. She went to a café by the opera, where students ate. She thought that if she went to her apartment alone she would go mad, but she couldn't bear to talk to Dieter; she waited until he would be asleep.

She lay close beside him tonight, much as she would once have hugged a toy bear, but concentrating on the rise and fall of his breathing against her breast and glad that he never wore pajamas. It softened the harshness of it, but by morning she knew it: her world had been stolen. The streets of Munich, the colors of the furs, her degree, her friends, her marriage in a kind and clever house, would be tainted forever if they were knowingly bought with cowardice and greed. They were gone already. Dr. Krel had kidnapped them and only through him could they be ransomed back.

Dieter looked at her in the morning with concern. "You don't look well. Where were you, anyway?"

She was still in bed, which was unusual for her.

"I'm all right. I hacked around with Inge."

He sat on the bed, dressed, smelling faintly of toothpaste. He held her shoulders and stroked her neck.

"Shouldn't you stay in bed? I'll get you a croissant from Dalmayr. You like that."

She shook her head. "I'm all right. I don't have a morning lecture. I'll get up later. You go on."

She went to Dr. Krel's house just before midday, when she knew he didn't lecture. She was shown to the library. She had just time before he came to think that the room, for all its sunlight and tiered books, was as cold as a hospital.

He came in. She rose and said at once, "I will do it."

He reached for her hands. She put them aside.

She said, "Would you please give me the details."

The Munich–West Berlin train, by Nürnberg in the West and Jena and Leipzig in the East, leaves the Munich Hauptbahnhof at 8:53. It reaches the frontier at Probstzella at 12:05. Passengers for destinations in the East other than West Berlin get off and cross on foot to take other trains. The West Berlin train then creeps through a complex of fences, baffles, guard towers, and electrified barriers. It is now a sealed vessel. It does not stop until West Berlin, and the station platforms it passes are closed off and lined with guards while it goes by. Renate almost missed it.

Because to dress on that morning began with the underwear and blouse that had been bought for her in a cheap store in East Berlin. She knew it was feeble and she despised herself for it, but to put on the bra and panties, remembering in advance their texture, both slimy and coarse, seemed to smear her body with Over There, and even after she shed her dressing gown she stood in the bathroom alone pressing her arms against her chest. She caught sight of her hand and the scar on its palm seemed to have deepened and darkened. Morning greetings and the starts of cars came up from Kaulbachstrasse. The windowsill was dusted with pollen from the linden tree. She smelled the corner bakery. The blouse was Bulgarian, and one button came off. She was to wear Western outer garments until later in the day.

Dieter, with much last minute disorder, had left by Lufthansa two days before for Frankfurt and Los Angeles. His affection, the last few days, had been ardent; it fact it had been exhausting and was fanned considerably, she thought, by guilt at his desertion. Still, it had been a warm distraction and when he left she felt the cold of her chances settle on her. His trip would be rather different from hers, beginning with the fact that it could be talked about.

She saw Dr. Krel from her own front door. He waited with his back to her on the bench under the beech tree in Kisskaltplatz, a hundred meters from her apartment and close to the subway at Giselastrasse. He had said to her, "Renate, I will not go with you to the railroad station. It is a small chance, but I am well known and one cannot know who is watching." She accepted that. But she saw the angle of his neck, and her heart sank a little more, for she thought, *My God, he is impatient because I am three minutes late.*

But when she sat beside him, her light suitcase between her feet, he looked at her with remote but solemn eyes and she thought. *No. It is anything but that.* He said quietly, "Good morning, Renate."

And he was right, it was easier if it was all done without a fuss. He passed her two envelopes. Three schoolboys with satchels left the house at number 14. The smallest knelt to tie his shoe and then ran to catch up to his brothers. There were squirrels in the tree above Renate's head.

He said, "The thin one is the first. It is the Bundesrepublik passport in the name of . . . what, Renate?"

"Gutrun Shack."

"Good. You will not be using that one long. The DDR visa is stamped in the proper place. You are visiting . . . whom, Renate? Once more."

"My aunt, Hilda Bucholz, who lives at Rosenbergstrasse 142 in Magdeburg."

"Yes. A short permitted visit. Gutrun returns in four days. That, of course, is why you cannot use this passport when you return. This part is very routine, and the passport is perfect. Do not worry about the passport control. They will be the most pleasant DDR officials you will ever meet. They need our money."

He paused. A man, stout and intensely dignified and smelling richly of cigar, walked slowly past, steered by a Pekinese on a leash. The Pekinese stopped a few meters away and relieved itself slowly. The man studied the architecture of the balconies and absently held the leash. The Pekinese moved on.

Dr. Krel said, "The second one is much more important. It is your DDR internal passport."

"Yes," she said. She looked at it in fascination. The paper was softened and rubbed with use. She looked through it. She nodded slowly. It was just like having her old one back.

"Yes," she said. "Renate Lugner. Lugner. It is an ugly name. Like Gutrun Schack." And then, "For how long, doctor? For how long?"

She looked him in the face. It was, as always, like trying to read a language when you do not know the verbs.

He said, "That is partly in your power and partly luck. Finding Konrad's friends should not be difficult, but I do not know how long it will take you to make safe and persuasive contacts. You will use your instinct there, very carefully. You are not an innocent, Gutrun, you have survived before."

He was watching for her to blink at the name, but she didn't.

"Good," he said. "But that is the first step, because we do not quite know how direct is the contact those friends have with dissent within the army. You will have to be guided. Fortunately, there is nothing odd in any of Herter's fellow officers spending free time in East Berlin or spending it with a pretty girl like you."

He smiled at her. She found it like having ice drawn down her back. She did not react.

He said quickly, "At any rate, not much more than a month, I am sure. Though you will have money for much longer—just to be safe. As I promised, this passport will stand up to any examination that does not involve a thorough check with central records. There was a Renate Lugner about your age, but she is dead. It is the best we can do. Are you sure you know what to do at Jena?"

"Yes. When I get out of the train to Magdeburg, I walk back toward the center of the station. I will be on platform three. I take the underpass. The women's toilet is between platforms three and five. In there, I flush the Bundesrepublik passport, torn up very small, down the toilet." She looked at him again. "Then I am trapped," she said.

He held her look with bleak eyes. *I should not do this to him,* she thought. She went on. "I leave the jacket hanging on the peg. If it is cold, I put on the sweater in the suitcase. I go to platform seven and then wait a few minutes for the train to Dresden and then East Berlin. I am this Lugner. An ordinary East German girl."

"Good," he said. "An ordinary East Berlin girl going home, and not on a train that originates at the Western frontier. Nobody could possibly think of any connection with the Western train to West Berlin. Now tell me about your room."

"Taunbergstrasse 148. My landlady is Frau Grundler."

"Why do you need new lodgings?"

"I have been working in Dresden as a grocer's girl. My passport shows it."

"Why are you returning to Berlin?"

She almost smiled. "I am a *Berlinerin*. We always do. Frau Grundler will understand that, whoever she is. The room was found by a Berlin friend. I gather he didn't look very hard."

"What is his name?"

"Max Lebkochsler. A young electrician. Nobody special."

"Yes, all quite proletarian. It is safer so. There is nothing special about the room. It is wiser not to put you with a sympathizer, because one can never know who might be under suspicion. It is just a room where a girl like you might live. Frau Grundler will make the reports on you she has to make, but nothing more. As you say, don't expect too much of the room."

"I have lived Over There before," she said.

"You know how to communicate? You have no questions about that?"

"No," she said.

"We have done what we could about a job," he said. "It is the hardest part, for it is closest to central records. We have a friend who manages a food shop. If one of his girls leaves, you will be told to apply there. That is why we made you a grocer's girl in Dresden. At your age, your employment can be vague for a little while. You must leave your room during working hours, of course."

"Yes," she said.

He sighed. "I am afraid that you must hurry now. It is not long before the train. Do not worry too much about the crossing. I believe that your only danger is the money in the suitcase—and the suitcase was made by people who know their business very well."

She nodded dumbly.

He took her hand. He said, "Renate, you are making the greatest sacrifice that you could make, and for the noblest purpose. We do not know how great the result will be. But this I do know: Germany has had no heroine greater than yourself."

She found the words utterly without comfort, and she threw her arms around him. He flinched at first and then carefully folded his arms around her back. She got up. It was like hugging a monument, and she felt embarrassed and ashamed. The Pekinese's master, now across the little park, looked on in disapproval. She picked up the suitcase. She walked toward the subway.

At every station after Nürnberg she looked at her watch. This was Ebensfeld, 11:20. The country was growing dark and meager.

There were roofless buildings in the fields and decaying engines on the tracks. The East grew nearer. But a beautiful abbey crowned the hill.

She shared the compartment with a young couple, warm with each other, nicely dressed. They were going on a jaunt to West Berlin. The woman said idly to her, "The frontier must be soon. Do you take this train often?"

"No. I have never taken it before."

"We always fly. We thought this would be interesting, once. Are you going home?"

To a Bavarian, her Berlin accent was strong, though she usually forgot this. She said, testing the words in her mouth, "No. This time I am visiting family in the East. In Magdeburg."

"Ah. We are staying at the Savoy in Berlin, this time, on Fasanenstrasse. Do you know it? Is it good?"

"Oh, yes," said Renate. "I know it well. It's very good."

Which was the crossing, she thought, of the first frontier, from truth to lies.

The woman sat back with a click of bracelets cozily beside her husband. "There!" she said. "I told you it would be good."

He smiled and nodded down at his wife. It was clear that he liked her cashmere breast.

He handed down Renate's case. She stood on the platform at Probstzella. She wanted to take his arm with both her hands and never let it go.

He smiled. "Good visit," he said. The train hissed and creaked.

It was cold; they were in the hills. The pines were dark. On a summit behind her an enormous radar bowl stared into the East. A mile away, on an opposing hill, another one stared back. In between was the frontier, here a triple fence with gates. A massive concrete beam across the railroad track now slid aside and an East German locomotive rumbled through with soldiers hanging from its footplate. Deutsche Bundesbahn's traction was exchanged for Deutsche Reichsbahn's. Straggling through all this was the main street of Probstzella, mostly in ruins. The station sign was broken. She picked the suitcase up.

"Thank you," she said.

She offered her passport to the Bundesrepublik officer in green. He waved it aside. She walked into the East. There were not more than six other passengers on foot. Though she was on the soil of her homeland, the fences and the guards in gray were fifty meters on. The platform was decayed and creaked beneath her feet. The train moved beside her. Her compartment friends slid by and waved as they picked up paperbacks.

There were two passport controls, one for West Germans, one for foreigners. Renate waited behind an old woman in bulging black with a scuffed suitcase which she dragged along the ground. The woman's passport was handed back and she walked on through a blank steel door which at once swung back and locked behind her. Renate entered the booth.

The officer was middle-aged and mild.

"You are visiting relatives?" he said.

"Yes, I am visiting my aunt in Magdeburg."

"Have you already a visa?"

"Yes."

"Have you visited the Democratic Republic before in the last twelve months?"

"No, I have not."

He looked at her politely, closely, and took the passport from her. The booth was so arranged that she could not see what he did with it. He did not hurry.

But she was not at first afraid, for the great fear, the obvious fear, had been laid at the very beginning by Dr. Krel. She had said, "But they will recognize me. There will be photographs of me in Potsdam on file. They will pick me up at once." He had shaken his head. "I do not think so, Remate. Not unless they suspected you already. Look at the photograph in your old passport. Then in the mirror."

He was right. The hairstyle made a difference, that of course. But the old photograph was of a different girl. There the mouth was drawn and tight, the chin hard, the shoulders sharp, the eyes narrow and askance. A tough kid, actually. She had blossomed since. There was no other word. But she looked in the mirror at the softened lips, the creamy skin of cheeks, the open and even bedroom eyes, and thought suddenly, *Could this girl have climbed the fence?* She had certainly changed.

But the officer still had it, had kept it too long, and she was suddenly drenched by a terror that standing on this soil, even for minute, had changed her back. She saw herself not even resembling the photograph taken three days ago. She saw herself as a grainy picture: Enemy of the State.

He raised his head. He looked at her more directly.

Could she run before they dragged her off?

"You are from Berlin?" he said.

The words "No—from Potsdam" rose in her throat and strangled her. She had all but spoken them. Her mouth froze with fright. She swallowed. She tried to breathe.

She whispered, "Yes."

He looked at her, surprised. He shrugged. He gave back her papers.

He said, "I too. Better than this place. Have a good trip."

She blundered through the door. It clicked behind her. She felt him looking at her as she went.

So she put her hands behind her as they searched the suitcase. Surely they shook. She had failed even the easy part, the part when she could still perhaps have fled. The suitcase's false back seemed as transparent as glass. The six thousand Eastern marks inside it, money for a three-month stay, would have been a real West German's ticket to "currency crime" and jail. For her, the unimaginable. She thought, *You must all be blind. Can you look at me and not arrest me?*

The inspector was young, with a face like refrigerated veal and eyes like marbles. He looked her in the eye and asked, "Is this all you have?"

She tried to answer in a normal voice. She had forgotten what her normal voice was.

"Yes."

He looked at her closely.

"You are bringing nothing else?" West Germans visiting family in the East usually travel like packhorses.

She shook her head. He nodded, grudgingly. She thought. *They are playing with me.*

She walked toward the exit. He called sharply, "Currency!"

She jumped.

He said, "You have forgotten to buy currency. It is over there."

She stammered something. She went to the currency booth and bought a hundred marks, the compulsory amount, twenty-five for each of her four days' stay. The bills were small and limp. Her hands were damp. The woman at the counter had gimlet eyes.

But she was on the platform. By the time the train came, her fear had just begun to dry from her body. She was back. She began to look around. Newstand: "Read *Neues Deutschland*, Organ of the Central Committee." Few people. They were deep in the exclusion zone; there would be no civilians until Saalfeld. Gray uniforms. A stall for sausage, beer and schnapps. Grease and disinfectant. A Bulgarian beach. "Class Consciousness Is the Dignity of the Workers." She knew it all. The glass on the clock was cracked. The wind was cold. The train came in.

By Rudolstadt it began to fill. She watched people get in. She had forgotten about the doors. West Germans are generally polite, though rushed. Here they hurried less but they pushed around each other impersonally, like crabs. People looked twice at her tailored Western jacket. The man beside her, whose dark hair smelled of grease, gave her space and looked away from her.

The train lurched along the roadbed. She had the impression of a countryside seen through the rain, though it was not raining. There were no suburbs, advertisements, traffic jams, fresh paint, or flowers. Beneath her coat, her body remembered an old sensation, between weariness and grit.

They were still on the Berlin line. There was a shriek ahead, and the window was filled with the red-and-cream coaches of the West German railway. The Munich express, southbound. She looked at the shiny magazines and easy people whirling by. She touched the glass. They flickered away. The police came through to inspect the passes.

Jena began with a bare brown hillside littered with apartment buildings in raw cement. The train slowed. A smell of soot and sulfur in the air. The thought was huge beside her: *For a few minutes you can still go back. You can be at home this evening. You can see a movie. This has hardly happened.* She ached suddenly for Dieter. She pushed it aside and thought of Dr. Krel. Herself, a German heroine. She rose from her seat. The man beside her was getting off here too. She tried to think of small things. He did not quite smell German. He had quick, small brown eyes.

She made herself hurry. The platform was busy. The underpass smelled strongly of fried fish. In the women's toilet it contended with chemical. Her gorge rose. She hung up the jacket on a hook, a gift to the next occupant, who would be unlikely to question her good luck.

The passport was only paper. It tore. The eagle tore. The visa tore. Half her face fluttered down into the bowl. It floated. She flushed and waited. One half of an eagle's wing and her address drifted back, now sodden. She flushed again. They were gone.

She combed her hair straighter in the mirror. There was no soap. It was chilly in the hills, and she pulled the sweater on. It was baggy, and a little grimy, and the label had been taken out. She looked in the mirror.

"I'll do," she said.

She walked between two platforms; that her destination not be obvious seemed somehow wise. But she was no longer precisely afraid. It was done. And a sense of dull depression seemed merely right—perhaps the best disguise of all. She was back with her people. They had not changed. The man beside her on the train was on the platform. That was slightly regrettable. She would not get close.

The trains came in almost together—Erfurt on platform six, Dresden on seven. The crowd moved both ways. She got on the Dresden train and turned around in the corridor, looking out. She saw the dark-haired man in the middle of the platform look quickly around him, as though alarmed. He scanned the crowd. A thought reared inside her, but before she could move his eyes had locked on her. He looked quickly and relaxed. He joined her train.

She shut her eyes. Her chest hurt.

"Oh, my God!" she whispered.

8

The general had of late become accustomed to rise from his desk just before noon each day in the Soviet embassy on Unter den Linden in East Berlin. He had made it his habit, commendable in a middle-aged man, to stroll during the lunch hour. He stood up now, obscuring the portraits of Lenin, Andropov, Ulbricht, and Honnekker, and called to his adjutant in the next room, *"Reinagle, ich gehe weg."*

He was a big man and he had the easy voice of one who is used to raising it—a sergeant, a sailor.

His adjutant's voice was thin. There were bumping noises as though he half rose to his feet, then abandoned it.

"Sehr gut, mein General," he answered.

For the general was not Soviet, but German. Though he had once fought, his rank, unlike his uniform, was not army but secret police.

He walked through the embassy, through that unique Soviet grand architecture, half palace and half railroad station; through the corridors where chunky peasant girls, stuffed into military uniforms, chattered behind typewriters; past the group portraits of inscrutable geriatrics saluting kilometers of rockets and the little pictures on the desks of schoolgirls with ribbons in their hair; through the smell of rank tobacco and disinfectant and armpits wiped with cheap cologne. The embassy stretched two blocks. He was greeted as he walked, in Russian and accented German. He was greeted by most as Comrade General, by some as General Sucher, and by a senior few as Hans. Before some who greeted him were born, when Berlin still smoked with war and stank with death, he had crawled out of the rubble into the Russian cause.

He was a starving ragged corporal then. Now the stately pace of the high polished boots, the gold-and-crimson Order of Lenin against the German field gray, the shining silver hair, and the eyes that bestowed upon each greeting a glance leisured, courteous, and sharp were all superbly of the plenipotentiary of a great nation at the embassy of a chosen ally.

His function was to spy for the Russians upon the German secret police that spied upon the army that held down his people.

He hesitated upon the steps. Summer of sorts had reached Berlin; the sun was warm, though the air in the shade stirred by quick breezes was sharp and damp. To the left was the Brandenburg Gate, closed off by the Wall, and beyond it, in the West, Bismarck's column and Mercedes-Benz's star. The Bulgarian embassy across the street was having a festival. "All Bulgaria is One Ceaseless Agitation for Peace," read the undulating scarlet streamer.

He turned right. At the second block, his head turned slightly toward the corner of the United States embassy and a flicker of the Stars and Stripes just visible up Clara-Zetkin-Strasse. He quickly looked away, like a man refusing an acquaintance. At Friedrichstrasse, which leads to the subway station to West Berlin, he looked straight ahead. He passed shops stocked with unearthly Balkan liqueurs, the colors of aniline dyes, suitable purchases for returning Westerners still encumbered with unexchangeable, unexportable, compulsorily purchased Eastern marks. He passed a shop offering records of folk dances from Moldavia and Romanian commentaries on Marx.

He was now on the grand block, the Hohenzollern legacy, the one street of East Berlin that does not look like Stalingrad or Belfast. Library, Opera, university, and museum, the dome of St. Hedwig's just behind, carried the Age of Reason triumphantly eastward into Middle Europe and ended where the slabs of Alexanderplatz carried Stalinism triumphantly west. The old buildings were crumbling like cheese: the pretty sentry boxes of Humboldt University were stuffed with trash, young elders had seized root in crevices of the library; nonetheless they had weight and courtesy and it was to the general's credit that where most of his calling would have looked rancid among them, he looked magnified.

He turned in to the Opera House square, which embraces both the Opera itself and St. Hedwig's Church, a pleasing balance of Palladian and baroque. It is busy. It is the first place that Western tourists photograph, the Eastern coaches without exception stop there, there is a parking lot beside it, it lies between two major streets. People loiter, walk fast, or sit on benches. Like all the center of the city, it is full of uniforms.

General Sucher walked like a man taking mild but conscientious exercise, but a little later he sat down on a bench just vacated by two robed Africans. The sun was warm. The view was pleasant, if one ignored the strew of petty trash—old film wrappers, a sheet of *Neues Deutschland*, a scrap of wax paper with a smear of mustard and hardened strips of onion—that disfigured every crevice of the city.

Also a child's limp, dog-eared, dirty school notebook. The general, tired of looking around the square, looked down, and picked it up apparently with curiosity, though some distaste.

A child's writing looped through the neat, forbidding squares. A boy's: a MiG dive-bombed, spewing bullets like knitting needles. General Sucher smiled, though he turned the pages with deliberation. In his day it had been Stukas. Geography: from Cuba we get sugar and tobacco, from Nicaragua come bananas. Russian: the boy had trouble here; the Cyrillic letters were ill-formed. A stick-drawn helicopter hovered overhead. Reading assignment: begin at Chapter 5, second paragraph—the book was not specified. The general closed his eyes a moment.

Homework: he read, "Your last is valuable. Breakdown probability in high-throttle use?

"Attach highest importance to possibility of recruits at divisional communications level, especially between their army and yours. Possibility in your network? Status of this would be appreciated.

"Please begin focus on late-summer WP maneuvers. Any new tactical thrust maximally important, also interservice or interforce disagreements on same.

"First priority continues unchanged. Keep the faith."

It was not easy to read. A battleship, topped with spiral smoke, was blasting it with shells.

General Sucher dropped the notebook back into the litter, a foolish nostalgia satisfied, an incriminating document disposed of. His lips barely mouthed once, "Fifth chapter, second paragraph."

He walked back on the other side of Unter den Linden. He walked past the New Watch, Frederick the Great's pretty Doric guardhouse. The present regime had renamed it Monument to the Victims of Militarism and Fascism. Soldiers in field gray with submachine guns at the shoulder goose-stepped among the columns. A coachload of Russian tourists was harangued by its guide. The general watched and looked faintly puzzled, like someone struck suddenly by a long mystery of life or love.

That night, at home, General Sucher took a book to his desk. An elderly dachshund followed him and, when the general sat down, yawned in his face and lay down on his feet. General Sucher opened the book. Chapter 5, second paragraph, beginning, *"So kam ich denn zurück and fand . . ."* The book was *Colin*, by Stefan Heym, an East German writer of whom no country would be ashamed but whose book no East German would be afraid to own. But the general did not read. Instead, he copied the passage out in block capitals, numbering each letter consecutively as it first appeared in the text. 1 signified S; 6, I; 11, N; and so forth. Having done this, he very slowly, and with a great deal of pointing with his pencil at the numbered alphabet, wrote a message.

Since the book reference would be arbitrarily changed for the next message, this particular code would never be used again and was thus very nearly unbreakable.

The room he sat in was spacious and without the decay of the city's older buildings or the almost hysterical shoddiness of the new. It was furnished in the best official taste, elliptical tables of light-colored wood, lampstands festooned with copper tentacles, pink mirrors on all doors. The only visible, believable connection between the general and the room was the dog, who clearly belonged to the general and made its home in the room. There was no trace of a woman.

General Sucher wrote, "High-throttle data no doubt available. Assume not urgent.

"Communications personnel always a target. Heavy counter-security to overcome. Concur fullest in desirability. Success possible.

"Main thrust of exercises so far is again refinement of deep-column fast penetration. Your defense in depth deemed very vulnerable. Counterargument is vulnerability of our rear supply lines, especially through Poland, Czech'a, and your air superiority. Will detail as available."

He stopped. The foregoing had been set down fast for a medium so encumbered. He now stopped and looked at the wall a long time, his arms folded across his chest, his head bowed. He reached down and scratched the dachshund, who sighed contentedly. General Sucher straightened his shoulders and wrote again.

"As to the first priority, in this my life may be in your hands. The penetration of your PSYCHIC is a KGB operation, not ours, and I cannot confirm or deny agent identification except as member of your own armed services, special technical branch. PSYCHIC briefing in Berlin is limited to KGB *Rezident*'s staff and self and thus is highly traceable in case of detected counteraction. Early suspect would be self, as non-Soviet. Please wholly forgo or most strictly limit counteraction or all else may fail."

He hesitated, his pencil over the paper, and added, "Please understand this."

He stopped again, this time as though organizing his thoughts.

He coded: "Extent of PSYCHIC technical penetration as known to me." The following two short paragraphs took him an hour and a half.

When he finished, he crumpled the paper up and pushed it into an empty cigarette package. This was clearly not impulsive, but he did it with satisfaction.

The general composed himself again and said, quietly but out loud, a short Lutheran prayer. He stayed still in silence almost a minute before he stood up, went to the kitchen, and poured himself a heroic malt Scotch whisky.

Very early in the morning, he went out. His apartment was on Karl-Marx-Allee, just off Strausberger Platz, in a neighborhood austerely elegant and gray as the dawn light. His apartment building housed high officials and Eastern diplomats of rank. The dachshund trotted down the steps behind him. Sucher carried a leash but did not use it. There was no traffic; only an old soldier would be up so early. The Stasi on the block, discreetly in a doorway, discreetly but rigidly saluted.

He took his walk on quiet Blumenstrasse, just off the *Allee*. The houses here were prewar, the color of excrement, and sinking from dilapidated to ruinous. A little stone window box, in which a trace of gritty earth was covered by a scattering of rain-bleached litter, spoke of better days. General Sucher stopped beside it, pulled a loose cigarette and the empty pack out of his pocket, lit the cigarette, and tossed the packet in. It landed just in the front left corner.

This drop would not be used again for a month.

That evening, just before dark, a young man in a shiny leather jacket walked down Blumenstrasse. He loitered a little, not hurried, or enjoying a walk. In fact, he had serviced many drops since he had begun to work for the Americans and found this one awkward, unaesthetic. He looked quickly at the window box, picked the cigarette package up, and put it in his pocket. There was no way to make this gesture invisible or entirely unremarkable. He supposed that there were only a limited number of possible drops in this neighborhood. He walked on to his apartment.

Once there, at his kitchen table, he smoothed the paper out and refolded it. He did not know who had left the package and could not read the message. He liked to think, though he knew it to be unlikely, that this weary and cryptic paper held something not only lethal to his government but able to bring despair and ruin upon at least one of its leaders. His closest childhood friend had died on the frontier fence, one eye hanging from his face, lacerated by the shrapnel of a mine. He patted the paper with his hand.

The next lunch hour, on the Alexanderplatz, he stood in line before a baked-chicken stall. He carried a folded copy of *Neues Deutschland*. He received his meal and stood at an outdoor table, reading and eating slowly. He was about to drop his paper into the trash when the man next to him asked pleasantly if he might have it.

This man in turn finished his chicken, which, though a little greasy, was nicely flavored with carroway. He then, with no hurry, walked back with the newspaper under his arm, browsing the windows of the hard-currency shops for binoculars and sporting guns, to his office at the U.S. embassy. As it happened, on the way he passed General Sucher on his invariable lunchtime stroll. Neither man knew of any connection with the other.

9

A week after Geneva and Zermatt, Brindle Woods said to Wop Stears, "I have just enjoyed the hospitality of the United States Defense Intelligence Agency, station London. I was its guest for lunch."

He spoke the title syllable by syllable, without enthusiasm. Stears said, "Notable cellar there, I believe."

Brindle Woods smiled shortly. The DIA was dry. "There are problems there concerning ELBEMAN," he said.

"Did I ever tell you," said Stears, "about the gunner who was invited for dinner to a cavalry mess? His friends asked him about it afterward and he said, 'It was quite extraordinary. There was one officer there so stupid the others noticed.' "

"You did," said Woods. "I keep it in mind at DIA. Quite serious problems."

"I see," said Stears.

The loden coat was back on the hook in Brindle Woods's office, where its presence throughout the summer, unchallenged by any coat in use, made it the more emblematic. Outside, Middle Eastern nannies wheeled diplomatic babies through Grosvenor Square. Woods sat behind his desk in a leather chair so ample for him that he looked like the brightest scholar of the class taking the teacher's place. Over his head, nineteenth-century Munich raised its gold spires toward the alpine morning.

"They think it was too easy," said Woods. "They don't see how you found the KGB's payments to its man in PSYCHIC unless the KGB meant you to. In other words, this man Mays you found is a sacrificial lamb whom we will easily prove to be a traitor, thus authenticating ELBEMAN's bona fides—which will really be false, of course. Meanwhile their effective source in PSYCHIC goes on working. That gives them uninterrupted access there as well as a high-level source feeding us crap from East Berlin. Nice operation. They make the point that all that represents a known KGB geometry. The Comrades even have a word for that tactic. They call it a bolvan."

"The DIA thought of all that?" said Stears.

"Don't be such a snob. The point is valid. Argue it."

"The truth is," said Stears, "that it worried me too."

"Good," said Brindle Woods. He looked at Stears across the desk, like a nice owl waking up for its night's predation. "I'd be sorry if it hadn't."

And Geneva would have been just the place, thought Stears, to hide a poisoned trap within the mazes of the banking system. A trap built specially for Giovanni Stears. Baruchi was a tool on the shelf, available to any buyer.

"I did not find that payment easily," he said. "The KGB would have regarded its agent's pay as secure. For such a small sum it was intricate, very professional. I found it through a bright idea and my own private contacts. The KGB could not have predicted my contact—I didn't choose him myself until quite late. And the KGB had no reason to expect a focused pursuit of Mays."

"Circular argument," said Brindle Woods.

"Agreed in principle. But if the Comrades wanted to give us Mays on a plate—and please remember that almost all we know so far is that a man called Mays in Berlin with access to PSYCHIC is getting money from a false-name KGB account—they would not have given us a lead that would have been inaccessible to most in the CIA."

Woods said, "The first tentative contact from ELBEMAN, the postcard that led to our getting Herter, did not come to the Company. It came to me, to Brindle Biddle Woods. Why would that be?"

"You were a legend in Germany," said Stears. "You've often told me so yourself."

And was stabbed by Woods's eye. "How kind," murmured Woods. He began to remove the weapon and then thought better of it. "This legend's—what? factotum?—is Giovanni Sidgewick Stears, once a financial man based in Geneva. Maybe this billet doux was tossed to you, not to me." He removed the weapon and wiped it with a careful smile. "It could have been meant for you, Stears. It's not impossible. Clever but not impossible."

"Flattering," said Stears, "but doubtful." He thought over the three days in Geneva, trying his memory for the positive scent of a trick. The idea of one was there but not the reality.

"I don't think so," he said. "Anyway, it will not be hard to find out. So long as ELBEMAN keeps up the traffic, the Mays business will remain strictly passive. We watch Mays quietly through binoculars—which is what ELBEMAN is quite understandably begging us to do—and get ELBEMAN's reports on what he's sending.

As long as those check out and it's stuff of any significance, then ELBEMAN's bona fides is proved by itself, and conversely, of course, so is Mays's guilt. The Comrades aren't going to go to the trouble of penetrating PSYCHIC and then telling us all about it. If the flow from ELBEMAN dries up for no good reason, then perhaps we think again."

"Yes," said Woods. "Yes, indeed. Now we come to the real problems. The DIA does not want to watch Mays through binoculars. They are not concerned with what ELBEMAN wants because they don't believe in ELBEMAN. Even granting that he could be real, the DIA insists that PSYCHIC is worth a regiment of him. Apparently PSYCHIC has many attractions, almost in a class with STEALTH." Woods had touched his blotter at each point with the head of a silver pencil. Now he laid the pencil down.

"The DIA wants Mays trapped, broken, debriefed, and turned."

"Jesus Christ," said Stears.

"Right now," said Woods.

"It had escaped me," said Stears, "that the DIA gives the Company orders."

"DCI gives the Company orders." Woods meant the Director of Central Intelligence, who, among other things, commands the CIA. "The DIA persuaded the Department of Defense and the Pentagon persuaded the director."

"We can stall them," said Stears.

"We will not stall them," said Woods. "Would you like a drill sergeant dealing with Mays instead of you?"

And Stears, finding to his vast relief a high card in his hand, said, "The DIA can't crash in on a Company operation. That's one thing at least."

"Mays is a United States soldier. The DIA can do what the fuck it wants. When I got them to allow you personally to break Mays it was a favor from them. A considerable favor. It took work. I was able to use the fact that the Company had found Mays in the first place. Not to mention the penetration itself."

Stears said quietly, "If you had let me go in on your own authority, the DIA wouldn't even know who Mays is. The DIA's paying back a trick, even if they don't know it."

"No doubt," said Woods. "But the better trick is mine and the exposure is still theirs. If I didn't think of the next battle and the next I wouldn't deserve to be your chief."

"I am breaking Mays," said Stears. "Did you say that?"

"So quietly that not the cracking of a bone is heard. You can be sure the Comrades are listening. Do you know much about this fellow?"

"Not much," said Stears. "Only the basics. I should have all the files tonight. I didn't want to put a rush on them. Someone may be watching. He's a sergeant, highly specialized technical duties. He's married with two children. Lives in NCO married quarters in that military city of ours outside downtown Berlin in Dahlem. He's from down South somewhere. I gather he's black."

"Children can work either way," said Woods. "Remember. Quietly."

Marie-Sophie said, "It must be fascinating."

Wop said, "Umh?"

They were going to dinner at Cadogan Place. Their taxi sailed down Park Lane. The green of Hyde Park, in the milky innocence of an English summer twilight, vanquished the traffic. A breath of mist hung over the Serpentine. There were views not so unlike that in Dahlem, out beyond the Berlin grit where the subway surfaced and ran through silver birches ankle deep, this time of year, in bracken. Mays would be able to walk from his apartment, in the ranks of three-story flat-roofed buildings, either out to the Grunewald forest or into the largest 100 percent suburban Kansas City shopping center ever likely to be east of the Elbe. Maybe he did and maybe he didn't, the treacherous creep, the poor bastard. *Live with your operation. Know your enemy.* Well, that he was beginning to do.

He noticed his wife in the taxi beside him. She wore a summer evening dress of peach-colored silk; the diamond necklace marked the softness of her breast and the intake of her breath in vexation.

He recollected that she had spoken. "Sorry," he said.

She said, but with less rancor than he had feared, "It's the same business, isn't it? I've come to recognize it. It's like being shut out of the room when the grown-ups are talking. Strangely enough, my dear, I didn't like that when I was six."

He took her hand, which first hung back, then opened on his knee.

"I'm sorry," he said. "I'm worried. That's all." He paused, weighing his words for foolish melodrama, and then went on. "I think I'm carrying a brave man's life on my shoulder and I find it frightening. I think I'm carrying it across a river where you can't see where you're putting your feet. I won't drown if I fall, but he will. He's in handcuffs, you see."

She said, "I had begun to think something like that," and patted his hand slowly and gravely. And then, as the taxi slowed for their address, said quickly and low, "Whether I like it or not I'm not your enemy." And then they got out. "And not one of your disguises, either."

He kissed his hostess and shook hands with his host. They sat in the upstairs sitting room under a Gainsborough on the paneled wall. Through the open window came birdsong from the gardens and traffic from Sloane Street. His host silently mixed drinks. No chink of ice here.

Frightening, yes. But one could not deny a pleasure that guilt sharpened more than tainted—the pleasure of a secret and arbitrary power. Berlin, a foreign city that didn't know his name, was being stirred by him like an ant heap.

His hostess said, "Paddy only got home about two minutes before you came. He spent all day on our trout stream. I'm happy to say some of the trout decided to come home for dinner."

Wop smiled. She was sitting in a pale silk chair which made her skin glow with that English tint like the pink in apple blossom. She was a very old friend, and he recognized the stiltedness of phrase that indicated she was pleased. He was glad for that, and for the Gainsborough, and for the tint still in her skin.

Paddy said, "Good mayfly hatch. Earlier than usual. Would have had to have left otherwise. Jolly lucky."

Paddy cultivated a Coldstreamer's phrasing. This was misleading. His eyes were All Souls.

He put into Wop's hand a whisky and soda a little cooler than blood.

The size of the operation was the point. No finger, however invisible, could point at Mays directly. The most discreet surveillance could, by mischance, be picked up by KGB. Therefore surveillance, as well as discreet, was massive and directed at the whole PSYCHIC program. This was not an unnatural thing for the army to do and, were KGB to hear of it, would suggest, precisely, a nonspecificity of American information. It would also suggest this to any mole inside the army.

His hostess said, "Are you doing Ascot this year?"

They were in the dining room by now. A Philippine maid passed Stears the platter of trout.

Marie-Sophie said, "Absolutely. It's a promise. It's my reward for living in England and dying of rheumatism one day. Giovanni has to take me to Ascot every year for all four days and give me all the champagne I want."

The trout, as wild fish should be, were firm and faintly pink beneath the skin. Stears said to his host,

"Beautiful. Like salmon trout."

"It's the freshwater shrimp," said Paddy.

What would not be apparent to the KGB was that Mays was attended not only by his small share of the swarm of Army counterintelligence assembled around PSYCHIC but by his very own escort of expert CIA tails brought in from distant theaters and rarely used. There was the danger that Mays's contacts might simply cease, but Stears did not think that that would be for long. The Comrades wanted this badly, wanted it quickly, and would be confident enough to operate around an unfocused investigation. Mays would be confronted with his guilt, could be forced into a double role, and would never know how he had been caught.

Brindle Woods had considered it and approved. "Your geometry is very good," he said. "Remember some mental disciplines. Remember that no one, not even the people chasing Mays, must know that only Mays matters. That sort of knowledge gets telegraphed to anyone who's watching. If they have eyes."

"I know that," Stears had said.

"And speaking of disciplines, this Mays is not a person, he is not a citizen, he is owed nothing. He's sold all that. He is a collection of traits and weaknesses to be recontrolled. Do you fully understand that?"

"Yes," said Stears.

"The trick is to make him the most lonely human being in the world. He has nothing: no friends, no rights, no dignity, no hope, no value. You, on your side, have everything. Then you offer him one tiny crumb. I'm sure you can do it."

"Thank you for your confidence," said Stears.

"Oh, you have it, my boy."

"This is the worst kind of operation," said Stears. "It's cumbersome, it's dangerous, it's unnecessary. Is there no way out of the bloody thing?"

"No," said Woods.

Paddy passed the brandy once again to glasses that demurred politely. Marie-Sophie's fingers began to play with her bag.

110

His hostess said, "What are you up to now, Giovanni?"

"Oh," he said, "the usual sort of thing. Smoothing the Bank of England's feathers over interest rates. Telling Crédit Suisse that we'll clear up the trade deficit by next Wednesday. Making everybody think that what we want is going to be nice for them."

She laughed. "You were always good at that, Giovanni."

On the way home, Marie-Sophie asked, "What exactly did she mean by that?"

———

Sergeant Scott Mays, who rarely drank beer and had not held a rifle since boot camp, had been born in a black hamlet seven miles in from the sea on the soft and snaky banks of the Wando River. The hamlet was Huger, South Carolina. It smelled of mud flats and the oyster-shucking plant and, early in the morning when the crab and oyster boats set out, of the exhaust of old and leaky diesels. Scott Mays had spent his boyhood on one of these.

Sergeant Mays was at this present time the effective on-site technical expert for the computer component of the PSYCHIC project in West Berlin, his captain having left the army for MIT and his replacement having not yet reported. This was not alarming, since Sergeant Mays had designed part of the computer program on which PSYCHIC depended.

At the age of twelve, when he was a little boy in a ragged sweater on his uncle's clattering oyster boat, Scott Mays had fallen in love with numbers. His uncle had a compass he never looked at and two old charts he never used, Wando River and Charleston Harbor. One evening a fog came in quickly while they were in the middle of the harbor before the turn into the Wando River. He could see that his uncle was worried. Then the fog cleared for a moment and Charleston Light blinked to starboard and Castle Pinckney range to port. His uncle drew two lines with a broken pencil on the old chart and then another one under the bridge and up the Wando. He stood over the compass and pushed the throttle in a little so that the engine rattled rather than popped. "I got my bearings now," he said. "Praise God."

The foghorns in the ship channel passed by, the traffic on the Cooper River bridge thumped overhead, and Scott stood over the chart while the intimation of a new order took life within him. The oyster beds of grit and mud and the creeks with blue herons and Charleston Light and St. Michael's steeple had another life entirely of numbers and angles, absolute even when they were invisible. He had fallen into a second world. It was a world he loved from the beginning.

He began to read math books like comics; for him they had stories in them. The seasons moved by numbers. The pull on the anchor in the creek tides was governed by the square of the velocity of the current and the holding power of the anchor by the cosine of the angle of the anchor line relative to the bottom. The world was bound together by numbers like the interlocking girders of the soaring Cooper River bridge. Under the hot October sun, with heavy gloves up to his elbows and the deck greasy with mud from the oyster clusters and a smell of creek and diesel, he worked in a world as cold and perfect as the stars.

Life went on with work on his uncle's boat, and schoolwork. He was at the top of his class in math, but he did not give that much thought. He began going out with a plump, sweet-natured girl called Thelma, and before long, after walking her home one night, made love to her under the live oak at the bottom of her father's farm.

He knew that the black boys he went around with did not think as he did. He also knew they were idiots. He assumed that white people, or at any rate people outside of Huger, or certainly people outside of South Carolina, shared his world, because it was the obvious one.

For his eighteenth birthday, Thelma told him she was pregnant. It never occurred to him not to marry her. The occupations available in Huger were oyster shucking, oyster tonging, dirt farming, or scraping paint at the boatyard. He joined the army.

In the middle of boot camp they were given some tests, including one with numbers and shapes. Two days later he was called to his colonel's office. His colonel and his lieutenant were there and another officer. His lieutenant held out the test paper and said soberly, "Soldier, did you do this by yourself?"

"Yes, sir," he said, and then remembered and said, "Sir!"

They gave him a more interesting test. He was allowed an hour, but he was through in twenty minutes. The other officer looked at it and said quietly, "Jesus!"

Two days later they flew him to Washington for the day. The biggest place he had seen before was Charleston, which he was afraid of. He talked to people and did more tests. These tests were fun.

He went back to boot camp. After boot camp, he was trained solely in computers.

The joy of numbers was unlimited, for their light shone everywhere. The grander the world beyond Huger, the richer the tapestry they played over. After two years, the army sent him to Germany. By then he was ready to explore.

He walked past a church and heard the organ play. For two months, he was ravenous for Bach. The German language was clever, like an exercise for two fingers in logic. It amused him for six weeks and made life more interesting. He saw a picture in the paper of the Charlottenburg Palace and went there. He played with the formal relationship of curves in the high rococo. He was much farther from Huger than even he knew.

He was also getting further from the army. There had been a time, even long after it had dawned on him that he was brighter than the officers he saluted, when he looked at the army with overwhelming gratitude. It had plucked him up from the Wando, breathed on his wings, and set him free. He might have been shucking oysters. The little apartment in Dahlem, with dishwasher and a balcony, was unimaginably nicer than any place anyone in his family had ever had.

He never disputed the truth of this; he never forgot it. It became simply uninteresting. He was a citizen of numbers. The external military world of sentries and rosters and salutes became a lumpish distraction as far from his life as the muddy battlefields for which the projects he was assigned to were theoretically intended. The equations he worked with did not salute.

And dissatisfaction was gathering over him. His formal education was laughable. What the army had given him was not worth nearly as much outside. Within the army, he was beginning to compete with the best technical brains of the officer corps, and he was not competing on equal terms. When he had listened to Bach, he had had a tantalizing vision of his own gift soaring and turning with the music. It had made him feel cold. Now it occurred to him instead that the army had exactly what it wanted from him and that he would go on doing small mathematical tricks forever. It occurred to him that he was black. He started to feel trapped.

He was not a cold man. He adored Scott Jr. and the baby. He loved their mother because she had given birth to them. Thelma was a poor, sweet, fat, dumb, swamp black girl. She had nothing to say to him beyond what she had cooked that day and what the baby had thrown up. She could deal with nothing in Germany. They ate like poor blacks, and it was frozen from the PX at that. He knew that none of this was her fault. She was part of his trap.

She cried a great deal, which made him baffled and resentful. He did not quite understand why, but they had stopped making love.

If Scott Mays was nervously discontented, Thelma Mays was leadenly forlorn. Thelma hated Berlin, hated the cold, feared the Germans, had lost all idea of who her husband was, and wanted nothing but the only thing she knew, which was Huger, South Carolina. One day she stumbled on the tropical greenhouse of the Berlin Botanical Garden, quite close to Dahlem. To her wonder and delight, the Germans had seen fit to assemble there a South Carolina swamp about the size of a swimming pool. She began to spend all day there alone with the baby. It only cost three marks. There was a cypress pool and a mushroomy smell of earth and warm, dark water reflecting Spanish moss and everything there felt warm and alive and damp. It was so much like Huger there might almost have been snakes there.

And soon there were.

One day another black woman had come to the tropical garden where Thelma Mays had begun to be pointed out to people by the custodian. She came back twice in the next week. Thelma Mays knew she had to speak to her. There were not many black women in Berlin, and if this one was here she was probably like Thelma, cold and lonely and miserable and scared, though maybe not quite so much as Thelma because she didn't stay so long. Also she looked like a city lady, and one of the prettiest ones Thelma had ever seen. Thelma was shy. She looked away from the black woman as carefully as she looked away from the Germans who walked past her making their horrible sounds.

But one day she looked up and almost jumped off her seat on the wall of the cypress pool, for the woman had silently sat down beside her. But the woman touched her arm gently and said, "Honey, you must be from home. I've been watching you. I don't like to see homefolks being lonesome all the time."

She was called Gloria Johnson. After that, they talked almost every day.

She came from Baltimore. She had a husband, but he traveled all the time. Thelma never quite figured out what Gloria's husband did, but it certainly wasn't army; it was important and they were well-off colored people and they had an apartment downtown in Berlin in the middle of all the Germans. But Gloria knew what it was to have to live abroad. She told Thelma she was her only down-home friend. She didn't mind talking about children's diarrhea.

One day, Gloria asked Thelma to come with Scott and have supper with them. Thelma was proud. Scott would never have thought she could meet people like that.

The Johnsons improved the Mayses' life. Their apartment, in Berlin itself, had shelves of books, old furniture, and crystal bottles for the liquor. Scott had never seen such a place except in movies. It was beyond him that such people would talk for thirty seconds to his wife, but his host gave him a drink and he put the thought away. Thelma was terrified, but Gloria took her in the kitchen. She made a joke of it that she couldn't find all the kitchen things even in her own apartment. Thelma relaxed. The German food did not bite her.

Randolph Johnson was the first black man Scott had talked to who could think as well as he. Randolph was a bony young man with excited eyes like a jazz player's. But he wore an expensive jacket and they sat in the living room drinking Scotch out of cut glass, talking about the world. He was an interesting man.

He was crazily patriotic. He made the redneck sergeants sound like hippies. America was without stain. The civil rights movement had proved the bottomless wells of American virtue. America fed, educated, and comforted the world and was invariably abused in return. Scott had generally thought that his country, of which he had seen a coastal swamp and some army camps, was probably as good as most, but he was forced to rein this one in. About dinnertime he heard himself say, "Man, there are people in the army who *hate* niggers."

At dinner he sat next to Gloria. He could hardly keep his eyes off the front of her dress. She was rewarding to talk to. Her voice was low. He often had to lean closer. He waited to catch her scent.

The Johnsons evidently traveled a great deal. After that evening, they rarely saw them together. Scott saw a lot of them separately. Sometimes Randolph would come by for a beer after Scott got home. This surprised Scott at first, but he decided that intelligent black Americans were not common in Berlin. On weekends he and Randolph sometimes walked together in the Grunewald. Scott enjoyed at first talking to an informed man, but Randolph's nationalistic obsessions became irritating, like a cultivated mannerism. It made Scott in turn say—half annoyed, half humorously—things like "Afghanistan's a fucking joke compared to Vietnam, man. We had *five* hundred thousand people raping and burning over there."

Scott did not thoroughly believe these things and was not even much interested in them. But he found that saying them both relieved and excited the tightening coil of baffled resentment that constricted his daily life and that he found more and more convenient to call racial anger. He felt that it was dangerous for him to think such things, knew that it was dangerous to express them, and was impelled to express then even more. This was the least of the reasons he began to avoid Randolph. It was embarrassing to be in his company.

For he was seeing a great deal more of Gloria.

He lay beside her on the bed in the apartment on Bleibtreustrasse. Her hair spread across his shoulders like a wing. Her breast rested warm and silken in his hand. Her long waist stirred gently against his side. The neon light of Ku-damm skipped and flickered through the heavy lace curtains like lights through falling snow. The traffic rumbled gently. Randolph was away. Her mouth hung above his. Her arms tightened gently around his neck. He put her mouth to his and closed his eyes and lay in the warm, moist, breathing, perfumed dark. His lust grew again. He moved and she moaned and kissed him more deeply still.

She had captured him completely; she magnified him. Her jeweled hand upon his chest, her eye softening for him, her voice on the pillow by his ear, the high ceiling and dignity of her room, the happy lilt of her fur coat when she saw him on Ku-damm, all banished forever the bumbling rustic with one prodigious gift. With Gloria, he was suddenly on a level with his own brain. Her sexual adventurousness, which had shocked him at the beginning and then made his years with Thelma seem like fumblings in the cow stall, finally made his body seem clean and winged.

The last did not quite come out in the photographs. Lying beside him in deep languor about six weeks after all of this had begun she whispered in his ear, "I've got a surprise for you, darling."

He raised his head, smiling.

The long, exciting mirror at the end of the room opened and Randolph came out. Scott had a quick glimpse of the camera and sound equipment in the closet. His first act was to cover himself. Gloria did not. Randolph advanced toward the bed with the serious modesty of an amateur photographer with some really good work. He put prints on the sheet, as though dealing cards.

Scott's first thought was of ordinary blackmail or even of perversion. He looked dumbly at the two of them, whose manner was methodical but whose eyes seemed pleased.

"What? What do you want?" he said. "Why?"

Randolph said, "PSYCHIC."

His stomach froze. He had never even said the word to them.

Gloria, who never took off her rings, laid her jeweled hand on his shoulder and said earnestly, "Honey, it doesn't have to be so bad. We just had to get your attention."

It took two days to force him. He lived them in darkening nightmare as his life slid toward its ruin and in growing excitement as he wondered what the ruin might offer.

The "Johnsons" called him back to Bleibtreustrasse the next evening. They received him soberly but pleasantly. He had the feeling of being tentatively received into a club, if he kept on his best behavior. Gloria opened an album of photographs on her lap and made him sit beside her. They showed her with other blacks dressed in the clothes Cubans affected with slogans in Spanish behind. They showed her bundled up in fur in a place that was probably Moscow, since she said it was. He vaguely recognized some of the blacks as radicals and Panthers from the old times.

"I went over years ago," said Gloria in her low and pretty voice. Her scent was as always. "The army knows all about me." She turned to the end of the album, where she and Scott disported on the bed next door. "It's not just your wife and children," she said. "The army will never believe it's just, you know, *that* with you and me. Not with the tapes."

He was sickened. He was terrified. "What tapes?" he said. He was fascinated.

Randolph played them. The voice was certainly Scott's, making wild, embittered denunciations of his army and his country. The other voice was different, accented, cautiously sounding out the genuineness of this crazed American black's implied offer of treason. It was a brilliant performance.

Randolph gave him some more photographs. He said apologetically, "These were on a different film." They showed Scott, a little fuzzily, receiving money from Randolph in the woods. He remembered: he had picked up Randolph's dinner tab one day and had been paid back in small bills.

Randolph said, "They will really crucify you."

Gloria said, "A white man might just get himself out of this, though don't ask me how. But not you, baby. Deep in his heart, it's what the white man knows we'll do. Isn't that so, sweetie?" She looked straight into his eyes. He discovered he had nodded.

*　　*　　*

On their next meeting, a blond young man was present. His manner was chilly, but he greeted Scott as though Scott had endured great perils to be there. He had a light accent. Scott realized with the feeling of having swallowed a carving knife whole that, all the way from the swamps of the Wando, he was finally in the presence of a Russian.

"It is time to talk of arrangements," said the Russian over coffee and a lemon cake. "You have no alternative, but that does not mean they will be harsh. We have absolutely nothing against you, unlike at least some of your compatriots. It is a good thing that has happened to you. It is your opportunity."

"That's just what I said," said Gloria. But she and Randolph both quickly left the room.

———

The reports and tapes came to Stears daily by courier from Berlin. For ten days, he knew where Sergeant Mays had been at every quarter hour of each day, every step that he had walked, and every human being he had been in contact with. He knew the sound of the Mays toilet flushing and the hymns that Thelma Mays hummed under her breath at the stove. He knew how Scott Jr. said his prayers and what bedtime stories his father told him. He wondered what Mays thought about now while he told them.

He rather liked Mays.

He said to Brindle Woods, "Do we need some kind of authorization for this? German law and all?"

Brindle Woods said, "To hell with German law. Anyway, it's not Germany. It's the American Sector of Berlin. Ultimately it's a military government. Ours."

"I don't like it anyway. It's a risk."

Woods said, "It's a necessary risk. What I said about DCI was true."

On a Monday morning, the thirteenth day, his eye stopped on the page. He went in to Brindle Woods.

"Contact," he said.

"Positive?"

"Circumstantial. My people were not crowding him. Of course. And it's a strange little setup—you'll see. But it's got to be it."

"Pattern?"

"Regular as to Sunday. That's inherent—which is the only weakness, I suppose. He did the same thing last week but nobody noticed the contact. It's that good. We have the worst possible description of the KGB's man this time, and since nobody has any recollection of him it's possible they're using different men. We just have to follow Mays."

"And next time you plan to join the party?"

"I thought I would tag along, yes."

"Good, Stears. Very good. Be careful."

He nodded. It disappointed him that Mays was using his son. Probably he had little choice. Soon his choices would be even fewer.

———

The sack contained ripened dead canaries. The vultures craned their necks, slapped their wings against the roof, flopped down, and waded into lunch. Two little boys on Stears's bench forgot their ice creams.

"*Prima!*" said one, deeply impressed.

"*Wie Lunch in unserer Schule.*" Both giggled.

Close by, a marble Zeus decorously raped Europa. Stears forbore to photograph any of this, since his Kodak was a radio.

From two hundred yards away, the galvanizing accents of German public address came from the Berlin Zoological Garden Station, where main-line trains, S-Bahn, and U-Bahn come together.

The little red "ready" light on Stears's camera quickly blinked twice. The subjects had arrived on the U-Bahn.

A rhinoceros behind relieved itself massively.

"*Er stinkt,*" commented the bird fancier.

Three minutes later the light blinked three times. They were at the zoo gate. They could not have loitered.

Scott Jr. liked the deer. The deer, with their species's predilection for kitsch, hung around an Indian tepee. Scott Jr. was a chunky little boy in stiff new jeans with liquid, wondering eyes. He looked domestic and vulnerable beside the mischievous, quick young Germans. He held his father's hand. His father was quite black, with a soft, broad face and a quiet voice. He bent toward his son as he talked to him. He wore his uniform well.

Good, thought Stears. *He's doing it in uniform. That's another thirty years.*

The German boys conferred. "*Ami Neger,*" whispered one.

The other screwed up his courage. He pointed to the tepee and said to Scott Jr., "You have Indians where you live, black boy?"

It was probably not meant badly, but Scott Jr. shrank back against his father. His father held him as though he perfectly understood.

"*Nein,*" he said politely. "*Die Indianen wohnen nur im fernstem Westens. Bei uns, gibt es schwartz oder weiss.*"

The little boys, impressed, regrouped.

Oh, damn it all to hell, thought Stears.

There must be a variable time for contact. The Mayses wandered off to the polar bear. It was the wrong direction. Stears let them out of sight. They would be tailed, but not by him.

At 12:23, his camera blinked twice, with a pause of two between. *Turning toward contact.* He got up. The signal of five rapid blinks, *Contact at gate,* had not come. So the contact was unrecognized or different and Mays himself was their only target.

His goal was a circular, flat concrete building. On the circumference were cages, and from the cages came the voices of large and toothy predators.

He saw the Mayses enter the building past a panther that looked at them with flat, amber eyes. Behind them followed John Falls from the CIA, Langley, with an infrared-loaded Minox in his pocket. Stears entered himself. Somewhere in the procession would be the KGB contact, identity unknown.

The building was full of the sharp, protein reek of cats. Stears sought the stairs and went down the unlighted steps. At the bottom, he opened the swinging door and stepped into the dark.

He was in the Night Zoo.

A blue velvet light, like a moonless night in August, barely glowed in the ceiling. On either side of the winding corridor were glass-fronted cages dimly lit. Inside them, creatures of the night hopped, slithered, and flew. It was crowded. Up against the cages, the shape of a face could be seen. Elsewhere one barely saw silhouettes, or bumped into them. People whispered.

The Mayses had simply vanished. Blue jeans, dark sweater, bottle-green uniform, black faces. Brilliant. Mays didn't look the type to grin with big white teeth.

The cages were the cue. Last week had been the fennecs. He fumbled toward them without confidence. There they were! Tiny little white foxes trotting through the gloom on dainty feet. No Mays. No KGB. John Falls brushed his sleeve and Stears murmured, "Do a sweep!"

The layout of the place was circular. Sooner or later, Mays could be found. By then the contact might be over.

120

He started off. Well ahead, he glimpsed two silhouettes, tall and short, by a cage. He softly hurried. In the cage, a jumping hare moved big-eyed and stiff on tiptoe like a husband in a French farce. A German mother and daughter watched it. Damn!

He stumbled over nothing. A soft, scared young American voice said, "Sorry." He stifled a reply in English. Scott Jr. Alone. No double shape to look for, then. He wished he could tell Falls. No Falls.

He passed a cage done as a literary garret, full of bats.

A tiger screamed upstairs. Heads turned.

Something glittered in the darkest dark and caught Stears's eye. He moved toward it. It glittered again. Then dark. Stears stealthily hastened.

No glitter. He moved forward. His shoulder caught another's. Mays would not spend long here. The contact would be synchronized. This was likely nothing anyway. He turned back to look for Falls.

He saw it behind him. He had gone too far.

He almost knocked Mays down. Mays was standing well back from the loris cage, his head invisible. When he moved or breathed, one U.S. Army button kindled in the light.

Mays was obviously waiting. The contact had not been made. Stears backed away and looked carefully for Falls. Without the Minox there would be no record.

No Falls. But a shape was pressing toward them, visible more as movement than as form. Mays saw it too. His hand strayed toward his pocket and checked. The loris oozed through the branches.

A shape separated from the crowd. It moved toward Mays. A hat. A man. A man with a bland, fair, and oval face. A man in a jacket. He stood beside Mays. Behind Stears, jerboas bounced from ground to branch like hardballs.

Falls emerged. He was too far away and the angle was bad. But he saw them.

Mays's hand went back to his pocket. Stears thought the hand was shaking, but he could not be sure. The pocket was buttoned. He fumbled with it. Falls slid through a cuddling couple and changed his angle. Mays took out a packet and passed it to the man in the hat. As he did so, Falls's hand went from his pocket to his face and seemed to brush it, freezing for an instant. The man in the hat slipped into the dark. Stears and Falls stayed stock-still, looking into cages. After a minute, Mays faded back toward the last position of his son.

Falls touched Stears's back. "Game, set, and match," he murmured. Jerboas rocketed around.

———

Once again, Mays looked at photographs of himself. In these, which were infrared, he had a halo and was not black. Otherwise, he was recognizable. Now he was in an office in the medical wing. He had been told to report there in the lunch hour, purpose routine. An officer he did not know was in the room. The room smelled medical, but the officer was not in a white coat. The corpsman left at once. The officer said, "Do you enjoy the zoo, Mays?"

These photographs, though less lurid than the first, were more deadly. They showed an American soldier with classified duties, in uniform, surreptitiously passing material. They had been placed in his hand by an officer who introduced himself as Major Hamilton, from Washington. Major Hamilton was tall, and the decorousness of his manner scared Mays worse than the drill sergeant had at boot camp.

Major Hamilton, who was Giovanni Stears, said, "We tracked your friend back to the East. He crossed with a USSR passport. So I'm afraid there is no doubt."

This was not true. But Mays could not know it.

Major Hamilton was leaning against the desk. He crossed his legs and said, "You'll get life. A couple of navy boys had an idea about as intelligent as yours. They were tried three months ago. They gave the leader three hundred years and the sidekick got off with life and a day. Maybe you read about it."

He looked at Mays. Mays had the photographs in his hands on his lap and was looking at them in studied bafflement. The surface of Mays's face still held, but as though interior forces were pulling at the cheeks and mouth.

"They were tried as civilians," added Stears. "For you it's Leavenworth. Life and a day means they let your body out a day after its cold. The army gave you a lot. We won't be nice."

Mays looked up. By some effort, he had pulled his face into a semblance of smooth black grievance. Mays said, "You must be aware, sir, there's some mistake about this. You shouldn't make allegations, sir, like that." His voice was meek, with insolence in the far distance.

Not bad, thought Stears, and, leaning back, he touched the buzzer behind him.

122

Outside the door, there was clang as though a metal chair had been hurled backward. The door opened and through it came a craggy, bull-necked white top sergeant of MPs, a figure of mean piny-woods army camps, spat tobacco, and angry beer. Stears caught, and approved, an acrid trail of sweat. Mays flinched visibly.

Stears nodded briskly to the sergeant. The sergeant said, "Yes, sir!" He seemed to breathe hard. He crossed the room to where Mays sat rigid in his chair, pulled the chair against the wall, and pushed Mays's head against it by the neck. The photographs fell on the floor. Mays tried to guard his head. The MP caught his wrists and jerked him to the edge of the chair. He was breathing over him. He pulled out a small, spiteful knife. Mays whimpered. His head was held tight and twisted in the sergeant's armpit.

The MP stuck the knife into Mays's upper shoulder, under his sergeant's stripes. He sawed. Stitches came loose. He pulled, hard enough to twist Mays's shoulder, and the stripes came off, leaving a pale, ragged patch beneath. He did the same on the other shoulder. He released Mays's head and cuffed it back against the wall. He turned to Stears and straightened.

Stears said, "Thank you, sergeant." He held out his hand for the stripes and crumpled them lightly. "Wait outside, sergeant," he said.

The door shut. Stears, who had not moved, said to Mays, "Don't argue with me, soldier."

Mays said, "I didn't want to. I didn't want to. I didn't want to." He spoke as though a small, cheap machine capable of those words had been installed inside him. But what was worse, thought Stears, was that the face had lost the surface of intellect and cultivation that accomplishment had put there, leaving behind a humble and dismal terror.

"I hear a lot of that," said Stears. *Careful now,* he thought. "Did they pay you much?"

Mays hesitated an instant. "No, sir," he said.

"They didn't pay you much or they didn't pay you?"

The same quarter beat of hesitation. "They didn't pay me much, sir."

Stears said, half to the floor, "That's lucky for your family, soldier." And then, "And what did you have to give them? Try not to lie. It won't help."

"Two things, sir. First the program. Then the collected data, day by day. What did you say about my family, sir?"

Contact! thought Stears. He said, "Which program? The master program?"

"Yes, sir, the master program. About my family, sir?"

"I'm asking the questions, soldier," said Stears. "How much did they seem to know about the program before you told them?"

Mays's eyes were pleading now. Stears thought, *Don't let him twist too long. He's smart—he might start thinking.*

He shrugged and added, "The KGB doesn't like to lose its investment. When they've paid a lot and the intelligence stops, they try to get it back. With you locked away, they try to get it out of the family. They can be rough. It's a warning to their other people. Since the family usually weren't traitors, we don't like to see it. That's all." *I must have faked more in the last five minutes than this bastard in his whole career*, he thought.

Mays whispered, "There was money, sir. It didn't start that way, but there was money. What we gonna do, sir?"

"What you are going to do is talk," said Stears.

He said, "You should have reported this, sergeant. I'm not talking by the book. You really should have done it."

He was facing Mays in a chair. He had a notepad on his knee.

Mays looked up at him out of whipped eyes. He shook his head.

"Just the photographs, yes sir, I would have done that. But the tapes, they'd have sent me to where you're going to send me now."

"Don't pack just yet," said Stears. "You would have had some very frightening interviews. But we're not easy to fool. You know that now. The United States does not put its soldiers in prison without thinking about it. Your advocate would have had that tape taken apart. I'm not an expert in this, but the splicing would probably have shown. The pictures would have proved a setup. Men and women who should know a lot better than you have fallen for that trap. We could probably have convinced your wife that you were in professional hands. We've done it before with wives and husbands. The Russians can't make you do anything you don't want to do—not on this side of the Wall. They can only panic you. But they did that, didn't they, Mays?"

Mays nodded and sighed.

Stears turned his voice onto its edge.

"So to protect your ass, sergeant, you were willing to kill as many of your fellow soldiers as it took. And get some money for it. Right?"

And this was as a rule the moment of wounded, or even of shocked, protest, but Mays had become almost Mays again, the puddle of terror had reassembled itself into a face, the eyes blinked in reckoning.

124

"Yes, sir," Mays said. "That is the truth. I wasn't thinking like that then."

"Good. Then we can get on with it. You are a traitor. We can prove it. You do what we say. Right?"

The eyes blinked again. *Computer time*, thought Stears.

"Yes, sir. If what you are fixing to make me do is going to make them come after my family, then I figure I'll pack for Leavenworth. Thank you, sir."

"Bad thinking," said Stears. "First, it would not help. They'll figure you've cooperated to some extent. Second, while you work for us you're one of ours, and we take that seriously, whatever you've done. Third and most important, it is our absolute priority, for reasons that you will never know, that they never have an indication that we caught you. That is why you are not under arrest. That is why your immediate superiors know nothing about this. That is why your divisional security knows very little. That MP was rather special. You understand?"

"Yes sir. That computes."

"What you will do is precisely what you have been doing. Same unit. Same duties. Same crime. You do one thing more. You tell us what you tell them and what they have asked you. And, if possible, who they are. That is all. At some time in the future, you will be suddenly transferred, and that will be the end of this. No record. No guilt. It never happened. Okay?"

And Stears saw suddenly in Mays's eyes a little worm of pleasure, quite beyond relief, a pure pleasure in the complexity and upside-downness of it all. *Well, I'll be damned*, he thought. *Welcome to the club.*

He said, "You will be given your procedure later. You will usually not deal with me. You will deal with a technical officer whom you may never see. But you are my man, and if you need me, I am here. I will give you a number in Frankfurt that will get me in minutes."

Mays said, "If I make a mistake, sir, I guess there's no record you told me to do this."

"If you make a mistake, sergeant, we try to get you out of it. You're not out there alone. If you play games with us, you're right. And the KGB never heard of double jeopardy. Understood?"

"Sir."

"Good."

Mays said, "Do I go now, sir?"

"We have to put your stripes back, first," said Stears. And added suddenly, "It wasn't just the money, was it? And it wasn't even just the photographs at first. You enjoyed this. It was fun. It's easy to be bored."

And shock was quite real in every fiber of Mays except his eyes.

"It's all right," said Stears. "You'll enjoy the next part even more."

Stears drove to Dahlem, to Truman Center, and parked near the supermarket. Tired Chevvies, Mustangs with hot wheels and battered fenders, Plymouths with plastic laundry baskets in the back, made the Opels and Audis seem prosperous, alien, and smug. The supermarket gave out brown bags. He got out and walked around. Mothers with skins like Sunbeam bread dragged towheaded children after grocery carts. A black kitten was lost—reward offered in a childish hand. There was a special on chuck roast. Blacks glided in groups around a radio, calling jokes. A row of discouraged backs sat before the machines at the laundromat. It was an America, here east of the Elbe, that Wop Stears of the Central Intelligence Agency knew from movies or from the windows of cars on freeways into New York or Boston. Its unfamiliarity disquieted him. Giovanni Sidgewick Stears, son of an expatriate Boston poet and nephew of a Tuscan count, had spent much of his life pursuing an Americanism which, however tattered and ambiguous, remained his birthright and pride. He had pursued it to its Castle of the Holy Grail, the CIA, and become its warrior. He had carried it into the Secret Country itself.

But the Secret Country, like all lies, guards its frontiers, and your only passport out of it is the memory of the real country you left. If that is lost, or if it was counterfeit, you are there forever. And whatever flag flew over the Secret Country when you arrived, the landscape is always the same. It is the gulag.

He walked past the U.S. Post Office to a muddy strip of ground set with young pines. Across the street were army apartments, but he had to wait to cross while a stream of U.S. Army tank transporters ground past, escorted by one German police VW topped by a small blue light. The Mayses' apartment was somewhere here.

He found a bench and sat. From here, beyond Truman Center, beyond Lucius-Clay-Allee, he could see the broad forest of radio masts and dish antennae and microwave transmitters extending down Argentinische Allee to Onkel Toms Hutte. Hidden somewhere in that forest, he now knew, were the ears of PSYCHIC. He heard the playground swing squeal, around the corner, out of sight. Linda Ronstadt, on the second floor, sang, "I'll be your baby tonight."

126

The horizons of the operation spread. This too was now a humble province. ELBEMAN himself, redoubtable and in peril beyond the Wall; Mays set to juggle the knives of the KGB; the Sunday zoo invaded by signals and spies; the sorcery of PSYCHIC; August Herter crawling to the West—all was part of Stears's invisible domain, populated by his needy and precarious subjects. He thought about it. It had a queasy seductiveness. He shook his head and walked back past the playground to the car.

10

The Bulgarian found his job dull, but better than unskilled labor. He was to stay in his room in a grubby alley in the Steibing section of East Berlin and watch the room of the girl across the street. He was to report any visitors. She had no visitors. He was to report late-night absences. There had been none. He was especially to report any appearance of German police, uniformed or possibly plainclothes, to a Soviet Major Karpov at the Red Army barracks just north of the city. All of this he was to do by telephone. There were no police. He was to keep a written record of her daytime movements, her clothes when she left the house, and of anything she carried. The Bulgarian stayed in his room and ate cold sausage and drank a bottle of slivovitz a day. It was better than sweeping up at the stockyards.

This Wednesday afternoon, he pulled the limp school notebook embarrassingly stained with slivovitz across the windowsill into the dim corner where he sat. He wrote in an uneven looping hand: *1525 leaves house, orange blouse blue skirt carries bag like women do.* Three glasses of slivovitz thought it would be funny to add, *and has a nice ass;* his memory of Major Karpov thought not.

Renate's bag contained her first report to Dr. Krel. It was in plain German, which, as soon as she was on the street, frightened her even more than the method of contact with the carrier. Dr. Krel had said, "There is no worthwhile code that looks like innocent writing to a professional—codes only mean that you were carefully trained," but this dictum did not help. Her handbag, she felt, had become a radio of new design built to broadcast loudly in the presence of police.

She walked down Lautingen Strasse, past the betting shop with a picture of a dewy-eyed foal in an emerald meadow on the door, past a cubbyhole in a wall serving schnapps in dingy glasses to two or three workmen on the street, past the shop window given over to a single iron household meat grinder. This was an old working-class district of Berlin, patched back together out of the rubble after the war. She left the sidewalk frequently to get around scaffolding blackened with age. It was not a neighborhood where she had been known.

128

Four blocks later there was a fast-food place on the corner. She was now near a light-industrial district along the Spree; there was truck exhaust and a smell of grit in the air. She slowed her pace. When she could smell the grease from the shop she looked at her watch. Three forty-five, just right. She went in.

Her man was coming from the counter with a sausage roll and a tin mug of coffee in his hand. She recognized him from the photograph: forty years old, thick brown hair, spectacles more delicate than his face, a Windbreaker with the insignia of Deutrans, the external trucking line of East Germany. He carried his food to a counter, where one stood.

Renate bought a hot salami sandwich. When she paid, she took the envelope out of her bag as well. She walked over to the counter by the driver and held the envelope under it. Chewing her third mouthful, she felt a calloused thumb on hers and only then realized that her hand was shaking. The envelope went. She kept her hand there, but nothing was put into it. She quickly swallowed her sandwich, which under the circumstances was making her sick. She left. She wiped her fingers on her skirt.

And that, though she couldn't believe it, was that.

The report, which had taken her all morning, read:

First a terrible thing on the journey here. I was almost sure that I was watched. A man was by me on the train from Probstzella, and when I was in Jena, he was on the platform. When the train came, I am certain that he looked to see if I was getting on it, then got on himself. I was almost too frightened to come to this house but I did not know what else to do. Nothing like that has happened since. Maybe it was just my nerves. I do not know. I do not think I am being followed now.

It took me three days to dare to begin to do anything here. I am sorry. Finally I found one of my friend's friends. He has told me to go to a certain place on Friday evening and perhaps certain military men he knows of will be there. I have decided after much thought to be no more specific here, even if it is less than you wanted to know. I also do not really know if my friend can send these people or even if he means to try. But I shall be where he said to be.

The room is all right. Nothing has happened since Jena that is actually bad, but my confidence does not grow. Please do all you can for me.

Now that she had sent the letter so easily, she was a little ashamed of it. Until she turned the corner and saw two burly men in leather jackets sitting in a gray car. They were not looking at her, but she thought, *I have come to the most dangerous place in the world for me—why am I ashamed of fear?*

In fact, fear came and went. Her room was not so bad. The window fitted in the frame. By stuffing her robe under the mattress's left-hand edge she could moderate the slope. She had found two wire coat hangers in a drawer. She even had her own handbasin in the corner, though this luxury was qualified—she had forgotten that all faucets here dripped day and night and that all basins were consequently brown. She barely registered by now the enduring smell of coal and cabbage. Fear had lived at first on the stairs outside her room, ready to turn at any second into heavy footsteps, a pause on the landing, a rap on the door. But it hadn't happened and maybe it would not.

Outdoors, fear ranged around the streets of what is still, even cut in half, one of Europe's largest cities. It would leave her quite alone in the subway, then come roaring out of an alley as a man looked at her from a bus stop. It had leaped at her throat in a pharmacy where, asked what toothpaste she wanted and thinking of the next thing on her list, she had answered, *"Colgate, bitte."*

When she had gone looking for Konrad's friends, fear jumped around her in small circles.

Müggelsee. A lake on the edge of the city, a poor cousin to West Berlin's pretty Havel within the Grunewald. A place of somewhat forlorn merriment—battered pedal boats, gritty flowerbeds on the quay, lemonade tepid and sticky in the sun. Renate had gotten off the U-Bahn here just before dusk. To the north of it were a few streets where the city's insistent grimness was very slightly touched by the suggestion of a resort. There were cafés and beer places here where by tradition mildly irregular persons and behavior might not be remarked.

Such as a student called Konrad with the sort of beard one does not trust sitting at a table with other dubious types while a blond schoolgirl, obviously underage, holds his hand.

Less than three years ago. Not an adventure, just daily life. Konrad might be dead now or might as well be, and through the gathering dusk on these same mournfully jolly streets walked the schoolgirl's criminal ghost, looking through the windows, peeping in the doors.

She couldn't hang around too much. Unless things had changed, the chance of finding one of the old crowd around here was high. But she could not think of even slightly trusting every familiar face—very few had been as dedicated as Konrad to begin with, and three years was time for any kind of change of mind and for marriages and babies to cement it.

So she tried to look like a slightly scatty girl keeping a loose rendezvous with her friends or boyfriend. If these cafés produced nothing in two more days at most, she would have to start ringing doorbells and asking for names. That terrified her.

It helped that it was just warm enough, even in Berlin, that café doors were open and some people sat outside. She stepped through the terrace of the Drei Ruderer and looked quickly through the door; no one, and it hardly bothered her that a young man looked at her hard—her stomach was learning that there were looks and looks.

Outside, three Red Army corporals huddled together in the dusk, frail Slavic boys in long-skirted greatcoats looking for somewhere cheap enough to go into—after God only knew what act of bravery or bribery sufficient to get an evening's leave. Renate almost felt for them. They seemed shrunk inside their coats as though there were room for loneliness in there between cloth and skin. And they made good stalking horses. While they loitered outside the Seeaussicht, and were stared at with pity or contempt, she checked it out.

But no one.

And no one at the Schindler. And no one at the Quai, where the little Russians finally gave up and wandered off. And at the place on the corner one face that made her almost jump back through the door because she had pegged its owner even in the old days as a snake.

And then the dusk that had shadowed her face became the dark that made a girl alone noticeable. So she took the U-Bahn home, thinking of the next day but one when she would start to climb stairs and a ring at bells, trapped indoors, with some kind of story, with an easily recollected face. People she could trust would not have telephones. And telephones could not be trusted.

At 2053 the Bulgarian had logged her in, then closed the notebook and picked up the bottle.

The next day she had found Rudi.

She saw him through the window of the Quai before she even

walked through the door. He sat sideways to her, a little fatter, with a better coat, undoubtedly a little drunk. He was with two men and two girls she did not know. She stayed by the window, though she shouldn't have, for her heart had winced in memory and loss as though a bandage she didn't know she wore had been ripped from its skin. Then she began to think. But still she almost clapped her hands upon the windowpane when, like a gorgeous present to her, like a lovely welcome home, Rudi laughed at something and picked up a beer mat and drew a funny face.

Then she walked away. Dangerous to go in. But Rudi tended not to have a girl, and there were two there at the table with three men. Luck might be with her. Rudi had often gone home alone. At worst she could somehow follow him.

She didn't have to. Her problem was waiting, but she found a bench where one could reasonably sit awhile and keep the café in sight. They came out together, but the foursome split off toward the lake and Rudi walked slowly up the street alone. She had seen him do that a hundred times before, but never then, when he was younger, had it seemed a lonely act.

But he was drunk enough tonight that a pretty girl's hand suddenly upon his arm was just the proper present the evening should be giving him. He smiled at her warmly and missed his footing on the sidewalk so she held his arm quite close. " 'Scuse me," he said. She said, "Hello, Rudi," and he looked at her in benign bewilderment.

"Do I know you, sweetie?" he said. And it occurred to her on the instant that if even Rudi didn't, drunk or not, she must be safer from recognition than she had thought.

"Don't you recognize me, Rudi?" she said. And added quietly, "Renate."

Then his face began to come together and his eyes to register.

And changed to sheer terror.

On Friday the Bulgarian logged the girl out at 1925. She was tarted up a bit tonight: *yellow blouse short blue skirt, heels, small bag.* His thoughts about her were increasingly lascivious. He guessed she would stay out awhile. He sighed and corked the slivovitz and put it in the far corner of the room. He was a man who knew his own weaknesses. He knew Major Karpov, too.

Renate refused to wonder if she could still trust Rudi Schreider, because if she couldn't, she would rather have it over with. But still, even after she had made him sit with her on the subway bench, even after she held his hand and talked very calmly, he had

132

almost yelped with fright when she asked whom Konrad had known in the army, who was left, where they might be found. He had said, not accusingly, just in horror, "But you're a foreign spy."

And she had squeezed his hand and said, "I can't be foreign, Rudi, I'm just Renate."

Which was probably about how Mata Hari would begin.

And then more firmly, "I don't want military secrets, Rudi. I wouldn't know what they were. But there's a man Over There who claims to be a refugee from the NVA, and people who ought to know think he's a Stasi spy. That would be terribly dangerous, don't you see? People talk freely Over There. Dangerous for people like you. I've got to find out. That's all. That's my whole job. Do you think I would do it if it didn't have to be done?"

Then he talked sense. Men whom Konrad had really known, if they had not gone the same way as he, were out of the NVA altogether now if they were not commissioned, and buried rather deeply if they were. She needed younger men. She needed men her own age, not old men like Konrad and himself. He knew one man who had gotten out of the NVA, from a unit near Berlin, six months ago, knew what was cooking, and could be trusted. He would try to talk to him. He would describe her as a "valuable link." He would suggest that somebody meet her. His friend might do nothing whatever, but he did not think he would betray her. Was that all right?

Yes.

He suggested that the contact, if any, would be at a place called the Pagoda, because that was the place now, had good music, was liked by young officers, and above all was always crowded. She might as well go that Friday, and if nothing happened then, the next.

"Thank you, Rudi. I've got a yellow blouse. I'll wear it."

At which he rescued his hands from the spy's, nervously squeezed her shoulder, and left the subway without turning around and without saying anything about where he lived. So that, she guessed, was the last of Rudi.

So now she sat at the Pagoda, listening to the music, and scared to think what eyes were on her yellow blouse. The music was Hungarian right now, and pretty terrible, but she guessed the place had not warmed up. It was a big place, half bistro, half dance hall, in a windy suburb off Prenzlauer Allee halfway to Pankow and consequently midway between the central city and the barracks. She had been scared at the sight of it, wondering if a single girl not patently a tart could go there. But it seemed all right. There were uniforms in groups drinking beer. There were couples at tables near the dance floor. But there were also local people placidly eating, and she was at a table with seven of them, seated with strangers in the German way and not, she guessed, particularly conspicuous unless you were looking for a yellow blouse.

Lieutenant Peter Hocholz, of the First Motorized Rifle Division of the NVA, thought she would have been conspicuous in a sack. He looked over the gray serge shoulder of Lieutenant Buchler and avoided as far as possible the face of Captain Klingenberg, and watched her eating with the local peasants. Her hair was a heavy smooth blond, not the light kind that feels like cellophane. She wasn't saying much. When she breathed in deeper, Peter felt his own breath catch as the important yellow blouse first swelled and then dropped back and the form of her breasts took shape for a whole blissful second before effacing themselves again. He was certain it wasn't just the bra. He also liked her smile. It would be a lovely smile if she kissed him in the morning and got out of bed and put on a furry, warm dressing gown to make breakfast. Warm because no nightgown. That hair would be uncombed. Peter Hocholz pulled himself together. He had had three schnappses and a beer to work himself up for this contact, and maybe it had not been wise.

On the other hand, the more lascivious he really felt the more natural his pickup of this girl would look, even to the cold eyes of Captain Klingenberg. To use the company of Sepp Klingenberg, who of all the fellow officers of his unit was the most open secret Stasi, as cover to find out what this girl really was was brilliant. Up to a point.

Stefan Buchler turned around and saw her too.

"Not bad," he said. "Maybe a brigade."

Peter, indignant and acting more so, said, "Army group."

Stefan turned back and shook his head, smiling and miming scales with his hand. "Maybe a division," he said. "Not more."

This joke had begun in officer school and seemed built to last.

Peter saw the waiter jerk her plate away and the girl give a slight, offended frown which he thought enchanting. The plate had been a dessert, so she had finished eating. With the other part of his mind, he had seen that she was spinning it out.

"I'm gong to ask her to dance," he said.

"Good hunting," said Stefan.

Sepp Klingenberg just looked. The thought that she might be working with Klingenberg hit Peter Hocholz like ice and drained

134

the schnapps right out of his body. But he could not truly believe that.

Away from the lighted square, the tram swung shrieking around a curve, then voyaged down the empty Prenzlauer Allee as a rocking capsule of light. Renate watched herself inside it. She watched herself do almost everything now.

She'd done it. She'd all but done it. Her fragile net had caught and held. Even the totemic name Herter had been lightly mentioned and quietly received. She was much further along than she had expected.

She could be out of here in ten days.

She saw a smile on her face in the tram window and realized that she felt an elation almost as of sex. The officer had played his part well. His approach had had so blatant a mixture of randiness and hesitation that she almost shrugged him off as the wrong man. She would have if she could have done it quietly. But on the way to the floor he had said, "I like your blouse. I like yellow." And looked meaningfully straight at it.

Which was clever, and she answered, "Do you? How funny—I put it on for tonight." Which gave considerably more charge than the usual to his putting his arms around her on the floor.

He asked only her first name. He gave only his, Peter. Almost nothing either said could be shown to be guilty.

Almost. The name Herter was a dangerous, slippery rock that could not be walked around. At the end she had said, "Do you know an officer named Herter? August Herter?" And then, "I should like very much to know more about him. We may have friends in common."

"I do not know him," he said, and had not stumbled on the tense, so perhaps he really didn't. "It should not be difficult."

That was the first guilty moment. The second was when they were dancing and she saw cold blue eyes upon her from across the room and he knew what she had seen and swung her quickly around and whispered in her ear, "Be careful of that man. His name is Sepp Klingenberg. He is the most dangerous man here." She was certain that he had not meant to do that and had scared himself by doing it.

They would meet next week. The same time and place. She would be his date. He would tell his friends it had gone well. There was nothing odd about it. Next week there might be some other girls.

Could her Peter be a traitor? Yes. Did she doubt him? No. He was of her own people and her own age. Raised in blindfolds, they had learned to pirouette through the dark. A tone of voice, a choice of words, a lift of the eyebrow hearing them, could guide her to her own species as a fox scents a fox in the night. Traps were everywhere, lethal, and easy to avoid. Stool pigeons stood out like Chinamen; they were dangerous only to people who would rather talk than see. Two kinds of spy were really dangerous: the very recently corrupted and the true believers, the incorruptible. She had never met one of those.

She got off the tram and walked toward her street. Caked cement and rusted buckets from an abandoned house repair littered the sidewalk, and she watched her feet. Pale yellow light still blotched some windows. Now that the end of her mission seemed in sight, the East stopped in its slow encroachment on the normal in her mind. She let herself think of Munich.

The moon hung over her own street. Here she did not have to watch the sidewalk. The window diagonally across from hers was dark as usual but now half open for the midsummer night. *So somebody lives there after all*, she thought idly. She searched for her key in her handbag and looked up again.

A face watched her. She stopped, then forced herself to move. She looked straight at it. There was no one in the window. But there was. It was dim as a ghost. She realized then: a face was reflected on the half-swung pane, and it was a face hidden in the shadow watching her. It pulled at her eyes, and she pulled them away. She governed her steps to her door.

A lonely neighbor. A crazy neighbor. A lecherous neighbor. She took the key from her handbag. *Concentrate on that.* The door stuck, as usual. And who shouldn't sit in the window and watch the street? Police. The end. A spy. The platform at Jena.

Think! Nothing has happened. You never saw the man on the train again. It is only a neighbor, just across from you, just as you come home after you met that officer, watching because he has nothing else to do. That is all it is.

Captain Klingenberg moved through the maintenance sheds of the First Motorized Rifles in the smell of oil and drill bits and under the anxious eyes of his men. The command vehicles were the most intricate, the most vital, the most susceptible to sabotage. His inspections of the maintenance were rigorous and sudden.

He considered the girl who had had Peter Hocholz panting like a spaniel last night. There was something notable about her, though unidentifiably so. He filed her, and the question, in his mind for further thought, as he had trained himself to do. Hocholz had more taste than sense, and he filed her with some pleasure.

He inspected a transmission filter, a site for sly sabotage that would show up disastrously after a few hours of operation. The gray sides of the vehicle loomed above him. His eye traveled on. It stopped on an electrical connection barely held in place.

He snapped his fingers. A scared private scuttled to him.

Captain Klingenberg said, "This is your work?"

"Yes, sir."

"This is carelessness, soldier. At best it is carelessness."

He looked at the private hard in the eye, then walked away.

Best to keep them worried.

He stopped suddenly, and the satisfaction left his face. He murmured to himself. "I am a fool," he said.

Over the weekend, Renate could reasonably stay in her room. From its shadows, she watched the shadows of the room across the street. She saw movement from time to time. Why should she not? She saw nothing to suggest that she was watched. She saw nothing to show she wasn't. What would show she wasn't, she had no idea.

She wrote a message to Dr. Krel. She wrote it foreknowing the eyes that she would feel on her back as she went to the greasy spoon on Monday afternoon. But she had learned something from her first two craven days here: anything was better than quaking in her room. *I will not be a little animal in a trap,* she thought.

It did not occur to her to fail to meet Peter. To do so might possibly increase her danger, but to fail to do so made her danger pointless. She had no way whatever to change the time or place of meeting.

Unlike the Red Army, whose soldiers may go for two years without leave from barracks, the NVA is not secluded. Even conscripts receive evening and weekend passes. Unlike the Russian soldier, whose month's pay would not buy a sandwich and a beer for himself and a girl, the NVA man can use these. Officers, duty permitting, may enjoy the nearest town more or less as their Western counterparts may.

But not alone, if one is wise. Only the most ominous view can be taken of the motives of a man who wishes to be unaccounted for; such a man will have no friendly witnesses when the inevitable accusations are made. Both officers and men, therefore, tend to form loose continuing groups for their liberty periods. They are not always close friends, but it becomes convenient. This can complicate things with girls, but then so does prison. Since one man in eight in the ranks of the NVA, and more in the officer corps, works primarily and usually secretly for the Administration 2000 military counterintelligence unit of the SSD, this control, though outwardly mild, is rigorous.

This is why Peter Hocholz, though he thought about it, did not dare to avoid his usual friends when he next saw Renate. Or especially to avoid Sepp Klingenberg.

Renate, looking back at their table, tried especially to avoid Sepp Klingenberg. They were a party this time, five officers and five young women. She knew their names by now. They knew each other fairly well. The men were happy to like her; with the girls she was a far outsider. She had been with these people now three hours. They had left the Pagoda, for reasons no better in the East than in the West, to go to another place to eat and dance. They had, for Renate, been far too much together as a group.

Now she had Peter Hocholz. There was a slow song playing by Alla Pugatschjowa, the Soviet idol, and Peter was giving a good impression of holding her tight. She was sorry that she noticed that his uniform smelled of old sweat and cheap cleaning, but she forgot it as best she could and snuggled against him.

He said close to her ear, "Your August Herter is dead."

And she wished for an instant that he had not even said the name, for her back had been warm under his hand and now it was cold.

"I think not," she said.

"He is listed as dead."

"Then he's listed wrong," she said and felt his whole body tense and asked, as though he had spoken, "What is it?"

"Then I have been asking questions about someone who is officially called dead and isn't."

She understood that and kept his tension out of her arms and folded him more against her and did not speak until her breast was warm against his chest. "Can you ask more?" she said. And felt him jerk like a hooked fish.

"Only to know if he is ours or theirs," she said. "If he is ours, that is all I need to know."

He said, "You don't know what you're asking."

After a while she put her hand on his lapel and said very slowly,

"Once I was told that a bit of the National Defense Frontier a little way from Plauen had no automatic mines. It turned out that was quite true. It wasn't possible to find out if they used dogs there, but apparently they didn't. The top of the fence was very sharp." She turned over her hand on which the scar, though largely gone, was still wider and darker than her lifeline. "I know what I'm asking," she said.

"Dear God," said Peter.

But it used up all her skill. They went back to the table when the music changed. Their party, not quite fawned on but privileged, had pulled two tables together in the best part of the room. The place specialized in pigs' trotters and sauerkraut, which were brought intermittently in piles on trays. It was mainly a crowded place to dance and drink beer. She tried to look lighthearted and relaxed and not aware of Klingenberg.

The couple on the other side of her from Peter had gotten up to dance. The feature of the evening, a live Cuban band, had come on. Two chairs away from her was Stefan Buchler's date, a thin blond girl with a tight sudden smile. She slid quickly down to Renate and smiled brightly in her face.

She just wanted to know her better. How had she met Peter? Just like that? Peter was a very nice man, a good friend of Stefan's—so she was sure they'd be seeing each other more. She smiled with a pleasure that stopped just short of her upper lip.

The voice signaled girlish inconsequence. Had Renate always lived in Berlin?

Renate's dazed alarms all rang at once. She moved closer to Peter's rigid flank. She had been so careful of Klingenberg that she had not even thought of danger from her own sex.

What did she do? Where, actually, did she work? It was difficult to find interesting work, didn't she think?

Renate put her hand on Peter's. "I love Cuban music," she said. She became aware that someone was standing over her chair.

Sepp Klingenberg smiled at Peter and herself. "May I ask your lady to dance?" he said.

He looked at her leisurely, full in the face, as they danced, smiling, daring her to flinch. He did not have the odd, furtive haste of the *stukachi*, the stool pigeon, of Stefan's date. It did not console her. She had never thought him that. *He is one of the real ones*, she thought. *I am finished.*

"Peter is a very lucky man," he said. "To have found such a jewel eating all alone at the Pagoda."

Well, she would play it to the end.

"I moved here from Dresden," she said. "I do not know that many people. I like music. Am I supposed to spend my life in my room?"

"Ah, Dresden," he said. "Not a lucky city, is it?"

She met his eye and found it cool and amused. *Bastard!* she thought. She put her feet hard against the floor and tried to stop dancing.

"Don't do that," he said, and pushed her off balance. "But your voice sounds much closer to here," he said.

"I was brought up in Potsdam," she said. "I went to work in Dresden."

"Don't dance so stiffly," he said. "You'll draw attention to yourself. Potsdam, yes. Potsdam, East Berlin, West Berlin, I had thought something like that."

"Potsdam," she said.

"I believe you. It is really none of my business. A security officer of the People's Army has quite enough as it is. Which brings me to one question. It is not personal and I think you can answer it. Then we can forget the rest."

"Yes?" she said.

His hand tightened on hers. It hurt.

"Where is August Herter?" he said.

11

The waitress of the George at Shepton Mallet said to Wop Stears, "And what will the foreign gentleman have, sir?"

Stears said to August Herter, "Try the treacle tart. It's very English."

Herter said, "*Das ist eine Empfehlung?*"—That is a recommendation?—and smiled. "Please," he said.

Wop said, "*Pleez*. Not *pleece*. S is as in German when followed by an e. You're getting better, though. How are you getting on with the Brits?"

"They are very professional. They have a good army. There is a difference in style, I think, between their army and yours. The questions they ask are a little different."

It was August Herter's day off. Herter, transferred out of Germany for security and with all traces of the ELBEMAN operation scrubbed off, was undergoing military debriefing in depth as a clean-run defector from the NVA. The British army had been invited in. "Helps to pay the rent," Brindle Woods had said. The Bundeswehr would get the data but not the man. "Too dangerous," said Woods. "They've got people in the Bundeswehr. The boy's not a pro. Somebody might twist something out of him. Safer over here. We'll even let the Brits take care of him. Nobody's going to look for him with them."

So Captain Herter of the First Motorized Rifles of the NVA was at Warminster with the Queen's Own Hussars, and Stears, that summer morning, had taken the Jaguar from Aldford Street out past Heathrow and through the Vale of the White Horse and Salisbury Plain where the motor coaches of summer ran over the shadows of clouds. It was somewhat like taking one's nephew out from school.

The waitress returned. Bits of brass harness glinted on the wall. The moonlight of the Aylesbury Midnight Steeplechase of 1856 had turned bilious in its frame. The waitress put down cream in a thick white jug.

Herter clarified, "I would prefer to fight against a division of theirs. I would prefer to fight against a platoon of yours."

Stears said, "That is very interesting. I'm not a soldier, though."

Herter smiled and said quietly, *"Nein, du bist Spion."* And still quietly, "Do you know the things they told us about the CIA?"

"Some of them," answered Stears. *And probably less bizarre than the truth,* he thought and looked away.

August Herter picked up his fork. "What is this, please?"

"Liquid sugar in pastry with cream. It's very healthy. Speaking of that, how's your leg? You're walking better, aren't you?"

"Almost well. They are going to let me go out on exercises soon. That will be good." He hesitated and asked tautly, "You must have news of my general. You can surely tell me something?"

"So far, he is safe. The operation goes well. You know that is all I can say."

"Yes," said Herter. " 'So far,' you say. That is what worries me. Time is passing. Everything that my general does carries risk. And I suspect something else too, though he did not quite say this to me—some of the things he has offered to do for you might be quite outside of his real purpose and even very dangerous for him. Stears, do not make him do more than he can do. Do not make him do what he thinks is worthless in order to be allowed to do what he believes in. That is actually contemptible when he is in danger and you are not."

"I understand you," said Stears.

"And that is all you are going to say. What is the phrase? 'One-way traffic'? Everything goes in. Nothing comes out."

"Right," said Stears. "It has to be."

He drove Herter back to camp. Herter's status was ill-defined but mainly sequestered. He did not get off base without Stears. His name had been changed to Captain Streicher. He had been allowed to keep August. He seemed to be holding up.

"It is interesting," he said. "The officers. I had thought that they would all be aristocrats, English Junkers, but they are not. I get on with them. And they are good men. I feel well beside them. I would feel better yet if some were women."

"Good," said Stears. No odd questions? No 'Whatever made you decide to come over, old chap?' "

"No. I think they have been told not to ask questions. I know that I should call you if that happens. Will you come and let me out again next week?"

"Perhaps not next week," said Stears. "I may be in Bavaria."

"How nice. You know, I hardly saw it. Just those mountains from my bed. Whatever I just said, I did not necessarily defect to England, Stears."

142

"We'll get you back. Just give us a little time. Most of those mountains were Swiss."

Herter firmly shook his hand. "You are a lousy travel agent," he said.

"Mystery Tours," said Stears. "Mystery Tours, Inc."

That July, Wop was a busy, happy spy. ELBEMAN was definitely his; he grew with his operation, rising from a landless younger son of the Company to a squire with neat villages of faithful tenants. August Herter with his discreet surveillance over the port of an English mess; Mays with his control and surveillance in Berlin and analysis in London; an ectoplasmically discreet contingency counterespionage operation against Mays's KGB handlers in West Berlin; all of it the mere groundwork and support for the collection and analysis of the flow from ELBEMAN; the slow evolution of plans to get ELBEMAN out by fall. He ran from Warminster to London to Munich to Berlin. He worked late at night over status reports and expense accounts. He juggled leave schedules. He told lies to old friends. He neglected his wife. In short, he got on with the business of espionage.

He liked to think while driving. The Jaguar poured down the Basingstoke Road past the hay-scented meadows and brick courts of stud farms and the glass extensions to village inns given over to Dubonnet and frozen scampi. ELBEMAN's intelligence was beginning to acquire the quirky character of a maturing operation: an agent loosely controlled is a reporter, not a camera, and, however unconsciously, selects. The characterization of this selectivity—from habit to intellectual bias to outright lie—is one of the principal arts of analysis.

ELBEMAN was a Kraut. ELBEMAN hated the Ivans. So much was clear. ELBEMAN was a professional officer, and one guessed that he had fought. Not a lifetime traitor. ELBEMAN was also a professional of the secret world.

It was a mouth-watering combination, and the flow reflected that. The intelligence ELBEMAN was sending was hard data of maintenance schedules, breakdown probabilities under different conditions of use, ranges in the field, communications bottlenecks. The promises at Reit im Winkl were being richly kept. These are the gritty realities of armies. It was like seeing past the marriage vows, past the front door, past the living room, and into the bed.

Which was not, it seemed, a frolicsome one. A picture was emerging of Warsaw Pact armies riven by atrocious problems of communications, surly petty indiscipline, and machines that lived up to their Western reputations only under the sunniest conditions. ELBEMAN was not the only source suggesting this, but he was a formidable and voluble one.

If it was true.

It was not all lies. That was certain. Some of it could be verified. It could nonetheless be highly misleading as a whole.

Misleading for what purpose? For no purpose. ELBEMAN was a contemptuous and bitter man and saw only the folly of his enemies. For a personal purpose. ELBEMAN was an opportunist, wanted a deal with the West, and was sending whatever he thought they would like to hear. For a grand purpose. ELBEMAN was a fraud and was buying a base of confidence for a grand deception down the line. In that scheme, Mays was a sacrificial pawn and PSYCHIC was penetrated somewhere else.

What grand deception? ELBEMAN's declared purpose was his network—the rest was rent paid for Western aid.

Why? To lull the West into false security? Unlikely and clumsy. Brindle Woods had made an academic suggestion: sooner or later, for the network's sake, the CIA's own knowledge of East German dissent would be called upon—by the KGB. That made one shudder.

But it hadn't happened. And Wop reached past the theological agonies of New England, the thought pattern of the CIA, to his mother's Tuscany and the angelic Aquinas. Or at least to Occam's razor. *What can be done with fewer assumptions is done in vain with more.* The simplest assumption was that ELBEMAN was telling truth as he saw it. And in his heart, and in Herter's eyes, he knew it to be so.

The worst of it was ELBEMAN's anonymity. To know who an agent is, where he is placed, to know something of his life, is to have a sporting chance of allowing for his perspectives and biases.

He returned to the issue of anonymity with Brindle Woods two days later, ending by saying, "We should honor the professionalism of the agent. If he asks you for anonymity, then he needs anonymity. Give him that much."

Brindle Woods's fingers stalked the last salted almond. "Do you know what agents are like, my dear boy? The best the Comrades ever had in Cairo took to calling on his friends and barking like a dog to be let in. There was one they were tailing in Washington once who wouldn't get out of the revolving door at the Mayflower. The doorman had to throw him into the street in the end. Stears, my dear fellow, your average agent is something out of Mack

144

Sennett. I ran one in Dortmund, once. Microfilm operation. He gave me the wrong film one day, which is normal enough for most of them. Do you know what it showed? Him and a friend in dinner jackets playing table tennis with a naked sailor as a net. Langley had to identify the sailor. Took them a while. Danish. Social Democrat. And if the agents of the world all went on the wagon together the distilleries would go on half shift. Yes, I know this one's better than most, but don't be pompous." His fingers closed around the salted almond. "Thank you, yes, I will have another sherry. No, it was La Ina."

The barman also brought the day's menu. There was poached Scottish salmon. The french windows of the bar downstairs at the Travellers' Club were open and the outdoors wafted in, scented of lilac and exhaust. Only six members were standing at the bar and no other table was taken. London was empty.

Brindle Woods said, "Are you in the Harvard Club?"

"No, Brindle. I'm a Yalie."

"Of course, I forgot. I could have put you up, you know."

It was a delight for snobbish Woods to be at the Travellers' Club and agony to be there only as his American subordinate's guest.

"Defense Intelligence is getting surlier every day," said Stears quietly. "I don't understand it. Our man's giving them a lot, not to mention what they're getting out of Herter. And I pulled PSYCHIC out of the fire for them. It's ungrateful."

Two more members had come in and the table was less isolated than before. Woods gave a small, tight shake of the head which meant, *Not here.* They finished the sherry. Woods prepared to rise but settled back.

"Odd that you should choose this table," he said.

"Ah," said Stears.

"I had a drink here a long time ago with one of their people from their embassy in Washington."

"Ah," said Stears. His guest was inclined to note that he knew other members.

"Who was it?" he politely said.

"It was Donald Maclean. Before your time."

Brindle Woods drew a line of *sauce mousseline* down the middle of his salmon.

"All right," he said. "The DIA."

The dining room was nearly empty. Silver, white cloths, and glasses gleamed unused on the tables around them.

"They don't like it," said Brindle Woods.

"What don't they like?" said Stears.

"What they're getting."

"Why? What they're getting is School of Realism. Slice of Life from the Warsaw Pact. The DIA ought to love it."

Woods said, "Nice little Chablis. You are still a little naive every now and then. The DIA is the Pentagon. What does that suggest to you?"

Stears said, "It's a Muscadet, as a matter of fact. An obsessive concern with complex hardware. They wanted to scuttle the whole thing for PSYCHIC—which, I am beginning to believe, may not be all it's cracked up to be. But that's just one area. DIA's getting surly about everything. They're getting surly about ELBEMAN himself."

"Because he's casting aspersions on their virgin daughter. Nobody guards the reputation of the Red Army like the Pentagon. They don't want to hear what's wrong with it. They want to hear it's ten feet tall, has tanks like Mercedeses, and picks its teeth with bayonets."

Stears said, "I know that that has to be the public picture, what with having to get through budgets for weapons programs and so forth—though it's often, in my view, self-defeating. But we are not publishing this in the newspapers; this is classified information and suggests that the situation may be a little better than they think."

"That's what scares them. As soon as you show that the Red Army can be stopped on the ground by land forces that the West could easily deploy, there's no excuse for not being ready to stop it. That means big increases in conventional forces in every NATO country, ours included, and for us it means the draft as well. Nobody will do it. Therefore we have the nuclear umbrella and a largely hands-off military. Anybody like ELBEMAN—and he's not the only one—who suggests the Warsaw Pact is a bunch of scared Russian conscripts—yes, of course, a very large bunch—with allies who hate them is rocking the whole NATO boat. At a certain level and with a certain logic, the Red Army is the ally and ELBEMAN is the enemy."

"I see," said Stears. "Jesus Christ."

"It's excellent salmon," said Bindle Woods.

Stears said slowly, "There's been a change at the center of this, hasn't there? It's not the operation I think it is."

And noted again his superior's knack of becoming smaller and still and difficult to observe as though he had stepped back into an invisible hole.

"Why would you say that?" said Woods.

"Because you're talking like a magazine, for one thing. And I don't like this Mack Sennett business. Intelligence is agents. If they're Mack Sennett so are we. Are we?"

"At the present moment," said Brindle Woods, "this operation is what you think it is. The director was impressed by your handling of Mays. That let me argue that PSYCHIC could remain the primary objective of the ELBEMAN operation within a strictly CIA context."

Stears arrested the ascension of a mouthful of salmon and laid the fork back on his plate. "PSYCHIC was never the primary objective. PSYCHIC was a sideshow."

"There is that," said Woods.

"PSYCHIC is a little counterpenetration job. The Soviets think they know something we don't know they know but really we know they know it. Even the DIA can't put that much value on that. It's a picayune. ELBEMAN is original intelligence at worst and a major active-measure play at best. You can't talk of them in the same breath."

Woods said, "ELBEMAN is biased and may be a disinformation source. His value may be negative. ELBEMAN's promise to sabotage NVA security may well be a trick. Since we don't know who he is, it's hard to tell. ELBEMAN's intelligence is military, of course. It is hard for the CIA to claim maximum expertise in that. Not when a more specialized agency has become involved." He had spoken as though reciting. He added, "I just told you all that. You should listen."

Wop said, "Yes. You told me that at Reit im Winkl, too. Before the DIA ever opened its mouth. So this isn't just the DIA, is it? It's Brindle Woods as well. Was breaking Mays your idea too?"

"Oh, not really," said Woods. "Not really. And don't forget, when I say it, it's a necessary hypothesis. Operationally, I would treat ELBEMAN as genuine until we knew he wasn't. With safeguards, of course."

"But you won't push it very hard, what with the DIA and all."

Brindle Woods answered from deep within his hollow. "I have been with the Company for thirty-seven years. I have never signed for anything I didn't know I could deliver."

"I see," said Stears. "Go on."

"Think in small stitches. The more dogmatically the DIA takes its line and the quieter I keep my objections the more likely the DCI is to accept our opinion of ELBEMAN's intelligence. It's called a 'corrective.' Take our line on something military once in a while and the Pentagon's on something civil. Ends up with a lot of crap, of course, but there you are. That's what I'm hoping for."

"Ah," said Stears. "And if we don't get it?"

"You still keep control. Then PSYCHIC becomes the absolute priority. It will make a difference to schedules. ELBEMAN may have to stay in there longer than he thinks and he won't be doing what he thinks he's doing. The DIA has been rather specific about this—PSYCHIC needs six months, which would mean another three months for ELBEMAN."

"Why does PSYCHIC need six months?"

"Because in six months the collection and processing of data will have ceased. The program that Mays created will cease to have relevance and he will have nothing more to send them. The circus leaves town. I am quoting except for that.

"You don't like it, and I don't blame you. You have a choice you may not have thought about: you could drop the whole thing straight into the DIA's lap. ELBEMAN, PSYCHIC, Mays, everything. You wouldn't win but you couldn't lose."

"No," said Stears. "I got Herter across. I found Mays. I put ELBEMAN in whatever position he's in. I'll back out for someone who cares more than I do, not the opposite. They're owed that much, bugger all though it may be. Incidentally, am I right that this has happened already? You may as well tell me now."

"No," said Brindle Woods. "But assume it will."

"They're not in there already, are they?" said Stears. "There's not somebody crawling around over there I don't know about?"

"I think not. The DIA is not really set up for that." He looked toward the sideboard. "I've never understood why the English think so much of their strawberries. The Germans have much better ones."

Stears said, "What is the fascination with this damned PSYCHIC? There's something there I don't understand."

Brindle Woods looked at him with great clarity. "I don't know either," he said. "That is the absolute truth."

"Gosh," said Stears.

———

Until six months earlier, Sergeant Scott Mays's experience had consisted of this: he had grown up in a black hamlet of two hundred souls; he had oystered around the immemorial rhythm of the tides and seasons in a manner so tedious that it got into picture books; he had romanced an amiable and pudgy girl whose bottom left a characteristic imprint on the ground under her father's oak tree and who had modulated with effortless hormonal skill into mother and wife; he had lived and worked under the care of the great Dutch uncle, the United States Army. That his career had changed from heaving hunks of muddy oysters to spinning fugues of algebra and its background from the Wando's squashy, snaky banks to Berlin had entirely improved his life's periphery but left its center unchanged.

None of this was good training for standing with a film of classified data in a remote part of the suburban forest of the Grunewald waiting for the KGB to make clear why it had chosen this rendezvous instead of its usual one of subway and shopping mall and zoo.

He heard a motor approaching. He was standing up to his knees in bracken among the trees of a small wooded hill near the intersection of two forest tracks. Half a mile away, the Autobahm thumped and rumbled. A mile the other way, the wives of U.S. servicemen shopped for pot roast. On the hillock, a squirrel hid behind a tree from Scott Mays, and Scott Mays, without quite admitting it, hid behind another from the motor. He had left the computer banks of PSYCHIC half an hour before. He carried in his pocket a Minox film of the printout of the analysis of several days' interception of random electronic pulses from Warsaw Pact aircraft matched with radar sightings of the aircraft's responses, if detectable. He carried a life sentence at Leavenworth.

The car came into sight around a bend of beech trees. It was a gray Volkswagen. That did not seem so bad. It stopped beneath his hillock. Three men got out. That frightened him, for since his entrapment, he had never met more than one. He recognized one of these. He was a small man, not so much furtive as sideways, who had met Mays before, once in the subway, once at the zoo. The second one, his own officer, whom he had seen only once since his recruitment over lemon cakes on Bleibtreustrasse, stayed in the car, but put his feet out on the road for comfort. The last, who uncorked himself from the back seat, was like a big-necked sergeant who causes trouble drunk. He was like a Slavic version of Major Hamilton's horrible apparition. In all of them, Scott Mays saw mayhem, disorder, force, the trampling of his family, the ripping up of his life. He wished that he had told Major Hamilton about the new rendezvous.

He stepped out from behind the tree hating himself for thinking that. Every corner of his life was now full of fear: fear of the army he belonged to; fear of the enemy he worked for; fear of Major Hamilton and his bland minions who controlled him; fear of new combinations of blackmail and punishment; fear for his children, that he might somehow lose them. He was disintegrating with fear and disintegrating into something he despised and loathed. His uncle with the oyster boat had been an upstanding man and a deacon in his church and a mean hand with a hickory stick, and he himself, as a patched little boy with a muddy dialect, had looked his uncle in the eye. The discovery of his mind had been a gift on which he soared out of Huger, South Carolina, with amazement and gratitude. And now he saw himself: a scared, puzzled darkie, licking his lips with fright, and whimpering for a distant white man, Major Hamilton. So he stepped from behind the tree, looked them all in the eye, and didn't move.

The officer beckoned with one finger. Scott Mays went down the hill.

The officer held out his hand. Mays fished in his pocket and brought out the little plastic box of film. He put it in the officer's palm. The hand closed tight.

The officer said, "A great treasure. Like the rest. Thank you."

He looked at Mays. The officer's voice was rich with the irony of those who are never victims. Scott Mays did not quite understand the irony, which was new, but the officer's expression was just as usual. His eyes and chin held the automatic challenge of the professionally assured, a police lieutenant, a pilot. He seemed intelligent, though not deeply so. He was neither nasty nor nice. He had the bland but focused look that Mays associated consciously with all officers and unconsciously with law and the white race.

The officer said, "It is pleasant to see you again. Of course."

Scott Mays said nothing. The courier was on the other side of the Volkswagen, looking away into the wood. The big sergeant stood beyond Mays, close but not crowding him. The officer sat sideways in the car, the open door of which was near Mays's chest.

The officer said, "You are having no problems?"

Mays said, "No, sir."

"Naturally we have to assure ourselves from time to time that you are not in jeopardy. You have no indication that your security organs are interested in you? You do not wish our help?"

"Uh-uh," said Mays. The officer looked at him. Mays clarified, "Nothing wrong that I know of. I work scared but don't nothing happen."

150

The officer said politely, "We all have to deal with our fear." And then, "How exactly do you obtain this data? Tell me a little more precisely."

"The raw data comes in from the radio and radar receptors. It is analyzed by the computers for sequences in ways controlled by technical people. That's me, when I'm on duty. It comes out of the computers in printout and goes into a safe. In between the computer and the safe I photograph it, when I can. That's the dangerous part. I thought I told you people all that."

"It is useful to hear it again. Obviously, then, there is no suggestion that the data itself is being tampered with. By some other person, of course."

Mays felt himself lick his lips. "No sir," he said. "No way. Comes right off the machine. Why?"

"No reason. Only an obvious question. A very important one, naturally. Well, I am glad to see that you have so few problems. Your recruitment was embarrassing for you—but you were undoubtedly recruited. You are one of ours. We do not forget that, or our responsibilities."

He dropped his eyes as though in conclusion, then raised them sharply.

"Nor should you," he said. "If you cheated us, it would not be the CIA who did so, but you. There were things that worried me, but now I am sure it is all right." He looked beyond Mays and said, gathering up his party, "Kurtz, we are leaving."

The car door leaped forward and struck Mays in the chest. It pulled back again and he felt an arm around his throat. He gasped as a knee drove deep into the small of his back. Then he was spun around and slammed against the side of the car. He saw very little, for a hand struck one side of his face and then the other. He felt the grain of the hand, he felt an icy pain in his neck as a muscle pulled, but he saw only the water of his eyes.

"No blood," said the officer. "These people's skins don't bruise."

The sergeant held him by his neck and piled his fist into his abdomen, as though covering it with endorsements. Mays could neither breathe nor think but he could feel his stomach rise and hear his lungs moan.

The officer said, "Enough."

One of Mays's legs was knocked aside so he stood straddled. A heavy, blunt knee rose into his groin. The hand left his neck. Mays fell forward on the ground. He found he was bent double.

The officer spoke very clearly, as to an unintelligent foreigner.

"If I knew you had played us false, this would have been much worse. This was a sort of question. Remember you have a family. Remember your duty."

A small piece of gravel struck the corner of Mays's mouth as the car drove away.

The nearest subway stop was Onkel Toms Hutte. This occurred to Scott Mays as he tried to call Major Hamilton from there, but he was too frightened and hurt to stop. As he put the coins in he saw a man looking at him. He dialed a completely different number and hung up at once. He took the subway home to Dahlem. It was not far, but he was too sore to walk. Thelma and Scott Jr. and the baby had gone off in the yellow Pinto.

The apartment, which he rarely thought about, seemed to him like balm. His family had not come back. He sat on Scott Jr.'s bed and, with one hand, retacked the corner of a baseball pennant to the wall. He did not like to see things awry. He stopped in the living room in front of a glass peacock on a shelf. It was fragile, cheap, bright, and innocent, and Scott Mays, who by now knew the Charlottenburg Palace well, did not so much look at it as remember when they bought it. He picked up the telephone and dialed Major Hamilton's number, then dropped the telephone as though electrocuted. He felt as though he had all but led the legions of the damned into his home.

He went outside to a public telephone. It was Friday evening. A young corporal was soaping his car while his wife sat on the curb close to him with a beer can which she stroked the air with as she talked. In a space encircled with Prussian pines, there was an informal game of basketball, mostly black. Mays's back was hurting and his neck hardly moved. He dialed the number in Frankfurt. A young female voice answered, "U.S. Army Cultural Enrichment Program." Mays asked for Major Hamilton. "Are you calling with reference to the tour of major European cathedrals in October, sir?" No, said Mays, by arrangement, only the leading art museums in January. She did not ask his name. "What number are you calling from, sir?" Mays gave it and the voice went on with its sunny imitation of a car-rental girl before dropping it completely with the last words: "Precisely eight minutes."

So he waited in the booth. The Camaro dripped strings of foam. The basketball game yipped. Scott Mays could see the door of his own stairway and the attendant parking spaces. Yellow caught his eye. His own Pinto nosed around the corner, the dented bumper and the soggy tennis ball impaled on the antenna giving it a look gawky and tame. It parked and Thelma struggled out, picking up the baby from the back. Out of his presence she looked softer and merrier than he had come to know her. Scott Jr. carried the laundry basket. He watched them go inside.

The telephone rang, and he jumped.

He said to Major Hamilton, "You got to get them out of here. You got to get them out quick."

It was not what the had meant to say at all, and he cursed himself for babbling.

Stears, as Major Hamilton, said, "Who?"

"My family," said Mays.

"I see," said Stears, and Mays heard and hated in his voice a soothing tone as to a scared hound. "Has something happened?"

Mays told him quickly.

Stears's voice changed. "What were his questions exactly? In his own words?" he said.

"I gave you his own words. I done that already."

"All right," said Stears. "Was there anything in the data you've been giving, anything odd, anything changed, that might have puzzled them?"

And on his side he heard Mays's voice become steady and precise.

"Numbers got more interesting, maybe," said Mays. And went on, now a professional talking to an amateur. "Remember, major, I don't know how they got those numbers, except it's radios and radar, and I don't know what they're going to do with them, except it's a gun. I am not an engineer. All I do is put them through the computers and look for sequences, then I pass it on. Now if you're a numbers man like me you get a feel for things. Some numbers are interesting, some just ain't. Now the numbers we were getting back in the beginning, weren't nobody could have done much with them. They were like hash, major, you get me? Wasn't any shape to them. Things are getting just a little different now. I've got a little bit to work with. Wouldn't matter if it was to do with guns or insurance or football games. They're just better numbers. Not much better. Just every now and then there's something."

Stears said, keeping his voice to an amateur's vague musing, "No way anybody could change those numbers on you? Like the man said." And felt a horrible, half-formed idea mercifully die as Mays said, "No way. No way, major. I told that man the truth. That's the raw data. You could louse up the computers somehow, maybe, but that's crazy. I'd know it anyway."

"Of course," said Stears. He thought fast. He said, "So all we're dealing with could be improved collection of data. That would be normal in a project. As it matured. Right, sergeant?"

"Maybe. I don't know about that." Mays paused. "I know about my family. We ain't talked about that yet."

Stears said nothing.

"There are animals out here and they'll do anything," said Mays. "Maybe that's what I get instead of Leavenworth. But maybe next time it'll be my kids."

Stears said, "No." He said decisively, "It won't. And there won't be a next time. What that bastard of yours said was true. It was a question. He wanted you scared. There'd been a change and they weren't sure about it. You've explained it. They know they've got your attention now. They know you won't try any tricks. And you hadn't been anyway. They'll go with it now. It's the way their minds work."

Mays said, "You won't get them out?"

"No," said Stears. "We'll put a guard on them. You won't see it but it will be there."

"I'd be a whole lot happier if they were out."

"No," said Stears.

"It's my family. Maybe I'll do it myself."

"Don't do it," said Stears.

He hung up.

Brindle Woods said, "Of course you're right. Of course we can't. Pull those people out and we might as well take an advertisement in *Pravda*."

"Yes," said Stears.

"Your absolutely right in what you told the boy. It's how their minds work. They've never been sure of Mays. They got him by intimidation. They think the pictures might be wearing off. They want that boy shitless."

"Yes," said Stears.

"If there's one man who would know how secure that data is, it's Mays. He's not stupid."

"No, he's not," said Stears.

"You did exactly the right thing. Took the right tone. You're learning."

"Good," said Stears. "I'm glad you think so."

Then he said, "You think there's anyway we could rotate them out? Part of a group or something?"

"No," said Brindle Woods.

"There's nothing we know about that links up with this. We're sure of that?"

"Yes," said Brindle Woods. "There isn't."

12

When General Sucher of the SSD was summoned to the office of his *de facto* superior, Colonel General Fyodor Alexandreivitch Karshkhov of the KGB, he was surprised. General Karshkhov's office was at the other end of the Soviet embassy. He reported there every Tuesday and Thursday morning. Additional summonses were common enough, but usual only when there was an urgent matter at hand. General Sucher knew of none at present. ELBEMAN of the CIA, who lived within General Sucher, knew of several—all terrifying.

In consequence, the iron bell that hung over Hans Sucher's doom began just perceptibly to swing, and the vibrations made his scalp creep. But when he called to his adjutant, *"Reinagle, ich bin beim Rezident,"* his voice carried as though across a field and his step down the corridor was grand.

General Karshkhov was *Rezident*, or chief, of the KGB in the fraternal capital of East Berlin.

General Karshkhov indicated a deep armchair. General Sucher relapsed into it, below the level of General Karshkhov's eye. General Karshkhov looked at his watch.

"We have a little time," he said. He did not say for what.

"Would you like some tea?" he said. His uniform was lustrous and trim, the crimson shoulder tabs rich as rubies, his face was smooth, his voice was correct as a schoolteacher's, and his goat eyes were coarsely amused by all of this.

Hans Sucher turned a little in his chair toward the pleasant summer day. Karshkhov's office overlooked both Unter den Linden and the Brandenburg Gate—the latter, sealed fast by the Berlin Wall, demonstrating that the KGB does not blush at reality. Nor did an ax-faced tourist guide opening and shutting her mouth in front of a gaggle of Bulgarians—opening it wider as a silent diesel bus swam by. Double windows. Bulletproof. With a practiced twist of memory, Hans Sucher removed Karshkhov, the Bulgars, the embassy, and the Wall; swept up the rubble, the swastikas, and the bombs; quickly planted spreading linden trees and stood beneath them moistly holding his father's hand and licking a Sunday ice cream. It was a trick he had stumbled on once, and it made both General Karshkhov and General Sucher an unholy accident.

But Karshkhov said, "Have you noticed anything unusual lately, Hans? In the way of contacts, for example? Surveillance? Just generally."

General Sucher received his tea. The cups were tiny and the saucers unrimmed. The scaffolding of the iron bell began to creak. He saw General Karshkhov look coolly at his hand. It did not tremble.

"That's a new set," said Karshkhov. "From Sans Souci. Early Prussian State porcelain. About 1756—Frederick the Great's time. I sent for it from the Hermitage. It belongs here, don't you think?" He added in the same tone, "Could be CIA."

"Very nice," said General Sucher. "No, I don't think so. Nothing that I'm aware of."

"Ah well," said Karshkhov. "Probably it's nothing." He looked at his watch again. "Still, when you finish your tea it will be time to go."

They went to Karshkhov's private elevator—for no special reason, the *Rezident*'s movements around the embassy were elaborately secret. Karshkhov said to the KGB trooper, "Down."

He said it flatly. Hans Sucher knew at once where they were going: the interrogation room. He tested his own strength, whether it would withstand the agony of a stranger, a friend, himself. He waited until the elevator passed the ground floor and then, observant subordinate, said to Karshkhov, "You've got someone, then."

"Maybe you'll know him," said Karshkhov. "Maybe not."

Outside the elevator, they were in the secure basement, separated by solid, doorless walls from the utility side of kitchens and garages. The fresh Berlin morning was replaced by the eternal 3:00 A.M. of nightless rooms. They passed the cipher room, the armory, the files, each a steel-barred door with a KGB lieutenant at a desk, flanked by two guards cradling submachine guns to their breasts like iron babies. Karshkhov's eye became quick and his step more taut, like that of a gun dog among boots.

Their door was at the end. As they reached it, two men came out. Both were majors. They were brisk, but red-eyed and bristl cheeked, and they smelled of tobacco lungs and coffee stomac Both saluted General Karshkhov and General Sucher.

"Get anywhere?" said Karshkhov.

The first shrugged.

"He's burning out. The next eight might do him."

They were an interrogation shift going off after eight hours' work. It was called the Assembly Line.

Karshkhov nodded. He opened the door. Sucher's memory bolted down a long, grim tunnel: jaws caved in with chair legs, fingers crushed in doors, spines cracking under boots, boots smeared with vomit. His own voice echoed down it—the questions meaningless, the voice meaty and strong, and answers screamed or babbled. Desolation swept through him like a flux. He delicately adjusted his spectacles. He sat down by Karshkhov.

He mildly said, "Don't know him."

Karshkhov said, "Think hard."

No horrors like that here. Stalin is dead. The suspect stood against the back wall, but did not touch it. His face was easily seen. Strong searchlights were focused on it, leaving the KGB trooper on either side almost as if in the dark. The lights' reflected heat warmed the room, brought stale smells of sweat, and made the cigarette smoke that strayed into its path leap into sudden sarabands as it shot toward the roof. The suspect looked at the light as if at a drill in his face. He was a young man, his eyes now red as a partridge's and his face gray. His mouth was open. His arms were tied together and held out in front of him. Both were swollen, but one was purple and tight as an eggplant and the angles of the upper and the lower arm did not relate.

"Listen," said Karshkhov.

The new interrogator, with a crisp shirt and a brisk voice, scanned through his notes and said, "Where were you about fifteen hundred hours, Wednesday, July seventh?"

The suspect rocked his head inside his caldron of light as though seeking the voice in the dark.

"File room," he said.

The suspect's voice was croaking and frail, as though a cheap artficial device had been put in its place.

"What were you doing there? It was less than three weeks ago. I am sure you can remember."

"Routine work. German liaison. It was just routine."

In a satisfied voice, the interrogator said, "You were looking at unauthorized files concerning liaison between the KGB and the SSD. Files of senior officers. We have established that. Do you agree?"

"It was a mistake. I was following something up. It was just routine."

158

"I see." The interrogator fell silent. Pencils and ashtrays whispered in the room. A faint, dry sound, like a cricket on paper, and a burning smell came out of the searchlights. As well as that and tobacco and sweat and coffee kept too long, there was another smell that Sucher could never quite describe. It was somewhere between ether and urine. It was fear.

Karshkhov whispered moistly in Sucher's ear, "The little prick's one of ours. Have you seen him nosing around you?"

Meanwhile, the young man's eyelids had closed and jumped up again as though electrocuted. They closed a second time and stayed. The young man rocked against the wall.

The KGB trooper beside him was smaller than he but he was as bandy as a badger. He moved, and a heavy white truncheon could be seen in the shadow. The young man settled against the wall. The trooper took the truncheon in both hands and swung it over his head onto the young man's arms. There was a noise like a stick hitting a chicken carcass. The suspect screamed and rocked his head and staggered forward, his legs beginning to crumple. The trooper brought the backstroke up against his groin. The suspect drew in his breath and staggered back and doubled over. The trooper pushed his chin up with the end of the truncheon.

"I don't think so," said Sucher.

The interrogator said, in the same voice, "How long had you been collecting this information? We have the answer ourselves. We merely wish confirmation. Take your time. Then we can move on to all the other things."

It was the thirty-seventh time this question had been asked in fifty-six hours of continuous interrogation while the suspect stood against, but not touching, the wall. The young man made a noise.

"Water," he said.

The interrogator did not look up.

He made another noise. The interrogator waited.

"About a month," he said. He looked shocked to have said it, like a drunk who has fallen over a chair.

"Good," said the interrogator. "Under whose instructions? Who is your CIA contact?"

The suspect whispered, "No CIA contact. No contact at all." But he had begun suddenly to shiver and in his eyes was a foreknowledge of shame.

"Fellow was right," said Karshkhov. "He's getting ripe."

They soon left. The door closed upon another soggy *thwack* of the bludgeon, which brought this time not a scream but a long moan.

Karshkhov said, "Up to my office."

Karshkhov said, "All right. Funny business, Hans. Little fucker's a file clerk. We'd had him under surveillance for a while because he seemed to be sneaking looks at things. Nothing specific. We were just about to give up on him. Then suddenly he got busy, Hans. Looking at this, looking at that. And do you know what, Hans? It was all about SSD officers of general rank specializing in liaison with KGB. What do you think of that?"

General Sucher frowned and said weightily, "Where there's a join, there can be a leak. It makes sense. I should think we'd like to get our hands on the Americans' liaison with the French."

General Karshkhov nodded. "Funny you say the Yanks, Hans. Because then—what do you think?—he made a contact. American, of course. Contact had diplomatic cover, so we can't do much there. But we'll get whatever this little cocksucker knows, as I don't have to tell you. You never saw him?"

Sucher, truthfully, said, "No."

"Maybe he was only records," said Karshkhov. "Maybe they've got some other lice crawling up your ass." He looked at Sucher with flat eyes. "Let's cut the shit, Hans. SSD has three general officers specializing in liaison with the KGB. Hasenfuss is in Moscow. Sentling's an old fool we give security orders to when a dignitary pays a visit. You're right here at the embassy and you know about things that count. They're looking for you, Hans. Why?"

Sucher shrugged. "Maybe it was my turn," he said. "They're always looking around. It's what they do."

Karshkhov smiled and nodded, his eyes still on Sucher's face. "Maybe," he said. The smile faded. Karshkhov said, "But it's funny, Hans. They never seemed to care about you before." He spread his hands dismissively. "I just thought I'd show you what was up. And what we're doing about it. Maybe we'll find out. Take care, Hans."

Sucher turned to go, but Karshkhov spoke again. He had adopted an expression reflective and leisured. "You know, it's another funny thing, Hans," he said. "The CIA and us, we're at each other's throats every day, and yet, here in Germany, we're still allies if you think about it. In some ways. Ways where the last war gets involved."

He looked Sucher straight in the eye and held it a long time. Then he said, "The Yanks wouldn't have found everything about you in those files, would they, Hans? Not the things that would really and seriously have hindered your career. January 1945 in

160

Poland—it wasn't your best moment, was it, Hans? A narrow sort of person might even say 'war criminal.' My predecessors thought the matter over and made an exception for you. I wonder if the Americans would have been so generous."

He withdrew his eye to the window and went on. "There were things we Soviets were supposed to share back then with our American allies—and with the British and the gallant French as well. I wonder if it's time to catch up on the paperwork. Especially if they have such a sudden interest in you." He feigned to ponder and dismiss it. "Well, they kick our ass now and we kick theirs. Times have changed. Why bother? Just a thought. I'm sure you're busy, Hans. Good day."

Sucher turned again to go. As he reached the door he heard Karshkhov say, "I've heard of all sorts of crazy reasons for trying to defect. I've never heard of anybody defecting to a Western prison."

It was not exactly said to Sucher.

He walked back through the embassy, a gray-and-silver personage lighted by the Order of Lenin, crimson-and-gold. The iron bell tolled above him, not faltering, not tocsin. From trust to first suspicion may be time measured in hopes, in loves, in years; terror in the night measures time from first suspicion to the cells.

And the CIA had cheated him.

He was not naive. He himself, in their place, would have accepted his plea for anonymity with difficulty. But they had accepted it, and accepted his reasons, just now appallingly justified. That his stated reasons were only half sincere, and their breach of trust only half a betrayal, was true in itself, but he had earned his condition with the risk of his life. In volunteering the matter of PSYCHIC, he had sent the CIA material close to himself, traceable to him, setting up operations that doubled his peril now that its hour had come.

So quit.

Karshkhov's behavior had certain aspects of a warning. General Sucher was a valued servant. The proven treason of General Karshkhov's chosen liaison in the heart of the Soviet Union's only strong ally would not be good for General Karshkhov. If General Karshkhov merely suspected that General Sucher had as yet merely wetted his toe in the shallowest waters of treason, then a warning, complete with this morning's bowdlerized enactment of the really bestial treatment in store, might suit him better than action.

Thus, if he stopped now, abandoned his network of patriots, turned a deaf ear to the CIA, he would probably survive.

He had covered half the distance to his office. His heels clacked in military rhythm over the Russian floor. The Soviet machine spread out around him, corridor by corridor, floor by floor, a principality in itself with its councils of war and courtiers, its marble salons where champagne and caviar filled dewy urns, the floors of pounding typewriters and scurrying clerks, the flicker of red shoulder tabs on the easy and insolent KGB: a greased and mechanized court. He shuddered and pulled himself to order. It wasn't the point. Not their big embassy. It was just a good excuse for cowardice. As cowardice was an excuse for hatred; for he hated them because they had used his guilt and fear over a villainy he had committed as a maddened and exhausted boy to press him into their own safe crimes.

He reached his office. There were two rooms, his and his adjutant's; he entered with a slight relief as though into a little peasant plot of German settlement on the vast and hostile *boyar* estate. Purely animal. His office smelled German—tobacco and polish instead of disinfectant and sweat. The Russian wolf could say "huff" and not even get to "puff" before it blew it all down. He sat at his desk, which asserted a more lofty Germany. It had been made by a French cabinetmaker at Sans Souci, and embossed on its leather top was the ghost of the Hohenzollern eagle. The curtains on the window were silk. Hans Sucher was a glossy general.

But he took his glasses off and wearily laid them down. He needed to think deeply about his situation and found it difficult here in the embassy. He came to a decision. There was a degree of foolhardiness in it but also of assertion and even of defiance. *And that,* thought the old KGB hand within him, *might make it the best thing I can do.*

He called Major Reinagle, his adjutant, and told him he would be gone for the day. This was not unusual. General Sucher had another office at Normannenstrasse, the headquarters of the SSD, and often gave explanations later or never. He called for his car and driver.

He had himself driven to his hunting lodge in the woods, eighty kilometers outside Berlin. It had been one of the great perquisites of his rank, one of his few real pleasures, and he had almost abandoned it for the past months. He had infected it with himself, with his cowardice, with his drunkenness, with his Russians, with their whores. Any KGB man of colonel's rank or better had been obliged for the asking with "a little party at Sucher's place." It had earned its keep.

But it had consumed the villa in the end until the pine fire lighting the walls on a frosty morning could no longer drive stale drink from the air, until the midnight cry of geese from the Baltic, Danube-bound, was stranger than a lickerish grunt, until a crisp new sheet did not prevail over the crushed perfume of Berlin whores. Inspiriting, by then, as a seedy nightclub on a Sunday morning, it had still suited him; he used to go out alone to morosely drink and see in the wrecked and slutted villa the face of its provenance, and Germany's, and his own. It had been passed from a Jew to a Nazi to a KGB thug to him. One gassed, one hanged, one shot, and one to go. Why should he accuse himself, what cause for squeamishness in the great barnyard of the Soviet, de-Nazified East?

So, finally, he had shunned it and withdrawn to the flimsy monasticism of the Karl-Marx-Allee apartment. He had been about to go there now, but its coldness offered nothing to his need. So he risked the villa.

They passed out of the pines as the lowering sun turned the lake to a hard copper disk. It was cooler out here. Beyond the pinewood, out of sight, the lowing of cattle moved across the field toward the barn. The limousine's tires crushed dandelions by the house, and he got out into their faint, astringent smell.

His driver stood in stiff query. General Sucher said, "I shall stay the night here. You may go to the servants' quarters or return for me here in the morning. It does not matter."

The driver said, "If my general permits, I will return to the city."

General Sucher nodded and turned away. Evidently, he was not under surveillance, or not yet, or not by his driver.

He walked up the steps to the porch.

The house was wooden. The porch creaked quietly. There was a spiderweb in the corner of an armchair. The house was silent and smelled of nothing but old timber, as though it had forgotten about humans and all their ways. He opened the front door, and the antlered deer skulls on the hallway wall led him in.

He sat stiffly at the dining table, which was bare. He had opened the shutters but turned on no lamp. What he had to plan should not be committed to paper, even here. Until full darkness, the sinking light was enough. The house barely took cognizance of him; a field mouse trotted in the kitchen like a busy waiter.

His full task could not be achieved in the time he had. First to consider how much time that was.

It was more than hours. It was more than days. If Karshkhov had had proof of his guilt, he would have been left strictly alone until a sudden pounce. If Karshkhov had, not proof, but conviction of his guilt, it was unlikely that he would have tipped his hand unless he believed that Sucher was playing a picayune game. He did not have to fear a whimsical, experimental arrest. The KGB was imperious and lawless but it was still an intelligence agency, and no intelligence agency finds the denunciation of a senior allied officer palatable or easy.

Karshkhov's was probably a long game. This morning's show had not absolutely assumed his guilt. The CIA, as Karshkhov knew, could have reasons for peering at any general of Warsaw Pact counterintelligence. And Karshkhov's sour adieu had been more and less than a taunt—it was a fact that the West would not receive Hans Sucher with a dimpled smile if it knew the whole truth about him.

This morning had been meant to unbalance him, frighten him, bring him to leash. The KGB would not consider this wasted even if it eventually decided that he was without guilt. More probably, there would follow a slow undermining of his position, a gathering of every sort of libel about him, grotesque or not. Then his fall.

The torture of the file clerk was, in this scheme of things, of very little moment. The boy would confess all he knew—and it would fit on a postcard. Never, never would the CIA have told him the reason for his search or given him a focus that indisputably defined it.

All that was easy. A croupier's understanding of a simple run of cards. Bet that he had three months to six, though with freedom rapidly narrowing toward the end. Lay off two side bets: any action of his own might be discovered and bring disaster at any hour; ditto any action, probably unknown to him, by the CIA.

He did not move. The setting sun, reaching the top of the pinewood, broke in through the window toward the lake. All at once, the corner of the room burst from dusty wood into gold. The glow reached him and lit the table. He turned and watched it, the cool fire flowing across the wall, the grain of the pine leaping and spinning in fanfare. He watched it seriously and respectfully, a gray-and-silver general alone in a schoolroom. When the light narrowed to a single beam, turned to molten copper, and went out, he sighed and reached slowly for a lamp.

Now to use his time—which meant to use the complex and trivial expedients of the secret world to prosper the real world. Not easy. Like using a screwdriver to mend a woman.

His fingers stopped short of the lamp, and he got up suddenly. He walked to the stairs and climbed them, rising above the horned and polished skulls. His uniform was now paler than the light, and his face had lost its hard angularity. Had there been anyone to see him, he would have looked translucent, mild, and almost old.

He walked past the doors, open, closed, left casually half shut, of made-up bedrooms waiting for their guests. The rustle of a wasps' nest came from one. He went to the end of the corridor and opened the door of the largest room, windowed on three sides. It was lighter here. He sat down on a chair beside the bed. Except that his hand was on the pillow he might have been sitting by the bedside of someone sick.

Himself. Himself, he realized, having forgotten the beat of time, two years ago this month.

"A little party at Sucher's place." Who? It was not sharply engraved in him; that night was only the fumbling beginning of the way back, an accidental turnabout in a black moist wood, not even noticed at the time. Vinoshevsky again? Lublynkin of the GRU. Chemulka. And Krebbs of the SSD. Yes.

In bed with his tart, whom he had first laid eyes on when she was bundled into his car in the Russians' basement. Loose, tawny hair. She was chubby, but not in the city way; breasts, hips, and stomach moved with your fingers and then sprang back, her nipples supported the weight of his hand. Broad face, full lips, her breath at first smelling of cheap candy, round eyes with no coquetry, pretended enthusiasm, or dismay. A Brandenburg farm girl mildly surprised behind a hedge. Not a pro. She worked, odd thought, in the ministry of pensions. Needed clothes or cash. Gretchen. If there'd been time he'd have sent her back for something glossier.

But there wasn't, and after midnight he rambled with her up the stairs to bed, which brought applause from Lublynkin and woke Chemulka in his chair. In the corridor, they passed a forthright, military pounding and panting from Krebb's room, where an efficient unit proceeded in good order in advance. She was drunk, but not near as drunk as he. He grabbed her inside the door, using her hips for handles, and kissed her with brief, salivary enthusiasm, seconded by his hands on her backside. Soon on the bed, he rooted around on her, distracted, greedy boy ripping the paper off lots of packages, squeeze a breast, spread a thigh, reach in, move her hand around him like a washcloth. And then unbalanced boozily off her, or at any rate slid away. She, good, patient Gretchen, took over then, dairy girl doing work like any other in the warmth and leaks of flesh, whispering in his ear what sounded remarkably like *whoa* and *steady up there,* sorted out their limbs and sat upon him equably and mildly as upon a milking stool with uneven, rocking legs.

And so into the black and cold and bloody country, sleep.

For the dreams were breaking loose, their claws were tearing at the loam of alcohol. In sleep he could feel them writhe and push. Underground, they knew where his face was. And he knew all their names.

This one was the worst. He was in a Polish wood. The dead were piled there. A woman's high-heeled foot stuck stiffly from the heap. Warm blood ate up the snow. Gasoline and wet ashes stank in the air. He stood alone deep within the wood with the dead. He stood there and in the silence in the snow their eyes at once all opened and looked upon him. And he knew that he was theirs. And they moved.

He didn't know how loud he cried. Perhaps not very. Gretchen was awake, but only half, half drunk. He was bolt upright, drenched, and cold. She looked at him, and he saw quite clearly that just then she didn't know his name and wasn't trying to remember it. She took his hand automatically and with sleepy care and stroked it gently, saying something like *bad dream?* or *poor old thing.* Stiffly, still shaking, General Sucher followed his hand and lay against her. She moved his down in hers to where it was warmest, between her stomach and her thighs, and stroked it there on a bed of springy fur. He could not speak, had not the heart to pet her; he lay against her trembling and breathing from her shoulder the scent of sleep-filled skin. She shifted her weight easily for comfort, and he fell closer and in due course stilled and warmed safely slept on the vast and anonymous forgiveness and care of heaven.

No longer dusk but almost dark, and he felt foolish sitting there but reluctant to move. His being at the lodge at all was, as things stood, a noisy demonstration. Karshkhov could certainly hear that he had run off there. Probably the telephone was tapped—but then it might have been tapped all along. Surveillance would be tighter now. That meant that everything would take more time, and there was no time anyway. He should go downstairs and plan. Light the wood stove. It was cool enough. Then he could make notes. Burn them in a moment if he heard a noise.

But he stayed a little with his hand on the pillow, leaning back against the wall in a sudden cozy intimacy with the bed, the house, with chance. He felt a good deal better. The fact was, he was making people act. His scheme might disintegrate, but its parts would be left. He, and they, could be defeated; they could not be canceled. They could not quite be defeated, either. Every act against the dead crust of depotism cracked it somewhere.

He went downstairs. He lit the stove. He sat at the table in a circle of light. It wasn't ludicrous. The CIA had blunderingly made impossible his plan to create yet another layer of deception, consubstantial with and parallel to the KGB and the SSD, but opposite, throughout the NVA; he now knew that it had always been impossible. In six months it obviously couldn't be done; in three years it more mistily couldn't.

But there remained the second plan. Create situations that turned the Soviet paranoia against itself. Create pretenses of deceptions.

He picked up a stubby pencil. He wrote the names of NVA units and his resources within them, grading them 1, 2, or 3 for quality. He needed to begin where he had most, where he could cause quick real effect. Then, where resources were fewer, he could create shadows, imitations, images.

He knew what he would find. He had used paper only to guard against assumption. One division had always been his best ground: August Herter's division, the First Motorized Rifles, Berlin. There he should begin. He crumpled up that paper. He began another. He listed names and functions. He drew lines between them.

He gave himself six months. He knew his own skill. The CIA had acted treacherously in spying on him, but it was a treachery that he had expected sooner or later, and he felt almost comfortable with it. He would abandon anonymity with them from now on; it gave him some satisfaction that he would do it on his initiative, not theirs. He had formed an image of his CIA control, and he felt respect for it. Quite likely—it would be the normal thing—his control had been given no veto over the breach of promise. He did not expect further perfidy, not soon, not if his intelligence remained valuable to the Americans. With luck and decency he had six months. He turned back to Berlin. He drew a line with a pencil and at the end of it put a name: Klingenberg.

13

So Renate, on the dance floor of the bistro where the music lurched and skated to Cuban rhythm and the air smelled of juniper in sauerkraut and the smoky fat leaking out of pigs' feet, heard Sepp Klingenberg, who could be nothing but a secret policeman, say, "Where is August Herter?" The implication was so awful that she could barely think about the question; it was confused with Klingenberg's arms dictating to her shoulders the movement of her legs and her breast punctiliously apprehended by his chest.

She only said, "I don't know where he is." And cursed herself, but feebly, because in the present sum of things even the idiocy of saying that was trifling.

He looked down at her, from the patronizing heights of his shoulder, of his cleverness, of the might of the state asserted by his uniform, and said with an easy smile, "Yes, it's not 'Who's Herter?'—is it? So I am right. But maybe you really don't know where he is right now. Who knows?"

She could have thanked him for the smile, because it made her so angry that, moving her legs to his policeman's rumba, she wanted to change the step and kick him in the balls. She at least could come back in a voice with snap:

"How in hell would I know where your friends are? They're none of mine, thank God."

The smile went away and the blue eyes quickly deepened as though a cover had been taken off.

"You'd have been good with a little training. It's a pity. It's irresponsible of them to have sent you over without it. I don't respect that."

She didn't rest against his softening, because to have done so would have been the end. She said rudely, *"Was?"*—the uncouth style of *"Wie, bitte?"* for "What?"

He said, "This tune is about to end, which poses a problem. I have more to say. You had better cuddle against me a bit. But not too shamelessly. You will have to go back to Peter Hocholz afterward."

She stiffened sharply, but he said, "It really is the best thing for you to do. You are in terrible trouble, but it is not all here yet. We are usually not in a hurry."

The rumba broke up in a clatter of unconvinced hilarity. She saw a hand take leave nostalgically of its partner's haunch, saw Peter Hocholz looking in horror over his beer, saw the drummer flap the Cuban shirt against his streaming chest, but all through the wrong end of a telescope as she sank forever from the real world into the secret one.

Sepp Klingenberg occupied her hip with his palm, but his fingers were under discipline.

"First and most important," he said, "don't think of running. That has only one result. If you behave nicely, who knows? There are lots of possible outcomes. We can do anything, you see. Anything at all."

The army maintenance shed fizzed with fluorescent light and the air was spiced with oil. The vehicles stood lined up on spotless cement. They were surrounded by men, but the loudest noise was of heels on concrete—no ring of wrenches, no whirr of drills, above all no chatter. Captain Klingenberg strode to and fro, looking over lieutenants' shoulders as they watched their men, pushing without apology between the mechanics and their work. This was quite expected. The work in hand was electronic maintenance, the delicate adjustment of fire-control and communications gear. The task was so fraught with implications of security that only physical incapacity spared Sepp Klingenberg of Administration 2000 of the SSD the duty of doing the whole job personally, himself. Every movement of every finger in the shed was a chance for sabotage.

To commit sabotage against the armed forces of East Germany was Captain Klingenberg's intention. Captain Klingenberg had been August Herter's friend.

So his preoccupation was real and his worry even greater than it seemed. Sepp Klingenberg assembled General Sucher's order in his mind. He was proud of his self-command and he was unpleasantly aware that he was frightened. It seemed to him that there was on one side the state's edifice, many stories high, swarming with glossy, burly men behind guarded doors, and, on the other, the general's, made of bits of wood and old rope and operated by a boys' club, letting down a bucket on a string for messages. That part of Sepp that was at home with the secret police was repelled by the humility of this. That part that was a German romantic rebel was exalted, in a febrile but selfless way. So long as the romantic and the policeman stayed on speaking terms they were a useful team.

Klingenberg spoke sharply to a corporal mechanic who was closing up the electronic control box of a self-propelled antiaircraft gun. "That is filthy," he said. "Clean it."

His own fingers demonstrated the gentle application of cleaning fluid to an assembly before closing it up. The copper gleamed.

He said more gently, "Suppose an American fighter were coming over the hill and this gun hesitated because of a molecule of grease here. Would you like that?"

"No sir."

"Well then."

He moved on.

The fluid he had ordered to be used had been adulterated with acid so that the communications and fire-control devices would show random and increasing cantankerousness before widespread breakdown. With a little luck this should come to a head during war games with the Red Army next month.

Not much real damage, though disastrous on a battlefield. But how would it have happened? And when traced to cleaning fluid (and a whole vat of the stuff would be adulterated at that point), who would have wanted it? And how many who used it knew? Captain Klingenberg would seem to be rabid with frustrated officiousness then.

This part of the general's order was easy, not very dangerous, almost playful.

The officers' mess was large, shared by the full brigade. Coy intimations of the old Wehrmacht were affected here and there—a silver tray of schnapps in tiny glasses, but on a cheap metal table in a room like a hangar hastily gotten up with improving slogans, starched flags, and a totemic Russian gun. But lunch brought a wide mingling of officers together in a subdued but unpretended comradeship of craft. The penumbra of security around Sepp Klingenberg was still visible here, but thin.

He approached a logistics officer, a young man with soft, wavy hair and a statistician's abstracted eyes. A tray of cabbage was carried past with steam of carroway. The officer registered him like an unexpected but possible digit.

"I have what you wanted," said Klingenberg, rather loudly.

The officer's eyes opened wide and then censored themselves. Klingenberg gave the officer an envelope.

"Thank you," said the officer.

Klingenberg unaffably nodded. He turned toward the cafeteria, speaking briefly to others in his path. He selected boiled fowl, potatoes, and red cabbage. By chewing carefully, he made himself swallow it all.

He had given the officer a poorly typed list of names on civilian paper. The names were Polish. The list would sooner or later come to light between the pages of a rarely used book of secret standing orders on Warsaw Pact interarmy battlefield cooperation. The names were all of security officers in that division of the Polish army expected to fight on this division's flank. All had recently been dismissed for unreliability and sympathy with Solidarnosk. This had been done without fuss or noise, and it was highly improbable that any German officer below high rank could know of it. The paper looked older than the dismissals.

Sepp Klingenberg lay awake. Once every nine breaths, as he had established long ago, the corner of his room glowed from the searchlight far away on the barracks wall. Once in a while an engine hammered into motion in the transport pool and, a minute later, sent a finger of diesel into the room. Then the wind was from the north.

He was afraid as one is afraid at night, when each handhold crumbles in turn. His own most dangerous personal task was still before him, to steal a radio code book from the safe.

But he concentrated on that, because even here, alone, at night he saw it could be managed. The rest was much worse. He knew the power and resource of the secret organs. General Sucher's plan was to taunt and madden the organs, to stir them into a flailing attack against a phantom enemy which would prove the existence of what in fact could not exist, an inclusive and coordinated plot against them.

It would work. He really had no doubt. The plan might be riddled with informers from the start. They might all be calmly and coldly arrested. But he thought not. It would work. But what would happen then? The secret organs might do anything once stirred up. It was like standing below an earthslide and pulling out a rock. Here in the night, he missed the Sepp Klingenberg the world knew. The hard blue eyes, the tart courtesy, the polished boots, all due to report for duty at eight o'clock, would have been welcomed right now. From a far quarter of the barracks he heard a faint cry, sharp as a cock's crow, of orders breaking the silence, and then the small crunch of a detail marching. A dawn duty. The searchlight's lunations faded in the corner of his room. The bedclothes were a heap, his pajamas had abandoned the whole territory between his shoulder and his hips, his eyes were not fresh, and his head was heavy. Sepp Klingenberg, officer of the National People's Army and captain of State Security, pulled himself together to confront the East German state.

———

Sepp Klingenberg lightly brushed Renate's hand, then tapped it to make the point. He said, "But I had to frighten you. I had to terrify you. I had to push you far enough to find out if you were really what I thought you were. And if I hadn't taken control of you, God knows what you would have done. You know that too. Stefan Buchler's girlfriend, the little bitch, was about to take you apart. That's when I made you dance in the bistro."

She nodded. "Is she a Stasi?"

"An amateur. But they're often the worst. They need the business."

"Yes," she said. She drank some beer. "Well," she said. "You did terrify me. I threw up everything I ate for a week after the bistro. I'm really not that tough, you know."

"You puzzle me," he said. "You are sitting with a man whom you know to be a member of the security forces, who was obviously about to arrest you, and who turned out to be on your side. That is an extraordinary thing. How many people has that happened to? But you have never asked me my reasons. You are not interested in my political thought?"

They were sitting outside a small beer place, among tables like pieplates on spindly folding legs, on an evening that was experimenting in advance with autumn chill after a day of thunderstorms and had driven most customers inside. It was a Saturday. They were to meet others later at a movie.

She studied the ease of his body in its uniform, the sharp blade of the lifted chin, the conventional arrogance of bearing which the eyes, not quite successfully, refuted, and the lightness with which the hand rested on the table by hers. *That is easy,* she thought. *He became one of them because they are the people on top, then he found that he was really and truly better than they, so now he has the best of all—he is with them and above them too. It is just a little dangerous. He is a little like Dr. Krel, but not quite.*

"No," she said. "They wouldn't have much to do with it. How did you catch on to me? Was I so obvious?"

172

Another thought plucked at her, but it went by before she could see it.

"Because I was looking for anything, you see, anything, because something should have happened after August vanished."

She nodded slowly and said, "What was he like? Was he like you?"

"No. August was a romantic boy. That and a new churchgoer, which is always the enthusiastic kind. Whoever sent him showed good sense. He was a good officer and a brave man and he would have gotten across or died trying, but if he had done anything complicated here he would have stumbled sooner or later. He was honest to his fingertips, you see. Like your Peter Hocholz and his friends. They are genuinely brave young men and they are dangerous and they will not survive. Actually, they are dead meat."

"That is not a very nice thing to say," she said.

"It is the truth. I am terrified of those young romantics with their hazy nationalism. 'Just give us a clean socialism and let the Russians be our friends but not our masters.' That is the idiocy they are going to spend their lives in the camps for. I am very worried that you had to do with them. Honest people do not make good traitors."

She looked at him directly. "And a Stasi does?"

"Of course. As an Austrian emperor nearly said, it is just a question of a traitor for whom."

She looked far down the street to the lengthening line outside the butcher's shop. She barely saw it, for the earlier thought had circled back and pecked her shoulder.

I do not like Dr. Krel, she thought. The metal chair didn't either and turned suddenly cold on her back.

"How will they get me out?" she said. "My next letter will tell them what they wanted to know. That Captain Herter was exactly what he seemed, not an SSD plant. It was always left a little indistinct how I would leave."

"Better so," he said. "Always better so." His face changed, not by movement but as though a thin, hard casing had been slipped beneath the skin. "They have to think of their organization, which was there before you and will go on after you." He said more lightly, "No doubt a false passport. I know it can be done. It is the safest way. I do not know much about this Krel, but I know he has been in business"—he professionally smiled—"a long time. He could do that, I am sure."

He saw her look at him somberly and waited for her to speak.

"It seems so easy," she said. "It does not seem real."

"It is real," he said. And then, as though it had slipped out from the casing beneath the skin, "Though it is also a little odd."

The general should know of all this, he thought. *Beyond doubt he should. But every communication carries risk, and what this is, I do not know.*

"You must phrase your report to Krel very carefully," he said.

"Of course," said Renate.

"I mean specifically that there must be no mention of me. No suggestion of anyone like me. Just that you have acquired certain information. Krel gets the details when you get home."

She was about to answer, but he stopped her and went on. "I do not think you should suddenly put a certainty in your next letter to him. That can only mean that you have met someone like me. Say now that it does not *seem* as though Herter was SSD. Then be more positive in a few days. That will be much better."

The chair she sat on turned cold again, but she said primly, "That seems a shabby way to treat a patriot like Dr. Krel."

"There is risk in all communication," said Klingenberg. "One agent does not jeopardize another. That may not seem very gallant but it is fundamental."

She said, "I've already thought of that part. I didn't want to hurt Peter." She said it wearily.

"Very thoughtful," said Klingenberg.

"Even if he's dead meat."

He frowned and said, "I have asked something from you. I am also going to give you something. I am going to give you a telephone number to contact me at any time, and I will also tell you that I will help you as much as I am able. I am not quite sure why, but you might need it. It is a number for informers, like that little bitch of Stefan Buchler's, so it is quite secure. Remember it." He gave her the number. "Say it to me."

She did.

"Again."

She repeated it.

"Good. Use it if you must. Call yourself Gisella. They will ask no questions."

"Thank you," she said. Little as it was, it made her feel somewhat better. But she woke that night and thought back over the whole conversation. At night it made her feel somewhat worse.

14

Dr. Oswolt Krel spent his summer vacations in the Black Forest, not far from Freiburg im Breisgau, in a house belonging to the intellectual widow of an appliance manufacturer. This was not a dalliance. The widow was not there. She was represented by her letters; she was full of ideas about neutralism, and Dr. Krel's unofficial rent consisted of refining these into ever more rigorous but attractive constructs. Dr. Krel received visitors but lived alone there with his manservant, a Slovene with a lean face, watchful eyes, and a faint smell of brass polish and sweat, whom he had had the luck to find through Heinrich Nadermann.

The house had been a Black Forest farmhouse, set back into the hillside, with a huge barn which could be entered at ground level at the rear and which surmounted the living quarters—very folk, very woody, very snug—in front. The widow had no cows, and the barn had been redone accordingly.

This morning, the manservant, whose name was Mikhail, had been sent to Munich and Dr. Krel was alone.

He sat in the barn, which was still as only a noble space can be. A wasp knocked against a distant corner, and the August sun, free to enter through enormous, recent windows, brought out the sweet smoky mustiness of the beams. A small corner—a desk, a Bokhara rug, a breakfront, a lamp, all bounded by a sofa—was Krel's summer office.

Delightful. He found it so and was grateful to the widow for giving him his due. His angular handwriting, the scratch of the good gold nib, expressed the turns and ripostes of his thoughts to friends. The project of the summer, a neutralist symposium, *Germany's Involvement with the Great Powers: Lessons of the Thirty Years War*, was nearly finished.

All of which served to bury the thought that his servant would bring a communication from Renate and that Nadermann would arrive the next day. He broke off for a moment, laying the pen down on an unfinished confidential letter to a Polish intellectual close to Solidarity, whom Nadermann had wished him to approach, and watched the wasp waver through a sunbeam which turned it to pure gold. It did not relax him. It sharpened the consciousness like a nail in the back of his chair of a secret wedged between himself and the world. The professor close to Solidarity was an urbane and courageous man, and Dr. Krel did not trivially play with his confidence.

In the late morning he paused again. He heard the elderly gray Mercedes venturing up the rutted drive. He shook his head and turned back to his letter.

Once again, he read Renate's. Mikhail, with one of the gestures which from time to time reached brusquely from behind his servility, had walked in and dropped it on top of what Krel was writing.

> My friend's friend was as good as his word. I have made contact with an officer in August Herter's division though not his regiment. I believe that I am trusted. I do not have serious doubts about my contact. August Herter is apparently listed officially as dead. This contact and I have not exchanged names. Believe me. I shall not be rash.
>
> I have found a second contact who also knew Herter. Nothing I have heard yet makes me think that Herter was one of Them.
>
> I am to meet both again in a few days. I think then already I shall know all we need to know.
>
> I deeply hope this for I feel no safer than before. Sometimes I think I am being watched from across the street. Now I am not so sure. Nothing happens—that is certain. Perhaps I am becoming like an old maid who is always being followed. But this I beg you: next week I believe I will have all we need. Therefore please begin now to prepare to bring me back. I am not strong enough for this. I will think of you planning for me and feel better.

He read it a number of times. He was surprised to hear the luncheon gong ring faintly from below.

Unlike his own house, this one was dwelt in by a woman. The barn was neutral, but the steep staircase below turned corners where a closed closet sweetened the still air, a drawer in his bathroom held jumbled paraphernalia of creams and sponges, and the beds in closed-off rooms were frilled and fragrant. The mild summer heat drew out a faint trace of musk and violet, modesty and sex. It was hardly noticeable, but he was no longer used to it.

176

He sat at lunch with Renate's letter. The Slovene served him and lingered an oppressive moment by his shoulder: translucent slices of Westphalian ham, a chaste veal cutlet. The room ran to heavy farmhouse furniture and was half-shuttered against the sun.

That such courage and sweetness as had thrown its arms around him in the park could be a finger's width from the jaws of the KGB—could be already lasciviously looked on by their eyes—was disturbing, and he felt both restless and self-pitying as he dwelled upon it. Renate and he were comrades in peril. He had a vision of sudden disgrace, of powerful friendships withdrawn, maybe trouble with the law. Renate's danger was the more conventionally poignant, but he had much to lose. He was magnified by the strength of his resolution.

But the air of the house made him uneasy, as though his purpose in it stirred up an unwholesome vapor. After lunch, he climbed quickly back to the still, unperfumed barn. He took up his pen again and his letter to the Pole. The ease of the morning was gone. His words seemed clumsily and pitiably disingenuous, a schoolboy's excuses. He pushed the letter away.

The next day, Heinrich Nadermann arrived near dusk and with an air of courtly celebration. He presented Krel at the doorstep with a whole smoked eel, which he carried by the tail, like an upside-down and fermented bouquet. He looked around him, at the farmhouse window boxes, at the skirts of a small thunderstorm retreating over the hills, at a hawk sweeping across the pinewood; he put his head back and breathed deeply several times.

"Delightful," he said. "Oswolt, you are a lucky man. I should have looked forward to this even if it were not for your company." He gestured slightly to the fish. "Nothing," he said. "A trifle. But they are good with vodka and this one looked nice in the shop."

Oswolt Krel held the tail with his fingertips.

"This is very kind," he said.

Nadermann had come alone, in a younger Mercedes than Oswolt Krel's. The Slovene went quickly to it and returned with a large briefcase, a small suitcase, and a Burberry raincoat.

He spoke deferentially to Nadermann. "I have put you in a room looking over the meadow, my colonel. I trust that it will be suitable. Will please the colonel tell me if he prefers another."

"It will suit me well, Mikhail," said Nadermann. "You may take my bags there." The servant did not look at Krel.

Krel's mouth fell into an expression affronted and still and somewhat like the eel's.

Nadermann stood at his bedroom window, looking out at a fold in the meadow, like a bowl. The sinking sun lit the wild flowers. He picked out purple, red, and gold. *Meissen*, he thought absently. *No, Flora Danica*. He raised his eyes to distant female voices. A party of girls was hiking on the road. A low place in the hedge offered brief shirts, shorts rolled higher over thighs. Promise, undoubtedly, but he was too far away and gave up the inspection. He looked forward to these days in the country, away from the ashtrays and rivalries of Tass and the tour buses of Bonn.

His senses were alert. When he was much younger, in Bern, he had snapped at a colleague who airily likened the first tightening of control around a newly dominated agent to the first week with a new mistress. Nadermann had asserted, "You should be demoted in the service and then thrown out of your lady's bed." Nadermann himself used flippant half-truths skillfully because he despised them. But half-truths were half true; there was undeniably in this process a concentration on another that came close to sensuality, an intimate process both of invasion and discovery. Nadermann's vision was aroused.

For he had something to work with. For a long time now the creation of new agents, which is the specified and permanent first duty of a KGB officer, had become a chore like patrolling a public toilet; the people who slouched within the grasp of the KGB were the queers, the drunks, the malcontents, the puzzled failures. Nadermann now left this to his juniors, who had known nothing better, and spent his time at luncheons, in cozy talks, stroking wrists that could hardly ever quite be snared. He even wrote for Tass. But Krel was a return to the old heroic days, to the majestic cripples, Rosenbergs, Oppenheimers, Philbys.

Which had its creepy side too. Nadermann was not an insensitive man, and a close sight of the parade of conscience he had marshaled to the service of his country made him squirm. Such vigor of intellect. Such strength of purpose. Such discipline. Such misery. Such nastily sad neuroses at the root. With Krel one squirmed, all right. It would have been nice to have looked forward to a first evening with one's collar open and plenty to drink. *Two glasses, then stop*, he thought gloomily. He looked back at the hedge of the meadow, screwing his eyes up against the setting sun. The girls with thighs were definitely gone.

Nadermann settled his reading glasses and skimmed through Krel's letter to the Pole.

178

"Very good," he said. He looked over his glasses and passed it back. "A little stiff at the end, but mostly just the thing."

"It was not my intention that the Poles should arrest him," said Krel.

"They won't unless we give him to them," said Nadermann. "Which we may never do. He's worth much more as a source. You may have a long friendship with him." But he observed Krel carefully; he saw morosity—and though hardness was exactly what was needed now, he might be forcing him too quickly against the grain.

"The Polish situation," he said. "You wrote something very clever about it in *Die Zeit*. 'A resentful nationalism rigged up as the Madonna and threatening to raise East-West power games to the level of the Heavenly Host'—was that it? Very nice. Just what was needed to counter Solzhenitsyn."

Which only half fit the bill, it seemed. Krel showed a scholar's ire. "Solzhenitsyn is a superstitious Slavic peasant who thinks of latrine rumors as history. I do not bother to read him," he said.

This was the next morning. Still morning-pale, the sun moved around the rafters of the barn. Later it became gold and poured down the walls. A small bird, a swift or meadow lark, had gotten in. It fluttered against the beams, disturbing motes of dust, but so high up that it could have been a moth. Krel sat at his desk but turned toward Nadermann. Nadermann sat by the table in a high-backed dark armchair, and the Bokhara glowed beneath him.

"So," said Nadermann. "We are finished with the little things?" He resettled his spectacles with a graceful weariness and looked at his watch. "We have time to begin young Renate before lunch, I think. I doubt Mikhail is ready for us."

Krel's expression became both eager and solemn, like a young acolyte's. He passed him her letters. He murmured, "You have seen the first, I know."

Nadermann skimmed the rest. "Yes," he said. And then, "I keep forgetting to ask you—did you sleep with her?"

"No!" said Krel. Nadermann heard the intake of breath.

"It is usually wise," he said. "It increases both knowledge and control. And it would scarcely have been a hardship. She was evidently most struck by you."

"She was a student," said Krel. "Entrusted to me."

"My dear Oswolt," said Nadermann. "Your sensibility is remarkable." But Krel had rediscovered the pit of air beside him and was gazing into it, and Nadermann thought, *Damn! Go easy now.*

"She has evidently done remarkably well," he brightly said. "She may uncover this Herter and his crew any day."

"Entrusted to me," said Krel.

"So any risk she has taken has been amply repaid. Your plan was excellent all around. On the other hand, there are problems we must anticipate."

"What?" said Krel. "And what is this business of her being watched?"

"Imagination, I expect. She says so herself. Women love to think they're watched. That is not the problem."

"We must be ready to furnish her new Bundesrepublik passport and the other arrangements necessary for her return," said Krel. "She is right—she may be able to return soon. When she has found who controls Herter, who put him onto the CIA, she has done enough. The Americans will be paid back and punished. You will break their ring. It would be a great thing to accomplish so much with no injury done."

Nadermann said emphatically, "Exactly!" Krel looked relieved.

"That is exactly the problem," Nadermann said. He set rhetoric aside and continued swiftly, using his fingers to nail his points. "They are being very cautious with this girl. One step at a time. Intervals to discuss among themselves. Rendezvous they can simply miss. No names. What do these letters contain? Absolutely nothing. One could even wonder if she trusts you as much as you think—though I do not say she doesn't. Will this be the end of it? No. I am absolutely certain that she will next report on good authority that August Herter was no policeman but an honest deserter, traitor, and spy. But after that? Oh, after that it all gets harder. Who exactly did Herter report to? Now, that is hard to say. What exactly was his purpose? Well, he took it with him, did he not?

"I do not say, Oswolt, that she will achieve nothing. Right now there are ways I could use her to trap some quisling officers. It might turn out that the Germans know about them already. But maybe not. Perhaps some little group with a letter drop to the CIA. Not enough, Oswolt. Not enough."

Krel said, "But almost precisely what she was sent for. One doesn't often get everything one hoped."

"Sometimes one gets more," Nadermann said. "There have been developments." He changed his tone to a careful administrator's. "Have there been repercussions at the university around her disappearance? She wasn't entirely invisible, I would think."

"Not particularly," said Krel. "What developments should there be? She has a loose manner of life. She left after the end of the university term. There was even a rather lucky circumstance: the young man she is attached to went off to America for the summer. No doubt he has found an American *popsy*, I think is the word, and has no interest in Renate at all. The rent on her apartment continues to be paid. There may be some who wonder privately about her, but I doubt that anything will be done."

"The problem may arise when the fall term begins," said Nadermann. "Which is not so very far away. You must alert me in that case." Krel nodded. "The developments, then. Oswolt, as you know, in our relationship trust is essential yet must always seem doubted. I am going to tell you very little and then ask of you a great deal. To accept this is your discipline but also your dignity—do you understand?"

Krel hesitated and thought.

They always do, thought Nadermann. *This is where they wonder if they are being insulted or magnified. But there is always something in humans that makes this a flattery, and then it hardly seems to matter what it is all about.* He felt a flux of weariness. *I have done too much of this.*

"I understand," said Krel.

"Few would," said Nadermann. "In a nutshell, then. A poor dry nutshell. We have come to have a pretty good idea where August Herter is, and he may not be utterly unavailable to us. That came by luck and very hard work. We worked through every American contact this journalist Bessel has until we found one who is certainly not what he seems and who appeared to be worth following. Sooner or later we will reveal that Bessel trafficks with the CIA, which will not help his reputation. But that comes later. Clearly the best way to find out about August Herter would be to talk to August Herter at great leisure. I will go no further there, and anyway it may not be feasible.

"Secondly, there is a thought that Herter's lines may go very high, not far from the very summit of the Staatssicherheitsdienst. We are dealing with specialized matters here, and I can only say that the Americans seem to be behaving in an odd manner about one of their endless stream of horrible new weapons and that this raises certain suspicions."

From far below, spilling up into the barn, came a silvery bell rising in mild crescendo. Nadermann looked startled.

"Luncheon," said Krel. "My man. He can wait."

Nadermann shrugged. "All those who could possibly be suspect are very senior, very powerful. It is exceedingly disagreeable for an intelligence service to move against its top men and even more disagreeable for the KGB to move against an allied service. The wrong move causes every kind of embarrassment and damage. One needs a catalyst." He gestured acceptingly. "It is not so bad that your man has rung. There was nothing more I could have told you about this in itself, and we cannot work without a break. But bear in mind: a catalyst—a small thing that moves great ones."

Nadermann divided his smoked eel into oleaginous firm strips and anointed each with horseradish. The Slovene had brought out the widow's best Dresden for his stay; the table was elegant in blue and white. The wine was a soft young Baden. Nadermann breathed with pleasure both the air of tension within the room and the meadow air that stirred the curtains through the opened windows. He talked of this and that in Bonn, touched on the Köln opera, was amusing about Ronald Reagan. Krel spoke the word *Renate*. Nadermann lifted his finger in warning as the Slovene appeared with a small chicken with mushrooms on a silver tray. Krel shut up at once. From the meadows came the sounds of cows, but distant enough to be bucolic, not agricultural. The old house creaked grumpily to itself.

But Nadermann thought quickly and with diligence. Krel would certainly resist at first. He had taken him far enough that he could be blackmailed, but Nadermann abominated that. To use force on a promising agent was destructive and savage; it was like raping a wife. He had a glimpse—had had it long ago but had never been able to approach it—of an opening in Krel where a key should fit without damage. He hoped he was right.

"Ah, the first *chanterelles* of the season," he said, helping himself copiously and enjoying the French word. "The parting gift of summer. You have a luxurious forest here, Oswolt."

And Krel had relaxed enough to smile and say, "It rained all last week. You missed the rain. You have the mushrooms. That is luck."

The stakes were high. Krel, by academic and personal reputation, by his access to the prominent, was an asset only just below a senior politician in value. To place him psychologically and legally under the unconditional control of KGB would be one of the significant coups of the decade for the German office.

The moment was early; by classical models of development he

was rushing Krel. But Nadermann had put himself on the line with his *Rezident,* saying that Krel had been worked on already for many years and that there would never be a circumstance psychologically or in any other way so suitable for trapping him. "I won't only have his liberty and reputation in my hand," he had urged, "I truly believe I'll have his sanity as well."

After lunch, smoking one of two daily cigarettes (for he still liked the rabid Russian ones), Nadermann said, "Oswolt, it is a lovely day. Let us once again go for a walk."

Krel looked at him sharply.

Under the high sun, the flowers in the meadow were pale and it was trodden by cattle, but a little spring shimmered in the middle of it. The pinewood beyond was dark.

"A catalyst," said Nadermann.

"Not over there—I am wearing house shoes," said Krel.

"A catalyst," said Nadermann, deviating. "A small thing to affect a great. I shall not be mysterious. Your Renate to uncover a German high official who has sold his country to the CIA."

Krel looked down sharply but controlled himself. "For a young lady who will be unable to find out about Captain August Herter, that is ambitious," he said.

"A different method," said Nadermann. "Of course she could not find him. He will hear of her. It is very simple, a question of timing. It requires one small act from you. Listen well.

"My service will proceed against Herter. Perhaps we will take him—then we will have ample information but not ample proof. Perhaps we will fail, but then the attempt will be made known. Just before this, you will send a communication to the girl. It will say that much progress has been made here, that it is known that Herter is connected with a high commander of the SSD and that she should reveal her knowledge of this to her contacts and plead with them to pass upward to their leader the fact that he is in deadly danger. This letter will be found on her at her arrest."

"At her arrest?" said Krel.

"Which is also timed," said Nadermann, briskly and without emphasis.

"Which is contrived?" said Krel.

"Necessarily. This arrest will send a shock wave up the nerves of the SSD. It will certainly reach this man, whoever he is. He probably thinks of himself as relatively safe. The double effect of this and Herter will cause a movement. That is what we want. The catalyst."

The repeated word caused Krel to look up, but he had stopped listening and was holding to one safe point. He said quickly, "The idea is preposterous. She had been told never to keep my letters." He nodded, satisfied. "Never."

"You write two letters," Nadermann said. "One, no doubt, she throws away. The other is placed upon her before the arrest. It can be done. She will not be able to talk about it. But she will quickly be identified. Former illegal emigrant. Student of Dr. Krel, the *Fluchthilfer.* Totally convincing. And do not forget, if there is one person this high traitor will then be disposed to trust, it will be you. There may be more to this."

Krel stopped and turned and even placed his foot upon a tussock. "I forbid you to speak such evil to my face," he said.

Which was rather fine, thought Nadermann. He said, bowed down by its weight, "It is cruel to put such a decision on one who is not trained for it. And you in the shock of what was done to Ursula." He stopped, seemingly discouraged. "After all, you are a teacher."

But in Krel's face there really was the look of an animal led close to a trap and seeing it. Krel said, "When I was young I risked my life to escape from people who think as you do. Would I go back to you now? I should order you from my property."

But he abandoned his tussock—and Nadermann's one cause for optimism now was that he abandoned it reluctantly. Still, *This may not work,* thought Nadermann. *I may have lost.*

"We shall not speak of this again," he said. "You are a scholar. I was wrong to forget it. The world of action is not yours."

They walked back in silence, Krel not looking where he stepped. He seemed to have trouble seeing, as though surrounded by swirling clouds. He surprised Nadermann by saying suddenly, in a voice quite without its usual projection, "Do you really think that Ursula Hecht would want a twenty-year-old girl sacrificed to her memory? That is an extraordinarily stupid idea."

"Of course not," said Nadermann hastily. "That is not what I meant at all."

But by the time they reached the house, clouds covered Krel again.

In the evening he made no allusion to the conflict. His manner to Krel was as if to the unjustly bereaved. Krel, though puzzled at first, seemed to find this appropriate and soothing. They spoke mainly of a new production of *The Marriage of Figaro* in Köln placed in Franco's Spain in modern dress. This was lunacy, argued Nadermann. Countess Almaviva is emotionally not a modern woman, nor can Cherubino be called a teenager. As well place it under the Inquisition. He hummed two arias in illustration. He hummed them well.

He said, as though the thought overcame him, "But Oswolt, this appreciation makes our life so difficult. I suppose it is the same for the kindhearted soldier, but I believe that ours is harder. All is in cold blood. All proceeds from the intellect and the sense of purpose. The Soviet Union understands this very well. With us, the men of the Organs of State Security are recognized unequivocally as heroes."

They were sitting after dinner in the living room. The widow had had fun here. It was the house's most eclectic room, and the heads of deer on the paneled walls looked through lustrous glass eyes at a Matisse and at a Picasso sketch of Leda and the swan.

Krel looked at him sharply. Nadermann thoughtfully went on.

"But for every cost there is some benefit. I believe that we who face the logic of our duty even to acting at the outer limit of severity do acquire a knowledge of the human condition that is extremely deep. Have you not thought of that, Oswolt? You would put it so much better."

He saw most oddly and suddenly in Krel the look of a peasant surly at the fear of being tricked. He added quickly, "The magnificent discipline in which you live your life would make you able to."

Krel answered, "That. Yes. Of course, it is its own reward."

"There is a story I want to tell you, Oswolt, about my earliest years in the service. Perhaps you will understand me better then. An event that had a great impact on me. It is one that I tell to very few, for I have intensely conflicting feelings about it." He shrugged gracefully. "It is a story, of course, from a more severe time. Much happened under Josef Vissarionovich that was not for weak stomachs.

"1951," he said. "I was a very young officer in the Lubyanka. Abakumov was head of the service then, and I was attached to his office. He was very much a working chief. He was not unwilling to be involved with the prisoners, even in his personal office. There was a rubber mat we used to put down over the Persian rug on those occasions."

And I am right, he thought. *This may work.* For he saw in Krel's eye a flickering of fear and anticipation, both at once.

"On that occasion Abakumov was working, not for the first time, with a certain former general of the Red Army. He had been in the Lubyanka a long time and there was still no signed confession. Abakumov was a big man, you know, and heavy. He had the general trussed on the mat with his buttocks up in the air and he was kicking him as hard as he could, working up a sweat. I remember how the tea service on the desk used to jingle each time. It sounds rather funny, perhaps, like a comic book, but after a time in the Lubyanka there is no body fat, only hide over bone, and then the effect is very different. They say it is felt like a bomb in the skull. I was sitting on the general's shoulders and I could see his fingernails breaking on the mat. But still . . . no confession.

"Eventually he began to bleed through the anus, really like a dying pig, and Abakumov had to stop. I was told to take him away.

"It was messy, of course. I was half carrying him, half dragging him in the corridor—not an unusual sight in the Lubyanka then. I remember suddenly seeing the look of triumph on the old man's face. I perfectly understood. Nobody could be expected to resist what he had withstood, and yet he had, and not for the first time. I had a sudden idea. I don't know where it came from. The point is that I acted upon it without hesitation.

"I threw him down then and there on the floor. And I stood over him and I urinated on his face. I was very young then, almost a boy, and maybe that had something to do with it, but that man, who had endured the impossible, began to sob like a baby. And, it turned out, there was nothing more left in him. The confession was signed that afternoon.

"Now, Oswolt, how does one think about that? In many ways a terrible story of a terrible time—life should not be like that. It is not *The Marriage of Figaro*, is it? But yet in a way deeply instructive. By dominating myself I reached a state, for that moment, of omnipotence. And that omnipotence was properly channeled to the service of society, by which that confession was required. My failure at that point to act so would have created just the sort of feeble muddle that a Chekist sees in the societies that he will replace. And there is something else, more personal. I learned the reserves within myself, that I could step at will out of the limitations that we impose upon ourselves and achieve whatever was to be achieved. I have never regretted it. But, tell me, Oswolt, was I right?"

Krel looked straight at him now, transfixed. He said nothing for several breaths, then murmured, "It is a terrible story of a disgusting time."

But Nadermann saw in his eyes a mixture of fear and craving. He shrugged, inviting more.

Krel said, "It is a terrible story. I cannot discuss it." He rose and left the room, awkwardly opening the door.

Nadermann settled in his chair and watched the last twilight sink into the meadow. Krel had had a secret love affair with cruelty that Nadermann had sniffed out. An academic in love with ruthlessness. Attila with a blackboard, the poor bastard! He had encountered the story, which he thought stomach-turning beyond expression, in Solzhenitsyn. He supposed it was true, though Krel, had he read it, would no doubt have added it quite appositely to the "latrine rumors." It paid to read widely. He put it from his mind. Krel would do what he wanted now. He was sure.

15

Colonel Vasili Filippov, of KGB internal security, was never unaffected by East Berlin. Its gritty buildings, coarsely patched over the scars of war, its unattractive but illustrious monuments—like the Brandenburg Gate he was looking at now—its bleak prosperity, the tough, cynical resignation of its crowds all reminded him of Volgograd, late gallant Stalingrad, the home of his boyhood. He therefore detested it. Last week he had been in Sochi, where there were palm trees on the esplanade and girls on the beach and they gave you casaba melon for breakfast. The week before that, he had been in Budapest, where the nightclubs were terrific.

He tapped his pen while General Karshkhov, KGB *Rezident* of East Berlin, made excuses. General Karshkhov said, "Excuse me, colonel, but it is far from certain that there has been a leak in the PSYCHIC penetration project. At your first inquiry, Captain Smolsky here himself examined the American black who provides our intelligence. The data originates with this man, and he insisted that it was not being altered. Smolsky believed him." General Karshkhov smiled bravely. Captain Smoksky smiled uneasily. Colonel Filippov did not smile. General Karshkhov added, "If there were a leak it would not have been from Berlin." That was a throwaway line.

Colonel Filippov tapped his pen some more. Karshkhov was a leftover of the old NKVD. He smelled onion on his breath. Probably still ate them peasant-style at home, raw like an apple. Karshkhov was an Andropov man. Andropov was dead.

He said with transparently false patience, "We are speaking of arithmetic, not of Captain Smolsky." He motioned with his pen to the chair beside him. "Major Dr. Volodin will explain."

Dr. Volodin opened his briefcase and looked closely into it, as though inhaling from it.

"PSYCHIC is a system for receiving and analyzing the internal electronic impulses of our aircraft, correlating them with the movement of the aircraft, and building a mathematical model by which to predict the aircraft's movement from such impulses in the future. It's importance is obvious."

"We know all that," said Karshkhov. To a mathematician, even from internal security, he could talk like a general again.

Volodin did not break stride. "And its success very improbable. Too many signals are nonspecific, too many are identical but have different implications with different aircraft, too many may be altered by small changes in equipment. And so forth. I will not elaborate. We had to watch PSYCHIC, because the Americans surprise us from time to time, but we never expected them to have much success with it."

He shut the briefcase. Major Dr. Volodin was twenty-six years old, and his face, which was round and fat, looked like a cynical baby's.

He went on, "And they did not. The numbers we got from Smolsky's black man were completely uninteresting. They had hundreds of correlations, they fed them through their computers, which are very impressive, and they got nothing, or nothing interesting. No mathematical model." He used the words "mathematical model" as one might use "soporific" to a rather stupid child.

He went on, "We did get the computer program that the black had designed. It was interesting, but we got it right at the beginning, and if the project itself was not of much value, then nor was the program, or for that matter the black, even if getting them was the sum total of Captain Smolsky's achievements."

Filippov cast his eyes to heaven, purely for effect.

"Until about six weeks ago. Then we began to find sequences that were important—that is to say, we found precise and recurring correlations. We began to be worried. We looked at these correlations very carefully. It took some time, for our computers are not as sophisticated as theirs. Then we began to be surprised."

Volodin impressively drew breath. Filippov beat him to it.

"Because we began to realize that the correlations were fictitious."

Volodin looked sulky and went pedagogically on. "The sequences of impulses were not those of any Warsaw Pact aircraft in any probable maneuver. They very nearly were, but not quite. Do you understand—the Americans were adding imaginary data to make nonspecific, meaningless figures seem significant. This was very hard to detect at first, and as a matter of fact, the artificial significance was not very great. Both might have been overlooked by some people." He recovered and smiled at himself. "We were not certain. That was when we sent the first inquiry to you. Of late there have been some clumsier examples."

Colonel Filippov said lightly, "Now, it is possible that their technicians were lying to their own generals." Karshkhov and Smolsky brightened.

"But it is almost certain that they are lying to us. I do not need to spell out the implications of that. KGB, Berlin, had charge of the entrapment of the black technician, Mays. Mays is by far the most probable source of the CIA's counterpenetration. Who had knowledge of it?"

Karshkhov said, "Myself, Smolsky, Fetchurin of Operations. The agents who performed the entrapment. A courier, who knew Mays by sight only. No one else in the KGB."

Filippov looked at him a long time. "Do I understand you, general, that there was someone outside of the KGB?"

He saw the heavy mouth twist at the corner, like a old dog shown a whip. He showed that he saw it. He had nothing particularly against Karshkhov, but he did not like onions or Berlin, and Karshkhov's protector was dead.

Karshkhov said, "Also the German chief of liaison between the SSD and the KGB. General Sucher. His office is in this embassy."

Filippov said, "A non-Soviet."

"Of the highest clearance." Karshkhov rallied. "He has served the KGB longer than you have, colonel. And perhaps in more dangerous matters."

Filippov said, "His file." He waited and added, "General."

While the file was being brought, Karshkhov tried, "You are here at a nice season, Colonel. The Berlin fall is famous."

Filippov decided to punish him, looked out of the window, and said nothing.

He took the file. It was as thick as an atlas. From the last pages of it protruded a yellow ribbon. Such a ribbon shows that a security inquiry is in progress, outcome undecided. Filippov stroked it and looked Karshkhov in the eye.

He said, "And the non-Soviet you chose for your confidence was already under investigation? How subtle you are in Berlin, general."

Karshkhov looked at the desk. "He wasn't then," he said, and added, with a leap into bravado, "nothing is proved now." His bravado met Filippov's eye and fell in a heap on the floor. He added helpfully, "He is in this building. He could be arrested at once. He could be interrogated in front of you."

Filippov nodded thoughtfully. "That would be consistent, I think. If one has begun stupidly, one may as well go on." He let that add for a while to the pleasures of the Berlin fall and then said brightly, "Or we could try professionalism." *I am being a real shit*, he thought, with some pleasure.

He opened the file and read its later sections in silence and with exaggerated care. He put the file down.

190

He said gently, "No, it is not proved, is it, general? A man gives every appearance of servicing a dead drop, though he is never actually caught doing so; a man suddenly becomes an object of fascination to the Americans; a man has knowledge of an operation and the operation suddenly turns queer; but none of this is guilt, I think. Guilt for a private, perhaps. Even guilt for a captain. But this man occupies one of the higher position of trust in the Warsaw Pact. You gave him his last promotion yourself. I agree, general. Higher standards must obtained."

Karshkhov nodded weightily. Filippov went on, "Because if he *were* guilty, general, you yourself would become responsible for the security of the urinals in the seamen's home at Vladivostok. But you knew that, didn't you, general? And, if I am not mistaken, you retire next year."

He paused lightly and then went on. "First," he said, "it is obviously very uncertain what this Sucher is actually doing—assuming, as I do assume, that he is doing something. Is it PSYCHIC only? That is so much less than he could do. And yet, there exist examples of the betrayal of one thing only. We must let this develop. It is extremely fortunate that this has fallen into my hands. You will do nothing in this matter from now on, general, without instructions from my section.

"Secondly, since the Americans are patently involved in this, we must not discount the possibility of getting them into some really embarrassing position. It is worth a lot to catch the Americans with their heads up their asses. Seeing that PSYCHIC is a load of crap in the first place and that we are not in danger of being fooled by it anymore, it clearly does no harm to let this part of the matter run. Major Dr. Volodin has something to say, I think."

"I want a little more of the black's figures," he said. "I'd like to know what the Americans are trying to make me believe. That's all."

"And what the major doctor wants, he shall have," said Filippov. "Don't touch the black until you're told to. Then, of course, you get the description of his handler out of him. And the name, for what it's worth, and the other details. Does Smolsky think he can manage that, or should we use someone else?"

Smolsky stiffened.

"As for you, general," went on Filippov, "I suggest you make this Sucher a little uncomfortable, darken his name a little. This will make him try to speed up while it in fact slows him down. Both are useful."

General Karshkhov, whose forehead was now white and whose

cheeks crimson, said, "I have already begun that process, colonel. I thank you for your advice. It is similar to what I learned forty years ago."

"But one forgets so much," said Filippov, "with age."

———

General Sucher walked at lunch. He passed daily through the embassy, which Colonel Filippov had left three weeks before. He assayed the noonday weather from its steps, he passed down Unter den Linden to the Opera House square, where the sun reflecting off the walls now pleasured an old man in the early autumn, all with a regularity that had become ritual and metronomic. And there he serviced his dead drop.

This was not foolhardy. He reckoned not. He serviced his dead drop only once a week. Even if he was now their prey, he was still clasped to the security organs, and it was like a dance with a very old partner—a more ribald metaphor suggested itself, but only time would tell then who was on top. The organs of security could not be seen to watch him constantly or closely without announcing their attack of an officer at the summit of their own service. That did not suit them yet. It might never suit them. If he made no mistakes, if the CIA was not clumsy again, the case against him might shrivel up for lack of sustenance and end as nothing more than one of those little, fatal marks on the careers of recently important men living in remote small cottages with one odd servant.

So he walked through the embassy at twelve o'clock. He greeted Igor Kuntsayev, commercial attaché, and received the same askance, uncertain look as he had had from a general of the GRU two weeks before and from a colonel of the KGB a week after that. Generals no longer returned his greeting; colonels did so, but coldly. The clerks would pick it up. The Germans were learning now, through Reinagle. His degradation was being managed, in good KGB style, with the etiquette of a dancing school.

The traffic on General Sucher's desk reflected his fall. He, General Hans Friedrich Sucher, of the Order of Lenin, eighth-ranking officer of all the SSD, was asked his opinion in triplicate on some cases of malingering in Rostok. His work now took up about an hour a day, which left him more time for conspiracy and very little to conspire with.

He crossed Friedrichstrasse, looking both ways, once toward the subway station to the West. A customer came out of the liquor

192

store and followed him. He was clearly an Eastern tourist with rocky features that might well have been Czech. He carried a moderately expensive Hungarian camera. General Sucher crossed over Charlottenstrasse as a high cloud darkened the stone of the State Library and chilled his shoulders.

The possible Czech paused in admiration in front of the library, which would have been the ugliest building in Prague. A man in an unbuttoned artificial-leather flying jacket walked out of the courtyard. He had been standing around trying for an angle with his nice East German Zeiss from Jena. He nodded minutely to the aesthetic Czech and walked on behind General Sucher.

The cloud reminded Hans Sucher of another thing: this method would do only in good weather. Elderly generals do not splash around in the cold rain, even if no one is speaking to them. The thought was beginning to form in his mind, *Ask the CIA for a radio.* It formed like a black blob. The modern ones were greatly improved, small and capable of transmitting a report in a second or less. They were marvelous tools; he had seen several of them—and their former owners were in the camps or dead. The best transmitter in the world was a hard, square incrimination. And, besides, such tricks were not his field. He stopped in front of Humboldt University and waited to cross Unter den Linden. The poster in front of the Opera was for *Macbeth.* The cloud retired.

Communication with his network was likewise difficult. It was classically set up. Only one man in each of the four military centers accessible to him—the First Motorized Rifles here in Berlin, the Seventh Tanks in Dresden, the Eighth Motorized Rifles in Schwerin, and the Ninth Tanks in Eggesin—had direct contact with, or personal knowledge of, General Sucher himself. These were all clever boys and all officers of the SSD's Administration 2000. They, in turn, knew names only in their own division. A few others, like August Herter, with special roles had knowledge of the general but not of these key men. By very modest standards it was reasonably secure. But these key men were to have been eased into positions where frequent communication with General Sucher's office would have been unremarkable. And this had by no means yet been done.

This was all good to think about—better than his dead drop fifty yards away. Which scared the daylights out of him.

A man in a suit of the hard, electric blue favored by snappy Bulgars turned from the opera poster where he had been gazing doubtfully at the picture of a hairy tenor with a big sword and a checkered skirt. The aviator, walking faster, swung toward the middle of the square. The Bulgar made toward another poster, this one of a dagger levitating over a barren set. General Sucher was between them. The Bulgar uncased a cheap camera.

General Sucher reached the bench.

The blue Bulgar was directly in front of him, about twenty meters away. The flying jacket walked a little farther so that he looked at Sucher's bench, end on. They were not conspicuous. Of a hundred or so people in the square, nearly a third had cameras.

General Sucher sat down. He had schooled himself, above all on the days of danger, to take a real curiosity and pleasure in the square. Stones, too, change with the seasons. St. Hedwig's was drawing into itself with the first chill nights, changing the buttery gold of stone in summer toward the etched outline of winter gray. A cantata was heard within it whose faintness gave it the un-guarded sweetness of children's voices. The square was busy, as ever. Many foreigners. Many central Europeans. It pleased him that even this denatured rump of his boyhood's bright and green Berlin should again be a German beacon to the East; that Bulgars and Slavs, even in suits of offensive blue, should photograph its squares. He bent slowly down to reach beneath the bench.

———

Wop Stears looked at ELBEMAN's penciled numerals, crisp and enigmatic on the refolded page, and at the decoding, fresh from the printer of the code machine downstairs. He read the last sentence again and then the original. The numbers were as orderly and expressionless as the rest. It said, "It will be of interest to me to hear your voice."

He went into Brindle Woods's office. The loden coat, hanging on the stand, had had its ritual monthly brushing and looked welcoming on a damp October morning. Munich glowed on the wall.

"He is getting worried about the drop," said Stears. "He feels that it is insecure now and he has to think about the cold weather when hanging around outside the Opera will look damned odd. I believe it's getting cool up there already."

Brindle Woods thought and said, "Drops can be a problem," as though admitting a side effect of a children's remedy. "I don't blame him. What does he want to do?"

"He wants a radio," said Wop. "He can use a radio from outside Berlin. In other words, he's feeling pressure."

"It's a difficult environment," said Woods.

Stears said wearily, "For Christ's sake, Brindle, he's been feeling pressure ever since they caught that goddam spy of yours."

" 'Agent,' " said Woods. "Or 'asset.' Never 'spy.' That was unfortunate but necessary, and it was very nonspecific. You cannot run an anonymous agent at that level, whatever you promise. We've been through all that. Besides, the CIA is meant to watch Stasi generals. It's what they expect." He leaned back behind his desk. General Lucius Clay looked down at him from the wall, above a letter to Woods in Lucius Clay's own hand. "Anyway, he wants a radio?"

"Yes," said Stears. He opened his mouth to take up yet again the perfidy of having violated ELBEMAN's, now Hans Sucher's, promised anonymity, but the weariness of futility stopped him and he said instead, "I hate those radios."

"Wise," said Woods. "The problem with small scramblers is that they are no longer entirely secure. Run it through a big enough computer for long enough and you can reconstitute it. But, yes. There's no choice. Keep the transmissions below a second and maybe they'll never pick them up."

"He wants it at his country place. He's told us very precisely where. Harder for us, safer for him. Is that what we do?"

"The agent knows his environment best. Don't second-guess him if you can avoid it." Woods said it instructively.

"I'll try and remember," said Stears. "It's going to be difficult. Obviously. I'll give you a proposal."

―――――

Hans Sucher woke to find his cover's knee pressed warmly and damply against his side. He almost pushed it away, but did not. He had dreamed splintered images of blackened guns, an unremembered smoldering street, a bicycle hanging by its distorted wheel from a charred and solitary beam. Where? God knew. Perhaps inside himself. Better than the Poles. He accepted the knee's sharp warmth. His cover was small and blond. He watched her shoulders move at the edge of her breathing. It was just dawn. The old wake early. The stove had long since gone out, the pine room was cold, the fall's first flight of geese called high above the lake, the light was silver mist, he worried about her shoulders, and pulled the hairy blanket over them.

He lit the stove in the living room for breakfast. She saw him kneeling stiffly by it, a fistful of pine slivers in his hand. They were last year's wood and very dry.

"I can do that," she said. She had brought no warm clothes and was wearing his shooting coat, which swallowed her. Her name was Ilse.

"No," said Sucher. "We understand each other, this stove and I."

Smell of hot metal and roar of burning pine. The warmth of the little breakfast room flickered on the wooden walls. He saw her stretch with pleasure. It surprised him how much child was left over at nineteen.

He had invited two KGB men out to the villa with their molls. Offered to get them molls. He had been turned down contemptuously, of course. Powerless, rumored traitor, and pimp as well. So here he was with little Ilse. The villa was up to its old uses. Not new ones, such as clever radios.

He saw her coffee cup was empty and poured her more. There was a skin on the hot milk. She had taken the saucepan from him, saying, "You'll scorch it like that."

She said, "Where does this jam come from? General Barens has it too."

He said gently, "There are special shops. Maybe I'll take you one day."

She nodded enthusiastically. "Yes, I know. I've been to one. My suitcase came from there. It's pretty, isn't it?" And then reluctantly, a well-mannered child, "You don't have to give me anything, you know."

It pleased him to imagine that she had not said that to Reinhardt Barens.

She held the big coffee cup, cradling it between the shooting coat's wide cuffs, bathing her face in the steam. He smelled coffee, gun oil, soap, and a not very expensive scent. She looked slowly around the little breakfast room. They had used the living room and the bedroom the night before. Her eye stopped at the clock, riotously quaint—a chalet, a gnarled old couple, window boxes, squirrel for a pendulum, a cuckoo overhead.

"That's funny," she said. "Does it work?"

"It could. I don't wind it."

Ilse looked studiously at the general and laughed out loud. "I'd love to see you do it," she said. He smiled and shook his head. She was there as his cover for treason; her ease was balanced on a hair's width between innocence and depravity; and yet he loved to see her hand move around the cup, see her hair and the coat's collar cover and reveal her throat, and he remembered her limbs in the night almost as if they had been a childhood home. He realized, with surprise, that she was more real than the use he was putting her to, and realized it with humility and fear, for it was the thought of a poor man, without power.

She said, "Are we going to stay here all day? And tonight?"

"I think so," he said. "Would you like to?"

She put down the coffee cup. "Sure," she said. "That's fine."

"I have to see a man on the estate this morning. You can stay here while I do that."

"I'll come with you," said Ilse. "I'll get dressed quickly and do the dishes later. I've never seen an estate."

"No," he said. "I'll go alone."

She said, "Oh," quickly. She already knew all about secrets. "I'll play the record player then." It was Swedish.

Her eye, for the first time just a fraction ill at ease, traveled farther to the living room, to the skulls of deer.

"Did you kill all those?" she said.

"None of them." It occurred to him that he did not know who had—the Jew, the Nazi, or the KGB man. Probably the Nazi. Who had probably bought the clock.

"Good," she said. She smiled at him quickly. She began to pick up the dishes.

Mist hung over the lake, caught the trailing strands of the weeping willow. The tips of tall grasses, the keel of the upturned rowboat, were brushed with frost. He smelled the chimney smoke. A cow bellowed beyond the pinewood. That was his direction. He set off, imitating someone on a sensible and decent mission, to shoot a hare, to feed a cow, to visit a neighbor, and to come back to a wife.

His property was over a hundred hectares, most of it woods. It was surrounded by a wire fence overgrown with ivy, and there was provision for security at the gate but it was not rigorously sealed. He walked into the wood. It was mostly pine, open under the trees and covered with needles in a silky brown carpet that took no footprint, but the hollows were full of brambles and scrub hazel, and here he moved slowly. He moved with the care of an infantryman at risk. He had seen no indication of intrusive surveillance, but he could not be sure.

He came to a track. The wheel ruts were soft with leaves and grass, the center was overgrown. It had not been used in his time.

It was a forester's track, leading to a secondary gate, now itself closed up with ivy, but lower than the surrounding wall. He walked along it. He passed a small brick structure with a wooden door. The brick was covered with moss and the mortar was crumbling. It had to do with a drainage system, now disused. He looked down at the track, saw that there now were faint marks of disturbance in the leaves and grass, nodded, and walked in them himself. He walked carefully to the gate.

He left the track before he got there and crept up to it. Nobody there. He examined it. If you looked very carefully, the ivy had been pushed aside and trodden in places. There was a faint smell of crushed stems. But you had to look. He walked back to the brick hut.

The door opened easily. The cobwebs around its frame hung limply, broken. The inside smelled so thick with mold that it tightened his throat. He let his eyes get used to the dark. By the far wall there was a dark bulge on the floor. He went to it and picked it up and brought it into the half-light. A company of Stasis might walk out of the wood and surround the hut—but they might surround him anywhere.

A small canvas sack, the size of a large schoolbook, dingy and unremarkable. Good. Inside it, some kind of packing—a half-clear plastic sheet with boils or bubbles in it. Very unprofessional, he thought. He'd never seen it. It must be purely Western. He tore a little of it off. And there was the radio. He tore some more. It was as it should be. At first inspection, the radio looked like the most common popular domestic make, a cheap yellow metal grille, the brand name in letters which suggested lightning. The grille came off and the wizardry was behind it.

He pulled the plastic back and then the canvas. He had not the slightest pleasant curiosity about it.

He carefully shut the door. He went back quietly through the forest. Before he came out of it, he heard the record player. Ilse had found the Rolling Stones. He forgot the name of the girl he had bought them for.

16

Waiting on Wop Stears's desk each morning was the German press, which gave him the feeling of a second breakfast, richer than his first at home. This was not difficult, for Marie-Sophie's regime ran to two cups of coffee, two ripe figs, and one wicker tray, half of which regale was at the disposal of her husband as he talked to her, dressed except for jacket, on the far side of the tray but her side of the bed.

Stears had his favorites. *Neues Deutschland*, from East Berlin, snickered this morning, "U.S. Racketeers prey on Afghans." Stears wondered how they noticed. He loved *Neues Deutschland*, addictive as pickle. Then there was the rich smooth *Frankfurter Allgemeine* with its daring dash of Gothic type down the side—one teaspoon of healthy German nationalism in a nice nutritious pudding of Atlantic Euro-feeling. He read Munich's *Suddeutsche Zeitung* last. Franz Joseph Strauss had come home from Bonn and given the Russians hell in a beer hall. Quite right, too. Dr. Oswolt Krel announced a fall symposium titled *German Neutralism: Lessons of the Thirty Years War*. Stears wrote this routinely into a growing appendix of new white paper to the Oswolt Krel file whose covers he had first touched three months earlier. His fingers had developed a faint distaste for them lately, as though they were sticky. Noticing this made him restive and discontent in spite of his walk down South Audley Street and the scent of new-mown grass rising from Grosvenor Square. Back in the *Suddeutsche Zeitung*, the steeple at Landshut was being repaired. Even while scanning the back page, the local news, he began to fold the paper. Until a little headline caught his eye and he spread it out again, reading the article carefully and tapping his pencil while he read.

Later in the morning he said to Brindle Woods, "It's hardly the story of the week, I know. But the girl was an escaper. She took Krel's courses—the reporter noticed that. She's even from East Berlin. And she's done a bunk. Or she did a bunk and she's not come back."

Woods shrugged. "Ran off with boyfriend on a motorcycle," he said.

Stears looked back at the clipping: *Apparent Disappearance of a Student*. It was four inches long. "Boyfriend was in on this," he said. "Boyfriend and girlfriend went to the police yesterday when she didn't show up at the proper time to register for next term. Didn't do it by mail, either. Neither of them had heard a word from her all summer. She's got digs in Munich, rent all paid, and her landlady hasn't seen her either. They're worried about her."

"Ran off with other boyfriend," said Woods. "She's pregnant. She's gone Zen. She's gone to San Francisco. She's a student, Stears." It was a pleasant morning, and his humor pleased him. He smiled.

Stears nodded. "Yes," he said. Then, "But escapers don't do those things. Not often."

"Have you a theory about her?"

"No," said Stears.

"Don't go calling Krel," said Woods. "Whatever you do."

"No, indeed," said Stears. Then, "Brindle, how did he get that goddam servant? Why does somebody four removes from ELBEMAN, even if he doesn't know it, suddenly get a valet who was thrown out of the Dutch embassy for reading the mail?"

"You're very jumpy," said Woods.

"Yes," said Stears, "I am. Krel was my idea. But that's only part of it. I do not want to be embarrassingly naive or let down the Company style or anything, but have you noticed that this entire operation is infested with bugs everywhere you look? Nothing has gone right. Nothing. It didn't even look that difficult at the beginning."

Woods said slowly, "A long life has taught me that those can be the worst. Be that as it may, I'd never blame you for looking for a pattern, Stears. The problem is, you have to know which ones not to find—otherwise you find nothing else. The servant is not so odd as you think. He's on the embassy blacklist but he's apparently so far down it the Germans didn't even throw him out. Probably he does work for the Opposition—Private, tenth class—I'd go with that. He's burned on embassy row now, so Krel's is the kind of household they would try to get him into. A little bit influential but no security. Important telephone call every once in a while. We live with that. We don't use those people because they're more trouble than they're worth. It doesn't mean much.

"The girl I just can't give you. There must be a thousand children who go to Krel's courses. It's too vague. Certainly by itself. Maybe if there was another connector somewhere. There's an in-

200

telligence adage, *three equals true.* I'm inclined to believe in it. You're not saying Krel's gone Commie, are you?"

"No," said Stears.

"Thank God. Please don't."

Brindle Woods said, "Have you any conception of the damage you might have done?"

This was a week later. Stears stiffly stood, a move toward his usual chair in Woods's office having concentrated the beam of outrage in his chief's eye. His report lay on Woods's desk—he had left it in the safe the night before—open to the last page on which a pencil lay snapped in two. *Still life with Administrator.*

"Three equals true," said Stears.

"Damn you!" said Woods. "A nice respectable German widow, the Mrs. Hotpoint of West Germany, has a lovely house in the Black Forest. She is a friend of Günter Grass, of Petra Kelly. . . ."

"*Respectable?*" said Stears.

Woods contrived simultaneously to glare at him and signal assent. "It only makes it worse," he said. "She invites to her gracious home the conscience and intellect of neutral Germany, Dr. Oswolt Krel. And you now have the bloody effrontery to leave me a report that Giovanni Stears of the American war machine had flatfeet crawling all through the plumbing. Do you realize that those people think the CIA has midgets hiding in their beds? Do you know what they would have made it sound like in the German press?"

"One man," said Stears. "Working on the hedge outside the gate. A retired Frankfurt policeman on the Company list, cleared at that level. Taking license numbers. That's all. I wish I'd had him there earlier."

"I asked you a question," said Woods.

"God-awful. But it wasn't going to happen. It wasn't even breaking German law, much. And we find that Krel's guest for two days was Heinrich Nadermann. Right at the end of the summer vacation when professors ought to be busy. And the locals say that was the only guest all summer."

"Bureau chief of Tass in Bonn," said Woods. "He's known him for years."

"Bureau chief of Tass in Bonn," said Stears. "And no one else, unless you count the Houdini of the Dutch embassy. Whom he has *not* known for years. And he hasn't been at the far end of a trail that leads to ELBEMAN for years and he hasn't had former escaper students disappearing for years, either. It's a pattern, Brindle. A new pattern."

"Stears, Stears, Stears," said Brindle Woods, "I will not dispute with you for one second that there are citizens who walk around in riding boots with rubber truncheons who have less to do with the KGB than Heinrich Nadermann. But if you want to pull in everybody who's had a long talk with him, you'll have to start at St. Peter's. I mean that."

"Who would you want at that house?" said Stears. "Soviet generals in full uniform?"

Woods looked at him with the pardon of a patient man and down at the report. He muttered to it, "Have you taken your goon off the premises?"

"Yes," said Stears. "Because Krel is off the premises. I've got a goon in Munich now. I'd like to keep him there."

Woods gestured to the chair. "What's the cut-out?" he said. "Between Krel and Herter? At the frontier?"

"As a matter of fact," said Stears, "it's good. Krel never saw me, never laid eyes on Herter. One of his people saw me, I guess, but it was dark, you know . . . and you know the rest. In a way, I hate to say it, but the mine helped us in that way. We grabbed Herter, carried him through forty meters of wood, and threw him in an ambulance. Then straight to Fulda. The same man who saw me would have seen Herter for a moment—he grabbed his hand, as a matter of fact—but Herter was a mess just then. Obviously nobody knows where Herter is now. The poor damn woman was obviously dead, and anyway she was in East Germany. The last I saw, the frontier bastards were cutting through the wire to get to her."

"Did you see Krel?" said Woods.

"Barely. He was coming out of the wood as we were going into it. He was looking at the woman and nothing else."

"Maybe he doesn't like us," said Woods.

"He never did."

"Would he have known you were there? Not by name, of course."

"An American out of uniform, yes. Unfortunately, when that sergeant I had with me started his one-man invasion, I had to yell at him and even grab him. That was in the open, which should never have happened. It would have been noticed, even then."

Woods said, "Krel's escape outfit has been in business twelve years. I have looked it over personally. There is not one bad smell about it. I admire them, if you want to know."

"I don't doubt you," said Stears.

"Krel is just the kind of person that Nadermann would go and see anyway. Nadermann's a charming kind of pig. Krel's a neutralist—he doesn't kick Tass people down the drive. Nadermann's main job is influencing people, especially people like Krel. Heart-to-heart exchange of views with a thoughtful Soviet—that kind of crap. He doesn't take the castor oil along."

"And the servant?" said Stears.

"What I said last week is not invalidated. Nor proved."

"And the vanishing girl?"

"Well, what?" said Woods. "You have her down as KGB?"

"I don't see that one," said Stears. "But suppose she's gone back to East Berlin."

"Why in God's name would she do that?"

"I don't know," said Stears. "Suppose it. And suppose Krel sent her. Would he have any acceptable reason for doing so?"

Woods said, "It would be to do with the *Fluchthilfer* ring and it would be extremely rash. But that's his business, not mine. There's something else. Krel may believe in fairy tales about Mother Russia and One Europe from the Urals to the Atlantic, but he's a tough old bird in his own way. He escaped himself, and that escape-help ring works. He would not be an innocent about the KGB. On that level, I think he could handle Nadermann."

"At least one knows that he would not cooperate," said Stears.

"Exactly."

"Exactly," said Stears. "That's what anyone would know."

Woods looked at him hard. "One can play cat's-cradle games to one's heart's content, Stears. It's the intellectual curse of this profession, people diddling with everything including themselves. You have to start from somewhere. There's no focus here."

"There's lot of noise."

Woods looked at him sideways. "I would turn the noise down very low, if I were you. People are listening. We do at least know that."

"I had considered that," said Stears. "Don't worry."

Woods said to the window, "Including the DIA."

"Jesus Christ," said Stears.

"Keep your goon quiet, too," said Woods. "The one in Munich."

━━━━━

Stears again drove the Jaguar down the billowy road to Warminster, but he bullied the accelerator and the brakes and neither saw the

203

hay turning in the fields nor smelled the heavy summer contending with the fruit and fallen leaves of fall. He looked once in a while at an itinerary typed on expensive paper that lay on the passenger's seat. *Symposium on East-West Financial Structures, October 4–5, Palast Hotel, East Berlin* was the title. Once when he looked at it he thought, *I would be out of my fucking mind. And Woods would kill me.*

And how else, in God's name, do I find out?

Woods is right: Krel cannot be a traitor. And to a girl he teaches? A girl the age he was when he crossed himself?

I am not a divining rod. A prickling in my neck means nothing. I do not like the man and never did.

I do not like him because he has stood back and let people perish when their intellectual breath was not pure enough. He has stood back as though he took pride in it.

Why did I not say that to Woods? Because it's a load of balls, that's why.

Ten miles before Warminster he became sociably intermingled with a line of coal trucks. Violent and sanguinary overtakings brought him from eighth to fifth in line. A pale blue English Ford bucketed in and out of the line behind him until it turned off for Devizes just before the town. At Warminster he exchanged coal for tanks, a convoy of the Scots Greys' Chieftains on transports. The Jaguar gave up humoring him and began to stall at lights. It stalled at the barracks gate.

He pushed his pass—one of a collection; this one came from NATO—at the duty sergeant and said, "I am here for Captain Herter."

The duty sergeant said, "Captain *Herter*, sir?"

And Stears, after an undamned eruption of vituperation—*blockhead, sloppy, dolt, loose-mouthed cretin, amateur*—all silent and all directed at himself, remembered Herter's alias, mildly corrected himself, and said, "Excuse me, I mean Captain Streicher. Bundeswehr exchange officer."

The sergeant telephoned.

"Captain Streicher is observing on the artillery range, sir."

"My compliments to Captain Streicher and request him to report to me."

Herter shut the car door and turned to Stears at once. He had arrived in haste.

"Stears," he said. "Why are you here? I did not expect you. Does this concern my general?"

His eyes had lost at last the lingering self-concern of the injured. They were deep and clear and troubled.

"Maybe," he said. "But don't worry. I'll tell you soon."

It was too early for lunch at the George. They took a table in the corner of the dim and empty parlor. Wop ordered them beer. A Rover, richly smeared with mud, drove into the parking lot. Two crimson-faced gallants sporting the ties of minor public schools came into the parlor and made for the bar.

"Oh, she's hot stuff, all right," finished one. The gallants were at the far end of the room, but they were the sort who bray in pubs.

"She'll do that, will she?" said the other.

"Doesn't even breathe hard."

"Good Lord, old chap, that must make the old heart thump."

Wop listened, fascinated.

"That's in overdrive, of course. Won't do it in fourth." The gallants sank gratefully into gin and French.

"Stears," said August Herter, "what of my general?"

"He's fine," said Stears. "As far as I know." He had noted with approval that Herter now spoke without prompting in an even, clear voice that was not a whisper but did not carry. A simple but valuable trick.

"Questions, August," said Stears.

"I see," said Herter. He looked beyond Stears and said, "Do you understand that there comes a time when questions make you sick? That you have been turned inside out? That no one looks at you, no one speaks to you, except to get something from you? I was very willing to help. Now I must tell you that you all begin to sound like the Stasi to me."

And it was true, thought Stears, that seen in the dim and empty pub, in the make-believe uniform, Herter looked fragile, as though losing definition.

"These are different questions," said Stears. "You can use your imagination. If you were dropped in East Germany, how long could you survive?"

Herter's beer mug stayed level, though his knuckle turned white. Very tautly, very slowly, he replied, "I have no paratroop training, Stears. With my leg it is still difficult, but it is getting better. I would like to have the training first." He hesitated, giving off tension like a tuning fork. "Is this my general's order?"

"It isn't even mine," said Stears. "I said 'imagination.' You've got wings. You've just fluttered down but you can't fly back. How long?"

Herter thought and understood and smiled broadly, conceivably at Stears's joke. "Wings? Ha ha! Very good!" he said, to prove it. He took a long drink of beer. "All right," he said. "As well as these wings, do I have documents?"

"I think so," said Stears. "Probably good ones."

"I have to, really. Am I actually August Herter, the great escaper?"

"No. You are a girl. About your age, a little younger. But you did escape."

"And what am I doing here?" said Herter.

"I do not know," said Stears.

Herter nodded. Then the smile dropped from his face and he looked at Stears hard. "Stears," he said, "she's mad." He put his hand on Stears's arm. "You must not let this happen."

"It may not have happened," said Stears. "If it has there's not much I can do about it. But I need to know what I asked you."

"It is not an easy question. Was she well known?"

"I do not find any trace of her," said Stears. "Probably not. Most likely she was a student."

"Yes. At her age," said Herter. "Escapes are not publicized. Rather the opposite. There would not be posters. The policeman on the corner is not thinking about her—that is not his job. The Stasi has all those photographs and some of them have very good memories—but they are not expecting her back, are they?"

"I doubt it," said Stears.

"Where is she? Do you know that?"

"No, but my guess is Berlin."

"Better and worse," said Herter. "They are suspicious there and they have all the records. On the other hand, it is very big. A small place would be impossible."

He paused. "I am trying to imagine, to put myself in that position," he said. "Let us suppose that her documents are good and that she is not doing anything that calls attention. I mean of itself. Also does not go where she was well known—for her, perhaps, the university. How long has she been away?"

"Two years," said Stears. "About."

"It is not very long, is it? Maybe she has changed a little. There are particular dangers—to find a place to live, to stay at a hotel, to find a job if she wanted one. It takes only one wrong question here and she is finished, because as soon as they begin to look for her that is the end. But perhaps she is lucky, perhaps she has friends. In that case, the danger is not in one place but everywhere. One person who recognizes her and needs a favor from the police, as everybody does. One stupid answer she gives. Perhaps she never even sees what gives her away. One official in a bad mood. All right, here is my answer, Stears. If she is clever, she gets by for a month. Then something happens and they begin to look. Then she has a week. Then she is caught."

"If she is there at all," said Stears. "She has been there longer than a month already. Perhaps two months. Perhaps even a little more."

"Then she is very lucky. Or she is destroyed already. Or she is not exactly what she seems. That is really all that I can say," said Herter. "She could be destroyed and not know it yet—there is that. Sometimes the Stasis will watch someone for a while when they know they have him."

"I had thought of that," said Stears. "One more question. If she had known people over there, people like herself, like you, would they trust her if she came back to them? If they knew she had escaped? Could they trust her?"

Herter said at once, "Not if they had any sense." Then stopped and thought. "But that is not the whole answer. There is the nature of trust, and that is hard for you to understand." He thought again. "That sounds bad and I do not mean it that way. Trust is like scent. If you are usually safe, I think you lose the sense of it, but with us it is very strong. I told you of my general asking me in the middle of an interrogation to go to the West. That was obviously a trap, but I really had no doubt. The sense of trust is the weapon we fight them with, Stears, and they cannot defeat it because the more they stamp on it, the stronger it becomes. So maybe this girl inspires trust. Obviously, I cannot know that."

"I'm not sure," said Stears. "Maybe you do know. Renate Segla—do you know that name?"

Herter sighed. "Maybe one day you will ask a question without hiding what you know. As I said, you do not know much about trust. No, the name means nothing to me."

"Are you sure?" said Stears.

"Of course I'm sure. Renate is not a very common name with us. It is more Western, I think. Actually, it is not German. And Segla—no. Renate the Sailor—I would remember that. And I imagine the truth is that you know perfectly well what she is doing there, poor girl."

"That was my last question," said Stears. But he almost didn't ask it and only did so thinking, *Surely there will not be any answer to this that one could really use.* "If she was in East Berlin, where would she go to find out about you?"

His eye flickered from Herter, whom he quickly hushed. The gallants at the bar were settling their bill with much competitive fumbling—frugally cirrhotic, they had made merry on only two drinks each. They passed close enough to the table for Stears to see the shirt buttons straining on the second, who was vaguely familiar—as though spiritually modeled on a particularly vulgar English comedian, whose name he forgot. He turned back to August Herter.

"That is the only easy question. For a start she would go to the Pagoda."

17

Stears, like most West Berliners and foreigners not in love with the Cold War, entered East Berlin by the subway. The symposium had arranged a motor coach from the air terminal in West Berlin by way of Checkpoint Charlie, but many members of so competent a group could be expected to make their own arrangements. The subway is an ordinary West Berlin U-Bahn that goes its rounds of the city until it reaches Hallesches Tor, where it feints surreally into the City of the Dead.

For though only one of all the stations the train runs through in the East is in use, the others are by no means abandoned. A subway track would be a comfortable mode of escape, with much to recommend it over a sewer, a tightrope, or the gas tank of a car. So the other stations are lit dimly but with the shadowless light of aquariums, and on the platforms, with the slow pace of suspended purpose and blank rotation of the eye toward trains racing by, walk guards with submachine guns and walkie-talkies. It is possible to go straight under East Berlin and out the other side without seeing any East Berliners but these. Many West Berliners do this every day.

Stears got out at Friedrichstrasse and joined the foreigners' passport line, which is the shortest of the three, beside the long line of elderly West Berliners carrying food packages to family on the other side, which is the saddest. His overcoat was a banker's good gray, his papers were in order, his registration for an international symposium visible but not ostentatious, his slim suitcase held neither radio nor gun; he was through three sets of steel baffles and an ultraviolet scanner in a jiffy, rather faster than one goes through JFK in New York. He came up into the courtyard of Friedrichstrasse Station and found a taxi.

His visa, like all short visas to the Democratic Republic, would let him leave only by the way he came. Friedrichstrasse has traffic at all hours except the very middle of the night. It is far less conspicuous than Checkpoint Charlie for a visitor leaving alone, on foot, at an odd hour, fast.

He was a good boy the first night. There was a cocktail party at the Palast Hotel. Totalitarians build good, solid drinks and are lavish with the hors d'oeuvres. This, and the Palast's best assembly room—it had a pink carpet, chandeliers that sent out vagrant rays to make one blink, and pictures of somewhere in apple-blossom time—warmed the intercourse between chilly young Western money managers and their affable, watchful hosts to a point near freezing. But Wop was fortunate. None there knew him well enough to ask awkward questions, but there were plenty he could shake hands with and even call by name. Yes, London was going well, he generally said. One missed Geneva. He was branching out a bit. He felt quite unremarkable.

Later he went outside. Alexanderplatz was emptying, but its emptiness had neither grandeur nor peace. He did not feel menaced, he did not feel watched. He felt futile and depressed. The remedy would have been to stride out into the city and strike his blow. *Not the first night,* he thought with certainty. *Not on an impulse. Nothing on an impulse here.* And besides, August Herter had doubted very much that Renate would try to meet anybody on a Thursday evening. He walked a little way up Karl-Marx-Allee and back. On the western horizon, above the Europa Center, hung Mercedes-Benz's star. He ate a bad dinner.

Between seminars the next day he was an insatiable tourist. He dragged his feet around the Pergamon Museum, saw the Brandenburg Gate, priced Bulgarian fedoras at Zentrum and shotguns on Karl-Marx-Allee. He admired the cunning spikes in the Spree set to surprise libertarian swimmers. He splurged on an Astrakhan hat that smelled, for some reason, of jet fuel. He was sweating all this time, for he wore a bulky, baggy jacket, somewhat stained, and too warm for the very slight autumnal chill. Though the summer that had just left England was only a memory in Berlin, the last two days here had been warmer. To wear clothes unnoticeable in East Berlin might have caused him to be stopped entering the Palast— but he was anyway building the image of an informal type who liked walking about. In the hour between "East-West Bank Clearings: A Look at the Mechanics" and "Two-Tier Exchange Rates: The Future?" he took the subway to nowhere special and came back. In his wallet was the well-thumbed photo of a girl too blond to be his daughter, too young to be his wife.

In a dingy corner at the back of his mind, he knew that the photograph could be of a viper. It could not be ruled out that Renate Segla's escape had been arranged, that she had spied in the West, had come back now to her own safe home where the "es-

210

cape" would let her set off on a new round of deceit. In the West he had counted that almost for nothing.

It counted for more in the air of East Berlin. Though he could have picked up the telephone in his room and dialed anywhere in the world, though he had a visa in his pocket that would have gotten him to the West in fifteen minutes, he felt alone and infinitely far from help. If he found Renate Segla, he intended first to take a careful look.

———

When Scott Mays was taken to the car, he was surprised. When he saw that the Russian officer was in it, he was frightened. When he realized that the officer had sat far back in the seat, so that Mays would not see him until his leg was in the car, his stomach clenched so hard that he did not at once feel the steel muzzle pressed against his side. The meeting place had seemed unusually innocent: the wide sidewalk outside the Kurfürstendamm Station of the U-Bahn among crowds and traffic and cinnamon trails of coffee and cake from Mohring's tearoom.

He quickly gave the officer the cassette of film. The officer dropped it on the floor and crushed it with his foot.

The officer said, "The bullet in this gun contains sodium pentothal. It will not kill you and it makes no noise. So I shall not hesitate to use it." He said it complacently. He added, "If I use it, you will have less time to explain. That would be very bad for you."

They drove down the Kurfürstendamm. It was the evening of a mild fall day, and the smell of roasted chestnuts seemed unseasonable. The traffic stopped them at Bleibtreustrasse, and Mays looked up it quickly. Just fifty yards back, he had once seen Gloria's fur coat reflected upon the tables and waiters behind the Kopenhagen's window.

"No indeed," said the officer. "You are not going to her bed. She is not there anymore. All things end." Captain Smolsky always found pleasure in his own wit.

They turned onto Konstanzer Strasse and then onto the wide and barren Hohenzollerndamm. It was Friday and the traffic was slow. They were headed toward Dahlem or the Grunewald. The Russians could not, simply could not, dare to walk him at gunpoint into his home on an American base, murder his family and him, and leave. No way. There was no security gate there. They were going that way.

The officer said, "Why did you lie to me?"

"I told you the truth," said Mays. His voice was high, he had pronounced it *troof,* and he hated himself for both.

"Shithead," said the officer, as though trying a new phrasebook. He poked Mays hard with the muzzle.

On Lucius-Clay-Allee, he poked him again.

"The data transmitted by PSYCHIC is gibberish," said the officer. "It is pure shit. That is, the correlations that actually exist are made up. You know that. So you are working for them. We need two answers. How long have you been playing with us? How did they find you?"

Mays felt sick and hollow, as though his intestines had been taken out through the front.

"I don't know," he said. And realized with horror that he had told the truth. They were within half a mile of his home.

He said, "I never knew those figures weren't real. I swear to God . . ."

The officer cut him short. "You gave me a very good explanation of why you would know. I believed you the first time. I still do. How long? How did they find you?"

"I'm working for them. It's true."

"I told you that," said the officer.

"I don't know. I don't know how they found me. Maybe those figures were always false. It must be the data gathering. That's not even me. The figures are real. It's the data itself. Someone's making the whole thing up. They made me work for them."

"Who?" said the officer.

"Major Hamilton."

"That is more shit. It means absolutely nothing. We know of no Major Hamilton. Who is he? Where does he work?"

"I don't know. He got a telephone."

"He got a telephone?" said Captain Smolsky. "Isn't that extraordinary? We look for an American officer with a telephone." He jabbed the gun hard under Mays's ribs, where it hurt. "You asshole," he said.

"He found me in the zoo," said Mays.

"When you both lived in the ape house?" said the officer. "That I believe. The jokes will soon be over. You will tell me what you know." He looked away.

They turned right, into the Grunewald. Away from his home. He began to wonder what they would do to him, Scott Mays. A picture burst into his brain of a skinny Negro with charred flesh hanging from the bough of a tree. They could hardly do that here. The officer reached for something. The first muzzle went away from Scott's side and was replaced by another, wider one.

"This is a real gun," said the officer. "It will blow your guts out." He said nothing more.

———

The last seminar at the Palast Hotel—"Hard Currency: An Obsolescent Term?"—ended a little after five o'clock. Stears was in no hurry and had no desire to appear to be so. He went past the elevators to the hard-currency bar, where the term was not obsolete. Two Arabs sat intensely over coffee, and a party of Canadians brayed in the corner. He had already discovered that the martinis were good, and he ordered one now. The Palast Hotel was so precise a copy of a Ramada at one of the larger American provincial airports that Stears had decided the thing was done by projection. There was no connection whatsoever between this hotel, which did not accept its own country's currency, and East Berlin; to walk into it was like entering extravagant air conditioning in August.

He went up to his room, locked the door, and opened the map. August Herter had given him three places, one of them far off toward Pankow, the other two much closer in what seemed to be a tight neighborhood of small streets. He looked a long time at the map, closing his eyes to summon up the angles of the streets, going back over their names, and checking the map again. He had made no marks on it and would not take it with him.

A little after six o'clock he took off his tie, rumpled his collar, put on a pair of suede shoes with no shine, and pulled the lumpish coat out of the closet. He sat on the bed before he put it on.

———

Mays and the officer rode deep into the forest, turning several times. Once the driver got out and opened a gate. They stopped at a hill covered with pines. It was a deep and generous and pine-scented place. The trees were much larger than most in the forest and the moss on them was thick—they were some of the very few that had not been cut for firewood in the winter of 1945. Randolph Wilson, Gloria's "husband," had told him that. The Wilsons had brought the Mayses to this place for a picnic once. Even the baby came. There was an easier way to get here. The Wilsons had made a point of showing Thelma the way. Scott turned cold.

"Now we wait," said the officer.

But there were machines working near the road, two lumbering machines on tank treads with steel teeth out in front. They browsed and snorted through the undergrowth. Scott grew calmer. Nothing much could happen here.

The officer opened a window slightly, with an expression of distaste. Scott's clothes were sodden and he could smell his own sweat.

Scott's little yellow Pinto came suddenly bounding into sight, the tennis ball on the antenna swinging wildly on the rough road. Scott had not heard it come.

"Ah," said the officer. "How nice. All your family." He turned to Scott. "Your little pussy called them and asked them to a picnic here. It may be the last nice day this year. You are coming with your friends. But in fact you are only coming with me, I am afraid. No fun in the bushes afterward."

One of the forestry machines pulled out on the road in front of the Pinto. Thelma unhurriedly braked. There was no place just there for a car to get off the road or park. Scott saw that she was smiling. She was looking around for someone. She saw the Russians' car but it was not the Wilsons' Audi and she paid no attention to it. She smiled up at the driver of the machine. He made a gesture to be patient. She smiled again.

The other machine came out a little way behind the Pinto. Their steel teeth were the size of ice tongs and came halfway up the car. The machines were topped with blue smoke. Scott Jr. looked at them with interest and said something to his mother. She began to pull the picnic bag out of the backseat. It had pictures of Yogi Bear on it.

The officer said, "Now. Those questions."

"They had pictures of me, sir," said Mays. "They had pictures of me at the zoo. In the Night Zoo. That's the truth. Pictures of me passing the packet over."

"Perhaps. But that was how they trapped you. Why did they follow you? It was not easy."

"I don't know, sir. I don't know."

"Did Major Hamilton know about the money?"

"I don't think so. He asked me. I told him there wasn't any, and he believed me, I guess."

"What is his real name?"

Scott saw that the officer held a small black cube in his other hand. He saw that Thelma had said something to Scott Jr. and that Scott had turned to the baby in the backseat.

"I don't know," said Scott.

The officer raised the cube to his mouth. He spoke into it. The rear machine answered with a spout of blue smoke. It jumped a foot toward the Pinto. It moved as suddenly as a frog. Thelma looked up, startled and a little scared.

"I didn't catch your answer," said the officer.

Scott heard himself wail, "I don't know, sir. I swear to Jesus, sir. I don't know."

"That's very reasonable," said the officer. "After all, why would you know? Now some photographs. Photographs are fun." He opened a folder and passed Scott a thin stack. "See if you find any friends," he said. Scott's hands were shaking, and he dropped one picture on the floor. The officer stuck the gun under his ribs again in the same sore place. "Look carefully, asshole," he said. Scott picked the picture up.

The fourth photograph was Major Hamilton. The face hit Scott like a blow on the chest. It scared him so badly he could only keep turning the photographs. Major Hamilton was not in uniform. Major Hamilton appeared to be at an expensive restaurant with a pretty woman beside him. He was laughing. Scott went on through the photographs, which were not otherwise at all familiar. There were twelve of them. Then he went through them the other way.

A feeling of hatred began to rise in him, eating through the tangle of fear. He got back to Major Hamilton, who had singled him out and hunted him down, who had lied to him, who had done nothing for his family, who had caused him to cheat the Russians in deadly ways he did not understand, who was laughing at him over a bottle of Champagne. He looked at the self-possessed white face and the woman with jewels on her bosom and the hatred burst in him and he said, "That's Major Hamilton." For some reason, the words hurt his lungs.

"That's not a major," said Captain Smolsky.

"That's Major Hamilton," he said.

"Well, maybe it is," said Smolsky. He put the photographs away. "When did you begin to falsify the data?"

For a second, Scott could not grasp the new subject. Then he felt the world slip from his hands. What remained of it was in the Pinto between iron teeth.

"I never did that," he said. "I don't know."

The officer picked up the cube again.

"In June," said Scott.

"When in June? With what sequences?"

"I don't know. I can look it up. I'll tell you tomorrow."

"You are lying," said the officer. The machine behind the Pinto suddenly poured blue smoke.

Scott found that he had kicked the officer sideways and thrown himself against the door. He came out on his shoulder. There was a terrible noise behind him and a hammer hit his arm. He began to run, half on his knees. By the hood of the car, he had stood up straight, and Thelma saw him.

She saw Scott running and his arm flapping from the elbow in its sleeve. She saw a white man get out of the car behind him and aim a big pistol with both hands. She had the door half open when the Pinto rose off the ground and the doorframes squeezed together and Scott Jr. screamed "Momma!" and went on screaming as long as she could hear. Scott Mays saw none of this, for a bolt of white light had passed into his skull and out again through a hole the size of an orange.

The equipment drivers jumped out of their cabs and ran toward the officer. The officer said in Russian, "Shit!" and then, "Throw him into the woods. Leave the rest. Hurry!" There are Allied army facilities in the Grunewald and the sound of gunfire is common there, but he was worried. He had been frightened ever since the KGB security man, Filippov, had come to Berlin and stirred things up. It was not his fault that a German had turned traitor behind their backs, but it was General Karshkhov's fault, and whatever was General Karshkhov's fault would be Captain Smolsky's too. The plan had not been to kill these blacks, and it was going to look like a blunder unless he was careful. PSYCHIC had been a disappointment all along. It had looked like a big technology coup and now it was only bodies in the wood.

On the other hand, he had confirmed that Mays's control was the same man who was screwing around with a German deserter in England. He suspected that to be an important thing. He hoped it was very important.

The wreck was found that evening by a girl who had a taste for reading Rilke in the woods. She tried to open the door of the Pinto but, luckily, could not. The Berlin police found Scott's body by chance a hundred meters away in the bracken just before dark. The United States military police found a routine security notation on Sergeant Mays's file. Divisional security (Fourth Armor) found a notation from the Defense Intelligence Agency. The Pentagon informed the CIA at Langley. Eventually the news reached Brindle

Woods in London, but it was a thread not only long but intentionally tangled, and it did not reach him until the evening of the next day.

It was not featured in the East Berlin papers, and Wop Stears could not have read about it there, even had he had time the next morning to read a paper, which he did not.

Long, long before then Captain Smolsky was back at the Soviet embassy in East Berlin with the photograph that had caused such an unexpected coda to Marie-Sophie's thirty-fourth birthday, celebrated at the Connaught Grill in London three weeks before.

———

Renate Segla's life moved in discomforting jolts between her twice-weekly contacts with the Deutrans courier and her weekend meetings with Klingenberg. The latter in turn were complicated by the need to get rid of Peter Hocholz, who if left to herself she would have liked better than anyone here and who reciprocated this undeclared sentiment with dog-eyed ardor. The rest of the time she could spend as she wished, quaking.

The day before, by a news kiosk—a change of rendezvous after two weeks of using the greasy spoon—she had swapped newspapers with the Deutrans man and felt for certain the shape of an envelope under the first page. She knew from common sense, from Klingenberg's analysis, from her own heart, that Dr. Krel had sent her her release, or at any rate the first element of it, and she carried it home almost running. She was not sure if the envelope was thick enough for a passport. She thought it was.

So when she opened the letter that Krel had written in the Black Forest under Nadermann's instruction, it was like opening your medicine cabinet and finding a snake.

She read Dr. Krel's letter through four times even to make sense of it, which, to the end, she never entirely did. She realized in sequence that her release had not been begun, that it was not even close, that she was to begin all over again with something three times as remote and impossible, a high officer, dear God perhaps a general of the secret police, name unknown, linked perhaps to August Herter's friends. She was to find him. It sank in slowly and coldly that she was a prisoner here until she did so.

She looked at Dr. Krel's letter, at its elegant spiked handwriting. She felt with her finger the courses of the nib, trying to get more from the paper than was written there. There was nothing. There was just Dr. Krel's prerogative and justification to demand sacrifice, cold and unyielding as glass.

Faced with what to do, her brain felt physically empty. It contained the one word *Klingenberg*. This was Thursday. The next evening, she was to go through the accustomed gyrations of meeting Hocholz in order to briefly meet Klingenberg.

For the next twenty-four hours she felt almost too oppressed to move. On Friday evening it took her an hour of vacillation to decide whether to take Krel's letter with her. He had told her never to do such a thing. She understood why. But Klingenberg had to see it, and she could not bring him to her room. In the back of her mind she distrusted what the letter might do, left unattended.

At about six o'clock she began to go through the motions of turning herself into an attractive date.

––––––

This was just at the time that Captain Smolsky was driven into a small garage off Hohenzollerndamm in West Berlin and exchanged the car whose wheels still smelled of the pine needles of the Grunewald for one with the official number plates of the Soviet Union, an Allied Occupying Power. In an uncomfortable bathroom where kerosene fumes nearly gave him a headache he washed the cordite that had eliminated Mays off his hands and then put on the uniform of a Red Army captain, without the scarlet shoulder tabs of the KGB. It was thus dressed that he smartly exchanged salutes with the U.S. Army captain at Checkpoint Charlie and drove out of the occupied city of West Berlin across the protective Wall into the free East German capital, East Berlin.

At the Soviet embassy, General Karshkhov heard the story of the end of the family Mays with at least the same language to Captain Smolsky as Captain Smolsky had used to the deceased. But he took the photograph of Major Hamilton with ungracious satisfaction.

The photograph went first to the records department of the embassy. Given the context, copies went at once to the East German Staatssicherheitsdienst, the SSD. They were listed as *Hamilton, U.S. Major (alias)* and *Stears, Giovanni Sidgewick*. They were given the highest priority level provided: *Officer, CIA*.

From the SSD, they went straight to one of its subdepartments, the Visa Security Section.

––––––

218

Renate took the tram, for she was not going to the Pagoda in the windy spaces toward Pankow but to a place called the Drei Ecken, which was indeed near a triangular corner. It was much closer than Pankow in a tight neighborhood of small streets. When she left the house the streetlights were already lit, and the last daylight died while she was on the tram.

She opened the door of the Drei Ecken and looked in. She had learned to do this in a mild and hopeful way, as though her friends might well be there but she could not be sure. In fact she was not sure. Sepp Klingenberg had told her that he would try to swap the group around somewhat this evening.

Peter Hocholz was there. Sepp Klingenberg was not. She thought she saw the back of Stefan Buchler's uniform by the bar, but she did not know the men talking to him or any of the girls around them. This place was smaller than the place in Pankow and less straightforward; it played jazz, and students and the mildest kind of dissidents were found there. By an officer's standards it was bohemian but not degenerate, and a suitable place to meet university girls. Peter Hocholz saw her and looked at her with eagerness, wariness, and transparent guile. She crossed the room and sat down beside him. She was alone with him for the moment.

"Are you all right?" he said. That made her want to laugh, but she did not trust her laughter, which felt a millimeter from hysterics.

"Quite all right, Peter," she said. "Thank you."

"I've missed you," he said. His eyes said it too, with a gentle heat, and she felt warmer all over. But she said, "Are you any closer to Herter?"

It was of no consequence whether he was or not, but she had to keep up the pretense that he was needed.

"I am trying," he said. He said it with dignity, hurt feelings, and restraint, which did not lessen when he added, "It is quite dangerous for me."

"I know," she said. And she did and could not ignore it, for Peter was not one of the cipher citizens of the secret country even if he had stumbled across its border but a real man of warmth and sweetness and deserving of every honesty that she deserved herself. This struck her suddenly, and she turned to him with a quite different expression. He put his head toward hers as though knowing that what she was about to say would matter. She never said it.

For she felt that she was watched.

Her stomach clenched. But there had been changes inside her by now, and no eyes had emanations strong enough to turn her into a rabbit in front of a stoat. She made herself drain her fear, sitting very still, and discern, as if lying with her eyes open in the dark and tracking a sound through a violated house, what direction the watch was coming from. And then, saying something merrily to baffled Peter, she turned quickly, captured the face that hunted her, and brought its image back.

And brought the wrong one. She knew that at once. The face she had caught simply was not Them. She examined it in her mind, the steady eyes, the arrogance in the carriage of the head that could conceivably in itself have been some species of Them but that was removed from Them completely by a look of concern and behind that, humor. And grace. This one sat in a shooting coat with a beer in front of him and reminded her of Prince Wittelsbach when he had been pointed out to her coming out of the Opera in Munich; They always looked like toads or jackals.

So she had the wrong one, and she turned again, which would be the last time she could allow herself to do so. She felt something on her hand and discovered that Peter had put his own there. She wondered fleetingly why he would do that, recollected that it conveyed affection, and removed hers rather sharply. There were no eyes in the direction of the watch she had felt except an ordinary young man who had already discounted her as being with a date and the man she had picked out first. Who was certainly watching her. But now she saw, with confusion that quickly became ill-defined fright, that he had taken her second look as acknowledgment or recognition or at least as permission for contact.

She turned back, looking at the table and calculating to herself. She heard Peter say stiffly, "Pardon me for bothering you."

She answered, surprised and quite sincere, "You don't bother me, Peter," but he was hurt and meant to show it.

He said, sounding like a stage duelist, "Perhaps you will excuse me for a moment. There is a friend I would like to converse with."

She realized that he was getting up, knew suddenly what the timing of that would look like, and very nearly squeaked, *Stay with me!* but instead dismissed him lightly as though he were going to the bathroom and sat looking, she hoped, unapproachable and bored. She looked at three officers she did not know standing by the bar with their girls. One of them had his arm lightly around his date's back, and she thought, *That girl can spend an evening with her boyfriend and think about what she wants with him and nothing more—there really is a life like that, a real life, even here.* It seemed a revelation.

Then she felt someone above her and the man sat down. He sat as though he had considered asking in a normal way and at last decided not to.

"Miss Segla," he said quietly—her real name, her Western name, the name in which she had escaped the first time from the East. "Renate."

"No," she said. She said it to the table and then tried to look annoyed, invaded instead of doomed. "No," she said again.

She thought he looked uncertain and distressed and had the wild idea that her own feelings might count for something with him. *He can't possibly be one of Them*, she thought. *Even Sepp wouldn't think like that.* Then she thought again, *He can still be horribly dangerous.*

"Don't be afraid of me," he said. "I'm on your side. And I know we have no time." He was not German. He was much older than she was. She saw that Peter had turned around at the bar and saw them.

"Were you sent here by Dr. Krel?" said the foreigner. She turned cold at the name. Peter looked at them angrily and as though his worst suspicions were confirmed. She looked at him piteously. *Save me!* the look said. *I'm yours.* Peter looked away, but indecisively.

"Who?" she said. "I have no idea what you are talking about."

"He taught you in Munich," said the foreigner. "You are both former escapers. He helps escapers. Did he send you here? Please talk to me. I am truly on your side."

She should have been thinking as clearly as light, but qualms skittered around her brain, biting each other. She muttered, "I have heard of Dr. Krel. He is a national enemy," and looked at the foreigner out of the corner of her eye. Peter made his decision and started for them like an angry spaniel, but the bar was crowded.

"Why did he send you?" asked the stranger.

She shook her head minutely and fast.

"Was it anything to do with a man named Herter? Captain Herter? August Herter?"

She looked away, for she could think of no safe expression for her face. Foreigners came from the East as well. "No," she said.

"If it is, you must tell me. It may be even more dangerous than you know."

She was suddenly sorry that Peter was coming to save her. It occurred to her that she would not mind this foreigner being on her side.

"What?" she said. "Quickly."

But then, looking up to see where Peter was, she saw what made her almost cry out. A man at the bar, with Them stamped all over his cheap leather coat, was looking at the foreigner out of the corner of his eye. She hissed, with the expression as near as she could do it of a woman crudely propositioned, "There is a man watching you from the bar. You are more dangerous to me than anyone else in the world could be. Go away now and do not come back."

"Where can I find you?" he said, rising. But Peter was already there.

She had to give it to the foreigner that he did not lose his expression. He got up like a man rebuffed. "Your lady wishes only your company," he said. "It was not my intention to intrude." He made his German much worse when he said that, as though he spoke it quite badly. That was clever, she thought.

Peter wanted to make a fuss, but she laid her hand on his arm as though he were really dangerous. *Could this possibly look real!* she thought. *Is that how you do a fight over a girl in a bar! And who are they looking for, just the foreigner or anyone who talks to me!*

———

Stears imagined the eyes following him from Renate's table to his own. He sat down and slowly finished his beer, glancing up from time to time as though to find a waitress. He had no difficulty locating the spy. The man moved back toward the bar, toward the fringe of a group that seemed in fact to know him, though without enthusiasm. He was small, sharp, compact, in a tight leather jacket. A workman, but with authority of some sort—a foreman, a guard. From time to time he looked at Stears. He looked openly, turning his head, with no expression. Stears put down his empty glass.

Stears got up. He got up with the familiar feeling that watching eyes would turn into a concrete bludgeon and knock him down the moment he moved. He walked toward the door. There was a group of young men by it, and he had a sudden certainty that his way would be blocked. He found it difficult to walk erect.

They did not glance at him. He walked into the street.

No one followed him. He was sure of it on the street. He was sure of it in the U-Bahn station. He was sure of it on the train. He saw two possibilities. The first, extremely attractive and with pleasant manners, proposed that he had been wrong, the private victim of some xenophobic lout, and the subject of no official interest at all. The second, which wore heavy boots and carried complete conviction, stated that he was not followed because they knew precisely where he went.

And they had already achieved, damnably, more than they could have known. She had been about to talk, or, given the circumstances, signal with her finger, hiccup, or nod her head. No, she was not SSD bait; he was as sure of that as he had ever been. Yes, Krel had sent her; he was sure of that. For Herter? Almost certainly. So Stears—or his most farfetched, confident guess—was right. And try as he could to find an innocent implication for it, every implication he could see belonged in a sewer.

At least possibly she was warned. If she was hunting answers about Herter for Krel, he was pretty sure she needed to be warned, and pretty sure it would do her very little good. The warning might well be worth less than her being seen with him—though there was also, he told himself, no way to be sure that the tail had been attached to him. Considering what Renate Segla's real status might be, she was as likely to be watched as Stears. One could hope, just possibly, that it really had looked like an attempted pickup. He probably looked old enough by now to pick up young girls offensively, at least in foreign bars.

He formed a plan, immediate and valid. *When dealing with the confident, do what they do not expect.* At the next station he could change for Friedrichstrasse, bypass Alexanderplatz and the Palast Hotel. His visa was in order. The time was not absurdly late. In his present clothes, to cross at night with no baggage would not be odd. Even in East Germany, even with the SSD, there are administrative lags, often considerable. It was highly unlikely that any change in his status had reached the passport desk at Friedrichstrasse. In lieu of foreign currency, the Democratic Republic could enjoy his Hildritch and Key dressing gown, his good overcoat, his shoes. He was overwhelmed with delight at the idea. The concierge at the Kempinski on the Kurfürstendamm would have to find him a razor in the morning. The night clerk would have to find him a room.

Before the station, chill returned. To do that would be to pin a notice on his empty room *U.S. Spy—Inquire Within.* He would be safe; Renate's guilt would be certified. Giovanni Stears would have done for sure what Oswolt Krel had conceivably not even planned.

It was very likely as it was that he had done her more harm than good. He stayed on the train.

The underpass from the Alexanderplatz station toward the Palast Hotel echoed with footsteps. They were all his own, he thought, but he did not care to look.

The night concierge at the Palast gave him his key with servility oiled with insolence. *Many night concierges do that*, thought Stears. *It is why they are night concierges.*

In his room, he had the thought of packing his clothes and simply checking out. At eleven o'clock at night. That sort of thing would bring the police in Grand Rapids. *Seven in the morning, dawn*, he thought. He turned out all but the bedside light in case the room was watched.

If Captain Smolsky, as an officer of the KGB, had had a wife he could have had an apartment anywhere in East Berlin—for a KGB wife is a hostage for her husband's misdeeds and will naturally spy on him to prevent or expose them. But Captain Smolsky was a bachelor and had to live in the Soviet compound. His apartment had two white rooms with paper-thin walls and a heating system that left most of it cold but, in small sections, sent columns of scorching air up the tenant's pants. Captain Smolsky did not like his apartment. It did nothing for his mood after a bad day.

This had been a bad day. At eleven o'clock, Captain Smolsky was still sitting on the edge of his bed drinking vodka and picking at his foot. General Karshkhov had nastily said that the end of the Mays affair would be considered a blunder, that all files concerning the PSYCHIC operation now went straight to the desk of Major Filippov of internal security, and that it would be made very sure that the buffoonery in the Grunewald would go under Captain Smolsky's name as disobedience to orders. "What orders?" Captain Smolsky had asked. "Implied orders," General Karshkhov had replied.

The buffoonery in the Grunewald, General Karshkhov, now blocking the window with his shoulders, had gone on to say, came just at the time of the extremely delicate operation of isolating and eliminating a senior general of the German SSD without demoralizing the security organs of the East German army. If Captain Smolsky had mucked up the destruction of Major General Hans Friedrich Sucher he would find some differences in his life. At this point General Karshkhov had eyed Smolsky's captain's shoulder tabs.

General Karshkhov finished by commenting that if he had not

let the black sergeant jump out of his car none of the rest would have been necessary and that someone who could not keep an unarmed man in a car by holding a gun on him was not fit to walk dogs for a living even if that might be his next job. Captain Smolsky was very, very lucky that "Major Hamilton" had been among those photographs. "Which was luck, Captain Smolsky, not skill," the general had said.

Not only were Captain Smolsky's feelings hurt; he was scared. With each glass of vodka his retorts to General Karshkhov became cleverer and more improbable.

After midnight he woke up, still on the edge of the bed. The hairs of his thigh were damp with vodka spilled out of the glass, and he already had a hangover. The heating had stopped, and he was shivering. He went to the bathroom and drank several glasses of water, then rolled into bed.

Captain Smolsky did not have a large bladder. At four o'clock in the morning he was standing in the bathroom. There he had a horrible thought.

He went to the telephone. His German was not good; his head, at this moment, was dreadful. His knowledge of the telephone network of the East German secret bureaucracy was inadequate. His clerk had better German and better knowledge and he could have called and waked him, but he wanted no one to know that he had thought of this at four in the morning.

———

The houses at numbers 1 through 14 at Normannenstrasse in East Berlin are small and gray and dingy; they look out onto a narrow street through windows that need only a dusty aspidistra to be dismally at home in London or dying African violets to be unexceptional in New York. The house at 18 Normannenstrasse, by contrast, covers two blocks and has six floors of orange reflecting windows, and all its doors are steel slabs raised by motors from inside. It is the headquarters of the Staatssicherheitsdienst of the Democratic Republic, the SSD.

On the second level of basement at number 18, in a room where the fluorescent light has never varied by day or night since the moment it was turned on, is the Visa Security Section. Here lies responsibility for the daily updating of the security file, the size of an unabridged dictionary, which sits by the hand of every frontier control or consulate visa officer and lists the names of all those whose entry into the Democratic Republic would be of special interest or alarm. It is also the sorting station for the several thousand twenty-four-hour or short-term visas issued for East Berlin or the Democratic Republic each day. This work is drudgery, like post-office sorting. It is given to SSD juniors without much promise or to older men who have made a mistake.

In principle, the updating of the security files and the sorting of the daily visas is done in tandem. In fact, it takes place separately in two large adjoining rooms. Much of it is done at night.

In charge of a small section on this night shift was Corporal, formerly Sergeant, Walther Gügen, who was forty-three years old and had been made the scapegoat in a minor smuggling affair near Rostok. This was his fifty-third consecutive night shift.

At a little after four in the morning a telephone in the vicinity of Walther Gügen began to ring. He went out to get some coffee, and when he came back it was still ringing, so he picked it up. Out of it came a roiling current of vexation delivered in a thick Slavic accent. Walther Gügen laid the receiver down and went on sorting forms. When the voice stopped he picked it up again. *"Was?"* he said.

Captain Smolsky, whose ninth misdirected call this was, was now close to tears. He asked with peculiar humility whether he was connected with an officer of Visa Security.

Somewhat inaccurately, with no expression, and in the heavy accent of his native Pomerania, Walther Gügen said, *"Ja."*

Captain Smolsky said, "This is the KGB," and waited for the change of tone.

Walther Gügen said, *"Ja."*

Captain Smolsky gave up. He asked politely if a search could be made through the extant visas in the name of Hamilton or Stears and exit posts alerted if one was found. Walther Gügen said it could be done, which was true. Captain Smolsky said it was urgent. Gügen grunted.

"Please take action at once," Captain Smolsky said.

"Sofort," agreed Walther Gügen. At once.

He was as good as his word. He then and there filled in a request form and placed it in a basket by his side. Thirty minutes later, near five o'clock, the form reached a lieutenant charged with special action. The lieutenant added the names to three others currently occasioning a search which required examination of all the sorted and unsorted visas of that night and then of the sorted visas for the preceding days. The lieutenant went off duty at six.

The confirmation of *Stears, Giovanni S., visa issued Friedrich-strasse valid until midnight today,* thus came to his replacement, who knew nothing about the matter. In due course, the replacement asked for an explanation from Corporal Gügen, whose name was on the form. Corporal Gügen had gone off duty.

At a little after seven, the lieutenant decided he had better do something about it after all. He telephoned his superior. The superior considered the matter for a few minutes and then called the KGB.

———

Outside Stears's window at six-thirty, Alexanderplatz was gray and cheerless as the moon. It vanished as he turned on the light.

He found himself in the bathroom running the water at half tap. He cursed himself; furtiveness would serve him worst of all. He shaved with care and bathed his eyes against the red of a sleepless night. He packed precisely—no flapping corner of a dressing gown stuffed into a case would mar the confidence of expensive baggage.

He was downstairs at seven sharp.

The desk was empty. He rapped sharply on the bell. He heard the clerk's voice on a nearby telephone. There was some delay.

The clerk said with surprise, "You are leaving us so early? You will not have breakfast? It is included in the price."

"I have a busy day," said Stears.

"You were with the symposium on East-West trade, I think," said the clerk.

"Yes," said Stears, grateful that it had ended properly the night before.

He was on the sidewalk at seven-fifteen with his one suitcase and his pea jacket over his arm. As he went out the door the desk telephone rang again. For no particular reason it resonated in his spine.

This was no doubt why, there being no cab, he did not wait but walked and then, driven by a haste that he choked down as being close to panic, ducked through the underpass into the S-Bahn station and joined the beginning of the morning rush. At Marx-Engels-Platz he could have had a seat but he remained standing by the door.

At 7:25, at Friedrichstrasse, he got swiftly off the S-Bahn and went down the stairs to the U-Bahn toward West Berlin. This part of the station was unpleasantly empty, other Westerners having barely begun to arrive, let alone to leave. The currency desk provided a nasty moment. East German currency may not be exported. To relinquish nearly five-hundred Ostmarks suggested panic, to keep them risked arrest. He compromised and surrendered 275. A receipt was written slowly and by hand. There were more police than travelers. There was wastepaper on the floor.

Now he was at the visa desk. He handed his passport in. Like all such posts in East Germany it was designed so that he could not see what was being done inside. It did not seem a good moment to look at his watch, but Stears was sure it was taking longer than usual. A telephone rang somewhere in the station. The passport was handed back.

The steel gate clicked open. He walked down toward the train. He was still a kilometer inside East Berlin. He gained the platform and saw the red taillight of a train disappear into the tunnel.

He stopped telling himself that he was not afraid. He looked at his watch. It was 7:31. He thought the trains ran every five minutes. He heard heels of several people swiftly on the stairs behind. A family came out onto the platform. 7:36 came with no train. Perhaps it was every seven minutes. He heard the echo of a voice that sounded urgent and official.

At 7:38 there was a train. He got on feeling sweat chilling on his neck. The jolt of the train's starting was as sweet as a caress.

He averted his eyes as the train swam through the subaqueous light of the unused, guarded stations where no doubt a red signal sat poised on a hair trigger.

And saw next, with the joy of Christmas morning, a lovely Western cigarette kiosk, sparkling with gold and scarlet and silver packs, dazzling with candy wrappers, richly lit on the platform under West Berlin.

What a perfect milksop I have been, he thought. *That's just what they aim for. Absolute panic for no reason at all.*

He breathed deeply the scent of the flower stalls.

18

What Renate needed least on this night was a puzzled, lovesick warrior by her side, and that, in the shape of Peter Hocholz, was supplied. She waited fifteen minutes after Stears left the pub. Though she had absolutely to see Klingenberg, Krel's letter was turning into a hot coal in her pocket now that she was watched. She thought only of that. She realized dimly that she was waiting to see Klingenberg before she dared even think about what the foreigner had said. Klingenberg did not come. It occurred to her suddenly that under these conditions, she would be terrified to talk to him.

She said, "I think I'm going home now."

Peter said, "I'm going with you."

She saw that he was drunk or close to it, and since she had put all the control she had into keeping her face and her bearing under control from any angle of scrutiny she answered with more sharpness than it needed, "No!" She stood up.

Peter captured her waist. "Officer takes a lady home," he said. "Definitely." Since she was only half up and he had grabbed her harder than he meant to, she came back down again.

"Dammit, no," she said, while a chilly, unfamiliar little voice inside her said, *This situation might serve as a cover, but the asset is drunk, therefore unreliable.*

"I know a hotel," he said.

"*What?*" said Renate.

"Well, if it's nosy neighbors," he said. And then doggedly, "It's a nice place." He had not meant to say this at all, but inside him there was now concern for Renate, utter bafflement about her apparent actions, a generalized jealousy, the beginning of fear that she might be less or more than she seemed, and besotted lust. It had become clear to him at that very moment that all of these problems could be addressed best in bed.

"Peter," she said. "Listen. I'm not taking you home, and I'm certainly not going to a fleabag with you. Now be nice. You're making a noise. Everyone's looking at us."

Which was true. They were making just enough fuss. Stefan Buchler was walking over, concerned and trying not to show it.

"You would if it was Klingenberg," said Peter.

Oh, Christ, thought Renate. Buchler had not quite heard.

Peter was now ashamed to turn back. "I've seen you with him," he said. "He's a cop. A spy. A *stukachi*. A Stasi. I told you about him. Is that what you like?"

Everyone at the nearby tables was now looking directly at them or altogether away. Stefan Buchler stepped forward and took Peter by the arm. "Hocholz," he said. "For Christ's sake." Stefan was a brave boy, but his voice was low and scared.

Renate said, "Good night, Peter." She got up and touched his arm. She walked through the emptied space toward the door with the thought that she lacked only a limelight and a brass band. Peter looked around in sad confusion as though several people were setting upon him. He was only trying to find something to say.

But no one seemed to follow her. She walked fifty meters down the street, turned into a larger street, and into a square. There was an important tram stop here for several lines. It occurred to her to take a tram at random, to get lost, but as she arrived a tram for her own street sailed into the stop, and home seemed no more menacing than the streets, or not specifically so. She was exhausted anyway. The tram was empty. She got on.

The tram did not start at once. The driver got out to stretch his legs. Renate sat near the back of it. She was in a state of numb and listless stoicism on the far side of panic and, in this condition, had not begun to unravel the significance of the American. Except he had patently been watched, had obviously been seen with her, and she didn't think for a second that she would count with the watchers as an failed pickup. She discovered that she called him *the American*, which he had not. From that discovery stuck out the end of a thread which she undoubtedly ought to pull and see if made Dr. Krel unravel, but, and she knew this, it was a thought she did not want to touch. She sat still and hunched in her seat, lit up behind the windows of the tram like something exposed for sale. A spasm of loneliness ran through her body; it would not have been all bad to have Peter tucked up gratefully beside her. She thought this to a distant rhythm: *What if* Krel, *what if* Krel, *what if* Krel. Like it or not the thought began to settle upon her and, settling, began to look by no means new.

She was, however, no longer alone. Four rough young men, all muscles and musk and curly black hair, Romanian or Bulgarian laborers, got on the tram. They appeared to be drunk. They looked at her lewdly, and whatever language they were using, she now knew the ruttish words in it. She didn't pay much attention; East Germany is orderly and the dangers of daily life seemed uninteresting anyway. The driver looked at his watch and got back in.

Beyond the square, the streets were empty. An old woman in a cloth coat—she was like an animated Stalinist poster—stumped off the tram, leaving Renate, the driver, and the foreigners. It was late for this drab country. Once in a while there was a police car or a dutiful worker, approved of by the state, or rumpled and bemused young people, definitely not so and looking as though they knew it. The yahoos had moved two seats closer to her, and their eyes licked her over their snouts. Their conversation now had words of German, and she felt herself blush, even used up as she was—which angered her, for they were as witless as degrading. She looked furiously at the back of the driver's head, for he should be doing something about it, the worm. But she did not have the sickly fear that a New York girl would have felt, nor even the unease of a Munich girl. And this was reasonable. Bulgars for sure. Her stop was not far away. The streets were empty.

She got off, and as she walked away she heard the clanging sound of the tram moving off and then a scrabbling sound, as of quick heels on metal. Her back froze, and before she half turned she knew: the animals had gotten off behind her. One laughed as she turned. *"Kum, Frau,"* he said. She shuddered at the phrase.

The tram stop was at the corner, and she had already left the main street. The street ahead of her went uphill before her own little street forked off. There were no people, and almost all the windows were dark. She would have to dodge around the louts to get back to the larger street, and even that had been nearly deserted too. She was frightened now, but still only of the unpleasant. There were people behind those windows. She could run and scream. That was the point. They would jeer and vanish. There were lanes and alleys. She walked fast and straight.

So she was shocked as much as terrified to know them suddenly right behind her and feel the paw confidently knead her haunch. She jerked, clumsy with fear, smelling unwashed male bodies and sour wine. A hand with a big cheap ring and horribly separate fingers reached in front of her and grabbed her breast. She felt something run up between her thighs. *This can't happen,* she thought and saw the alley they were dragging her to and the hand rising toward her mouth. She screamed once. Her noise astonished her. She tried to bite.

231

And the headlights rose over the brow of the hill and glared. Her ravishers seemed too preoccupied to notice; she was still being pushed toward the alley when the police car was halfway down the hill and its blue light lit up the street.

They dropped her. They ran. Even that was confused. She felt one of them trip over her and stumble against another. The two policemen were out of the car by then. She shouted, "I'm all right, get *them*." But the police came straight toward her, ignoring the yahoos, who were still not even far away. She liked it that the police cared about her, but she wanted the swine caught, so, sitting now on the street and gathering her legs under her, she tried a brave smile at the officer in front. "Really, I'm all right." Then she saw the expression on his face.

He was coming at her like a dog. Her brain heaved. She whimpered to herself, *Oh, no!* and scrabbled off the street. She was almost in the alley they had dragged her to. She pitched herself into it and ran. She knew it was no good.

A door opened in the street behind her. Its yellow light poured out into the police car's blue. She heard a voice, its authority quavering against its age, shout, "Idiots! Whippersnappers! Get after them, you young cowards!" The pursuing steps faltered. Another voice, like the same one doing duets with itself: "You're not needed there, you young fools. Go after the bandits!" She took one look back and saw two figures in the street, like a split image of a single figure improbable in itself, two erect old men in dressing gowns, mustaches white as the moon, faces with the fierce innocence of boys or old men, pointing stiff as railroad signals down the street toward the flying heels of the Bulgars. Turning around, she had taken her eye off the alley. She half fell against a garbage can, which fell itself behind her. She ran. She had an impression of more doors opening and voices in the street. The alley turned a corner.

Someone had been too clever. Two quiet men in leather coats could have tapped her on the shoulder and led her to a car and not one person on the street, in Berlin, in the whole DDR would have dared to lift a finger. But they had dressed it up as crime, and that made it the business of every German burgher, and the police, whatever they had really been supposed to do, had ended up shamed into behaving like police. At least for a minute. She wondered who the Bulgars were. For she saw it now. They had not assaulted her until the lights were over the hill. Just for a second. But it was true. The alley steepened and went down steps. She still ran. There was a street at the bottom of the steps. She slowed.

A small street, like her own. Mean brown housefronts and infrequent lamps. Her danger was great. The police would know where the alley went to. But if she could become hard for those particular police to find, her chances should at least for a little while improve. Every new street widened the circle. She walked quickly up this one, turned into a second alley, and quietly ran.

And stopped in the dark. Get rid of the death warrant. Her hand went to her pocket and found Krel's letter, more rumpled than she had remembered. She looked at it a second and tore it small, scattering the pieces with her heel. She started off again. The pocket was still not empty, and, not stopping this time, she put her hand in it. She took out Krel's letter, folded just as she remembered. She took out Krel's letter—the needle was stuck in the dream. She unfolded Krel's letter. She looked at the pieces in the alley behind her. Borne on a draft, one scrap ran after her feet like a puppy. She looked at the letter in her hand. Neither was a copy. Both were in Krel's ink, and her fingers had felt the imprint of the nib. She tore up the second letter and scattered the pieces. She considered being sick. She ran instead.

The "Bulgars." *Kum, Frau.* The corrupted phrase used as mating call by Stalin's baboons in Berlin, 1945. It had passed into the nightmares of German women and into Russian latrines. No one else remembered it. Not Bulgars. Some sort of Russians. KGB. And, oh, oh, oh, how could she have been such a fool? *Always destroy my letters as soon as you read them. Remember that, Renate. They are too dangerous.* She could hear the bastard now.

Klingenberg had said the same. There was another street. *Do not be seen running in the street.* Was Klingenberg part of the trap? Two streetlights were out to the left, so that was the way to go. Past the shuttered news stall. There was another passageway ahead. Almost obviously Klingenberg was in it—except there seemed no point. There was a blush of headlights around the corner. It was coming quickly. It would be the police car. *Run.*

Her heels slipped on the sidewalk. Her shoes were askew. She heard the change of gear just around the bend. She ran awkwardly, her legs going out at the side. As she dived into the passageway, the light separated into headlights. She dropped behind a garbage can. A rat squeaked, and its dry feet scuttled across her instep. The car braked by the mouth of the passage and then picked up speed again, hard. She found that her hand was in her mouth.

Hopeless. Hopeless. Hopeless. She could not last. She had to have a friend. There was only Klingenberg.

She had to have a telephone. She could remember the number.

What was her name, though? Gertrud? Gisella. But she had to have a telephone. Not so easy as in the West. Public telephones existed here, but in very public places, and they were not made for privacy.

She was special. She could see that. Probably those were not ordinary police. If she could stay out of that one car's way there might just possibly be some brief indecision about what to do with her. And one car could not search a city. And she would not have the letter. After the indecision passed, if there even was any, she would be finished. Keep going. Find a telephone. And do not think about what came next, because it was all so hopeless that if she did she would walk out into the middle of the street and wait for the police car to come around again and wave her arms at it and say, "Here I am."

The hall of the post office stayed open all night. It was not the central post office but a major secondary one serving a sprawling and featureless district of apartments. Its concrete steps were palely lit. Renate climbed them feeling as exposed as on a glacier. The hall smelled of chalk and tobacco. At the far end of it, under the wavering fluorescent light, was a block of telephones. One was in use. She had thought of telephones in restaurants, all closed; in hotels, suspicious for a young woman alone so late at night; on the main square, very dangerous; at the railroad station, even more so; at her landlady's, suicidal. This was dangerous too, but the best she could think of. Her steps echoed on the floor.

A young man turned from the telephones. He looked at her directly, and her heart stopped. He went on by. But he would remember her.

She put in a coin. She dialed. A sharp female voice, a voice of pincushions and applications refused, answered with the number.

"Captain Klingenberg, please," said Renate.

The voice said with pleasure, "Captain Klingenberg is not on duty. You will call tomorrow."

Of course he wasn't. It was the middle of the night. She had not thought of that. The voice would love to hang up.

She said, "This is Gisella." She paused a second to authenticate the falseness of the name. "The captain will wish to speak to me."

The voice said brusquely, "You will wait."

And she did. She had visions of the barracks night: brightly lit, lonely offices, heels in long corridors, passwords and gates. The door of the post office opened behind her and sighed shut. Would a soldier shake Sepp awake?

234

A voice spoke behind her and was answered. She half turned. She all but cried out. Two policemen were circling the room.

She stared into the telephone, beseeching its help. She had not seen whether they were her own policemen. She could not look again.

Sepp Klingenberg said crisply, "Yes."

She said, "This is Gisella." She said it as though he might come to love Gisella.

He said coldly, "Yes."

Oh, my God, she thought. *He is one of them, too.*

Steps came closer behind her. They were probably in earshot. She said, holding on to her voice, "I have important information."

The steps stopped not far behind her. She stopped, as though listening to his reply. He said, "Yes."

And he began to talk, in a voice still without a flicker of warmth. "Yes. I see. That is very interesting. Also that? That, I must say, seems doubtful to me."

And she realized, *He understands. He is pacing it so I can break in when I want.*

The footsteps moved, not closer. She said quietly, "I need to speak to you. I need a place to meet you. I can wait for you there as long as need be." And prayed that he would understand.

"I see," he said. "Can you go to Zuppinger Strasse?"

She said, "There is no way to know." It was not close and was in a district she did not know well.

And thought his voice darkened a fraction as he said, "There is really no better choice. Zuppinger Strasse 48. It is quite quiet there. It is a little house. If you use the back door you will not need a key. I think you should try. No one will disturb you there."

"I will try," she said.

He hung up. She held on to the telephone. She did not know it, but the back of her shoulders was close to despair. She waited for the footsteps' unappealable verdict.

Max Bessler and Toni Eberhardt, two young Volkspolizei, completed their circuit of the post office and went back out through the door.

"What was wrong with that girl?" said Toni. "She looked miserable."

Max shrugged. "Boyfriend stood her up."

Toni looked back over his shoulder. "Some people are real bastards," he said. "Nice girl like that. Should we do something about it? That's a lonely place in the middle of the night. We're supposed to be helpful." He had been on the force two months.

"No," said Max. "It's not police business." He said it sternly. He had been on the force for four.

═══════

Sepp Klingenberg said, "I can keep you here a few hours. No more."

"Of course," she said.

She had found the house, the back door, a can of soup, some tea, sleep on the sofa, the possibility of hope. She had cringed at the opening door. But it was Klingenberg. She found a tray. There was powdered coffee and damp cookies. She gave him a sort of breakfast. And this improved her spirits.

"Am I a danger to you?" she said. It was also heartening not to simply bleat.

"Not for that time," he said. "One has to have a certain autonomy, handling informers and so forth. We get it. But thank you."

"What is happening to me?" she said. "I would like to know."

"I think I understand, but I am not sure."

"I trusted Krel completely. In the end I was not sure that I liked him anymore, but I trusted him. My best girlfriend said I was in love with him."

"Maybe you were in love with something that did once exist. It can happen." He had not meant to get into such depths, and he felt a shiver in his spine. "It may be a complicated story. It may even be a tragic one."

"Yes," she said. "At least it will be. I shall kill him."

He stared at her. He said, "After you leave here, your position is extremely bad."

"But I will only kill him after he has had time to dread it." She thought, *And I mean it. That's good.* "Yes, I can see that it is extremely bad."

"You cannot hide in Berlin. It will be a matter of hours or days. You cannot get out with a false passport, even if you could be gotten one, because your photograph will be posted for months. Your letter carrier with his truck may possibly be Krel's honest dupe, but I doubt it. Even if he is, carrying a letter and a woman are very different things. The Berlin Wall is impossible. You could try the frontier beyond Berlin. You did it once before. But to succeed twice would be a little improbable. Besides, they were not looking for you then."

It was when he said that that she knew it. The West had died in her. She was the same girl who had climbed the fence two years before and would have killed to do so.

She said, "I know. I have gone through all that myself."

"But perhaps," said Klingenberg, "you could help us."

She laughed. It was theatrical, and she knew it. "That strikes me as a very poor idea."

"In such a way that it would also help you."

She deliberately raised her coffee cup and said across it, "If it mainly helped me it might just possibly be different. It would have to help me a great deal."

He said, "The truth is, it is the only hope you have of ever getting home."

She shrugged. "Well then. If it is the truth, of course, and if you can show it."

He said, "The man you were meant to find exists. He is a senior general of the SSD. August Herter worked for him. So do I and so do quite a number of others, though I do not know how many."

She cut in, "Is he another fake?" She had been a good little lamb for so long that it warmed her just a bit to be a bitch.

He looked her in the eye. "No. He is braver and better than you or me, and he has put together the nearest thing to an effective conspiracy that has existed during the Soviet occupation."

She heard his conviction and shrugged gracelessly. "Perhaps." *I'm good at this,* she thought.

"I am not going to tell you very much, because it is much better that you do not know."

"Oh, yes," she said. "The cyanide tablet."

He looked at her irritably. *Right,* she thought. *Sorry.* And didn't blame him for the edge in his voice. "He also trusted Krel," he said. "August Herter. Can you work that out?"

"Oh, shit," she said. And then thought. "Why can't Krel just denounce him, then?"

"Because he doesn't know who he is. The general has survived because he is cautious. He would have pointed Herter to the contact. No more. Probably Krel expected to get something out of Herter. The Americans must have been too quick for him."

"Have you told the general this?"

"No. You will."

She again had recourse to the coffee cup. "I see," she said. "That's what I do. I drop in at his office at Normannenstrasse, I suppose?"

The philosophical Klingenberg had been exchanged again for the pedantic and he said, "That as it happens, is the problem. He does not appear to be at Normannenstrasse. I have a means to make contact with him there—a means at least to initiate contact. It is more than a week since he has responded, though there is news from me that he must be expecting."

"Perhaps he's changed sides," she said lightly.

It gave her some conviction that that made him truly angry. He said, "If he were in the cells being"—he spoke it icily— "*interrogated*, I would know. There are limits to secrecy, even here. The general has an estate north of Berlin. I know where it is but I have no means to communicate with him there and I would not dare to do so anyway. There would be only one telephone line."

"Why would he go there now? It seems a strange time for a holiday." But she did not say this flippantly.

"Only for the most inauspicious reasons. I think he is in great danger and knows it. He has gone to stay very quiet. They would not fear him there and they would not move against him there as quickly as in Berlin. Perhaps he has a hope of escaping from the country. In that case, do you not think he would turn to someone he trusted?" He looked hard at her. "Maybe he would turn to Krel."

"Ah," she said.

"Your danger is greatest in Berlin. It is very great between Berlin and the Western frontier. At the frontier itself, your case is hopeless. If you do this, you will be leaving Berlin with me to help you, and you will go first east and then north. That is my plan for you, because no one would expect it. The general's estate is about eighty kilometers north of the city, though you will be going a much longer way. It will not be easy and you may not succeed, but I believe you have a better chance in doing that than in anything else you could actually do."

"And when I get there?" she said. "What then? You have forgotten that the advantage must be to me."

"If there is anyone in Germany who can get you out, it is the general. Compared to me he is like God, even if he is in danger. He has contact with the Americans. I am certain of that. There is something else. You are going there to denounce Krel. The general has contact with the West. Krel will be destroyed as soon as you tell him. If you stay here, and are picked up as you will be, he will have won."

She thought a moment, tasting it. "Yes," she said. "There is that." She put her prop back in its saucer. "What is his name?" she said.

"General Hans Sucher. Major General of SSD."

"How do I get there?" she said.

———

That afternoon, Klingenberg said, "The beginning and the end will be dangerous. The rest will be all right. I really believe that."

He changed gear. They were in a Trabant, driving to the eastern outskirts of Berlin. The two warm days had ended in chilly rain, which was increasing. Renate had forgotten the Trabant. It had a gear lever like the end of an invalid's cane and a ride like a tractor.

She said, "It's all dangerous. It doesn't matter."

"You know I would drive you to Frankfurt if I could." He meant Frankfurt on the Oder, on the Polish border. "I cannot explain the absence. All I can do is take you outside the city."

"Of course I know that," she said. "Don't worry. So long as I am outside Berlin." The smell of a Trabant's engine always made her sick, and it was raining too hard to open the windows. Her knapsack was uncomfortable in her lap. Her feet and collar were wet with rain.

"So a bicycle is really the only way. I cannot let you go anywhere near the railroad station here. I could not know it was going to rain like this."

"That is really a detail," she said. "I am not made of sugar."

"Harder to explain why you are bicycling."

"Yes," she said. "But on country roads, you know. And what else am I to do if I only own a bicycle? At least I have the right accent up here. Maybe the rain will stop."

"At least by nightfall. You will not reach Frankfurt by nightfall."

"If I sleep in the rain," she said, "then I sleep in the rain." She touched the slicker he had given her. "This is very waterproof." Indeed it was. In the warmth of the Trabant's heater she was sweating freely inside it.

"At Frankfurt," he said, "I think it is quite safe. Why in the world would you go straight east? And between Frankfurt and the general it should be safe, because I can think of no reason why anyone should come to the general from Frankfurt."

"We have not talked about that," she said. "Will they expect me to go there? If so, all this dodging about is silly."

"How could they? I have thought about it a lot. How could you know who or where he is? There was no name in that letter. You were meant to be believed to be trying to find the name, and you couldn't have. It was meant to draw his attention to you, not the other way around. The general's is the last place they will expect you. Try to believe me. I am really convinced of this."

"I know, Sepp," she said. "I have thought about it too." She surprised herself by laying a hand on his knee.

"But do not underestimate the other end. If I am right, if the general is in danger, he will also be under watch. With so senior a man, they will spare nothing. Do you understand? Any farmer, any hiker, may be a spy. They will surely watch the station. You must not go all the way by train. Only to Angermünde. They will watch his land. You will probably have to get in at night. Be careful of dogs. Suspect everything."

"I'm good at that now."

"We are not superhuman. Sometimes we are quite stupid. If you are careful and lucky you can succeed."

She patted his knee again. He was a lot less redoubtable than she first had thought. That tended, she had decided, to be the case with men.

Berlin ended suddenly, as Eastern cities, even Moscow, do. No suburbs. No shopping malls. A last harsh apartment building on the edge of a flat field and they were in a countryside of wet hedges and despondent earth.

"About another kilometer," said Klingenberg. And then, "The news you are bringing him about what I have been able to do here will make him very happy. He has not worked in vain. That is a great thing."

"That's very nice," said Renate.

The bicycle was behind a hedge a hundred meters down a farm track. It had a tarpaulin over it. She made Sepp stay in the Trabant, tightened up her slicker, and got out into the the rain. The bicycle turned out to be a sturdy, unpretentious machine with a nicely oiled bright chain. She put the knapsack on. It slipped on the wet oilcloth, and she quickly took off the the slicker and put it on underneath. The rain made her no wetter than sweat had already, but it was colder outside the car. It cleared her head. She said through the window to Klingenberg, "Right, then."

He nodded stiffly, the old Klingenberg again, and said, "I wish you good fortune."

"Thanks," she said.

The Trabant, turning, blew its fumes in her face. She felt sicker for a moment and then much better.

By the outskirts of Frankfurt, her clothes squelched, her thighs screamed, and her backside was rubbed raw. None of which was serious. Some good socialists spent vacations like that. She had had a long ride in the rain and a wretched night, but she had seen no sign that she was followed or observed. She dumped the bicycle in a rack near the station, where it would have to make a completely new life for itself.

She went to the station toilets and washed her face and brought some order to the outside of her clothes. This was Sunday and to be hiking wretchedly was not suspicious—it is almost patriotic. She bought a sausage roll and a meatloaf pastry. Both were greasy and delicious. She bought a glass of schnapps, which was even better. Her good humor surprised her. Under the modernistic clock she saw three Vopos watching the platforms. She hung back and her heart reflexively thumped, but then she walked by briskly. She thought suddenly, *This is the first time since I have been here that I have not been watched. I know this.* She got on the train for Rostok.

At Eberswalde she got out and waited for the train for Stralsund, on the Baltic. It was colder in the north; the wind swept down the platform, and although it wasn't raining she drew her slicker tight. In two hours, the train would take her to Angermünde, ten kilometers from the general's village. The wind gusted again. The Baltic gray was in the sky, and she shivered. *You've got to go on with it,* she thought. *You just do. Think about Dr. Krel.* She did, and had a melodramatic vision of herself, a woman in a long gray cloak coming closer and closer to Krel, her hand on the silver hilt of a knife. It cheered her up. It was now three in the afternoon. She would get to Angermünde in the early dusk. It would be a two-hour walk to the general's estate. Her legs had no enthusiasm for it at all.

Flat, hard country with etched details of water and rock. Cows and pine trees and potatoes. Pure Prussia. Her own country, as creamy gold Bavaria had never quite become. The voices on station platforms and tractors in the field were not quite like Berlin but much like Potsdam. She fitted in. She even took a short ride on a cart piled with gritty turnips. Sepp would not approve, but her legs did, and she was not so very near the general's village. The sky was gunmetal overcast, and the wind was steady and still spitting rain. The night would be dark and noisy. Good.

She had the crudest possible map, drawn in pencil on torn paper. No names. The larger village, two kilometers beyond the general's place, was Greiffenberg. There was a smaller village, Dunsfelt, on this side. The gate of the estate was on the country road between them. Drawn vaguely and without much confidence was a farm road around the side of the estate and a hamlet, or something, up it. The place was mainly woods, she thought, and the house was in the middle of it. *"Das wäre ein Schloss"*—a castle? she had asked, rather awed. Sepp didn't think so. Just a house.

If the entrance of the estate was on the road between two villages, then the village main streets would be a place for discreet surveillance. Sepp had said, "Look for a man in the window of the tavern, a workman who doesn't do much, anything like that." She saw the sense of it. She could try to skulk through Dunsfelt at night, but it seemed a very bad idea. This was a passably pretty landscape, and it was not so late in the year that a young Sunday hiker with a knapsack was altogether odd. The farm road on the side of the estate seemed the most hopeful entrance. "I believe there is a gate there that is never used," Klingenberg had said. "That is perhaps your best hope."

Perhaps everyone in Dunsfelt was a spy. Perhaps no one was. She was not stopped. She went through it well in time to reach the next village before dark. Beyond Dunsfelt, there was a man on a tractor near the edge of a wood. He seemed to be busy. She could not be sure.

There was a car. She heard it before it came. She debated a second. Walk calmly on, or hide? The ground decided for her. The ditch was deep here and the hedge was brushy. There was no one watching. She hid.

The car was a plain Trabant, a farmer's muddy car, but it drove past slowly and the two men in it stank of police.

From then on, she did not move until she had picked out a hiding place ahead. The car came past twice more. It was truly raining now, but her yellow rain slicker stood out like a beacon and she stuffed it into a culvert. Her clothes sucked at her skin.

She saw the beginning of a long fence, stretching as far as she could see. By the corner of it, a lane led off at a right angle through the woods. Just at the limit of her sight, she saw the Trabant stop, turn, and travel back toward her. She was a sodden, dark figure now, and light was fading. She crouched under the hedge. The Trabant paused by the lane but did not go up it.

She did not move until dark. The rain had ended, but the wind was high. She watched for an hour and once saw the trace of headlights far up the fence, perhaps at the main entrance of the estate. She slipped into the lane.

242

It was dark, but not difficult for walking. She could see the line of the fence, which was overgrown. After about a kilometer, the line dipped a little. She came carefully nearer. So she was there. The gate. It was hard to see through it, for it was choked with creepers, but an overgrown avenue seemed to lead into the woods behind it. She looked at it. *Well, here goes,* she said.

It was not difficult. The gate was full of ivy. She stepped heavily at first, and felt it give beneath her feet. The crushed stems reeked in the night. She thought quickly and afterward pushed the ivy aside with her toe. Not much damage, she thought. She was up in a jiffy. At the top, suddenly wise, she looked for a hidden wire, an electric eye. Nothing. Just an old gate. She threw her leg over it, considered climbing down, and jumped instead. She had a sudden vision as she went of a snarl in the wood, bared fangs, hot breath on her throat. She landed. She stayed still. No dog. She was scared of that.

There were still wheel ruts, but the center of the avenue was overgrown almost to her shoulder. She walked softly, in spite of the wind in the forest and the creaks and knocks of branches here and there. The avenue was straight, but she could not see much.

Until a shape emerged beside the track. It was man-made and square, suggestive of a guardhouse, though it wasn't lit. Nothing moved. Closer, it was windowless and smelled of mold, an old brick shed. She walked on by, prickling only a little as she passed the door. She saw a light twinkle as from a distant house. The trees quickly shut it off.

She could not see twenty meters into the trees, which was reassuring in theory though not in practice, since she filled the forest with ravenous and silent dogs. Theory proposed that even dogs couldn't hear or smell much in the wind. The light appeared again. She had a quick fear and stopped still. Could it be a light that moved? It couldn't. She went on again. It could only be the house, and she had crossed half of Germany with all its guards and spies to get there and that was not a small thing, she thought, not a small thing at all. Heartened by this, she crept down her wheel rut stealthily as an Indian. When the light next showed, it never quite disappeared again.

So there it was. The wood ended. She looked out onto a hundred meters or so of grass. Forlorn hope, impossible challenge, suddenly changed into a wooden house with a porch with shadowy chairs upon it and a light in the window not for "the general" but for a man who might wear spectacles or smoke a pipe. After the wood, the meadow was almost light. She did not move. She watched.

But, whatever Sepp had said, there was nothing sinister. The driveway entered at an angle and ended in pale gravel. To the left was a sheen of water with a dark mass jutting into it and something bulbous by its side. A dock and a boat. Her eye knew exactly what it feared to see: the sentry pacing quietly with a shaggy shape leashed beside him, the jeep in the shadow of the wood. But the lighted window shone out on perfect stillness. So the surveillance was all outside the fence. Which made sense too. Well, it was over. She was here.

The grass was to her calves. She saw a small animal scuttle through it. She saw the smoke above the house's roof. She saw the porch steps. She saw a movement in the lighted room.

She saw a speck of light flare up near the lake, beside the boat.

She felt it in her chest, which pulled almost in two, and in her face, which turned cold. The light flamed yellow for a count of three, went out, and was replaced by a smaller, dimmer, redder one.

She was standing still listening to a didactic voice inside her say, *A man with a cigarette, watching from the lake. Maybe he can't see well yet. Get down.* She did. The grass covered her head. Seeds were in her nose. The voice said, *And maybe he saw that quite well.* Her limbs dissolved. The voice had another thought: *If you sneeze, you're finished.*

She lay still. There was no sound, but there mightn't be. She imagined the steady pace, the raised rifle. She imagined the slipped leash, the gray chest flying across the grass, the jaws appearing above her neck. Nothing happened. She began to think.

The man was well placed. He was invisible. He could watch the housefront and the drive. No doubt he had been doing just that and so had missed her own dim figure coming out of the wood. He would have seen her as she neared the house.

And now, whether she crawled through the grass, burrowed, or flew, he would see her as she climbed the porch and knocked, polite girl, at the door.

She did not think he could see the back of the house. This could well mean that there was no door there. It could well mean that some other man could. She had no idea whether she could crawl through the grass without being seen.

She thought some more. This was a great man's house. Surely it had a kitchen door. Her choices were not great. She could spend the indefinite future lying in the grass, crawl back to the wood, or try for the back of the house. Even counting doubling around it, it could not be much above a hundred meters. Not much.

Renate stood by the back wall of the house. Her arms shook uncontrollably from the shoulder. Her knees were skinned. She was smeared with grass and soaked. This was two hours later. She had spent an hour lying by the edge of the graveled drive waiting for the flare of another match by the lake.

There was a window near her head. It was lighted and there was a dull noise of movement from within. She looked into it.

A gray-haired man in a woolen sweater stood by the sink washing a small saucepan. He did it carefully and not well. She looked longer than she meant to.

She knocked at the window. He looked up at once. It was late at night. He was perhaps a man near the end of his tether. He must have known his house to be watched. But he looked up with none of the clumsy emotions—fear, surprise, bafflement—only a grave and focused attention. He could not see her. She brought her face nearer the glass. He looked closely and his eyes became concerned, as at a wounded comrade. She motioned for quiet and to the door. He nodded.

She stood before it. He opened it. His hair was silver in the house light. He was taller than she had realized and very straight.

She said, "I was sent by Captain Klingenberg in Berlin. There is a man watching your house from the lake."

He took her hand gently and brought her in. Her arm was still shaking, and he laid his hand on it.

"It is kind of Captain Klingenberg to tell me that," he said, "but it is a long way for you to carry the news."

19

Stears caught a cab at Hallesches Tor U-Bahn and went straight to Tegel airport, where he found a seat on the early British Airways flight to London. It is a tawdry flight, protected from competition by the Four-Power division of Berlin airspace, which excludes all but Air France, Pan Am, BA, and Aeroflot, each to its own routes.

But Stears watched briefly as the airliner banked and rose above Mercedes's distant star and as the Berlin Wall drifted by less than a thousand meters below and as the Elbe River flashed on its way to Hamburg and the West; then he retreated into discomforting thoughts.

For he had slept in brief snatches the night before with predictable dreams of eccentric escalators, blocked tunnels, and ill-intentioned dogs. But one dream had been quite different.

A fat, drunken baby dressed in loud English checks reminding him of an offensive, forgotten English comic until its smile turned into a moist and evil leer and it started popping up around corners and peering at him, pink and flaccid but always a little bigger, always a little closer. He had waked up even faster than from the SSD's own special repertory of dreams. And then realized that he had seen the original of this figure in real life: one of the two roaring vulgarians in the pub near Warminster when he had talked to August Herter.

And now, in daylight and security, knew that he had seen him other times as well. It was as though a man from some other context (*a pinstripe suit*) had for some reason (*with a dignified walk*) wished (*and food, and a wineglass*) to borrow a character (*you don't walk with a wineglass*) completely contrary to his usual one (*shotguns*). Shotguns and contact! South Audley Street—Stears's own neighborhood. Just a Londoner. More or less a gentleman. A neighbor, or perhaps he worked or had a club nearby. Stears had seen him coveting the guns in the window of Purdy's blue-gold heaven. On pleasant days he had seen him lunching, *Telegraph* propped against a carafe, at the outside tables of a wine bar on Stears's way home. He had come out of the Ambrose delicatessen with a small white package just behind Stears. He had walked, preoccupied, led by his umbrella tip, across Grosvenor Square as

Stears went to work. He had seemed to admire Stears's Jaguar when it was newly waxed.

Never near Stears. Not inevitable. Not watching. Just often there. But the clearer his memory the more out of focus it became, for the man had had that ambiguity of a tailor's clerk—quite, quite the perfect gentleman, such a gent. But still far from the braying jackass in the pub.

The stewardess offered him coffee, and he barely heard her. That kind of Londoner did sometimes turn drunk and funny in a country pub. A coincidence was possible. Shepton Mallet was not quite the back of beyond. The second vulgarian struck no chord of memory, none at all. The main thing was to avoid false conclusions, paranoia, haste. Even when the first link in this chain, Oswolt Krel, was looking ever more strange and might well be rotten. One must be calm and clear. Even when August Herter might be in deadly danger and with him all else, and Stears was fifteen thousand meters up in the air without a telephone.

He turned to geometry. How far back did this memory go? Indefinite because hazy, but certainly not beyond the beginning of ELBEMAN, not before the spring. Of what had it consisted? No known attempt to penetrate his office or his house. No apparent telephone tap. Just a tail, then—where was he, whom did he meet. He met Herter, didn't he?

Spies are spied upon. That he was followed did not mean that the followers knew the context of anything he did. He had not outwardly met August Herter of the NVA; he had met Captain Streicher of the West German army.

Where was the point of access? What was the potential danger to the keystone, to ELBEMAN? The stewardess menaced him with a plastic beaker of yellow fluid; Stears defended himself and tried to separate his operation into strands and isolate the moments when surveillance might have tied two or more together.

First, Berlin. There was no way whatsoever to know whether his surveillance in East Berlin, if there had really been any, had been random, or Renate's and not his, or his and focused. This point was vital and unknowable.

Next, Mays. If the Opposition could connect Stears, August Herter, and Mays, then ELBEMAN was surely done for.

He had been in Mays's presence twice: unseen in the Night Zoo and then in the room in Dahlem. Mays knew Stears only as Major Hamilton, accessible through a number in Frankfurt which he had only once used. Even if the KGB were to learn that Mays was the

CIA's, even if Mays had doubled again, only a precisely located traitor in the Company could connect him with Stears. Furthermore, he agreed with Woods: there was no good reason to think that the KGB suspected Mays, or even had accessible reason to do so beyond the KGB's morose and usual paranoia. Discount Mays.

But the certainty was this: he had begun to be followed not long after August Herter had been hidden in England, and had been followed to August Herter, who could well have been photographed and whose whereabouts were undoubtedly known.

And if the KGB got August Herter, they would soon get ELBE-MAN, though Herter would first be brave and the end would not be nice.

Herter, to the SSD and the KGB, was an East German national and so a traitor, a deserter, and a spy. Short of attacking a British army camp they would do anything they needed to get him back. They would play rough. They would move fast. They would take the heat afterward. The base at Warminster had proved its insecurity.

That in itself was not surprising. Treachery was not even necessary, though it was possible; armies are large, loose things full of ponderous innocents. Nobody had ever thought that August Herter could not be found, given time, at Warminster. But he was not going to stay there forever, and one had thought that it would take more time than the Comrades would be given. A defecting officer of the Warsaw Pact is a hot property even if he is only a young man in a sulk; still, the Comrades must have worked up a sweat if they had found him by any means except following Stears. That in turn, either way, meant that they must assume that Herter was a good deal more than a young man in a sulk.

None of which was nice to think about.

Hanover passed below them. He had not noticed the frontier, which from this height was probably not even visible; strange to think that a structure only four meters high and easy to see through could support a garden of lies and fear from here to Vladivostock. He remembered the inn at Lüderbach the night that August Herter had crossed and his own pleasure then in his sport of merry duplicity. He turned from it now in dismay.

But as the vague and muddy Belgian coast was replaced by the channel and the ruled wakes of ships, he turned to geometry again and to the axiom that all surveillance can in principle be turned against itself. He turned his thought to the attack. By the white cliffs of Kent he was pleased enough with his plan to regret his slighting of the stewardess, call for a glass of Champagne, and be told that the bar was closed.

When KGB Captain Yuri Marchenko, who turned out to be a participant in Stears's plan even though Stears had not known that he existed, told the story to Grigori Priabin in the KGB mess at the Soviet embassy in London he made, like many storytellers, a discovery about himself. This was two days after the event. What Yuri Marchenko had done near Warminster was, he realized, connected with Afghanistan. Also with Ethiopia, Mozambique, and Cambodia. Marchenko had been in none of these manly outposts of the Soviet Empire and envied those who had, as an English police constable, trudging with his bull's-eye through the gaslit drizzle of the Old Kent Road, would once have envied the bronzed heroes of the Khyber Rifles or even Captain Scott.

At Warminster, he had merely seen his chance: not to just watch the CIA man and the German deserter while a plan of abduction was made up but to do the job himself here, now, like a thunderbolt. He still felt the rush and risk of that stroke, and it depressed him that Priabin nibbled the rim of his vodka glass and said finally, "You're meant to have initiative. Yes."

"Fuck it," said Marchenko. "He was going cross-country on little roads. I had three cars on it. That CIA bastard drives fast, but there's always some obstacle on those roads—sheep, tractors, whatever. I knew I could take him."

"And you were right," said Priabin. "You did take him."

"Fuck it, yes," said Marchenko.

Priabin licked his vodka like a cat and smiled. It was peppered vodka, pink and hot, and Priabin treated it like medicinal drops.

Marchenko's KGB surveillance force had been almost at the level of an action squad. The decision had been made already—on what precise grounds Captain Marchenko was not told—to face whatever diplomatic wrath the careful recapture of the former Captain Herter of the German NVA entailed. "Careful," in this case, excluded situations in which Soviet operatives openly took on the forces of British law and, obviously, assaults on a British base. It also excluded those that might leave former Captain Herter dead. It did not exclude kidnap witnessed by civilians or accomplished with violence. Herter never left the base except in the company of Stears, his CIA control. These sorties appeared vulnerable and might indeed be so. But not for sure. There might well be unseen escorts close at hand, and the CIA man, according to his dossier, had a deceptive penchant for trouble. It was these matters that Marchenko had now to elucidate. Marchenko, of the "wet"—or Department 8, or violent—section of KGB, would also be in command of the abduction.

Today was both promising and ominous. The CIA man's arrival at the camp was expected—a telephone at the base normally used by Herter had long been tapped. On the other hand, though what had been said on the telephone was a little obscure, it seemed to imply an imminent removal of Herter to some other place. It also implied, the conversations being on an open line and cautious rather than impenetrable, that their surveillance of the CIA man had not been detected. That pleased Marchenko.

He saw the Jaguar. It came down the road from the barracks gate toward the first significant intersection. Marchenko, in the forecourt of a filling station, motioned his driver to start the Audi 5000 carefully—no sudden exhaust. A hundred yards down the road, Kolchov would do the same in a Peugeot 505S. A third crew, in a Mini-Minor with a Cooper engine, was out of sight, half a mile away. These were all fast, inconspicuous cars. Each carried two armed men. They had radios. A fourth car, a Rover, carried two English operatives and was several miles away, toward the village of Shepton Mallet, where Herter and the CIA man frequently visited an inn.

Marchenko looked at the Jaguar. As the angle of light changed, he saw Stears's profile and Herter's peaked cap and characteristic stiffness of neck.

"He's there," said Marchenko.

"Kraut shit," said his driver. He did not like Germans, even fraternal ones.

The Audi fell in behind the Jaguar. The Peugeot stayed well back. They would switch in due course. The Mini-Cooper was called in.

As the Jaguar approached the turn for Shepton Mallet, Marchenko's foot touched an invisible brake. The Jaguar neither slowed nor turned. Marchenko called back the Rover, though the likelihood of its catching up was small. The Jaguar continued toward Salisbury. The road was open and busy, though by no means clogged. The Jaguar stayed at just under eighty, above the speed limit but not extravagantly so and a nice hand canter for all concerned. The Peugeot overtook the Audi and the Mini-Cooper closed up. *He's moving the son of a bitch right now*, thought Marchenko. He felt his hands tense on the radio.

The Jaguar turned left toward the village of Heytesbury. It turned off fast, benefited by the arts of left-hand driving, and picked up speed. Marchenko frowned in surprise, reined in the Peugeot, and sent up the Mini-Cooper before repassing the Peugeot himself. A truck full of sad-eyed calves, smelling of silage, lumbered the other way. The Jaguar was rolling now. Marchenko's driver said to himself, *Where the fuck's he going?* Marchenko shrugged.

They were on the edge of Salisbury Plain now, not very far from Stonehenge—high, short-grassed country with austere, rare farms and a sky haunted by fretful ghosts. They passed a field with rocky outcrops imitating its sheep. Marchenko saw the sparse traffic and the swooping plain and glory began to grow in his brain. He did nothing about it.

The Jaguar slowed hard for a tractor pulling bales of hay, flowed around it, and slowed soon again for Heytesbury. It passed the post office and the Fox and Hounds and turned left at the church. Marchenko looked at his map. They were going straight across the plain. A vision of grandeur filled Marchenko: the high plateau of Kabul and the mujahedin fleeing like snow.

The Jaguar took off hard. Marchenko told his driver, "Pass the Peugeot but stay back." The driver floored the Audi. Marchenko pulled the automatic out of the glove compartment and checked the loading.

The driver looked sideways. "You think we can?" he said.

"Just maybe," said Marchenko. He took his eye off the road and reached into the backseat. He picked up a case. It would have done for a small telescope or something else expensive and long. He opened it on his knee. It contained a sort of gun, similar to an underwater speargun, and a cluster of darts. He closed it up again and put it beside him. The Audi rocketed over the crest of a hill he had not seen, and only the seat belt held him fast. In most cases he would have known now that the Jaguar had seen its plight. In this case, he was not yet sure.

The driver said soberly, "How do we get past? That thing can move."

"We don't," said Marchenko. "Something has to stop him. Move on up." He spoke quickly to the other cars. They closed up behind. The Mini-Cooper was laboring.

They were now traveling slightly south in a wide, shallow valley. The shadows of clouds flowed across a stone farmhouse on the right, making its stone alternately bright and gray. Far to the left, four British Chieftain tanks, line abreast, sent a haze of torn grass and diesel smoke into the air behind them. Their incalculable, useless might pleased Marchenko as a spice of risk. The Jaguar's rear wheels danced on the rough road. The farmhouse changed color and rushed past. They were doing well over ninety. The road turned downhill ahead. The Jaguar crested it and vanished. Marchenko pushed himself into his seat. The nose of the Audi dropped.

They looked into the brake lights of the Jaguar squeezing up to them. They looked to the bottom of the dip where a farm lane entered the road across a cattle grid and a tractor pulling a thresher like a huge injured moth crawled onto the road in front of the Jaguar. It was two hundred yards away. The Jaguar inhaled the gap. "Son of a bitch," said Marchenko. "We've got him." The Jaguar slewed slightly and corrected. Herter put his head down. The Jaguar's rear pushed to within twenty feet of the Audi and then stayed steady. Marchenko shouted on the radio to the Mini, "Get up on the shoulder. Block him." He pulled the automatic out and snapped open the dart gun's case. The Mini skated past. Marchenko ordered generally, "For fuck's sake don't shoot Herter."

The Mini slithered sideways off the shoulder and struck the Jaguar. Marchenko saw Stears spin the wheel away and then fast back so the Jaguar feinted and swung into the Mini, driving it halfway back up the shoulder. He saw the Jaguar tense under its acceleration and Herter sit suddenly back up. *He's going for a gun,* he thought.

The tractor had pulled half off the road and there was a hole for the Jaguar to escape through. He considered ramming it from behind. But the Jaguar rebounded off the Mini just enough so that one rear wheel, under full throttle, hit the soft grass shoulder and dug in hard. The Jaguar slewed across the road, rocked, half climbed the other side, and settled back, at bay.

The Mini scuttled in front of it. The Peugeot was stopped on Marchenko's bumper. Kolchov ran past, crouched on the Audi's bumper, and aimed a revolver two-handed into the Jaguar. Lyscho, from the Mini, brandished a gun at the stopped tractor, waving it on and shouting quite unconvincingly, "Police!" And Captain Marchenko, twenty-eight years old, who had brought the glories of Afghanistan single-handedly to Wiltshire, got slowly out, picked up the dart gun, stuck the revolver cavalierly into his belt, and advanced upon his beaten foe. He was not a nasty boy and his expression was polite.

"Yes," said Priabin to Marchenko, "tell me again. The end."

At the Soviet embassy, the KGB had its own dining room, not as nice as the ambassador's but very nice. Priabin signaled to a mess-man, who brought a plate of pickled herring. Priabin pointed to Marchenko's glass. Priabin's was still half full. Marchenko nodded. Priabin very slightly frowned. All over the world, the KGB is corking the decanters.

Marchenko said, "First I thought Herter was badly hurt, and I was worried. The CIA guy had his arm around him, sort of holding him up. I was worried. Then I thought maybe the guy was trying to protect him, which would have been pretty stupid. I was near the car then. Kolchov was holding the gun on it. No guns in the car that I could see. The CIA guy was looking at me. Herter was looking away. I was almost sorry for the little shit. I mean, we had him. No doubt of that.

"Then I couldn't believe it. This Stears guy took Herter's cap off and started playing with his hair, like a girl, you know. I swear to you, for a second I thought, *They're a couple of goddam faggots.* I swear to you. It's what it looked like.

"And then I started looking at Herter. In the face. That's one thing I can say. I knew it before Stears did it. Only a second. But I knew it."

"Did what?" said Priabin, smiling.

"Took Herter's head off and threw it in the backseat. Then pushed the rest onto the floor. A fucking dummy. He was still looking at me, that CIA bastard. He lifted his fucking eyebrows. I remember that."

Priabin smiled and sighed, a story known already, well retold. He speared a rolled herring and ate it slowly.

"These are better at home," he said. "That's one thing for you. Look on the bright side. Russia's not all bad, even if they don't let you into Moscow." And then, in the same tone, "It's a simple trick, the oldest in the book. Obviously they moved Herter while you were playing around."

Marchenko agreed. "Yes. But it was out of context. You expect that kind of stuff in Berlin, you expect it when you've got some real cat-and-mouse going. This just didn't feel like that. We were only observing him, anyway, until I saw where he was going."

"He screwed you, you know," said Priabin. "You've lost Herter. The ambassador's at the Foreign Office now. The British are shit-ting bricks. You'll be *persona non grata* by this evening. You and God knows who else. They're going to start wondering how we got onto this Stears in the first place. He screwed you. They'll probably send you to Murmansk."

"Yes," said Marchenko. "He had balls, though. He couldn't quite have known what I would do. I had some tough guys with me. When I told them to get back in the cars and go away they nearly lynched me."

"It was the professional thing to do," said Priabin.

"Granted. It was what he'd think I would probably do. But he couldn't quite have known it. Not for sure."

"There's that," said Priabin. "My brother likes English shirts, the kind with stripes. If I buy some this afternoon you could take them home. There's a sale on Jermyn Street. I'll buy you lunch." He added kindly, "Murmansk isn't so bad. They say it's pretty in the winter."

"Fuck you," said Marchenko.

"If it makes you feel any better," said Priabin, "they canned someone else because of Stears as well. Some asshole in Berlin called Smolsky. Let him walk in and out of East Berlin like it had revolving doors."

"I knew Smolsky in Helsinki," said Marchenko. "I didn't know him well."

"Maybe you'll know him better in Murmansk," said Priabin.

———

Stears had returned home from all this with a feeling that his substance, which had been growing closer to lead the further the ELBEMAN operation went, had moved up the atomic scale toward helium. It had gone perfectly; someone had been spared, the operation significantly secured, no one had been hurt, and Wop Stears was more visibly and simply ace than at any time since the Yale Skiing Team in 1963. Deeply and shyly he felt as he always felt when once in a long while a vision of his uncle and idol, the great Ferrara-Ugolino, the partisan marchese, became approachable enough to sit down with by the fire.

He was exhausted; he had reached London from Berlin in mid-morning, spent the rest of it in artful telephone calls to Warminster; the afternoon had been given over to adventures behind the wheel. But his exhaustion was the kind that spun like a flywheel; it bundled Marie-Sophie into an evening dress while he fended off precise questions by helping her painstakingly with the buttons over the bust, and got them both into a cab for Annabel's. For sophisticated juvenility, London is a world resource.

Marie-Sophie, as he knew, liked Annabel's, liked being warmly looked at, like Champagne, and got all three. A party of delin-

254

quents connected with the palace arrived with their police keepers and bayed and giggled in an alcove. Marie-Sophie watched them with the unconcealed delight of a child at a zoo. She put her legs cozily around one of Wop's.

He took her home, breathing through her hair in the back of the taxi. He sat on the bed stifling tremendous yawns that left his brain clear and his concupiscence unblunted, pulled Marie-Sophie half over him, and began to disassemble her dress while her head lay on his shoulder and her scent rose from her breast. She had worn a bra, and he detached it as delicately as if it covered petals.

At which point, like a family dog shut out of the room, the telephone began to yell.

———

Stears said to Brindle Woods, "You bastard." Ineffectual rudeness seemed fitting to his race through the drunks outside the wine bars of South Audley Street to Grosvenor Square, to Marie-Sophie sitting abandoned and disordered on the stairs, to the empty building where Brindle Woods's office and his own seemed to blink in the sudden light. And to the photographs. Especially to the photographs.

Brindle Woods, at his desk, opened his hands a millimeter and permitted the insult to strike his chest.

"Later," he said. "The important thing is ELBEMAN. What to do."

Stears pushed aside a photograph of Scott Mays, whose face ended in a jagged edge just to the right of the nose, and looked again at one of the Pinto as the girl who liked Rilke had found it. Another picture, of the Pinto after it had been opened, he had already turned upside down and never wanted to see again.

"Yes," he said. "After all, Mays was only a sergeant, wasn't he? And this does seem rather final."

Brindle Woods spread his hands again, but not smugly. He said, "How are you going to get your asset out?"

"Sucher? I suppose there is no possible doubt that Mays was killed because they knew we had doubled him and were feeding him trash. Or that that will lead them to Sucher."

"Damn little," said Woods. "It will lead them to Sucher in the end. We don't know quite how fast. And they may hold back a little. They often do."

Stears said, "I don't know how I'm going to get him out. Emergency evacuation of a well-known man under suspicion from a point outside Berlin. It takes a little imagination, don't you think?"

"You had better think fast. You have a few days at best."

"I may have a few hours," said Stears. "In that case you've murdered him."

"Yes," said Woods. "It might be hours. That is true."

"I have had an idea in the back of my mind," said Stears. "It will not work well and it may not work at all. I'll need a couple of hours to know even that much. I take it you will be here."

"Yes," said Brindle Woods.

"I will be in the map room," said Stears.

At one in the morning he came back. He carried a pencil and a legal pad marked with notes of kilometers and estimates of hours and minutes carefully on top of a pile of satellite reconnaissance photographs and maps of Prussia. They were unfamiliar tools, and he looked at them yet again before he spoke to Woods.

Woods raptly listened. He said, "Sit down, please. You can loom over me later. What happened is not as simple as you think."

Wop said, "I don't know if it will work. It's just the best I've got." He sat down. He went on. "Schematically, there are three ways to get Sucher out. Snatch him—light aircraft at his house or something like that. It might work, but it won't be authorized." Woods nodded. "Or false papers. Won't work—he s too well known and there's no way for plastic surgery. Or surreptitious exit, and that's the only one left. So we look at geography and assets. For some reason I'd rather not have a fifty-odd-year-old man trying to climb the goddam fence with the whole country chasing him."

"Yes," said Woods. "All right, what are your assets?"

"Geography first. Sucher's place is near Angermünde. Twenty kilometers south is Finow, which is a canal port on the Elbe-Oder system. Finow serves some of the northern industrial suburbs of East Berlin, so it's fairly busy. Here are the satellite photos." He placed a sheaf of photographs on Wood's desk. Taken from space, they looked like diagrams of a radio. They were the port of Finow at different resolutions.

"Now look at the port perimeter. There's not much security. I mean, there's plenty, but by their standards it's loose. I don't know why. I guess it's in the middle of the country and it's not in Berlin. There's an ordinary fence, three gates, and the guardhouses are just cubicals. It's night that interests me. There are two searchlight posts—see, there's one just above that stack of pipe sections and

256

another to the left of the three cars and a bicycle by the warehouse. Unless I'm much mistaken, parts of the perimeter are going to be quite shadowy at night."

But he saw it all suddenly, not the figures and the etchings from space but the long kilometers of country road, the tightly strung fence, the roving searchlights, the police with photographs and dogs, an old, hunted man. He looked at Brindle Woods.

"I don't know," he said. "Maybe. There's still a chance. We could have had him out easily without this damn game with Mays. Two or three weeks lead time was all we needed."

He thought again of what had been done behind his back and added acidly, "Maybe you'll still be lucky."

But Woods looked back at him drawn and small, the bright prosperity shrunken in, and said, "Maybe. A chance. And there he meets your asset?"

"Yes," said Stears. "First mate on an Elbe barge. Big thing, twelve hundred tons. Runs between Hamburg and Stettin. She'll be carrying Polish coal on the westbound run. About thirty-six hours between Finow and the border at Lauenburg, plus two for the crossings. I say 'crossings' because there are two. They check her once when the south bank of the Elbe becomes West German near Wittenberge, then again when the river passes fully into the West east of Lauenburg. There's about fifty kilometers in between, but the frontier's the Western bank, not the middle of the stream. They've got guns and boats and everything. He's got to stay on until Lauenburg. That's where I'll be."

"Can he?"

"I don't know. If he gets on board, I think he's got a good chance. They're big vessels and three fourths of it's bulk cargo space. Crew of four, one of whom is our man. And it's our asset, the mate, that makes the difference. He's gotten two men through for us. One in '79 and one in '83. That's good."

"They weren't bolting generals. Can you contact him?"

"He's in Stettin tomorrow. That's Poland and it's a lot easier. Yes, we can contact. I've checked with Polish Section at Langley. Fortunately it was only six P.M. over there. They've got Solidarnosk people to spare. Sucher's got to hold for three days, though."

"Sucher's got to get out of his house."

"Yes. We don't know anything about that. So far, they've not been crowding him."

Woods said, "How does he get off the barge?"

"The sensible thing would be for him to stay on until Hamburg and get off like a gentleman. But that may compromise our asset on the barge too much. Hamburg has tight port security and somebody would find out that there was an unexplained man aboard. The other two were taken off surreptitiously at night. That must have been the reason."

"Surreptitiously, how?"

"Jump in the river. Preferably quietly. As I recollect those barges, they have almost no freeboard. I'll have a little boat."

"Oh," said Woods. "When's your next transmission?"

"That is not very good," said Stears. "There was one last night, which we didn't use because there was nothing to say. He will not expect us until tomorrow, Monday. He's got a time he could transmit himself this afternoon—but only in an emergency, and since he doesn't know of any emergency, he presumably won't transmit. I've been very strict about transmissions. They scare the hell out of me."

"Yes, indeed," said Woods. "Well, as you say, the barge won't be there anyway. Not tomorrow."

"When we transmit, I'm going to give him the general situation and the plan and ask him only if he can hold for three days and then get to Finow port. I want to keep his transmissions under half a second."

"Quite right," said Woods.

Stears placed all his notes one on top of the other and his pencil, like a compass needle, on top of all. He said, "But we don't know how quickly the situation is going to change there. Because we don't know their side of it. We don't know how long they've had our Sergeant Mays and his wife and his little boy and what seems to have been a baby once, before it came pâté, in their sights, while we kept setting him up. We don't know how long they've known we've been betraying our own agents. We don't know how long it would have taken them to work out that the famous Brindle Woods is not operating as a chess master but at the level of a third-rate numbers runner pulling a scam in a public urinal. Those are all unknowns, wouldn't you say, Brindle?"

"Yes," said Brindle Woods. "They are unknowns." He looked at him, Stears thought, as though counting him up.

"All right," said Woods. "PSYCHIC never worked. The theory was interesting and it got in as a pilot project, but the Department of Defense nearly scrapped it two years ago. Then the DIA got hold of a dim echo that the Soviets had heard of it and that it scared them stiff. It's computer stuff, you see, and they get irrational

258

about that because they don't know how far ahead we are. Their technical people are fairly level-headed, but not the generals. To them it's sorcery, as Sputnik was to ours. So the DIA got the DOD to keep working away at it. The contractors liked it, the DIA had its own little private baby, the Comrades hated it, and maybe it would make a bargaining chip one day.

"Then we got ELBEMAN, you see, and then we got Mays. The DIA discovered two things. First, it was finally plugged right into the Soviet PSYCHIC operation. Second, they now knew what material the Soviets were getting, and from that they knew it wouldn't be long before the Soviets threw the whole thing out with the trash. So they decided to change the material the Soviets were getting. Do I have to go further?"

"Yes," said Stears. "Did you authorize it?"

"Strictly, no. If the army wants to fake an experiment and pass the results to a serviceman who happens to be run by the CIA, they don't need to ask me. I knew about it. I knew about it from the beginning. And I did not try to stop it. Do you want to know why?"

"I suppose so," said Stears.

"I was categorically assured that it could be done without the Soviets catching on. It was explained rather carefully to me. It is again the question of what our computers can do compared to theirs. On that basis it was worth it. Assets are there to be used. And for quite some time, it appeared that I had been advised correctly. I believe there was a mistake near the end."

"Mistake. Yes, I see. Odd, isn't it?" said Stears. "The DIA never did like ELBEMAN."

"Step a little more carefully," said Woods. "That was what I told you. Don't fall over it. Imagine a mistake that isn't quite corrected. That gets repeated. Overlooked. Think in small stitches."

"And Mays was a sergeant and all, but he really belonged in Leavenworth. Rough on the family, of course."

"I don't think you can go that far. I am honestly surprised that the KGB did that. There may have been some kind of mistake there as well."

"Such a muddle," said Stears. There was a sharp sound and a pricking in his hand. The pencil, which he had picked up again, had broken and there was a point of blood on his palm. "What about you, Brindle?" he said. "You and Sucher. Do you think he's a joke too? Are we trashing him? Perhaps you could tell me the truth."

"No," said Woods. "I had my doubts about him once, but not for quite a long time. I'd like to meet him. I did not wish him harm, Stears. That is the truth."

"That's good," said Stears. "That's nice. That's really very nice." He assembled his materials into a precise rectangle—order promised some refuge. He stood up. "Good night," he said."I'll be back to draft the first transmission a little after ten. We can do the requisitions then. I'd like to clear August Herter. He may come in handy. Do you mind?"

"You may have what you wish," said Brindle Woods.

"I'll leave for Germany on Monday."

<hr>

On Sunday morning, Wop Stears took the clandestine radio transmission blank from his office safe, smoothed it with his fingers on the desk, and very methodically wrote. The top of the paper was decorated with a format of boxes in heavy ink, like an illuminated manuscript of inauspicious content, and he filled them up with cabalistic markings: ELBEMAN; 109.7mh; 1143; 3AB17; 4—agent, wavelength, time, scrambler code, secrecy classification.

Then he wrote quickly: "Your position has deteriorated badly. Emergency removal forthwith. Can you arrive by your devices at canal port of Finow by midnight of ninth? Asset available, details next. Suggest you hold in place until latest but on full alert for sudden action. Reply next scheduled transmission. Expect emergency transmission at 1548. Keep transmissions shortest. Ends."

The message would be sent the next day, Monday, two hours after Stears had left for Germany. He stood up. He went to the window and sat on the sill. In Grosvenor Square, the fall wind was brisk, the Stars and Stripes were as bright and wind-snapped as on New England hill. The streets were quiet. Sunday is the day on which cities celebrate themselves. It was getting considerably colder.

There existed no asset that could be used to help ELBEMAN to Finow. Langley had instantly vetoed extraordinary methods, thus sparing the Security Council from doing so instead. Thus the only asset was the mate of the barge *Marija Kulska*, due to leave Stettin and any possible contact with the CIA before this message would even be sent. That die would soon be cast.

And otherwise? Nothing. Nothing would serve the geography, the time, and the degree of exposure. The lack of time was it—the time ripped up by the murderous games played with Mays. The blood seeping from the car in the Grunewald trickled all the way to Sucher.

He went back to the desk. He took an envelope marked "Radio Traffic: Top Secret" and put the slip into it. He took the slip out again, wrote at the end, "Good luck," studied it, and scratched it out again with a grimace. He sealed the envelope and wrote on its front only the time of its transmission.

He went back to Brindle Woods's office. There were requisition forms to sign for the vehicle, for the radios, for the medical bags, for the boat. He still needed people, Herter aside, to work them.

He said to Brindle Woods, "We're under way." His voice sounded inanely bright. He looked away from Woods.

———

August Herter met him at the U.S. Air Force base at Greenham Common on Monday in a raw and dismal dawn. He had been brought there in a closed army truck. Stears had also assembled a communications man and a fourth man, balefully athletic and patently Special Forces. His specific task was to handle the boat. They would all fly to another USAF base near Kassel and thence by car to Lauenburg. The base was cold and smelled of kerosene. Warplanes screamed like banshees on the runways. Outside the gate was a filthy meadow covered with old toilet paper, health-food wrappers, and literature from the last demonstration. Stears perceived this with an aching head.

When he had returned from Brindle Woods's office at three in the morning, Marie-Sophie had been in the guest room with the door shut. Her bedside clock, peignoir for the morning, and current novel had all been as though surgically removed from the bedroom.

When he got home the next evening, he had found her wrapped tightly in a dressing gown nursing a cup of consommé in both hands. "There are things in the refrigerator," she said. She used a stiff and lofty French, réfrigérateur instead of frigo. He was laden with the anger and gloom of a ravaged operation, of a repair that he knew already to be squalidly inadequate. His anger rose at her, but he controlled it and put his arm around her.

"Sophe," he said, "don't be like this."

She looked at him a long time and said precisely, "You look like a hangman. I could not help it if I wished." She moved away.

He said in English, "Shit!" He did not take off his coat. He went

261

to the Travellers' Club. He had intended to go for dinner but he did not make it past the bar.

At Greenham Common, August Herter took his arm. He said, "Stears, if possible you look worse than the circumstances." He said it with no humor at all.

"That is not possible," said Stears.

20

General Sucher's driver no longer came. The caretaker had gone from his cottage, gone so abruptly that the cottage door banged unlatched in the wind. The telephone worked but it spoke into echoing caverns, haunted by clicks and whines. The underbrush had been cleared around Major General Sucher. The axman would come soon.

He roamed his empty house, face to face with the cold accounting of his acts. His severance from the world, which had reached this last stage suddenly, indicated a judgment on him. He knew neither what the judgment was nor what evidence it was based on, and he held fear and the suspicion of betrayal inside him like a stomach wound. The Baltic winds began; October started to strip itself of gold and turn to armored gray. He watched the forest from the windows, feeling its daily impoverishment creep from his groin into his soul. His rich provisions from the Party stores—malt Scotch, Prague ham, jars of asparagus and figs, smoked eels and caviar—dwindled slowly. The neighboring farmer had brought eggs and milk until three days ago; perhaps he would come again. The CIA communicated on a complex schedule through the clever radio: short messages in which he found a frightening lack of specificity. He transmitted back only the barest codes to show himself in place. Transmission was dangerous, and he had nothing to say. The CIA, unfed, was possibly deserting him. Communication with his own network, with Klingenberg in Berlin, was impossible. His campaign, prematurely opened, was beyond his reach. He began to realize that he might never know whether he had destroyed himself for nothing.

If he moved, the trap would shut. The Soviet Empire had its claws around him but would prefer not to strike until he was just perceptibly a figure of the past. The balance was delicate; if he ran he would be hunted ruthlessly. He might conceivably get out of the country without the CIA, but almost certainly not. The CIA would not move until it had limited in advance the damage that showing its hand would cause. All sides watched the trap and waited. Only Sucher was inside.

He said as gently as he could, "I know. It is always done that way. You have beaten them so far. Please go on."

She screwed up her forehead like a child preparing to recite. "All right," she said. " 'The book is taken. The eyes are blinded. The false neighbors have been introduced. Two more will leave in a month. The maps are left for your friend to find. On the rest, I am working still. I keep the faith.'

"That's all," she said.

"It's enough," he said.

He stood in a room that had changed as though the beleaguered house had been reprieved and the firelight warmed his risk and labor. He had not failed; had not been failed. *This has not been in vain*, he thought. *Whatever happens now is not quite in vain.* And knowing it spread slowly through him.

"Is it all right?" she said.

"Yes," he said.

"Sepp said that it would please you."

She dropped her eyes sharply and said, "Can you tell me what it's about?"

"No," he said. He looked at her and then, as though the possibility of such a thing had just occurred to him, stepped forward and took her hand. She was startled, and he himself held it awkwardly like an unfamiliar small animal. But he did not drop it and said, "It is yours to know and I will tell you. But not now and not here. Do what you began to do. Tell me about Krel. Tell me how you came here."

Her eyelids pulled at her. Sleep rolled behind her forehead. But, "Yes. Krel," she said.

When she had finished, he said, "Dear God, girl, one should wear you like a rabbit charm."

She said, "Why? Because I am in a trap?" And then, "And why should you believe me? This entire history is about nothing but lies." She had long since finished her bowl, and she put it down gracelessly on the floor and pulled the blankets tighter. Fatherly cheer was not what she wanted, and whatever good news she had brought from Berlin, that was far away and she and the general were here, and stuck. She wished he would go away and let her sleep.

He said, "We do not have much sense of humor. It would be fun to send a girl like you covered with wet grass to my door with a rigmarole like that, so I do not think that we would do it. And I might as well believe you."

She closed her eyes. She did it firmly, so he would see. He went on in the same unhurried voice.

"Yes, you are in a trap, it is true. But sometimes one gets out of them. You seem to be good at it, and I have more powerful friends than you. This is where you ask, 'What friends?' and your thugs come in behind you when I have answered. But I don't think that is going to happen."

If he was trying for a smile, he didn't get one. She really was almost asleep and only nodded. She heard logs thrown on the fire. He said, "You will be as comfortable here as anywhere else in the house. I do not sleep much anymore and I am not going away just yet, but you need not pay more attention to me." He said that gently, and she opened her eyes and smiled.

"Thank you for the milk," she said. "There is still more to tell you."

"The morning," he said. She shut her eyes again. He went away. She thought she heard him pour from a bottle. She was distantly but well aware that her situation had scarcely improved at all, but the fire and the blanket against her cheek were closer. He came back near the fire. Now that he had stopped talking she was glad that he stayed.

He looked down at her. She lay with her bundled hips pushed up against a cushion. Her hair was dirty, and her breathing bubbled a bead of mucus on her reddened nostrils. But one shoulder was partly bare, and he looked at it with joy. He felt the need to speak and heard himself whisper, "It's over now." And then, as though he had not understood until he said it and the words were now set free to chime, "It's over. It's over. It's over."

She had released him. Released him from the hypnotic aloneness that he, the professional, only now clearly recognized as the first act of his interrogation. He was back from the outer chill into the current of trial and life and loss, like her own ramshackle journey. He felt a soldier's careful courage replace metaphysical doom.

And so she had released him from his trap. There was no reason for him now to stay. His powers were ended. The time had come to demand the risk from the CIA—give him an escape route and let him try it. They would have several possibilities by now. None would include a second person, for which the CIA would have no enthusiasm at all. Thank God the girl had information that was probably accurate and, if so, exceedingly important.

And she had released him from himself. He had struck back at his bad masters. He had paid with everything, the privilege, the safety, the power that they had given him, and then added the risk of his life as well. And he had not struck in vain. Insofar as such a sum could be calculated, the nightmare that he had hatched to haunt the secret brain of SSD canceled all the use they had had of him from the beginning. The bargain was broken, the pay returned, the cowardice repaired. He had nothing and was free.

She moved on the sofa, disturbing her wrappings further. He took the felt cover from the fireside table, shook crumbs and stale ashes off, drew it gently over her, and tucked it into the sofa cushions.

He drank slowly. Of late he had drunk until his sense of the world came to a grating stop. Tonight, he achieved a warm diffusion. After the fourth tumbler, he took his glass toward the kitchen. He stopped halfway and came back for Renate's bowl. Her bedcover was smooth and well tucked in. He approved his work. *Funny*, he thought. *Never done that for anyone before.*

═══════

Hans Sucher came downstairs quietly in the dawn but with a sense of purpose he had lacked in weeks. The CIA would communicate in four hours and he with them two hours later. By the end of the day, the preparation of an escape should be under way. There was much else: keep the girl concealed, coach her, hone her morale. And he must be cunning—the CIA needed time.

He stopped on the stairs. He had expected to find the girl drowned in the sleep of youth. Instead, her silhouette was erect in the gray light by the window and she had found her own clothes. They still had the fiery smell of hot dried cloth.

He said curtly from the stairs, "Get back from the window."

"The man by the lake has left," she said, "and I do not think anyone else has come."

She did not turn around, and her voice was not the weary child's with a bowl of milk. He went to the window and stood behind her. There was frost on the grass, and her breath made a pulsating cloud on the windowpane. He saw footprints on the frost between the boathouse and the drive, never near the house. "They watch the road by day," he said. "They will do nothing obvious until they come and get me." He saw her neck stiffen, but she controlled it, and he added, "In which they may very well not succeed. I should think that you are hungry."

"Yes," she said. "Very," but as a statement and not a plea.

"We could make something together. It will be rather barrack-room, but there is plenty to eat."

She cut the Prague ham, holding it fiercely in a firm white hand. She watched him rake the stove, allot wood precisely to its belly, and took pleasure in the smell of new fire. She took the pan of eggs from him. But her composure needed props. She avoided his eye or looked secretly at him, with doubt. He was pleased, though guiltily; another's fear had been his lifelong tool, and he was too well used to it. *Let's find out what she's made of,* he thought.

But food helped her if he didn't. Breakfast was grand. On top of her homely ham and eggs he dumped a jar of beluga and laid by its side a stiff bronze smoked eel. The bread was piled with foie gras or Swiss wild cherry jam. She ate first like a lumberjack and then like a lady and fleetingly like a fascinated little girl.

"Where do you get this stuff?" she said, licking eely fingers.

"I am a Guardian of the State," he said. "I need prodigious strength. So there are special stores to feed me."

She laughed. But not for long. She said abruptly, "Are we trapped here? Both of us? I came here in your service. I have a right to know."

Her voice was steady, but he looked at her giving nothing and said, "You came here for help."

"That too," she said and did not back away.

So he turned to her. "You have seen the situation," he said. "You want to be told that it is better than it seems."

"I was told that you were a very powerful man even if you were now in difficulty." But the thought shot suddenly through her, *Another one who's less than he seems,* and she added with prickly enunciation, "Sepp Klingenberg said that compared to him you were like God."

"That was certainly very kind of Captain Klingenberg," he said, "but he should know that God does not run this country." She didn't smile, and he said, "Sepp Klingenberg knows that there have been changes or he would not have had to send his report by you. He does not know how great the changes have been. But that does not mean that I have nothing. I am in communication, by radio of course, with the American CIA, and they have known for a long time that they would have to bring me out one day. That day has come—in large part through you."

She said as though testing ice with her foot, "The Americans can do almost anything, can't they?"

He saw how fear had worn her down and how hard she bore up against it. So he said, "Oh yes. They have a lot of tricks up their sleeve. They are powerful masters." But that was empty and she saw it and he added, "Sepp Klingenberg could better have said that I was a tough old fox. That would have been the truth."

But she only nodded and quickly said, "And you will tell the Americans about Krel?"

He said, "Yes. But the main thing is to get us out. The radio is quite different from what you think. The transmissions take less than a second. It is all recorded first. I don't talk to them when they talk to me. I transmit to them later. Transmissions close together would be very dangerous. So it is quite cumbersome, and getting us out will be about as much as can be done."

She brushed that off the table with her hand. "I cannot accept that," she said. "We may never get out. I know that very well. I know that you are trying to keep up the spirits of a child. You could do that better by showing me that Krel will be torn apart."

"That man in the café in Berlin," he said, "whom you called a 'foreigner.' Can you not be more precise? Could you not say 'American' perhaps?"

She stumbled from drama to detail and said, "How? I don't know. Of course I have thought. He did not seem quite like the Americans one sees, but I do not know much about them. I do think he was Western. Now I am sure of that. I wish I had been then."

"Indeed," he said. "For someone so bloodthirsty, you did not handle that very well. Maybe the Americans already know all about your Krel. Perhaps you were being told that."

"It did not sound quite that way," she said. "Perhaps he suspected. He was worried. But he truly wanted me to tell him things. I am sure of that. Perhaps he was American." And then, as though she had been diverted from the real issue, "Anyway, Krel had not betrayed me yet. Not that I knew."

This one's odder than she seems, he thought. He said, "Very well, Renate. I will say something of your Krel, but not much. And that is not all because of the radio. You must bring something with you when you cross, and you have only Krel to bring. Krel is your ticket."

She said, "I understand. But it must not happen that he goes free." She nodded sharply as if to cauterize that and then said more thoughtfully, "If they think that you have turned against them, why do they not come for you now? Why do they let you be here?"

He said, "I would have done the same. Time is theirs. They can wait. I was part of them, a claw of their hand. It is not pleasant to rip out a claw. It hurts. It disfigures. Better to let it wither, let a new one grow, then throw the old one into the fire; that's almost painless. There are other things too. They can have very little proof against me. This is a game of nerves. Perhaps I will do something foolish. Best of all, perhaps the Americans will do something foolish, then they can have my guilt and embarrass the Americans too. It's all logical."

"So nothing will happen."

He stroked the grain of the kitchen table with his fingertips and heard the fire settle in the stove. He said, "Unless something changes. Something like this could happen:

"The house is secretly watched at night. A woman comes out of the wood. The guard would like a cigarette but he remembers his orders. He watches the woman cross the grass and enter the traitor's house. A messenger, a contact. Maybe even the CIA. Now they act. They arrive in about the time it takes to heat a pan of milk, but not to drink it. By morning, the interrogation is really only beginning, but already the traitor and the woman are not in good condition. That could always happen."

When she spoke she held his eye. "It was not my idea to come," she said. "I did not even know you existed. And I was never part of them. Never."

"I was answering your question. There was a reason for you to come. You did me a great service." And as he said it, the awareness of bounty spread through him and his dwelling on the harshness of his secret world seemed suddenly graceless, a meanness of spirit drawn from the eternal 3:00 A.M. of the police. He got up and went behind her chair and held her shoulders in his hands.

"You have given me back my life," he said. And then, surprising himself, "It has been gone for longer than you have lived."

She almost responded to him, but her shoulders quickly went sharp and pulled away. "There is still Dr. Krel," she said.

———

Four minutes before the CIA's scheduled transmission of the message that Stears had recorded in London the day before, Hans

Sucher crouched close beside Renate in a narrow closet under the stairs. He felt the slenderness of her body, the firmness of her thighs, and the force of her preoccupation, as though his hands gratefully upon her shoulders had opened her to him in spite of her. He took the radio from behind a peeling oilskin coat.

Before the radio, the closet had been given over to guns, old rain gear, and obsolete langlauf skis tied together with twine. At first, General Sucher had kept the radio in full view on a shelf of books in the hall. Its expensive disguise as a cheap set available at any store was as effective as concealment; concealment would work for a few minutes, and any radio whatsoever, hidden or not, would be taken apart if the house were raided. He had not been able to take his eyes off it in the hall, and his back had crawled whenever he used it. He felt better with it in the closet.

Renate looked at it and said, "That's all?"

"Wait," he said.

He took off the cheap gold grille. Under it, knobs and dials glinted, small but lustrous and smooth. He turned a switch to where *Empfang* had been taped in yellow plastic above the engraved *Receive*. The other position, *Send*, was untaped, the word being the same in German, and the effect was slapdash or even raffish. A red lamp lit. The wavelength was calculated daily somewhat as he had used the book *Colin* as a master code for written messages. He set the machine with care. It was now 11:41. Two minutes to wait. He felt the daily doubt that he had rightly set the machine; he felt resentment, hope, and fear here at the end of his imperious, immaterial lifeline; he smelled the soap in Renate's hair and herself beneath it.

"You will hear nothing," he said. "If they transmit, this light will wink and this spool on the left will move. That is the recording tape. It will be so quick you will hardly see it. Then we play the tape back through the scrambler and hear the message at a normal speed. If you do not have the scrambler, the right scrambler, it does not even sound like voices, just noise. Maybe nothing will come at all."

She nodded. Deep in the closet, something scratched and stirred. She moved her leg quickly, rising her haunch off the floor.

"Only mice," he said. "They are the next tenants." Her thigh still touched him, but did not seek protection.

"Eleven forty-two," he said.

"When do you speak back?" she said.

"In two hours. One thirty-six."

She nodded once, as if ratifying his arrangement.

"How do you do it?"

"I'll show you then."

"Show me now. Suppose sometning happened."

"You turn that to *Send*. It must be the same word in English. You set the wavelength. But first you record the message through the scrambler. Now be quiet."

He held his breath. The green lamp lit. The spool moved. He let out his breath.

He felt too heavy a tension, and he said, "The truth is that most of what they send these days is of very little consequence." But it was still too heavy, and he said, with a shrug he knew was ponderous, "It would not surprise me to hear them singing nursery rhymes. What I shall be sending them later will stir them up quite a bit." His hand went to the upper switch where *Spiel* was taped.

He said, "Let us hear it then." She looked doubtful, and he said, "It is in German. I do not speak English." He picked up a pad and pencil. "One must listen carefully. It does not repeat. It plays once and then it is gone."

The message came and left silence behind it. The lights of the radio went off by themselves.

Renate said quietly, "So they are taking you to the West."

"Yes," he said. The implications swirled upon him, and he said to buy time, "We must think as one, they and I."

They sat in silence before the immensity of the idea's reality: death for sure, perhaps rebirth. Until Renate thought, *It's only another place. I live there.*

She said, "It is frightening when it becomes real. I was very frightened. But it can be done. You have the Americans to help you." He heard a trace of bargaining in her voice as she said, "Two people can go to Finow as easily as one, can't they?"

He saw in his mind the kilometers of road, the patrols, the fences and searchlights around a port, the watch on the wharfs. The vast apparatus of the CIA was throwing him, as his fragile sanctuary caved in, the resources of a boy's game.

"Perhaps," he said. "Perhaps so. Sometimes it is better to move separately. The Americans will have to decide. That will go in our transmission."

She looked at him for a moment not exactly in distrust but as though on the lookout for a warning sign.

"All right," she said.

He governed his face. Nothing was less likely than that the CIA would or even could enlarge a plan that had so obviously been thrown together out of rough planking at the last minute. Still less so to include a companion of such dubious status. She sat beside him, a young woman made for every joy and purpose of life. He wondered what would be the precise and squalid shape of her destruction. His memory held a fat album of the fetid faces of women in the cells. He moved to put his arms around her and stopped, not only because he could not have explained it to her; his memory held another album too: the legion of women, forced, blackmailed, or bought, that his hands had played with. Now that the world of the cells had been invoked again, his own flesh seemed to him contagious of abuse.

He said, "The problem is that things are evidently suddenly moving quite fast against us, and I do not know exactly how. That makes everything more difficult."

"Yes," she said. "I realized that." He heard her voice struggle not to plead. His constraint fell before a surge of comradeship; he stretched out his hand to her and began to say, "You'll be there," and stopped as an alien noise came upon the house.

A rattle, as of something cheap and insecure. A heavy throb. Separate from either, a whine which seemed to move faster. Though he knew it at once it was out of context here, and he listened until it had grown to a clatter sweeping past the roof to frame the words: "A helicopter." Its shadow of flickering axes crossed the front outside.

Renate whispered, "What is it doing?" And then deliberately raised her voice. "Has it come for us?"

He thought and answered slowly, "It is a shadow on the stairs to frighten children."

"Is that an answer to a child?" she said.

"No, I think it is the truth," he said. "It could be looking for someone such as you, but this is wooded country and it would not be an efficient method. Perhaps it is hoping for that, but it is mainly to frighten. Maybe I will rush to the radio and they will have a better chance of intercepting me. Perhaps I will bolt. It is all part of the game I told you of."

But the game's last part. They were putting the dogs in to flush him. They wanted him to bolt, and they would give him a little time, but they would take him whether he bolted or not. So they were shouting at him with their helicopter and shouting loud enough for the CIA to hear. *Kick your rabbit. Make him run.* The CIA had not waited to be told.

274

He said, "However, it is not a good development. They are certainly watching closely now. It will not be so easy to get away."

She did not answer at once, and when she did it was as though from reflection on a long life. "It was not easy to get to Munich," she said. "It was not easy to get back. It was not easy at all to get away from the police and come here. So maybe once more—the last time. But you see why I cannot leave Krel to that chance."

"Why do you hate him so much?" he said. "The world is full of tricks. What was done to you was not extraordinary."

At that she opened her eyes wide, then shrugged. "Not here," she said. "I knew that. I thought there was an end to here. He showed me that there isn't. And I had thought that it was because of people like Krel that there was an end to here and would always be one. Instead he carried it with him like a fly."

He looked at her somberly. "It is good to have a strong need. I have known it to keep men alive. Retribution is not the worst." And more briskly, "One also needs a plan. There is only one thing to do now, and that is to draft a message to the CIA. Let us go back to the living room. Be very careful of the windows from now on. They might have people in the woods. No way to know."

He wrote, rejected, wrote again. Renate sat beside him, looking toward the window in a preoccupation of her own. He saw the rise and fall of her breathing, her hair brush her shoulders as she turned her head. The indifference of the CIA and the power of the forces that would hunt her down seemed to focus upon her. The helicopter circled back, but farther away. This time, its shadow axes chopped the heads of the pines. She raised her head and watched it, but said nothing.

21

Wop Stears sat alone in his hotel bedroom in Lüneburg with the door locked and the chain up. He sat at the dressing table, which aspired to rosewood and was under a mirror with a sycophantic tinge of pink. His two American crewmen, the radio technician and the Special Operations man, had rooms in the hotel. August Herter was in a rival establishment down the street. They had landed at the USAF base at Kassel that morning. All were presumably enjoying "the architectural legacy of notable brick houses in a variety of medieval and Renaissance styles" recommended in the guidebook on Stears's bed. Lüenburg was twenty-five kilometers, combining caution and convenience, from Lauenburg on the Elbe, where General Sucher would conceivably jump off a barge that had brought him through two frontier inspections from a guarded port. Outside in the parking lot was a VW camper containing communications equipment and a concealed inflatable boat.

Stears pushed out of the way his ebony hairbrushes and a card that gave the hours of the dining room. This made room for a briefcase that opened to show a tape player able both to unscramble Sucher's messages and play them at audible speed. He put into it a tape brought to him two minutes earlier by his radioman from the camper in the parking lot. The transmission had been received simultaneously by Brindle Woods in London. Stears picked up a pencil and put a sheet of notepaper on top of a copy of *Time*. He breathed deeply once and said quietly to himself, "Okay." He switched the machine on.

Sucher's voice, denatured by the scrambler, said, "It will be difficult to get to Finow and then difficult to get into the port. I find your plan inadequate and request revision. Can you assist in travel to Finow? Surveillance here has been intensified but is not yet open. Please inform me of what has caused this change."

The voice paused an instant and went on with studied authority. "It is imperative at all events that your evacuation be extended to include a coagent, now present here, who possesses parallel intelligence of great importance to you. Await provision in your next transmission. Ends."

Stears played it once again. He put his hands over his forehead, saw himself doing so in the dressing mirror, and took them away as if finding the gesture theatrical. He noted the duration of transmission, eight tenths of a second. He closed the player into its case and put it into a suitcase, from which he took in turn a smaller case. In this was another device, a scrambler also, this one designed to fit a telephone. Stears looked at it with a mixture of puzzlement and distaste and took it to the bedside table, where he pushed aside a Cartier alarm clock and a French novel and a photograph of Marie-Sophie in a crocodile frame. He put the machine by the telephone, placed the telephone receiver experimentally in its embrace, and took it out again. He dialed Brindle Woods's number. When it answered he said, "Secure, please," put the receiver back in the scrambler, and picked up the scrambler's receiver, which was bulkier.

Through this concatenation of equipment, Brindle Woods spoke and gave judgment. "You have no way to contact your asset on the barge," he said. "Am I correct?"

"Yes," said Stears.

"Then we can give him nothing. You know that, don't you?"

"You could hide a battalion on one of those barges," said Stears.

"The asset has been told to expect one man," said Woods. "If you cannot contact him, you cannot change it. You do not know his arrangements. It might be disaster for all concerned. That's fundamental."

"Yes," said Stears. "I know. I knew."

"What's your plan about this coagent and his intelligence?"

Stears said tonelessly, "Instruct Sucher to send the basics in his next transmission and bring the rest with him. Tell him that we will work on evolving an evacuation for the coagent."

"Have you got one?"

"No. Unless he runs to the frontier and jumps over it."

"That was my conclusion too," said Woods.

━━━━━

General Sucher returned from the closet under the stairs to the fireplace and threw the written message into the flames. The tile with the picture of the bear at bay was cracked, and the tile of the coursing hound was broken at the corner. Both had been so for twenty years. *Old men leave their houses and their work*, he thought. *So do I.* But the policeman quickly pushed the sage aside as Renate strayed closer to the window. A hare was exploring the grass in the shadow of the trees, and the tips of its ears cruised above the melting frost. Sucher reached for Renate's arm. "Get back," he said. "I have warned you."

She sat at the table, shrugged, and said, "I shouldn't think that animal would be out there if there was an army milling around." But she said it resignedly and it was not an argument.

"Probably," he said. "But still. Always caution, still more caution. That way, you survive."

The fire settled and sent a robe of sparks flying up the chimney. Even the gray antlers on the stairs were touched with gold.

"I was thinking while you were writing," Renate said. "This has been your life, hasn't it? I mean, we are sitting in a room, you and I, a nice room, by the fireplace on a frosty day, but really it is not like that at all—it is a terrible place. And the only things that are important to us are things that barely exist. What lie so-and-so has told. What someone else might be made to believe. And that there are spies somewhere with a radio who may let us be able to live or not, that's normal for you too. Like buying food or making love. And there must be thousands like you, armies of you, who spend their time taking the real things out of other people's lives and changing it for these ugly games. Because you weren't always what you are now, were you? You couldn't have been. I just can't believe it. You're a Stasi general. The opposite side of this—that's what your life has been."

She stopped and opened her hands as though her thoughts had unraveled and spilled out of them.

Hans Sucher said, "I have done things I would rather not have done." He said it to the coursing hound.

"I have no right to question you," she said. "Here we are, after all. I was just thinking. I thought of this once in a different way. I have nightmares about my first escape, of course. Once I dreamed that I was lying on the ground, as I really did, and I saw the frontier guard coming closer and heard his footsteps, as I did. But in the dream he knew exactly where I was, and as he got closer he began to change into a huge dog, still with a uniform and a gun but also with wet teeth. And I knew that I could not move and that he would come and tear my throat out. I am frightened of dogs anyway, so that was very bad and I woke up in a terrible state. Then lying there in bed in the dark I thought, That was the most dreadful, immeasurable day of my life and for them it was just work. If they had killed me or found me and sent me to the camps it would have been like a grocer saying at the end of the day, 'I have sold some sugar.' That's what they do. They are willing to live so that other people can't. It almost made me dizzy. And that has been your world."

"But you are here," he said. "You entered this world. You agreed with this Dr. Krel. You have done exactly what you were instructed to do. You have found me. Few agents do as well. I wonder what you will do next, Renate. Maybe you will join the CIA."

She said, "It was made to seem as though I could never again be what I thought I was unless I did this. And yet it has nothing to do with me. It is the opposite of me. Do you understand?"

"A little," he said, the simple soldier.

"No," she said. "It is not that. I was willing to be tricked. I wanted Dr. Krel to notice me. I wanted him to need me for his work. In my heart of hearts I knew that this was what people who were not ordinary did."

"Oh yes," he said. "Now I understand." He smiled at her gently, but it did not reassure her, for she had the idea that there was a secret in it that she did not want to hear. He did not smile long. He said, "This is very wise, very perceptive, very destructive, and rather cowardly. You are a soldier about to fight for your life, whether you like it or not, and these are thoughts for an idle Sunday. Save them for your Dr. Krel—he probably has many like them."

"Then how do we get to Finow?" she said.

"We walk. We leave at night. The very first part, we will have to go across fields and through the woods. The farther we get from here the safer we are. They do not know where we are going. Finow is only twenty kilometers."

"Jesus Christ," she said. "And with the life that you have spent in the police, these are the answers you can give? We sit here and then we try and crawl through the trees? This is what a general does? There is nothing else?"

"This is usually how it ends," he said. "It begins in ministries and it ends in alleys."

"Look at the hare," she said.

The hare had been feeding, moving fitfully but smugly through the grass. Now its movements were as tense as Renate's voice: ears shivering, small head twitching, a step to one side and the other. And then it leaped, the hind legs surging, leaped straight into another dimension and changed from fur and liquid eye to a shadow streaking to the wood.

279

"I think you should stay very still," he said, "though perhaps it is only a fox."

But the house remained in its facsimile of autumnal peace. The last of the frost melted and left the grass shining and the keel of the rowboat black and wet. The frost left unseen cigarette butts soggy by the bow. Crows flew out of the wood. The blatant helicopter rattled by twice more but farther away. The sun swam over the pine walls. Hope and doom snoozed comfortably together.

Hans Sucher and Renate had lunch.

"I do not know what is out there," he finally said, "but we cannot stay here until the end of time. We have to assume there is someone in the wood. I will go to the window rather obviously and then to the kitchen. You will go to the kitchen. Keep low."

Which, with intimations of a children's game, they did.

Belgian white asparagus, pheasant in a jar from Strasbourg, Glenlivet for General Sucher. A little after two o'clock. They were suspended between the CIA's response at 3:14 and the presence in the wood, if any.

Renate drew the pheasant from the jar with an unctuous sucking sound of jelly. She said to the platter she placed it on, "What do we do when we get to Finow?"

"That is what we do not know yet. The CIA said 'port of Finow.' Finow is a canal port and there are barges that go from there to the West. To Hamburg. That is almost certainly what they intend, a barge. It will be necessary to get into the port. We will know more when the CIA sends."

"There's the chicken," said Renate, who had never eaten pheasant.

At the table she was distracted, as though a thought were circling her and she were chasing it away. It caught her as she put down the pheasant thigh and she said quickly, "You have to volunteer to join the Stasis, don't you?"

"Yes," he said. "You volunteer." And then, "It was the end of the war. You have no idea what it was like."

But she was not much impressed and said, "I know about the end of the war. I've seen pictures of it. Everyone was hungry. I suppose a lot of people did things to get food. Was that it?" She spoke as though forgiving a boy's sin.

"No," he said. She looked at him again. He felt a closing trap and said, "I did not choose the world I lived in."

"I didn't exactly choose this one," she said.

He heard the pleading in his voice and the self-possession in hers. *Damn her,* he thought.

He said acidly, "Let me tell you a little childhood story."

For a long time Hans Sucher had thought only of the wagon ribs sticking into his back and the wind pushing ice between his gloves and his face, but the wind fell for a moment and he opened his hands and tried to speak to Uhlmeier beside him. He touched his arm. Uhlmeier turned to him and began to say something. He had gotten terribly thin, and his uniform, always too big, because Wehrmacht uniforms were not made for sixteen-year-old boys, now looked like a casual wrapping. But suddenly Uhlmeier rose up and flew across the wagon and hung over the other side of it like a chicken in a butcher's shop. Hans Sucher gaped at him. Then he heard the sergeant say, "Partisans! Shit!" All the men had their backs to the forest and the wind, and they turned around awkwardly, getting their rifles caught, but Hans still looked at Uhlmeier, whose uniform was turning red on the back. He saw the sergeant beat the horse, but they did not go any faster. This failure of the sergeant frightened him, for he relied on anyone who was a veteran and eighteen. He heard the truck speed up behind.

He turned himself. He got his rifle up and began to fire at the Polish forest. There was no one there that he could see. The horse stopped and fell down. It screamed once. A long bloody bone was sticking through its shoulder. Behind this captured farm wagon, a surviving unit of the Fourth Panzer Army, were open fields. Hans heard the machine gun fire from the truck and saw the truck close up. The sergeant jumped off the box and ran toward it.

Hans Sucher had been told to expect attack. The partisans were active. There was just the brain's whining, forsaken protest that after three weeks of beating by the Red Army guns, three weeks of grinding retreat from the bridgehead of Magnuszew, in its first full hour of quiet and apparent safety, the company should be harrowed by invisible civilians. Private Sucher, who was sixteen, tried to be a soldier and drive this from his brain.

The sergeant came back. He said, "Out of the wagon! Get down behind the horse!" The men jumped out. No one got hit. The wind had picked up again and the snow was blowing. The horse smelled of blood and latrines. The sergeant got down with them and said, "We're going in to take them out. Now, while the snow's blowing. Stay in line with me. There are some bushes between here and them. When you get to them, take cover, and when the wind drops shoot at anything you see. They won't expect us there and we'll have the vehicles behind us. The machine gun will cover us. Let's go."

There was snow in his boots, and it got into his coat. There was a bush at his chin. He heard the wind drop. Trees took shape. The machine gun on the truck ripped the air over their heads, and he felt it hammer his skull. Under the forest trees were bundles working rifles. One rolled over and then twisted back and forth. He fired at the one to its left. The snow came in again, but just as it did a bullet whacked through his bush and released a scent of myrtle. He heard the sergeant's voice: "We got two. Make the next count."

The wind stopped. A pretty Christmas forest at once sprang up with snowflakes falling onto branches on the ground. A holly tree stood in a clearing of its own; its top leaned a little to one side as though it were getting ready to disrobe and throw all its berries away into the wood. The partisans' rifle bolts were bright against their cheeks.

The machine gun did not fire. Over the cracking of the rifles its silence was huge. Hans heard a sobbing behind him and thought it was Lehring. The sergeant looked behind him to the truck. There were splotches in the snow beneath the forest trees, as though they were bleeding at the root, but there were still about a dozen partisans, and suddenly the head of the boy two places from him blew up and spattered all over the snow.

The sergeant said, "If it whites out, break for the truck." The sergeant sounded scared. Muller, beside Hans Sucher, made a loud, surprised sound.

The wind sighed. The forest blurred. Muller's breath whistled in and out, unbelievably loud, like an accordion. Sucher looked at him, but his face was turned away.

The wind increased and the tree trunks vanished. The sergeant shouted, "Back!"

Muller did not even try to rise. Sucher put his hand on him to see what was the matter, then his arm went around Muller and he began to pull him, though Muller complained like a hurt small cat. His foot slipped against the myrtle. He began to struggle back, pulling Muller with him. He saw the truck solidify in front of him and knew the wind was dropping. He knew that he was visible and would be shot down, but Muller's face was by his and Muller was trying to say something, but his breathing was louder than his voice. Sucher squeezed his arm and panted, "It doesn't matter,

Willi," not knowing what he meant. Privates Muller and Sucher, who had shared a piece of chocolate on their sixteenth birthdays, who had told each other about their schools, who had assured each other that it was a great thing to be taken into General Manstein's Panzers, who had showed each other photographs of their dogs at home, effected their last retreat against Polish partisans. Hans Sucher knew that he would die.

He stumbled against the truck. He turned to fire. The forest was quite clear and the only Poles were dead.

The sergeant was saying, "What happened to the fucking gun?"

"It jammed again," said the gunner.

Muller was whistling very quietly and not steadily.

"So they ran away," said the sergeant. "They killed eight of us and then they ran away."

"They'll be waiting somewhere," said the gunner.

The sergeant briefly looked at Sucher and Muller. "Good going," he said to Sucher. "Good man."

General Sucher said passionately, "It could have ended there. No reason not. It could just as well have ended like that."

"What?" said Renate. "What do you mean? What happened then?"

He had pulled himself from the story before it entered the dream country of death and darkness, but he had almost forgotten whom he was speaking to.

Renate said again, "I don't understand. Did your friend live?"

He thought hard and said, "This is what you must understand. There was something that controlled us in those days that was completely without reason. It was irresistible and utterly irresponsible. Things became their opposites. I had not meant to risk my life for my friend. If I had meant to, God knows what would have happened. You must try to understand that."

He saw that she was looking at him like a good young dog given a completely stupid order. He recollected that she had asked a question.

"No," he said. "Willi Muller died within an hour."

"That's very sad," she said.

"It was in the aftermath of such conditions," he said grandly and emptily, "that I made the bad decision to join the Staatssicherheitsdienst."

"Oh," she said.

Wop Stears sat in a new blue VW camper with German export plates on the heath outside Lüneburg. He drove. Beside him was the radioman, whose name was Lee McCoy. McCoy said, "You should stop soon, sir. Three minutes to transmission." He was a long-faced boy from Tennessee whose throat bore lush cornelian meadows of razor rash.

For transmission, the heath had no technical advantage over a hotel parking lot, but there existed a remote possibility of signal interception, and a van transmitting from random points made tracking impossible. The van, with the inflatable boat invisible within it, would also be the command post for the last stage of the operation.

Stears said, "I was looking for a stopping place. An official view. It looks more natural."

All around them was a plain of gray heather to which, close up, a few smoky blooms still precariously hung. In the far distance, the Hamburg-Hanover Autobahn shot sudden arrows of chrome or glass. Between, small clouds of birches floated on the heather.

"Gotta stay clear of high-tension wires and tall buildings," said McCoy.

"I think we can do that," said Stears. McCoy's adenoidal twang suggested that several of each might appear on the heath, for spite. He saw that the roadside here formed a slight rise with a bowl of myrtle in the hollow beyond. He stopped the car.

And sat, his hands cradling the wheel. McCoy opened the briefcase on his lap and plugged the radio inside into the dash. Ground and antenna. McCoy looked at his watch again and turned a switch. Stears had no picture of Sucher's house or of where the radio might be, but he saw it in the closet of an unused bedroom with an iron bedstead and a pitcher on a stand, and he had seen Sucher's shadow many times climb the stairs toward it.

McCoy said, "Ten seconds."

Stears thought suddenly, *He said once he wanted to hear my voice. So here it is at last.*

McCoy said, "Sending."

He touched a button. A green lamp lit. It lasted, numbers on a little screen confirmed, 1.05 seconds.

Which was what it took to say, "No alternative plan is possible. Only evacuation possibility consists of the barge *Marija Kulska*, port of Finow, night of ninth between oh oh three oh and oh four three oh hours. Wharf B. Asset is barge crewman in whom full confidence. You will be introduced into cargo hold. You must remain through first border check at Wittenberge and second check at Horst before final crossing. After second check, make visual recognition of Western port of Lauenburg, two kilometers after frontier. Expect yellow boat in vicinity starboard side of barge. You must leave the barge surreptitiously to protect asset. Jump in.

"Port of Finow perimeter security is light. Suggest area close to pipe storage, easily recognized. You will have to reconnoiter security details. Asset has night watch and will expect you on the wharf.

"Further communication with asset is impossible and inclusion of second party is impossible and forbidden. Send this asset's essential information in your confirming transmission. Will evolve later evacuation. Good luck. Ends."

"Okay," said McCoy. "That's it."

22

In the closet under the stairs, Sucher felt Renate's body stiffen and smelled the quick return of his old servant, fear. Hans Sucher shut off the radio in silence. But she walked ahead of him back to the hall with the stiff movements of a woman betrayed or shamed, and her first words to him were, "I've been a fool, haven't I? You expected this. You knew it all along."

He forced himself to meet her eye and said, "Expected, yes. Not knew. A barge, you see, it would have been physically quite possible at least for both of us. I hoped."

"I see," she said. And the fire, compulsively aping domesticity, crackled cheerily at the prospect of the afternoon.

She said, "And this thing that they will try and make a plan for me, it means nothing. Am I right?"

"In the ordinary way it does not mean much. Not in these circumstances."

"Should I try to leave now or wait for dark? There seems no reason to stay here. I can take some food. A map, perhaps." Her voice began in sarcasm and ended in quavering reality.

"Stop," he said. "You have better chances than that."

"How?"

"Because I shall certainly not obey them."

"You will take me anyway?"

"Not that. I would be leading you to disaster, where I may be going anyway myself. They can be made to care much more about you."

"How will that be?"

He said, "I will send them nothing about the intelligence you have except so much as will make them know that they have a traitor in their confidence. There is nothing that frightens spies so much. To get the rest, they must get you. I will say that you have not entirely given me your confidence and that I cannot tell them what you know for I do not know it. You are clever, you see, not a foolish girl who gives everything away. I said before that Krel would be your ticket. The only danger is that they will discount this—believe you know nothing of importance—but I do not think they will take that chance. I would not, especially if it is true that they already have suspicions."

She looked at him as though counting the pieces in a puzzle. "And then what?" she said.

"And then they try very hard to bring you out. They have plenty of tricks up their sleeves—it is a question of when they use them." He saw her face darken and went on, "I make them seem worse than they are. Intelligence is trade, it is profit and loss. If they spend what they have on things that are worthless they go bankrupt. Sometimes lives become part of the trade. They do not want this. They are on the right side, after all. They are not bad men."

She sat in silence. Her shoulders were hunched around her chest as though precariously holding warmth, although the room was not cold. Then she said, " 'I would be leading you into disaster, where I may be going anyway myself.' You said that."

"Yes. My case has been extremely odd. I will not say that the Americans have been without fault in it, but still there are reasons why . . ."

"You are a general of the SSD and they can do almost nothing. Please stop treating me as a child. You see why I cannot do this. You would see if you had any opinion of me."

"No," he said, realizing as he said it that he did.

"You will do as you say. Perhaps the Americans really will put together some plan. It will not work, I shall be caught or I shall die, and Dr. Krel will go free. Perhaps he will even hear something about it and laugh to himself. No—smile. He does not laugh. Then I have utterly lost, do you see? I am a little piece of dirt that does not even hurt the machine as it grinds it up. My escape, Munich, it all means nothing. They have won, as they always do. You should understand that if anyone does. Think what it would be to live my life in the camps knowing that I could have destroyed one of them and did not do it."

He knew that he should speak wisely, and not one word came into his head.

"Give me that much respect," she said. "From you it is worth something. I have not told you all that Sepp Klingenberg said about you. I know what you have done and what you are."

He said quietly, for a cold iron band had fastened around his chest, "It is some hours before we reply. I will do as you say then if you insist that I should. But do not promise yourself now that you will make me do it. If you were to change your mind it would not only be most certainly excusable, it might be right. It is harder than you think to choose between principles and life. Principles look finer, you see, but they are not always what they seem, and life is. Don't forget that the Americans may not fail you. You may have your principles and your safety as well. But I will do as you say. And from now on you are my comrade."

"Thank you," she said.

Half an hour before transmission, and before he needed absolutely to record the tape, he sat softly down beside her, without speaking. He realized with shock that she would not have been in his house a whole day until the middle of the coming night.

The time for her decision came. He opened his mouth to ask her but at that moment she looked behind him to the wall. His eye followed hers and saw that the setting sun had begun its dance across the pine. She sat forward, her lips just open. The sun's fire entered the courses of the grain, followed the vertiginous whorls, turned from copper to flame to molten iron upon the different shadings of the wood. She watched it in silence and with complete attention as though the messages from the clever radio had been superseded by a cantata played beyond the planets. The light narrowed, ending upon a single plank of pine, a finish of formal intensity. It went out. The room was dim. The light of the fire was dusty and scant.

He said, with great hesitation, "It is seven minutes before I must transmit. I must record it now, you know."

"Yes," she said. "I knew that. Send everything about Krel. I have been thinking about it. I can dictate it to you. It will be everything they need to know and it will not be very long."

When Sucher spoke, the words he intended had to do with a threadbare and probably worthless reassurance about the charity of CIA. Instead he said, "I told you it was not for food. It was for company. I was seeking people among whom I did not have to be ashamed." He stopped, appalled.

But he had intruded his stale drama on Renate's live one, and her first reaction was almost snappish. "Ashamed of what?" she said.

Which left him on the cliff face he had slipped onto. "You are very lucky," he said.

She looked at him in disbelief. "The Stasi was the only place where I could breathe," he said. "You cannot understand that, and that is why you are lucky."

"I do not understand at all," she said, and her voice was cautious as to a big dog that has begun to growl strangely.

He felt the prison they were in and the rising torrent of corruption that, once out of his mouth, would lie between them. He said, "You have seen the pictures of the end of the war. You said everyone was hungry. There were much worse pictures. Have you seen those too?"

She looked at him a long time. Then she said, "Oh, my God! You were not SS? Not Belsen? You were not one of those?"

"No," he said. "Not exactly. Not quite."

"Then what? How 'not exactly?' You cannot be 'not exactly' that."

He drew breath to answer, but he looked at her and the answer stuck in his throat. He said wisely and weightily, "I mean there is collective guilt, you see. All of us in Germany who did not actively resist the fascist lie share the guilt even of the SS. I accuse myself of that. That is why I say that you are lucky. You have never participated in the guilt of the state that replaced the fascists. I, on the other hand . . ." The safe words rolled across his tongue like soft warm clouds, but in his memory the Poles, who had moldered there of late, had become almost covered with earth, now came back in woodcut clarity. He felt physically sick, and his tongue writhed between two masters.

"I on the other hand," he said, "I on the other hand murdered women and their children in a cage. I shot them where they could not move and they lay tangled on each other in their blood. I did it because I preferred to do that than admit that I was a scared boy running from bigger boys. It seemed better to be a demon."

Renate said quietly and not as a question. "That is what came next."

"Yes," he said, "that is what came next."

Now the company fitted easily into one light truck. They pushed the wagon off the road, shot the horse, and put chains around it to drag it after them. The company of Manstein's Fourth Panzer Army moved on through Poland. Willi Muller died in the truck.

They bivouacked in a clearing. Other detachments straggled in by truck, by horse—one company had harnessed a cow to a howitzer—a few with tanks, on foot. The division was theoretically regrouping. Konev's pursuing Red Army forces now outnumbered it eleven to one. The Red Army was a day behind. This was between Leszno and Poznan.

Later the company sat around its fire. The wood was cold and green, but turning it released a yellow flame and a smell of horse fat. Young soldiers sprawled around it. Hans Sucher remembered quite suddenly how they had looked eight months ago, as bright as peeled twigs, and how a group of gypsies looked that he had seen being taken from one camp to another, blackened marionettes with broken joints. His friends now looked like the gypsies, and this made him feel more frightened than the rifles had.

Someone said, "They shouldn't have surprised us."

The sergeant said, "That will teach you to keep a lookout. You were thinking about the cold, not about the forest." And then, "That was my job too. Mine most of all." The sergeant said this like a schoolboy owning up to a theft. It was clear that he hardly any longer knew what to do.

One called Hausser, wrapped in a blanket with his arms clasped around his knees, said, "It doesn't matter anyway." And then paused, because it was a long time since they had eaten meat, and thought was abstract and slow. "It's over now. Fuck, we lost eight today against nothing. Against Polish farmers. So three more days and that's it. Then we're dead. Fuck, there's no Germany to go back to anyway."

The sergeant said, "That's cowards' talk. A real man can do anything." Someone snickered, and the sergeant blushed. But he didn't give up, and his voice got firmer. "You think we didn't fight in the old days? You think we didn't fight outnumbered? We didn't even count the Russians once. We didn't have to. A wolf doesn't count the hens. We were men in those days, and they weren't." But he had been too emphatic for his own conviction, and he finished uncertainly. "It's not being taken by surprise because you face the wood in spite of the cold and don't think about it. You stay warm from your guts, your balls. Then they don't kill you and you win. And if they do kill you it doesn't matter. You still win. That's a German. We had them here once."

They liked the sergeant, and no one said anything. Then someone said, "There should be coffee. After meat you want coffee." Then one by one they went to sleep. Some slept sitting or curled up like dogs, quivering with long impenetrable dreams. As hunger and cold and fear tightened, sleep opened and bloomed.

Hans Sucher did not sleep that night.

With the men still, the bivouac looked like a woodcut of faces pared to the last reserve, the rifles stacked in delicate attention, the outstretched finger of a shadowed tank, the dismembered horse like an icebound monster with hoop ribs. From time to time he threw a branch on the fire.

His terror and despair had much to do with the fight by the

wood, with Muller's death, and his friends' words and faces. But it had taken food and this evening's quiet—for once they were not under bombardment—to sharpen it. For a starved and exhausted boy with two months' training, he was a good soldier. His sergeant had praised him before.

He had never before this night feared annihilation, more terrible in German, the void of the word **Vernichtung**, benothingness, the abyss. He looked at it like a child before the ghost-wolf under the bed. He had understood death and wounds in a military context, to do with heroism, Germany, duty. All this, he knew tonight, was in a different time and planet. Here, where he and his friends were being tortured and would die, was soundless basement where they would fall and rot without purpose, without memory, without hope. He had once seen a soldier, not hurt, not under heavy fire, begin to scream in horror, more loudly than he had known a man could, without pause for breath, until a corporal clubbed him with a rifle butt. In the still forest, among the flickering fires, in the embrace of an army and alone as if he were floating in the sea, Hans Sucher screamed to himself.

It got colder. The wind had blown the clouds away and died itself. The stars came out in swathes just above the forest trees.

And so it was a lovely dawn. The army's rising had less of military blazon than of the stirring of a timid, dingy species of untidy nesting habits and stiff limbs. Squirrels ran out from the trees and feinted toward the gun caissons. Under grime and stubble the faces of the men as they turned over ashes, urinated, wiped their mouths with snow, looked as though they had been given as a present something like real cake—once perfectly familiar and now as strange as myrrh.

For it was quiet. There were no guns. The monstrous Red Army, whose pursuit with snarls and roars and thudding footfall had been the background to every act and word, must have curled up like a sleepy badger. Far away a single Junkers trailing gossamer commented on the purity of the sky. The army itself seemed to have no special plans, as though the lack of close pursuit had removed its purpose. Platoons and companies settled to small domestic chores.

A small, neat truck drove in from the wood bearing only an SS officer and driver, both in jet black. It circulated among the units, settling here and there and giving rise to small, faint altercations, like a wandering fly. It came to Sucher's unit. In the back of the truck there were now about eight men collected from various units. The SS major, whose perfect uniform distressingly set off wretched teeth and unpleasant breath, sought Sucher's captain. Hans Sucher heard nothing until his captain angrily said, "The Wehrmacht does not do that. Why do you not have your own unit do this?"

The major said, "I am my unit here. I need volunteers. I outrank you, and SS takes precedence over Wehrmacht."

Sucher's captain, whose uniform was as ruinous as his men's but who had that morning scraped his boots, came forward and spoke stiffly.

"This officer of SS requires men to execute a group of captured partisans. I order no man to participate in such an action. I am unable to stand in the way of volunteers."

Hans Sucher felt a powerful spring release inside him, something between sexual climax and fear. He stepped forward. He was almost beyond reason, but it distressed him that the SS major said, "There will be rewards."

His captain looked at him and stiffened.

They did not speak in the truck or meet each other's eyes. Hans Sucher had no curiosity about the companions of his quest. They drove away from the bivouac along a narrow way. Perhaps it was a hunting avenue in other days, for there were signs that they were in some province of a great estate. Oak trees turned whorled faces from them as they passed. A stoat slipped into the brush. They drove in the crisp tire tracks the truck had made in coming.

He rode with the fire of license crackling within him. It had come to him in a bolt; the major—whose collar beneath him he now saw to be greasy and pointed with specks of blood from erupted skin—had been only the necessary messenger: the brave dog in the farmyard is betrayed in the end; not so the wolf on the hill.

There was one corporal in the truck, a boy with the cocky, blackguardly look of a Hamburg pimp. The SS major placed him in command.

A structure came into sight in a square clearing, a cement hut with large, stout pens on one side. The surrounding concrete was sewage-brown. The snow in the clearing was mashed by trucks and feet. The pens were probably intended for hounds, conceivably for hogs. At the edge of the clearing stood a group of frowsy troops, armed only with clubs and shovels, in unrecognizable uniforms. They looked vaguely oriental. The truck stopped.

The major pointed to the troops with his thumb.

292

"Hiwis," he said, meaning cooperative Russian prisoners. "They'll help you clean up." He made a joke. "Don't shoot them." He pointed to the pens.

"You don't have many men," he said. "Best do it right where they are."

They got down from the truck.

The pens were packed. A steam of breath hung over them. Since a man could not stand straight there, it was difficult to see individuals; the pens could have been filled with bundles of shifting, murmurous cloth.

"Fucking murdering assholes," said one of the men mechanically.

They each picked up a dozen ammunition clips. They were heavy.

The corporal spaced his men in a line, twenty meters from the pens.

"Load!" he ordered. Once Sucher had drunk beer at a fair and then gone on the roller coaster. He had the same feeling now of the bottom dropping away and his gorge rising and electricity racing through his blood. He pushed home the magazine and felt the butt for reassurance.

The contents of the pen recoiled and moaned. He let go his grasp on the permitted and leaped to the unknown. His breath checked. He saw a body standing straight, its arms around another, its head well below the top of the pen; a blond child. He saw a woman's hair. He closed his mouth. His hand lowered the rifle. He looked for the major. The major was gone. The driver sat in the truck alone.

The corporal fired, a single shot. There was a scream and a movement inside the pen like the lip of an oyster. The pimp looked down the line, grinned, and deliberately picked his nose. The others raised their rifles.

Hans Sucher fired.

The pens held too much motion. They worked the bolts. The rifles kicked and roared. The bars reverberated with glancing shots. And still things flopped and shrieked inside. They stopped firing when the magazines gave out. Before they went into the pens, they went back to the truck.

He saw a blond young female face wipe blood from its eyes and look at him and flinch. He dared himself to shoot into its mouth, rejoiced that he could, was sick, and shot again.

The pens were designed to be hosed down. There was a barred corridor, a man's height, running the length of the hut and giving onto the pens. The soldiers stood there while the Hiwis worked bent double among the bodies. When a body moved under the frigid water, a soldier shot it or the Hiwis helped with their clubs.

A young man lay up against the bars with one arm around a woman, blond and long-waisted. She was dead. The other arm was around a child, only the back of whose head could be seen. Neither the Hiwis nor the hose had gotten to him yet, but Hans Sucher could clearly see that he was breathing. He was almost at his feet. Hans Sucher aimed his rifle. The young man looked him fully in the face. It was impossible to be sure, in the slaughterhouse, whether he was already dying or whether he himself, his family butchered, was not yet hit at all. He looked at Sucher in neither fear nor pain but as though to settle an imperative question and take the answer with him. His eyes were gray, there was a fleck of gold in the iris and a wire of blood in the white. They pulled on Sucher like a rope. He had a picture of himself falling to his knees by the face and begging from it. He never remembered when he shot the face or how many times he struck it with his rifle butt to beat whatever it thought away.

The Hiwis were ordered to pull the bodies out and stack them in a heap. The soldiers stood apart, rubbing their collarbones. Even the corporal looked at no one, and nothing was said.

The bodies did not achieve anonymity. It became evident that many were well dressed. Gold-rimmed glasses on a black silk cord, a carefully knotted tie, a woman's shoe becoming to its ankle appeared at random among tissue and blood.

There was a problem. The ground was frozen solid. The Hiwis demonstrated this by bouncing their shovels off it. The corporal told men to get cans from the truck and siphon gasoline. The activity was welcome but the driver stopped them before long. There was enough to make the heap smell strongly, but since all was wet it failed to light on the first thrown match. Even the clothes burned sulkily. The hair burned off the scalps.

"Let's get out of here," someone said.

They walked quickly back to the truck, leaving crimson tracks behind them where they walked.

The tide inside him slowed, receded, and dropped him freezing on a grim beach. It came to him that he had no idea how to get back to the world that he had lived in.

The men in his company treated him gently, as though he had been in a plague and lost family there, but they came nowhere near him, especially with their eyes. A rumor of some accuracy was spreading as to the facts of the case.

In the night he realized that a way back existed and was physically near to hand. He had to walk down the snowy avenue to the pens. If a way back existed it was to look on what he had done.

It could be done now. The winter night was light enough to see the balls of mistletoe in trees. He almost rose. But the danger of being shot by sentry, as deserter or as spy, was great. And he feared the pens by moonlight. He resolved to go at dawn.

But at first dawn the guns began again and by full light had the range. Trees split and deadly splinters flew. It was clear that Konev's tanks were perilously close. The division gathered up its belongings and staggered on.

Two weeks later, trapped between Konev's army and the Neisse River, the command disintegrated.

"Dear God," Renate said.

"So I was a criminal. To the world and to myself—but first to myself, for I was a criminal to myself before I even did it, when the thought came to me, before I even volunteered, and that was why I did it."

She sat absolutely still except that one finger ranged around her upper lip, as though it had lost something there.

He went on, "But also a criminal to the world, of course. They began to find people like me."

He was silent a long time. She raised an eye very slowly to his face, but when he spoke again it was not in response to it.

"That would be the simple view." He was speaking briskly now. "I was a criminal and a criminal must confess or hide, and where better to hide safely than in the secret police. And it is true. Stalin's service, and later the service he left us with a German name, was the only place where I could be quite safe. That is why I stayed in the East. I was trapped, Renate. Trapped."

There was a plea in that and she reacted to it instinctively, raising her head, but it was a baited trap and he met it with a hard grin.

"And the simple view is shit. I wanted to be near people like myself, or worse if possible. I covered myself in the Stasi like a dog on a coat with his master's smell. Do you know what we are like in the Stasi, close up, day in day out? We are made wrong, Renate. We have odd smiles we cannot control. Our hands twitch behind our backs. Our heads are put not quite properly on our shoulders. We're only impressive if you're terrified. I studied all of that. I looked for it. I made myself see nothing else. I looked for the worst

295

part of their natures. In the beginning, when there was not much that Germans could do, I worked for the Russian police as a pimp."

Now she sat looking at the table with one hand in front of her face and gave no sign that she heard him at all.

"I wanted to show myself something. I wanted to show that I need not be sorry for my crime, that I could repeat it over and over and only profit by it. So I did not only the worst things that the Stasi does but I did them for the Russians, and I began to rise very fast. So it worked. I was disgusting beyond speech, and I was first safe, then comfortable, then powerful and even honored. You understand, the nature of things changed a little. In the beginning I beat people, crushed their hands in doors, broke their backs with table legs, all those things, but there are only so many ways you can do that—and anyway I began to rise above it. And I discovered I could do much worse. It is really nothing to beat somebody or even kill him. You do not often change him. Sometimes you make him only more purely what he is, and if you kill him he is free of you forever. It is a much greater thing to corrupt, for then you are in that person until he dies. I learned to do that too. I tricked a woman who was genuinely good into betraying innocent people to me with a lie, knowing quite well what she was doing, for the sake of her husband's release. But I knew the husband was already dead. That was actually as far as I got. I could go no further. It was the limit of my strength."

Renate got up abruptly and stood by the fire. "That is enough," she said. "Tell me just this. What you are now, is it real or just another farce? I am used to almost anything by now, so you may as well tell me. There is nothing I can do."

"It is real," he said. "I do not ask you to believe it."

"I know it is real. I just do not know why. On the other hand, I don't suppose it matters."

———

When the lake had turned to pewter and the woods were dark, Hans Sucher quietly said, "The man by the lake will be arriving soon."

Renate said, "Should we draw the curtains then? At least we could move around."

"You are quite right, but I have not been doing so and it is wiser not to make a change."

"Of course," she said.

The fire to be fed, the lights to be lit, the kitchen stove to be kept alight—the ordinary performed its exorcism. He felt emptied, and his thoughts moved simply and one by one. A particular thought recurred, a little clearer every time; it had a glow about it, but it was too daunting to face quite straight.

He said, "This university, how much longer will you be there?"

"Less than two years. I had been there more than one."

"And then?"

"I am not sure what I would have done. Not a lawyer, I think, even though I enjoyed those lectures, Dr. Krel and all. I was not that ambitious in that sort of way. You may laugh, but I had thought of working for a travel agent. It would not have been exciting, of course, but quite agreeable. Or a flower shop, but that does not pay very much and I should have wanted a car."

"Do not use the subjunctive mood," he said. "Use the future. It must be nice when life moves at its own pace. I went from school to the army to the eastern front, and you know the rest—so I have very little sense of that. Will you marry someone?"

"I imagine I would have. You know perfectly well why I use the subjunctive. I use it because it will not happen."

"Don't be so sure," he said. The thought came back, clearer still, and he could face it all but for looking it in the eye. "I said I was a tough old fox. The Soviets have been trying to destroy me in one way or another since 1941 and I am still here. I can be a good teacher. Wait here a minute."

She saw him go to the closet under the stairs. He came back bearing, in full light, the totemic radio.

"It is anyway quite stupid to keep it there now," he said. He sat down and placed it between them.

"First you will learn to use this," he said. "you will learn it very well."

"I do not see what good it will do," she said.

"It does not matter what you see. Just learn. First the elements. First the scrambler control." He pointed to a switch. "Essential that it is on. Else you are yelling from the rooftops."

"Of course," she said. "That switch. Up. I see."

"This switches on the tape recorder so that you can record your message. Note that it is on the other side of the scrambler. Your voice is already gibberish when it is recorded. Even if they came right then, you see . . ."

"Yes," she said. "I do. How thoughtful."

But the issue is not simple, he thought. *She is an empty bottle now that she has spilled her Krel. She is not worth the trouble to carry—that the CIA will also think that does not make it untrue.*

"The tape erases automatically. Now here is the part where you may most easily go wrong—the wavelength. I shall show you all this many times and you must pay attention each time. There are four digits to set."

And for the Russians to know that I am alive and with the Americans crowns all that I have done. It was worth the risk of many mens' lives, not just my own, and this girl does not mean more than any of them.

"But how do you know which digits to set?" she said.

"That's a different matter. I'll come to it. Learn the machine first."

Sentimentality is a cheap coin. It pays no debt.

"Turn the numbers with the ball of your thumb," he said. "You will feel little clicks. Tune it now one oh seven point six."

"All right," she said. Her thumb moved tentatively over the digits. "One oh seven point what?"

"You are only told once," he said. "This time you have failed."

As I will probably somewhat fail if I do this. Nations and people are in different baskets. Like apples and oranges. You cannot trade between them. You can only choose. But I might fail anyway.

"But it was one oh seven point six," he said. "Do it anyway. Good. Now your message is recorded and your wavelength is set. Now you turn this to *Send*. Do it. Good. It is easier for you than for me—you have small fingers. Now you would turn the circuits on. Here it is, the red switch goes down—but do not do it now. You must do that at least a few seconds before the time. Now you are ready. To send the message is the easiest thing of all. This red button. Take off the safety catch with the tip of your finger—do not do it—and press the button down. That is all. The machine erases its tape and shuts off by itself."

And would it work anyway? Would they believe this machine could fail in just that way at just this time? Maybe. They may be like dogs who have been on point too long—they will jump when a leaf moves. I wish I knew who had my case, who's hunting me.

"It is a funny feeling," said Renate. "To push this button under my finger and speak to such people Over There. It is like having one arm through the bars of a cage. It is exciting, but I do not like it." She remembered suddenly that she was talking to a monster and thought suddenly, *Why don't I fear him? I don't even distrust him. How very odd.*

"Now do it all again," he said, "without my prompting you. Before you finish, you will do it in the dark. Change the frequency to one oh eight point four."

I do not have to choose now, he thought.

"And after that you have to learn how to receive," he said, "and after that you learn the wavelengths."

———

For a little while, she had slept. She awoke with the general's hand on her shoulder and the fire warm on her face. They were real and sufficient for a moment, then cold stretched inside her like a snake. His eyes were on hers; they had a way of changing from pure blue surface to the veiled depth of light in a forest, and she knew that he saw the stirring of her fear.

There was a glass on top of the mantel and she recognized the smell, like horses' feed, of the Scotch whisky. But his voice was steady, as always. He said gently, "I let you sleep here last night, but I am not sure that it is wise. The watch may tighten. Even by the firelight they could see you from outside if they came very close. I will put the light out and you should quietly come upstairs. There is a room for you. They cannot see in those windows."

She took his hand. It was strong and dry, and her fingers drew in its warmth. She said, "I will do whatever you say. But I made my own decision. I do not hope for very much. To creep from one side of a trap to another . . . that does not seem of very much use."

"It is of use," he said. She knew as she heard it that it was meant in some concrete way and that he did not want her yet to know this. She did not have the strength to drag it from him.

"All right," she said. And then, "What time is it?"

"Not late. Not quite ten. You were tired, tired all the way through."

Her thoughts came back to particulars. She frowned. "We were to send to the Americans. At eight fifty-eight."

"We did," he said. "I did it while you slept."

And if you had not been asleep, he thought, *would I have done this? At the next transmission? Before tomorrow night? I think not. The last strategic evaluation of General Sucher of the SSD was based on the way a girl's chin lay on her breast. Well, now it cannot be taken back.*

"And this time I could have done it," she said.

"Yes," he said. "You have learned quite well. Are you ready to go upstairs? I will start to turn the lights out."

"Yes," she said.

———

Stears dined early. By eight-fifteen he was back in his hotel in Lüneburg. There was more than half an hour before Sucher's reply would come, but he felt obscurely that he owed it a vigil. He hung on to the field control's last moral claim in a disintegrating operation: that his ruthlessness in condemning Sucher's companion after offering Sucher a nearly negligible chance was not the smug dispassion of a safe man but a surgeon's calm guiding of the scalpel in a desperate case.

It was an attractive metaphor, for it left quite to one side the fact that his operation had become a buffoonish farce from the moment he had cheated Krel into assisting a CIA operation. He thought back again to Lüderbach, to his tense, merry self-congratulation. Using Krel was not itself the crime; Krel's moral pose had for a long time been too contorted to take seriously. The crime was in having not merely signed Duplicity on for a necessary job but in taking pleasure in her company, being happy to go off with her for a jolly weekend. The weekend had ended soaked in Ursula Hecht's blood by the frontier fence.

Memories like this no doubt dictated the mature control's ultimate source of self-esteem. The ultimate source was drink. He had drunk little at dinner. He resisted now the bottle of German brandy on the dressing table. He could reserve it for later with confidence. It had the unreserved endorsement of the most senior professionals, both CIA and KGB.

It was true that Krel himself had ended up destroyed. The wires between the CIA and the BND were buzzing, Bonn was having the vapors, compromises were being oiled with soap. Krel might not fall very hard, but he would fall. That at least was sure; though Krel, unless he had friends one did not know about, was still in ignorance. Stears hung to it like the last thread of grace.

He set the room in order. He made space for the unscrambler. He moved Marie-Sophie's crocodile frame away from the telephone.

Lee McCoy arrived from the camper at nine o'clock. McCoy pushed the cassette into Stears's hand and mumbled, "Got some major problems, sir, you ask me. Something weird, you betta brace yourself."

Stears said, "What?"

McCoy looked away. His razor rash rippled on his throat. "Could be the scrambler fucked up. Could be your man's gone nuts."

Brindle Woods said on the telephone from London, "The first question is this—was there a scrambler malfunction or is he off his head?"

"No," said Stears.

"No," said Brindle Woods. He went on, "I have the advantage of you there. I talked to technical branch. If the scrambler breaks it stays broken. It doesn't go on and off."

"I wonder if he knows that," said Stears.

"I wonder if the Comrades do," said Woods. "Tricky if they do. Did you get the message straight? Gave you problems, I should think."

"It did," said Stears. "But I think I have it straight. In the end."

Problems, or at first blank refusal to believe. First, Sucher's message was insanely long, more than five seconds sending time— he had seen that at once. Time for a scanner to lock on, to hold it for half the transmission. It had carried conviction at first, nonetheless, the ragbag of an agent's last transmission turning now and then into a barely disguised plea for consideration.

But less than halfway through, Stears's senses tightened. For Sucher's message was not just inordinately long; it was patently padded. Sucher, in his extremity, was prosing on like the club bore. Things settled long before, things that could never now be taken up, on and on it rolled.

Sucher was advertising.

So Giovanni Stears, subtle control, concluded at once that Sucher had left the radio somewhere behind him on timeset and was drawing all his enemies onto a false trail. Dangerous, a little obvious, but maybe the best he could do.

And then it went berserk.

The voice changed to an electronic gibber. Stears stopped the tape, reversed it, checked his controls. The same. And then with pure horror and a prayer that he was wrong, rewound again and switched off his own unscrambler.

And Sucher's natural voice came on. Halfway through his peroration, Sucher's scrambler had failed and, unawares, he was speaking good plain German to all who would hear.

And then Stears's brain skidded again. For Sucher, having rambled on awhile, made references to his evacuation suggestive of the real plan, but garbled beyond recognition. He confirmed contact at Oderberg, on the same canal but sixty kilometers east of Finow and twenty-six hours later. He confirmed Hamburg. "Canal," and "barge" were never mentioned but the places and the timespans made this unnecessary.

Sucher was drawing the hunt onto a path almost his own, but not quite.

And then just in the middle of a phrase of this the scrambler cut on again. Perhaps he had kicked it. And in a little while more, the message ended.

To which Brindle Woods now said, "But why, goddamm it, why? Now he's told them he's bolting."

"They'd guess that," said Stears. "He's told them something they already know. That's good method."

"Too close. They'll jump the house."

"Maybe not," said Stears. "They'll want him with his contact. I think he's done the opposite. He's steered them away from the house. That's the one thing he's done."

"And they'll get his fucking contact too. He's put them on the same canal."

"Yes," said Stears. "The same canal. He has."

"Then, Stears, would you tell me what he's doing?"

"He's drawing off the hounds," said Stears.

"He's running a handicap? He's taking bets? He's drawing them off to ten yards behind his own tail."

"He's drawing them off someone else," said Stears. "Someone in his own house. The man I just told to drop dead. The man who gave us Krel."

———

Hans Sucher lay in bed. He had long ago turned off the lamp, but the dresser and the chair were plain in outline and the windowsill was bright. The night sounds came in: the clear bark of a fox, a cow as though abruptly kicked awake, owls. In fact the room seemed transparent to him; he was sure that human eyes were on it from the wood, and after his last message all the eyes of the state seemed to burn through the walls.

His plan was based on one premise and two aims: that they would much rather catch him in the act of conspired escape than drag him from his house or pick him up alone on the road; that Renate, who could now talk to the West and whose presence here was not suspected, should have the best chance of escape and that he should still have some.

He hoped, and could not know, that she was a sound sleeper. That she would wake and find him gone and find his instructions on the stairs. The instructions were the last poor legacy of his cunning and his power.

A smile covered his face as though it had dropped from the ceiling. It surprised him by its sweetness. That legacy made Renate his heir.

He hoped he had handled it as well as could be. His sleeve had been almost empty; the scrambler trick had been the best he could pull from it, probably. And it gave Renate a further vague claim on the CIA, his heir again—he hoped they would see it. He should probably not have turned it back on again. He did not really know how they worked.

Which was somehow appropriate. For his last decision in the secret world had been to turn his back on all its claims and put even the possibility of one real life in their place.

She stood in his door. She wore as a nightdress a gardening smock she had found in the closet downstairs and that made his heart cry out for such an illusion of domesticity. She must have seen something of it, for she crossed quickly and sat down on his bed.

"I was frightened," she said.

"Yes," he said.

She took both his hands on the bed cover and held them firmly and still. Her hands were dry and cool. She said nothing for quite a while and then, "It's not sensible for us each to be alone and frightened."

"No," he said. "Far better like this."

"Are those dogs in the wood?" she said.

"No. Foxes. It's a different sound."

She nodded. Although fragile, she seemed tall above him. He watched with neither disguise nor suggestion her breasts rise and fall under the smock.

She said, "I have been thinking about you."

She stopped, and he could think of no answer he dared make, so he lay there looking up at her.

"I don't understand it very well. The things you have told me are like having a terrible nightmare about someone that you actually know. It's impossible, but you can never quite wipe the nightmare off."

He looked away, but she tightened her hands on his and leaned a little over him so that he felt the faintest warmth from her body.

"That's not all of it," she said. "The nightmare's over. I know that. I believe in Sepp Klingenberg and what you are doing. And I have been with you for a day myself and I know it is the nightmare that was false, not what you are now. I suppose that what you are doing is truly heroic, though I do not like that word. But I suddenly saw that you were doing it with no friends, no hope, no future, nothing. I really don't understand what that could be like. Maybe like trying to do something tremendous if you were starving. And then I thought of this: the first time I dared to try to escape I did it because I knew they were robbing me of my life and finally they would take it all. They didn't succeed, and now I know they can't, whatever happens. But I think they did steal yours. Almost the whole of it."

He put her hands to his face for comfort, hiding his eyes, for to his astonishment and shame he was close to tears. Finally he felt her get up and pull her hands away. He looked then, dreading to see her leave the room, but instead she was beside his bed, her hands on the bottom of the smock, which, with that motion abrupt and unadorned that women attain and men never do, she pulled over her head and dropped on the floor. He looked at her still, now almost unable to move, surrounded by the young scent of her body, her breasts above him, her thighs by his head, until she put her hand on the bedcover and he remembered himself and helped her lift it. She snuggled rather agilely in and then lay softly against him.

"This is better, too," she said.

He was shy with her at first. He still felt his own contamination between them like a blade. But she melted it slowly. Her fear, his fear, even helped, both of them warming so gradually to simple comfort that by the time passion caught they might almost have been old friends. So, held back by no sense of infamy, pushed on by no anger, and received by generosity and youth, he was overwhelmed by a vigor of desire he did not even remember, and when he entered her it was with amazed joy. He heard her gasp and begin to moan and choke it back, and he placed his hand softly over her mouth as her moment came. He let it lie there longer, and she kissed it gently and wetly, several times.

He murmured to her breast, which fitted beneath his chin, "I told you about something else that you have given me back my life. Now I say it even more."

And felt her stomach move in swallowed laughter as she squeezed him and said, "But this was so much nicer than bicycling from Berlin."

It turned out that she had the tact to sleep like a log. She did not stir when he moved his legs or change her breathing when he crept out of bed. He even dared kiss her half-shown breast and only took the precaution of taking his boots to the next room.

He went downstairs. His instructions were on the top step. He picked them up, took the pencil from his pocket, and wrote at the end of them, "Pray God we meet in the West." He wrote in a large hand. The pencil was blunt and the wall he wrote against was rough.

23

General Sucher opened the kitchen door in the dark. On this side of the house, the forest began forty meters away. It was black and breathed fitfully in the wind. The inside of the house was darker than the night, and his eyes were already keen. He stood a moment, quietly shut the door, and relinquished the latch, his house, his rank, and the charade of waiting. Now the traitor ran for the state to hunt.

He entered the forest. Thickets and trees were black, but the pine-needle floor glowed in the dark. His legs remembered an infantryman's crouching lope, though they would not sustain it. The going was not difficult. His burdens settled in his pockets: bread, cheese, and sausage; map and compass; knife by the shin; Walther and six oily rounds. Supporting them, an aging body that drew strength from loins drained with the forgotten sweetness and unreserve of youth.

He headed toward his first bluff. By this far side of the estate ran a lane that connected to others that became in the end a farm road to Zeithen. That way was Finow. If they believed his objective, Oderberg, they would not look that way, even later. They could, of course, surround the whole estate and every nearby road with ease—but they wanted him at the last moment with his American escape. He was still, after all, a fallen chief selling this and that to the CIA, not the center of the comprehensive web they would discover in time. They might try to trail him, but not closely enough to head him off. Their craft was his too, and they knew it.

The fence took form in front of him, irregular and overgrown. There was no gate close by here. He stood under it, testing the ivy with his hand; he had to be far away by daybreak, but the fear of noise in the invisible lane stopped him. As did doubt of his body, not tested like this for years. He put his foot carefully in a notch of root, pulled himself up, winced at rheumatism and the noise—but rose. He climbed again. The top of the fence dropped suddenly below his chin and revealed the lane glowing innocently to itself under the night. He pulled himself awkwardly over the top; his legs, as he dropped down, flinched at the shock but did not fail. He landed, swayed against the fence, pulled himself upright, and set off down the dark margin of the lane.

It was 4:05 now. He did not plan to walk to Finow, though twenty kilometers in eighteen hours could be done. By first light he would be well beyond any neighbors who might recognize him. In the country there would be early trucks and wagons. His shooting coat of stained and baggy loden, his scratched boots, could be a farm laborer's. His objective, by foot, was Zeithen.

He feared precisely the outside of the fence—for their aim now would be to keep help out, and for that purpose they might have guards anywhere. He walked on the far side of it, bracken brushing his ankles. At first, the forest spread over from the estate; he could duck into it at need. But then it receded and there were fields. The line of the woods was safer—he could creep around its edge—but it doubled the distance. He did not have time. He crossed the lane and walked close by the fence he feared. Better come on them face to face than be silhouetted against the night.

And so he would have been. He reached the corner of his estate. Straight ahead lay his road; to the left was the unpaved lane with the gate over which Renate, and the radio, had come. He looked down it, saw no movement, took two steps, and froze. At the limit of sight, among the soft outlines of trees and ivy, was a rectangular squat shape. A truck. It was between him and the gate. He lay down. He heard a scrape of heel on metal. On top of the truck shape was another, rounder and darker, like a head, and he puzzled it out at last: a sleeping searchlight, trained on the gate. They would be looking that way, then. Very slowly, smelling the fallen leaves, he crawled across the lane.

Now his estate was behind him. He would not see it again. Renate still lay there in the warmth of his bed and the destitute protection he had left behind. He had lost seven minutes. He stood up and began to walk.

Lights sprang on in farmhouses. Vague rooflines woke up with clangs of buckets and rumbling barn doors. His hands were in his pockets and his breath steamed, but his body was warm with walking. Just when the hedges and the trees were black cutouts against a charcoal sky, a tractor with a wagon came down a farm drive and two boys swung milk churns onto a platform by the road. Hans Sucher greeted them but did not raise his head. Their eyes followed him. *This is dangerous*, he thought. *Too early to be walking*. He had not expected to be seen until after dawn. Having spied on his country for forty years, he knew very little worth knowing about it.

When there was enough light to show the furrows of plowed fields and the colors of berries in the hedges, he heard a motor behind him. It did not catch up quickly, but as he passed an audience of young farm horses, snoofing at him from the fence, it came into sight, a muddy truck with one fallen fender and a rattling cargo of churns. It caught up and passed him, then stopped. Hans Sucher walked briskly and braced his lies. The truck door opened and a red face with blond stubble and a blue wool cap looked back at him, chin tilted in hospitality.

General Sucher, the weary rustic, said, "Thanks, I will." He crossed to the other side and pulled on the door.

The driver said, "Give the dog a shove." And then, "Where are you going?"

"Eberswalde," said Hans Sucher.

"That's okay then. It's where I stop."

The cab smelled of oil, silage, and sleeping dog, but mostly the last. The dog was black with pointed ears and gray muzzle. It stuck its soft rump into Hans Sucher's side.

"You're not from here," said the driver. "Willi Stumpf." He stuck out his hand. Sucher shook it and it went back to the gearshift.

"Günther Brel," said Hans Sucher. "No, I'm not."

The driver looked at him sideways. It was a face with strong chin, well-founded nose, and open blue eyes. Sucher said nothing. The driver turned away with the beginning of a shrug.

"Riding beats walking," he said.

A German peasant, thought Hans Sucher, *the bone and blood of our country, the pretext of the socialist state, and all he cares about is that I'm not police.*

"You can help with the churns," said Stumpf.

They stopped by the farm drives. The milk platforms were built at about the height of the truck bed, and hoisting on the cans was satisfying work. At the third stop, among the cans, Hans Sucher lit a cigarette. Stumpf knocked it from his hand.

In the cab, Stumpf said, "Not a farmer, are you?"

"No," said Sucher. "Work on engines."

Stumpf nodded briskly. "Gets into the milk," he said. He did not quite look at Sucher. "Never said you were a farmer, did you?"

They drove through Serwest. The villages were awake now, and Stumpf raised his hand to acquaintances in the street. They drove past the tavern, in this country the first door to open and the last to close. Some men were coming out after an opening schnapps. Sucher remembered this place. Once he had been driven home in his big black Russian Chaika by this way instead of the main road (a whim, a roadblock, a flood—he did not remember). They passed this tavern on a summer evening when men were standing sociably outside. He had caught a look as he passed of anger and contempt. It spread quickly on alcohol through the little crowd, and he had seen lips speak, as plain as hearing them, the word *Bonze*—bigshot, boss.

"Straight to Eberswalde now," said Stumpf. "No more lifting. That's the depot for Berlin."

The dog had waked up. It sat up on the seat, taking in the landmarks of the daily run, and leaned against Sucher or its master on the bends. The gearshift rattled like someone inexpertly humming a tune. Sucher's seat, though crushed and with the stuffing showing, was comfortable. The flat country, seen from the height of the truck, turned past as on a platter—spavined barns, muddy fields, disheveled hedges, a meager, real, and various country beneath the banal visions of the State. Sandwiched between the mongrel and the milk, he felt a part of it as though he had suddenly fallen out of the sky, out of all connection with the State, neither its jaws nor its prey.

"'How far do you go every day?" he said. "Where do you start from?"

"Start at Gramsow, then through Greiffenberg and Angermünde. Serwest's the last stop, then take it into Eberswalde. Then back the same way with the empty churns. Twenty-seven stops, if you want to know. Doing it ten years."

General Sucher very nearly said, "And every day you've driven past my gate," but he said, "Not such a bad job," instead.

"Not so bad," said Stumpf.

Eberswalde showed ahead, a market town bullied by loutish concrete imitations of a city. It was just past nine in the morning. A brisk night walk and a cozy ride had brought him from his beleaguered house three-quarters of the way to Finow. From Eberswalde to Finow there was a bus that he could take with reasonable safety—he would be traveling in a direction totally different from any that they had reason to suspect. He would be there before midday. Fourteen hours to study the perimeter of the port. Renate, he supposed, would be awake, would have read his message, would be coming to what terms with it she could. She had a chance, he still thought that. As for himself, he entertained for a second the thought that he might simply walk out of his house, ride to a barge, and sail away like a citizen of some other country enjoying a trip.

Now the truck clattered through the streets. A shiny police car—two Vopos in field gray and glossy black belts—passed them. There had been none between his watched gate and here, and he felt the simplicity of the morning spoiled. But they turned off the main street onto one of small brick warehouses still labeled with the fading ghosts of family business names in Gothic script toward some kind of market hall or depot. The street was cobbled, and they drove in a metallic hysteria of chirrups and shrieks toward a long building outside of which were hillocks of turnips, potatoes dumped in piles, and milk churns drawn up in lines like a child's goblin army. The dog, preparing to disembark, trod on Sucher's stomach. The truck drove up to a loading bay and stopped.

"I don't know what you do now," said Stumpf, "but I have breakfast."

There was a building nearby that seemed to be a café of sorts, and he pointed to it.

Sucher, wavering a second between fugitive and homecomer, said, "All right." It was at least the last place they would look for him.

In the early morning, Renate lay with her eyes still closed knowing that the jagged lump of fear inside her had stopped cutting her for the first time in weeks and that its absence was a new kind of life. She knew that she could turn around into the arms of someone strong and wise who had reason to cherish her. She knew that her body lay smooth and warm and that none of this would altogether survive her fully waking up. She became aware that the bed behind her was empty and wondered how the general would appear. That she still called him "the general" made her smile.

Half an hour later she woke up properly and hard with a thought already made inside her. She sat up and listened to the house, which gave no sound. She got out of bed and saw that the general had taken his clothes. She was out into the corridor before she recollected that it was cold and went back and picked up the smock from the floor on the general's side of the bed. From halfway down the corridor she saw the glint from the living-room fire, and warm relief washed through her. He was reading, he was out for a walk. At the top of the stairs she found the message.

310

She read only the first lines then, but it was enough to tell her that the fire was without warmth, that the house was matchwood, and that she had no help anywhere.

Inside the café at Eberswalde, there was a line of agricultural backs at a counter, a smell of bitter coffee and sausage rolls. Sucher pushed into the crowd beside Stumpf, against shoulders stained by the flanks of cattle, chapped faces, fierce black pipes. He was served.

And, munching, he listened to the talk around: talk of weather and swine, balky tractors, luck at the lottery, ailing wives. He looked at the faces. The steamy warmth after his sleepless night woke stirrings of Renate's warmth, a fading sweetness in his loins, and he found himself drawn into a current of common life, into a sheltering and seductive communion.

One face looked at his. He saw it as it changed—first a plain round unshaven face, eyes occupied with the sausage the jaws chewed. The eyes passed vacantly over Sucher. Then they came back. And then they froze. And then they watched, first in puzzlement, then in bafflement. Then—and now all Sucher's warmth was ripped away—in fear.

He knew the man. A neighbor, a laborer; he had come to the estate to fill up foxes' earths. The general, strolling in the evening, had bestowed words upon him. And now the man edged away, looking in every direction but Sucher's.

Sucher swallowed his roll. He started to move himself, then forced himself to shake hands with Stumpf, whose eyes he could not meet. He pushed from the counter and was free of the crowd before he knew where he was going. The plowman had moved first and was now passing through the door, eyes down and head rigidly in front. Hans Sucher stopped.

For he had moved to kill. Not with a plan. Not even with a possibility, for he could hardly cut the man's throat in a busy street. But he had moved with the first instinct of the Stasi, to destroy anything in its way. He was afraid now. The man had recognized him without a doubt. The man himself was afraid of the unimaginable consequences of taking the wrong action in response: losing the chance to report a fallen Sucher, of reporting an unfallen Sucher and being guilty of meddling with the State. The fear would pull at him all day, and which way he would turn neither he nor Sucher knew.

Sucher watched from inside the door as the man crossed the

street toward the depot. He saw him half look over his shoulder and then think better of it. When the man had entered the dimness beyond the loading door, Sucher walked quickly out and set off in a direction different from his goal, which was the bus stop. He felt himself still watched, but was not sure. The morning's blessing was gone. Even as prey he awoke only treachery and fear.

So in the bus, he sat in chilly isolation and found it hard not to flinch when a man whose black leather jacket vaguely resembled the Stasi style took the seat beside him.

It was less than ten kilometers. The road ran beside the canal. The canal was on the other side of the bus, but he could see it in pieces between heads and shoulders. The banks were low; the water was gray and the reflections of telephone poles bridged it with length to spare. It looked an unlikely place to hide. It looked mean and cold. A little beyond Eberswalde, they overtook a barge. The cabin was shut up tight, the smokestack streamed bitter fumes, and the low black hull shouldered its way without grace. It was coming from the east, going toward Finow. He looked for the name but a pair of shoulders blocked it.

At 11:43 the bus reached Finow.

He was not expected at the barge for fourteen hours. He had never been in this place, but it was easy to see that it was a modest town, smaller than Eberswalde, and that the canal port took up much of the northern half of it. The central square, and the bus stop, were on slightly higher ground, and he could see the general line of the port perimeter, the warehouses, and the cranes from where he was. It was not a grandiose complex. He could walk the perimeter in fifteen minutes.

So he had time: too much time altogether. He had not expected to remain in Finow so long; he would have waited in Eberswalde had he not been driven from it.

He took stock. He could not haunt the perimeter for fourteen hours, though he could usefully take a first look at it now. Having arrived so early, he had a choice that the CIA had apparently not thought of: it might possibly be better to enter the port during working hours and skulk there until the night. He would have to think about that.

If his hunters had been taken in by his trick, they expected him at Oderberg, sixty kilometers east on the same canal, a day after his barge should have sailed from here. When they did not find him there, they would first rush his house. Renate should have left about midnight tonight, long before. When they found no one there, there would be a general alert. They might concentrate on the canal, and then he would be quickly found. But his hunters were almost his children, and he thought he knew them well; having discovered that the transmission was a trick, they would think the canal was too. A general of the SSD, in league with the CIA, might have, should have, more than one way of leaving.

But if General Sucher was known to have been seen at Eberswalde, then both ends of the trick unraveled, Oderberg and the canal. He would be hunted down in hours. The eyes of the man at Eberswalde bored into his back. Sucher was full of sudden self-contempt for his sentimental thirst for comradeship that morning. His own first thought had been to destroy, had he been able; the man's would have been to betray, if he dared. Repentance sat badly on a limping wolf.

So he walked the perimeter. It was across a wide, gritty thoroughfare, given over to trucks and rail crossings. The near side was warehouses and workshops very thinly interspersed with arid taverns and unsociable shops. All this faced a barbed-wire fence set between rust-stained concrete stanchions, behind which were dumpy cranes, sheds, strips of leaden canal, and guard towers. Only three of the last, and only one seemed manned. The CIA was right—security was mild. Only the eyes from that one tower, and the eyes of the policemen at the crossings, and the eyes of the policemen at the three controlled gates, watched in turn the solitary rustic loiter down an industrial boulevard in muddy boots. He turned back into the town.

The CIA was right again—to get in by day could not be done. Barbed wire was barbed wire and guard towers were guard towers, and what the schedule of manning would be by night, he could not know. But he had seen no insulators—the fence was not electrified. And what he had watched closely was the angle of the searchlights.

Renate sat in the living room of the house crumpled up with her arms wrapped around her. The fire reduced itself to embers. She recollected that there was a line in Sucher's message: "Do not let the fire go out—there must be smoke from the chimney:" *I can do that much, I suppose,* she thought. Also she was getting cold. She put on a number of logs, stacking them carefully. In due course the fire began to roar. This result of her skills made her feel better, and she made some coffee in the kitchen. Then she went back for Sucher's message.

She studied its details all morning. She became haunted by the fear of a face looking in through the window. It distracted her. She went back up to the bed, which was also warm, and vaguely comforting, and where no one could see in. She slipped down from time to time to fuel the fire and get some foie gras and pears glacé for lunch. She was punctilious about the fire.

The message was largely details of the radio wavelengths, times, and call signs. It was complicated, but it was like the general's lessons. She felt that she was making progress.

Corporal Werner Detz was technically a border trooper, but he had never served on the Wall or the frontier, he had not fired his machine carbine since boot camp, and, walking now under the pale electric illumination of a passageway between two sheds in the almost deserted port of Finow, mayhem was the last thing on his mind.

Finow was a port and thus in the Border Troops' domain; it was also in the middle of the country and served only barges that were rigorously searched before they crossed real borders. Werner Detz and his two colleagues, both off-duty, were stationed here to assert the Border Troops' prerogatives. The troopers' uniform and weapons discouraged pilferage; all arrests by the Border Troops are tried by the secret court system of the SSD.

The port was quiet at night. Barges might arrive but were not unloaded until morning, though they might be fueled at night if they had through cargoes. When Werner Detz reported for night duty, he picked up a list of the activity he should expect. A Western barge, eastbound for Prague, would put in for fuel tonight near 2300. A little later, a big Polish rig, the *Marija Kulska*, was due, westbound. Her bulk coal cargo went through to Hamburg, but she had deck cargo for Berlin, so she would tie up for the night and unload at dawn. It was her regular run, and Werner knew her well. Her first mate had taught Werner the trick of soaking breadballs in stale beer as bait for carp. The canal was full of carp, and Werner was a fisherman. He looked forward to having a word with the mate.

He liked night duty. He liked the throb of a barge a long way off, then its lights on the water, then the engine ripping into reverse and the thumps of rope and heel on the wharf. He liked to stroll out of the shadow, speak a moment with the crew, then disappear again with an official look. He liked to look at the marks on crates and speculate on what was inside. He was a dreamy youth, and the fact, of which he was quite aware, that he had this posting because he was considered substandard for his service did not bother him. Nor did the emptiness here at night. The dock gates were locked, one guard tower at least was manned, there was a Vopo posted at the fueling dock. Werner had come upon only one night trespasser in two years, and that had not been frightening. Even with only Werner Detz to wear it, the uniform of the Border Troops cast a shade.

But he was not apathetic, and when he heard a noise he could not quite place, like an untuned cello plucked a few times without rhythm, he stopped and listened. It didn't come again, but he changed course and walked slowly in its direction. This led toward the perimeter, to a dusky section where the fence was not well lit. There was no one around. He put his hand on a strand of the wire to show himself that he was thorough. Then he turned around.

Now he faced a high pile of industrial pipe stacked against a warehouse wall. He was end on to the pipes, behind which the light was better. He walked toward the light, though he was not alarmed. He saw the light through the pipes.

The pipes winked.

It took him a heartbeat to register, but there it was. Something had flickered behind the row of pipes. Something had moved.

He walked faster. He walked reluctantly. Three months ago, he had arrested a man he knew for theft and trespass, guaranteeing ten years' hard labor, and he had not enjoyed it. As he walked past the far corner of the pipes, he flinched.

At nothing. The shed wall stretched another twenty meters. The light was good, and there was nothing there. And nothing in the alley. Werner noticed that the palms of his hands were damp and disapproved of this, for he did not think himself a coward.

There was a noise inside the shed. A single clank, then a short, gritty noise like something rolling.

He squared his shoulders and moved. Far off, he heard a mellow throb. It occurred to him that this sneak thief was preventing him from watching the Western barge for Prague come in, and he was actually irritated.

The shed had no door, and the alley light spilled into the front of it. It was full of high steel storage racks going at right angles from a central corridor. Farther back they were dark. He felt for his flashlight. He had to choose between that and the rifle, because the Kalashnikov, arm of the Border Troops and excellent for the Berlin

Wall or a Thuringian heath, was awkward here. Anyway, he knew the flashlight better.

But he did not turn it on at once. He let his eyes adapt to the existing light, which was also an excuse to go no farther in. He began to walk down one of the racks. This was methodical, and besides, he could see almost the whole rack and there was no one there.

There was something gray behind a crate. He turned toward it. It moved. Werner Detz dropped the flashlight and, for the first time in two years, unslung the Kalashnikov and fumbled for the safety catch. The gray moved out from the crate and became a head, the head of a man, the head of a man with outstretched arms, the head of a man with a knife. Werner Detz waved the rifle, but a hand closed around his mouth and the knife followed it. He had just a moment to see the face. The last thing his brain registered, signaling a reprieve that did not come, was that it had an expression of horror and regret.

There was blood, though not too much, and Sucher looked to wipe it off the steel rack before it soaked into the concrete. He tore open the boy's jacket and used one side as a cloth, then buttoned it up again. It left a smear, and he found the kitchen towel he had wrapped around his sandwiches, used it, and stuffed it into the boy's neck, where, becoming wet and crimson at the edges, it hid the wound. All this time he held in his mind the insignia of the Border Troops on the shoulders—a real, a ruthless, a designing enemy—but the milky face and the down on lip and chin made the excuse crueler than the act.

So he sat beside the body. He heard no sound of further pursuit or any other reason to delay taking the body farther into the shed and hiding it as best he could, but still he sat there. He could see the screwdriver he had knocked onto the floor, bringing the boy to look.

At length he put his arms under the shoulders and the knees, felt the weight, and contrived, not easily, to lift the body. He left the rifle for a second trip. He could risk no noise and had no idea how much this shed would be used tomorrow. Straining at the weight, panting, he shuffled down the corridor into the gloom. He had a vision of himself so, gray and bent, bearing the body of murdered youth; it was not a pleasant one, and he pushed it from his mind. He doubted he could hide the body well enough to defeat an hour's search after the boy was missed. This would be almost pointless, and, putting it down on the floor to rest, he almost declined to pick it up again.

But there were shapes farther back which turned out to be tarpaulins, not in use and folded, and indications that this end was not much visited. He fumbled with a stack and pulled it in half, spreading out an oilcloth. He maneuvered the body in flat on its face. He went back for the rifle and put it in too. He folded the tarpaulin over, lifted the others on top, and draped the last one over all. There was a faint bulge in it, the policeman and the pea, but it was good enough.

He looked at his watch. It was near midnight, and he could hear that a barge had come in. But his instructions had been to seek contact after midnight. This might even be a different barge. He would have to wait. He sat down on the other side of the aisle from the stacked tarpaulins. Twenty-four hours ago, Renate had fallen asleep in his arms. In the meantime, he seemed to have come back to his old bloody service, though to an unpropitious branch of it. His own chances now seemed to him minimal and of doubtful importance. He felt for the thought of Renate as for balm, but the squat bale of butchery in front of him drove it off.

He thought, *No more killing.* He thought it as a wish, then at once understood it as a promise. He thought again, *It's killing that binds you to them.* He felt less deeply buried.

At two o'clock he got up. Time for contact. He thought of this quite abstractly—directions for someone named Hans Sucher which he was obliged to enact. In consequence, he behaved with consummate care, the layout of the port clear in his brain, the risk quite impersonal, so that he handled his movements as coldly as a hand of poker.

And thus arrived. Moving silently and slowly where he knew he could not be seen, moving officiously and swiftly and in the dimmest light where he was perhaps in the line of the guard tower's view, he was either unnoticed or unseen. He did not have far to go. Rounding a corner onto the wharf, hearing suddenly a quiet lap of water, he was actually startled to see all of a sudden, as though materialized from the brain of the CIA, the barge itself, huge and solid with anchor, smokestack, and paint and tied to the bollard by a piece of rope. He looked at the bow and there, like a gift wrapping, was really the promised name, *Marija Kulska.*

It made him conscious again of risk. This part of the wharf seemed deserted. At the end of the quay a second barge was docked under lights, had men around her, and, from a faint smell of oil, was taking on fuel. He pressed into the shadow. Still no one. He looked at the barge. He had not known they were so big. He faced a low, blunt bow with heavy winches inboard and a sheet-metal forecabin perched like an afterthought. Beyond that, she stretched back a long dark length of cold steel hatches flanked by capstans and cleats with a huddle of cargo in the center. Almost at the waterline, an outside deck a shoe's length wide gave the only uncluttered communication between bow and stern. There were handholds, but *Marija Kulska* was all business—though a light in the high wheelhouse aft seemed to shine through a colored curtain, she was a creature of engine and steel and by no means of pretty paintwork and fragrant smoke.

Also, she seemed deserted, and he wondered what to do.

He walked very slowly down the wharf in the shadow of a receiving shed, watching carefully for doors or windows that might give onto tenanted offices. So far so good. He could see the wheelhouse more clearly now, two low stories with the bridge on top, companionways on either side. Behind that seemed to be more capstans and winches and chains. Still no one, which was good and bad. The canal was smooth and still, and the *Marija Kulska* looked as though cemented to it.

He crept farther and raised his eyes to the bridge again and stopped. A figure stood there. It looked at him directly. It was blond and still and had appeared without the slightest noise. It wore a muffler. Hans Sucher looked back. He stepped into the light and out again. He held himself between hope and fear. He saw the figure nod.

He did not know what to do. He saw a hand materialize on the bridge rail and gesture slightly, drawing him closer, motioning him aside. He followed. Near the wheelhouse, a passage led through the receiving shed. The hand, which fluorescent light made frail as paper, motioned him to the mouth of it. He waited.

And almost jumped out of his skin as his spectral guide turned abruptly with a clang of boots on metal and sang out something in Polish, apparently to his feet. There was a dim reply from far inside. His man left the bridge, clacking down the companionway, through the light, turning into a fair, slight figure on which a duffel coat bulked like a barrel and whose face could have started as a librarian's and then been tanned and cured. He came down the low gangway and walked toward Hans Sucher as though he had sent him off five minutes before for a fuse.

But in the passageway he stopped abruptly and spoke quietly and fast. "Have you water and food?"

"Yes," said Sucher.

"You will be two days alone. I do nothing for you but this. You know that?"

"Yes," said Sucher.

"I have done this before. Twice. The men lived. So you may have hope. Perhaps you did not know that?"

The pale eyes took on suddenly an expression lacerated and intense, a priest at a famine station.

"I did not know that," said Sucher. "I thank you."

"Listen very carefully. Are they hunting for you now?"

"Not here. Not now." And this was true, he thought. The man at Eberswalde must have decided to do nothing, else the chase would have begun.

"Then we will not be looked before we go. The first dock shift come at six, and it will unload that deck cargo. It takes little time. Then we sail—before sun this time of year. No stops until frontier. We have one only cargo and it goes to Hamburg. The frontier is two days. Do they hunt you then?"

Sucher frowned. The Pole was speaking faster than his German allowed, and he had to listen closely. "Maybe," he said. "Quite possibly. I do not know."

"If they really hunt you they empty all the barge and then it is completely hopeless. What are you? Writer? Unionist?"

"No," said Sucher.

The flayed eyes passed over him again. "You are right. No time for that. You hide in the coal. It is not comfortable. Hide all day. There are three other men on the boat. Please do not trust them. They are good guys, they are Poles, but if you are found, you see, we are all arrested. By our own cops, at home. They cannot take that. They have families. Me too. You lie buried. At night you can come out a little if the country is quite dark. There at the bow, I show you. You understand all this?"

"Yes," said Sucher.

"Good. When we go on board we go fast. There are two border checks."

Sucher nodded.

"The first is much more thorough. It comes after Wittenberge, in the evening, the day after tomorrow. We will have been in Elbe River then for several hours, you will feel the difference. For God's sake you must be careful then. Bury yourself—they may lift the hatch. No trace—no paper, no shit, nothing. Understand? After that the south bank is West German but there are guns and wires and searchlights everywhere. Stay below always. The last search will be eight hours later, before dawn, at Horst. Usually it is not much, just papers. Sometimes more. This I must tell you, though—if it is very careful, many men, then I think they hunt you." The eyes looked at Sucher, imagining that, then quickly blinked it away. "When you feel us underway again, the engines normal, it is still forty minutes, almost ten kilometers, actually to the West. You must not come up at once. There are towers and patrol boats until the last meter. After twenty minutes you can risk it perhaps—it is dark still, see, and you are black—the coal. It works well." He smiled but gave it up at once.

He went on, "The first buildings then are West, Lauenburg. First a dry dock, then a town and wharves. This is where you must leave the barge. I cannot take you to Hamburg. If you get off at Hamburg, somebody see you, somebody make report, ears at home hear it. Then it is all finished—for me and the other men. You understand this?"

"Yes," said Sucher.

"You jump off there. There is a little boat for you—that is all I know. I shall have that watch, but please be quiet about it. Remember also, it is almost winter. The river will be cold, and I think the weather change. Let the boat be close. I will try to make it easy, but I cannot risk much."

"You are a good man," said Sucher. "I can never repay this. I am not even Polish."

The eyes tried to say all of something at once. The voice only said, its German collapsing under the strain, "German, Polish, is no difference. You have lived for freedom, you are my family." Then back to solid ground. "Now we have to go on board or I am too long. You go right behind me up the plank, only one footsteps. Then I go up the companionway, that ladder, maybe I call out. And you, look closely, you go through that hatch, down a ladder, to the coal. In port here there is a little light through the deck hatches. Go all the way forward. There you find another such ladder and a little hatch. That is where you can come up at night, perhaps, very carefully. Do not stand up there. Now I see if anyone come and if not we go at once."

He put his hand out. Sucher took it.

"Go with God," said the mate.

24

The hull encased him. The coal was large; here and there were very big pieces, like boulders in a stream. Sucher fell flat on his face several times and hurt his shins. Then he learned to move slowly, as though wading.

It was not utterly dark. The hatches let in fingers of light from the quay. He followed them up the hull, though facets of coal reflected them confusingly like mirrors. He went on interminably. He thought that he had turned around and gone back when the coal rose up suddenly, and he rubbed his face against the bulkhead and saw the spindly ladder from the bow inspection hatch a few meters away. He stood bemused and still a few minutes, then sat down.

He could hear very little, which, buried here, seemed reasonable. He began to experiment with moving coal to make a trench for future concealment. It did not go well. In a little while, he very clearly heard a big engine start. It was certainly not his barge. It must have been the other barge down the wharf, which meant that sounds carried easily through the hull. His stupidity frightened him. Afterward, he hardly dared move when his position became intolerable.

But when that fear subsided he realized he had never expected to come so far. The barge was here and he had gotten to it. He felt a startled gratitude that the CIA, this barge, this wonderful Pole should all be here for him. It was a weepy feeling, and he realized he had been stretched very thin. He wished he had not killed the boy. There was nothing else he could have done. He would hate to be found because of the boy.

He thought of Renate. He thought of her first with more self-satisfaction than seemed quite gallant and then less distinctly than he would have liked. He remembered her profile in his old living room and her shape by his bed and supposed he always would. He very much hoped she would get out. It would be terrible to think of her in prison. He had given her the best chance he could.

He realized suddenly that if they both got out he might see her once. Afterward he would be an old man in a government apartment repeating in numbing detail a life he had not much enjoyed to Americans who would be as inclined to disbelieve him as not.

In between then and now was the crossing. He would either be looked for in this barge or not.

He thought of his network, Sepp Klingenberg, everything that he had tried to do. He was no further away from it, and no less out of touch, than he had been the day before, but the barge shut out everything.

He was tired of his situation and wished it would end one way or the other. He had not known he was so tired.

According to her instructions, Renate was to leave the house between midnight and one in the morning. She wished it had been at dawn or nightfall. She waited through the long dark hours. She knew the wavelengths and their corresponding times by heart, her fingers had found them on the radio, she knew them backward; with a leap of faith she threw the instructions into the fire. Her watch was not a good one, and that concerned her.

She made herself do things. She found a loden coat smaller than the others and hemmed the sleeves and bottom; it still looked big on her but not absurd. She had a thought: she could tape the radio to her arm inside the ample sleeve. She carefully selected her packet of food. She tried Hans's whisky but did not like it, which was probably lucky.

At thirty minutes to midnight she wished she could stay for days. The house all of a sudden turned solid as a fortress. She decided she would go through the door at 12:13 precisely.

She built the fire up high with big logs for the last time and turned the lights out downstairs. She went up to the bedroom and turned the light on. She stood by the bed and wondered if she would see Hans again and what he would be like in more promising circumstances. She went downstairs and sat in the dark.

After she went out of the door and was in the wood and no one had stopped her, her fear began to leave. She found she could walk fast through the wood once she was accustomed to it, and the passing of distance cheered her. She would have liked more wind. Climbing the fence and hedge worried her. She stood below it, listening, but knew she would lose her nerve if she waited long. She climbed it in four quick movements, listening between each. She waited at the top before jumping down.

Her instructions were to move generally and slightly north. By day, she could take rural buses—the danger of exhaustion from walking being greater than the likelihood of her photograph being circulated nationally—but no other transport. She must not go from bus to bus to make a route that could be followed. She would have to do what she could about the nights, for she could not stay at any form of inn or knock at doors. She must not look odd or raise questions. She must get quite out of this area but not go near a frontier. She must survive for two and half days like this before she used the radio.

By dawn, she sat near a lake by a village called Wilmersdorf. She thought it wiser not to be seen walking at this hour; she was both footsore to the point of pain and anxious to be farther away. It occurred to her that all this had barely begun. She touched the radio inside her sleeve.

Huge things were being moved over him with grating noises like crushed bones. He sat up, stiff. A frightful crunch. The metal shook. They must be taking off the cargo. He must have been asleep. He had almost broken his back while sleeping.

The engine supplied continuity again. It woke with a roar and a shake, and from then on he listened to it constantly. It had a high, singing note, between a jackhammer and a sawmill, and he noted every variation in its stride: the nervous fidgeting as it maneuvered from the wharf, the imperious assertion as it pushed ahead at speed, the demurrals which he soon learned were accompanied by a horn and then a ponderous acknowledgement of another barge's wake, the frightening lapses into idle followed by voices and foot-steps and thumps upon the hull. The last were locks, he supposed, but he heard them like the totemic knock on the door at three in the morning. Otherwise they moved. He had no idea how fast these things went, but he had a pleasing vision of the countryside whirling by. He ate a sandwich from his pocket, his first food since the jolly trap at Eberswalde. Like everything else, it was gritty and tasted black.

He was ashamed of his fatalism the night before, though he remembered it dimly, through exhaustion. He made himself go through Renate's probable actions, he gave her courage and stealth, he willed her to make no mistake with the radio, he imposed upon the CIA an aggressive and swift response. He furnished himself with various roles evolved by the CIA and projected his network into the future.

He considered the boy again, pushing remorse aside. If Finow had received no notice of General Sucher, and clearly Finow had not, then the boy's disappearance would at first be taken for just that. Private violence is rare in East Germany, and men of the Border Troops, who daily contemplate escape, have a known tendency to try it for themselves. So until the body was found, or unless General Sucher became the subject of a general alert, the guard might never be connected with him. Both these things would happen, but maybe he had time.

He fell back upon soldiering. It had become afternoon, and the first crossing was twenty-four hours away. Very carefully, he began again to dig a grave for himself in the coal. He learned to fit one piece against another, to measure his own length against the trench, which very slowly deepened, to stack the coal by its edge so that he could pull it in after him. At night, away from a lighted wharf, it was totally dark in the hull.

A vision occurred to him with increasing vividness, rising from nightmare to hallucination—his helpless capture. He had foreseen his end, if such was to be, as an unspecified chase, a struggle, a scarlet finality. He saw it now as the confident voices of his SSD stopping above him, the search beam comfortably resting, the pleased, vindicated eyes upon him. And then his imagination could settle at will with perfect detail on everything that followed. He could put faces on his interrogators, cadence on his own screams, hear the night sounds of the cells. He knew that and the courtroom and the camps as a butcher knows his shop.

By dark he was close to a hysteria that he despised and feared and could barely push away. The hull had begun to stifle him. He could see far too much in it. It was a measure of his fear that he could put his foot on the ladder but could not climb it.

In the end he did. He put his head out like a mole. They must be in the country. It was full dark. He was in a sort of well beside the forecabin, littered with chain and one smeared paintpot. The hull was dark, and far astern the wheelhouse windows shone dully through curtains of different colors. He could just make out the bank, which seemed to move much more slowly than the engine's note had led him to expect. There was a breeze upon his cheek. From very close, a cow suddenly bellowed and made him jump. He smelled trees and manure. He felt a little better.

Far off to the right, he saw the lights of a village, but they floated past and came no closer. One half of the sky was clear, the other half streamed trails of fine cloud. From the unevenness of the wind on his face, he fancied it was rising. A dark bridge flew low over his head. The lights of a single truck or car kept him company for a little while, then veered away. He dared a little; he rearranged himself more comfortably and looked with passion he did not understand until it came to him that he was seeing his country for the last time. He let himself look as though he were leaving it in innocence, had never been its jailor, had not torn himself from it with butchered flesh. He had no right to this and he almost feared to do it, but he gave himself this night's grace.

He would have stayed until dawn, but late at night a pale glow rose up ahead, then split into the filaments of a town. He crawled back down. Even so, he stayed until the lights of an outlying factory almost reached the barge. He had not the vaguest idea of where they were.

He knew late the next morning. There seemed to be another lock, more complex than the others. Then the barge floated free, the engine hit a more reckless note than he had heard before, and the hull swung perceptibly as though into a home stretch. He felt it at once; they were on living water now, it struck back against the bow and the barge sullenly acknowledged it.

So they had entered the Elbe. He knew the map. They were lined up straight for Hamburg now. This wide water that knocked against the bow would roll from one Germany to another whatever became of him. There was nothing between them now.

He had been told late afternoon. Though there seemed nothing wrong with his watch, the hull gave him no confidence in time. When the engine finally slowed, he had been buried for two hours. His throat, his nose, his eyes were caked with dust. He was blind and numb; in this condition, the unvarying engine note was driving him back into a panic from which only the actual beginning of the crisis saved him.

They touched a dock. He could feel it down the side. There were heels and voices. He tried to count them. He tried to imagine where the people were. He listened as intently as a desperate lover for every note of urgency, of protest, of surprise. It did very little good. He was not sure that he could tell the Germans from the Poles.

Very little happened. Footfalls came and went. From somewhere a loudspeaker made remarks in metallic. There were silences, though there seemed always to be activity around. It had been foolish of him to forget that the unfailing instinct of authority here was to preface disaster with long waits. No doubt it would take hours to get an execution over, though he had never witnessed a legal one. Barges crossed here by dozens daily.

Then footsteps again, which was how he apprehended the universe by now. This time single, walking straight as down the street, walking toward him, closer, over him, past him. Stopped.

An awkward little movement was followed by a shuffling sound. Then by one more melodious, almost a scale, in fact a ladder. Feet on the ladder coming down. Hans Sucher's throat closed up, closed on a piece of grit, and left him hanging on for grim life to a retch. Then a considerable silence.

Then the tape was wound backward, the episode recalled with perfect fidelity, even to the feet receding down the same side. No doubt an unseen flashlight had played a role.

There followed an interval for torment. Then the engine started. The barge moved.

A short horror ensued while he was unable to get his hands into position to free himself. But he sat up. He coughed. He spat. He wiped his eyes and made them worse. There was no light. He looked at his watch. It was after eight.

He would not, he would not dare tempt fate by thinking of, by even touching, the word *success*. He held it off so rigidly that he sat as in a daze. He thought of the left side of the barge, the south side, as glowing now with a suffusion of freedom. *I could talk to people in the West*, he thought. *I could almost swim there before they shot me.*

But he owed a huge debt of gratitude to have gotten even so far, and he could begin to pay it by thinking constructively, which was not presumptuous but professional.

It would make a very good impression if a gray-headed general pulled out of the Elbe could sit down that morning and give an account of his acts. So he pulled it all together for the hundredth time, but now, what with half the hull steaming with freedom, it took on the earliest aspect of a paper operation, the seams neat, the channels distinct, nothing done because, good or not, it was the only poor damned way you could see to do it.

He could sit on his coal with satisfaction. He had made communications at the most privileged level suspect over half the NVA's armor; he had manufactured connections between highly suspect Polish officers and supposed party stalwarts of the NVA; he had sown an ominous crop of petty sabotage; and now, by unmasking himself completely, he had seriously compromised the SSD before its master, the KGB. He had been theirs for so long. What he had in fact done against them for three years carried the free addition of everything he might, for all they could know, have done against them for thirty.

It would never be listed in troop strengths, it would never show in orders of battle, but in the highest councils of war, East and West, the NVA was a damaged article for three years at least. And so he had promised the CIA and so he had done, and so he had kept the faith however they had broken it. And so he would speak.

It was dark again. The second crossing would be before dawn. That the second inspection was often perfunctory was clearly logical—it would be virtually impossible to get on the barge between the two. Still, he knew the mind of the police and knew with what fragrant joy the officer of the lesser post would uncover a libertarian missed by the officer of the greater. Besides, he would not dare tempt fate by carelessness.

The next day she could use the radio. The next day would be Renate's last if she did not get help.

Her task was fundamentally impossible. To live in holes and burrows and look like a young woman so unremarkable that villagers did not notice her. It had not occurred to her until now that this simple dilemma was one of the State's most commanding assets.

She had begun to inspect herself like an aging actress. Was her face too drawn? Was she dirty? Did she smell? She had washed her face in the nasty little hole that served the village or the bus stop near Ragelin in Mecklenburg as a public toilet and used paper to wipe mud from her shoes. She decided she was good enough for one more bus ride. But on the bus a rawboned woman, face humid with inquisitiveness and malice, had begun to look at her. When her curiosity became undisguisedly rude, Renate knew that the woman had come to it that she was looking at a person in trouble.

They soon came to another village. The arthritic bus showed signs of stopping. Renate abruptly but with what grace she could got up and stood by the door and almost at once got out. She was in a muddy hamlet with one street and a tavern. She dared not show indecisiveness, though she did not know where she was. She walked quickly along the road. She was tolerably sure the woman would make a report of her, but perhaps not immediately, and even that was better than being asked questions.

It would fairly soon be dark. The hedges and copses were already solid lumps. There was a smell of rain. If she lay in a field she would look like a Hottentot by morning. It occurred to her with one faint flutter of gratification that she needed a place to use the radio tomorrow. A way off she saw the roofline of a barn and eventually a path to it. On the way there, to her horror, she saw a large black dog ranging a field, but either the barn was not on the dog's own property or it failed to see her.

There was no livestock. The barn was full of old machinery and was not in a good state. There was some hay, which was old and smelled of must but was fairly dry. It seemed as good as she could get. She had run out of food, but that seemed irremediable.

If the first inspection had stretched Sucher on a rack, the second scared him by being so offhand that he could not be quite sure that it in fact had taken place. The barge touched a quay. He heard the gangway thrown, but nothing else over the engine's idling. He heard the gangway again, and ropes, and then the engine rising.

He was not elated. He did not chortle. He felt in the presence of the immensity of fate, of the mystery of judgment. He felt humble and still afraid.

He waited twenty minutes. He listened to the engine, gauging its speed. He checked his watch twice. *All right*, he thought. *Time.*

He moved carefully, with a sense of ceremony. He might otherwise have heard the drop in the diesel's note, but his mind was now on his own progress. He climbed the ladder with circumspection and checked his watch once more before becoming coming up.

Into a scene that was almost festive. His eyes took in the search beams settling on the barge like white moths, the two patrol boats pulsing with blue lights and streaming silver across the water; he heard a disembodied bullhorn whose hysteria seemed to mount with the dying volume of the barge's diesel. He had been for two days in blackness; this was so unlooked-for that it was at first no more amazing than the immensity of water, a kilometer wide, surrounding him. For a fraction of a second he actually saw a grand and pyrotechnic welcome.

Then he heard the bullhorn's words. "Vessel under arrest! Proceed no farther! Anchor where you are! Prepare for boarding party!" He saw two men flush from the wheelhouse toward the stern. He felt his breath choke up and freeze. He heard something whine across the bow, a bullet, and then the engine struggling for reverse. He saw a searchlight swing toward him, inhale his prostrate body, and pass on. He saw the men with rifles on the patrol boats. He saw the water still foaming at the bow.

It was two meters below him. He had no power of movement. He might have stayed there until the end if one of the boats had not now been close enough for him to see the officer's face, a look so precisely modeled on his nightmare in the dark that he heard himself moan and felt himself move. The boat was coming up toward the bow, on the other side. He grabbed for a link of chain and pitched himself over the gunwale. His hands slid bruisingly down. His feet touched the walkway. Water rose and chilled his ankles. He hung there, tried to get his bearings, and saw nothing but the other boat drawing near and searchlights settling in. He let go. He almost yelled at the cold.

But the barge swept past him. He heard the backing screws clutching at the water and a terrific noise, the anchor chains pouring in. Then he was farther away and saw it all, the huge hull, the boats pulsing with blue light at her side, the men wriggling over the side and running over the deck. He felt his body turning to stone.

He forced himself to think. Just a little. It's not quite over. He had not moved before time. He must be literally at the edge. And where else would two patrol boats be kept? And didn't that, the absolute edge of freedom, explain the hysteria of the arrest?

The cold around him was a busy ship channel. Couldn't be obstructed. The water moved with frightening speed, spinning him, pulling him down into the cold. He passed the barge again, but not closely. The water would carry him. It would carry him dead, but he could live through ten minutes of anything, somehow he could. And in the West, somehow all things were possible. The drowning swim.

A sharp thing brushed his face. His mouth filled with mud. His feet swung around. He was terribly cold but the cold was still. It was not twisting him or sucking him down. It was not moving him.

Everything around him was gray. He wondered about it and raised up his head and took it in carefully. He was at the edge of reeds, and the earliest light had come. The river was behind him, still sucking at his shoes, and everywhere else was reeds, a million reed tops black against the gray. He thought very carefully and raised his head farther, seeking the particulars of his country, towers and barbed wire. He looked a long time but could see none. Very probably, he was in the West. He felt as though he had been in the cold for hours.

He began to move. He pulled his feet into the reeds and tried to stand. They sank. He pulled them up through mud that sucked and stank, but they sank a little less next time. He was careful to go the right direction, with the river.

But it was very slow, and his strength was going. The reeds went on and on, grasping his feet, giving no purchase when he fell. He could just see the line of the embankment in the gray. It was above him, far off.

Then there was water in front of him again and reeds only on the other side. He tried it. It was shallow. Better to go through.

Suddenly, everything around him woke, the gray, still water boiled. He stopped. A chorus broke out around him, rippling from where he stood to the farthest edge of the lagoon. And all at once, everywhere were wings.

He stood astonished. The surface of the world seemed to be striving for the sky. He understood now that this lagoon was the resting place of waterfowl, that it was packed with wild geese and ducks and swans, that he had panicked them. But he stood in wonder as the wings beat around him, the flutter of a thousand ducks, geese striding through the air, the unfolding span of white swans rising. It went on and on, flight rising after flight until the whole surface had been drawn up before him, stretching forward like a Milky Way into the West.

Private Strelker of the Border Troops had been combing the marsh right at the frontier through his field glasses. The criminal and traitor who had murdered his colleague in Finow and might have gotten out on this barge if the story had been put together half an hour later had still not been found. They were still taking the barge apart. He was almost a hundred meters from the birds, but he, too, looked with a moment's pleasure. There was something about those geese. Then he saw the man in the lagoon.

The man just stood there, right in the middle, framed. He could only have come from the water. Strelker shouted, but he didn't move. Strelker did not shout again. He should not have shouted at all. The man would drop to his knees, be hidden by the reeds, and have an excellent chance of crawling the two hundred remaining meters to the West before anyone could get in there and do anything. Strelker had no choice. He raised his rifle.

But the light was bad and it took almost the whole magazine. For two long bursts the target didn't even move. Then it did, but only a shuffle as though disoriented. Before the last burst, the target even turned to face Strelker, but only as though it had been disturbed from something more important.

The body fell out of sight below the reeds. No matter. Strelker knew that he had hit.

When the first gray touched the Elbe, Wop Stears looked at his watch and said, "He's late."

He realized then that he could see the bricks of the old waterfront at Lauenburg, the mass of the castle behind them, and the yellow nylon cord holding the inflatable boat and Bob Keckney to the wharf.

"Barges aren't trains," said Keckney, the Special Operations man.

August Herter, standing quite still close beside Wop, murmured, *"Ich hab' lieber Dunkelheit."* Dark is better. He had abandoned his English at Greenham Common.

Keckney put his hand back on the outboard's starter. Ten meters away, by a gabled housefront, the VW camper sat with a patient air, like a nanny at a boys' game. Lee McCoy was in it, with his radio.

Stears let his eyes sink down again to the worn brick. A puddle duck, with the movements of an electric toy, paddled at the edge of the wharf. *Come on, come on,* thought Stears. *I don't believe this, but maybe, just maybe they haven't caught you yet.*

Brindle Woods had said, "We'll monitor every security frequency we know about in East Germany. If they start stopping every barge on the river, if they haul a general of the SSD out of one, there ought to be a traffic pattern we can catch. I think we'll know about it."

The camper door was open. Stears said sharply to Lee McCoy, "Anything?"

"No sir. Nothing since Frankfurt twenty minutes ago. Everything was normal then, like I told you, sir."

There was a bend in the river here. He could just make out the emerging shape of a dry dock upstream, still in the West, and an abandoned highway bridge just beyond. Then, invisibly, the East. It was flat country. Smudges beyond the far bank were farming villages. The Elbe was wide and silent and fast and smooth. Stears looked again at the far reach of the bend, willing a blunt bow to materialize upon it.

The radio murmured in the camper. He swung his head that way and then walked over. Lee McCoy sat embraced by the earphones, as though in prayer.

Lee McCoy lifted his head. "What?" said Stears.

"That's Frankfurt, sir. Monitor at Lübeck is picking up some stuff right about here. They can't make much of it. It's low-power stuff, like walkie-talkie. It's a Border Troops frequency."

Stears said, "How unusual?"

Lee McCoy spoke back, then listened, then said, "Not unusual, sir. Pretty common. But you might not get it for several days."

Herter walked quietly over. "*Bitte?*" he said. Stears told him. Herter looked away, then put his hand softly on Stears's arm.

Windmills on the skyline grew out of the dark. The cobbled street going up to the castle emerged from the houses.

The radio murmured again. Lee McCoy said, "Lübeck says that activity's intensifying, sir. Good bit of talking going on over there. They still can't get it."

Neither Herter nor Stears moved or spoke. Then Stears said, "Can you get it?"

Lee McCoy said, "I've got two frequencies, sir. One's on Frankfurt and the other's open on your agent's frequency. I'd have to close out one of them to even try."

"Don't," said Stears.

He thought the radio spoke again, with a different sound, but Lee McCoy did not react. He listened again and knew it came from the sky, a faint multitudinous sound like a distant pack of dogs, flying. He listened again and remembered late fall over Massachusetts Bay. Geese. He looked up. He squeezed Herter's arm.

Over the river, from out of the east, the sky began to tremble, then turn white. The sound had turned to honking now, geese for sure. Then they came, not in echelon but in a rippling trail with smaller wings pulsing in between the swans with necks outstretched beside them. The honking grew actually loud. The wings whispered behind it. The line sailed overhead, strung out over the river, finally gone and squeezing down upon the horizon into the distant marshes.

"Jesus Christ," said Stears.

Now there was another sound from far away, like a sudden, peremptory knocking. Herter stiffened. Stears looked at him. It came again. Stears knew, and his back turned cold. It came a third time. Then they listened with held breath, but heard only the last voices of the geese.

Herter took his arm slowly from Stears's. He said, "A light machine gun. A Kalashnikov. Three bursts." Then he said, "That is not the whole of the magazine. He hit his target." He said it without inflection. He stood by Stears a moment more and then walked slowly away toward the shadow.

332

Stears caught up with him. "Maybe it's Sucher," he said. "Sucher firing. Maybe he had to fight. It must be right at the edge. The river would bring him out." He turned to Keckney. "Let's not wait," he said. "Let's get the hell upstream."

Herter turned slowly toward him. Stears thought, *He looks eighteen. He's going to cry. Don't let him cry. I may be right after all.* Herter said, "No, Stears. That was a rifle. The general could not carry a rifle. A sidearm, maybe. Not a rifle. My general is dead."

They heard the door of the camper, but neither looked that way. Stears heard Lee McCoy say, "Sir, sir!" He ignored him and followed Herter in silence. Lee McCoy called louder. "It's very important, sir! It's the radio." Stears looked back at him with irritation. Lee McCoy was out of the camper and running after him. "It was the other frequency," he said.

"What other frequency?" said Stears.

"Your agent's frequency. It was a high-speed burst. From his contact radio. He's just transmitted."

25

Renate took the cover off the radio and for a moment felt Sucher beside her, scent of tobacco and whisky, rough hand guiding hers. It didn't last. No Sucher, no fireplace. Certainly no foie gras. She was alone in a cold barn.

Suppose I use it wrong, she thought, and held to that, because it was better than the thought beneath it: *Suppose I use it right and nothing happens.*

"I should cross to the West by dawn on Friday," she had read in Sucher's handwriting. "Call then. Call at 6:18 because that would theoretically be my call time. If I am not there they will be listening. If I am there, I can explain you. Do not waste calls. They are dangerous."

So on Friday's dawn, eighty kilometers from the house and still far inside East Germany, she had checked her watch again and prayed that it was right. She pressed the button to transmit.

And there was no reply.

She waited. The general's times and figures, crystal-clear in her head throughout every travail of the last four days, began to fog and fade. She waited three minutes.

She sent again. The temptation to try another setting was great, but she resisted it.

The radio sat there as useless as a brick.

So the third time she tried it her spirit was already coming to terms with hopelessness, and she sat looking dully at the dead little toy thinking, *Do I walk out and get arrested or sit here until the end?* She picked up the radio with the idea of throwing it at the wall, but she lacked the energy or interest to do it, and that made her feel still worse.

Which gave her time to see that she had neglected to set the instrument to *Receive* and that nobody in the world could have called her on it.

Now when she pressed the button her hands were shaking, for her watch said 6:26, long after the call time, and Hope had undoubtedly shrugged and walked away.

The green lamp lit. The receiving tape moved.

The voice said, "Position and circumstance? Transmit shortest."

It sent a wave through her like love.

To reply was not so easy. "In a barn" did not seem to meet the case. She had not thought about her answer.

She struggled to remember at least the name of the last real village she had passed through on the bus. *Ragelin* came foggily to her, and she had picked up the radio when a cold thought sprang up that the voice that had answered her could have come from any direction and belong to anybody. She compromised and made her reply even vaguer than she had to.

"Near Ragelin," she said.

Which was swallowed by the air. She waited ten minutes, then more. She thought of messages clicking through the country, police cars hurrying to position, the net drawing tight.

The green lamp blinked. The voice said, "Are you on high ground?" The question made no sense to her at all, but the voice was balm. For now she knew it; it was the voice on the radio at the general's house.

"Yes," she replied. "In a barn on a hill."

The answer made less sense still: "Look to the west. Can you see an Autobahn? Keep answers shortest." She had no memory whatever of seeing one and would have to go out of the barn to be sure. Outside it was already light. She very nearly answered no, but she crept out of the door of the barn and then around its side. She saw a gray, flat ribbon a few kilometers away with rare dots of dawn traffic.

She crept back. "Yes," she sent.

And the voice, of which she had begun to have an older memory than at the general's house but could not imagine how that would be, said, "Go to Ragelin. Be in the churchyard by twelve hundred. Stay where you are now until time to go. If you are not contacted by fourteen hundred you are on your own. Discard and hide the radio when you move. Reply if imperative within thirty seconds. Communication ends." She did not reply. *I should have asked about Hans,* she thought, but she thought too late.

The village was small and poor. It took her an effort to remember that she had been through it only yesterday, had washed her face at the bus stop. Though she had been able to see Ragelin from the barn, it had been a long walk during which she had been buoyed by the thought of magical properties which Ragelin apparently possessed. They were singularly unevident when there. Ragelin was gray brick on a foundation of mud.

She was a little early. There was nowhere to wait but a dirty tavern. She looked at it seriously, for she was light-headed with hunger, but it was deserted except for three idle farmhands, extremely male. The only clean vehicle was a police car parked by the village office, empty but terrifying. It was unlikely that there was any stranger here but her. She walked on. There was a place by the bridge where it seemed possible to loiter. It was now 11:47. She saw that the church was toward the edge of the village and that the churchyard lay beyond it. It occurred to her that the churches were shown prominently on maps and that might be all the voice on the radio knew about this place.

Ten minutes later she moved. The churchyard wall was fallen in, and she stumbled over a rusty fragment of wrought-iron railing. The churchyard was secluded. It was also unattractive, cold, and dark, and it would have been as easy to explain her vigil there as on the church steeple. She waited.

If he had not trodden on a broken piece of gravestone, he could have touched her shoulder before she knew he was there. As it was she jumped and turned around. A young man was there ten meters away, looking at her.

"Good," he said. "You are here. Has anyone been watching you?"

"I don't think so," she said.

He was about twenty-five and fair-haired. He looked as though moving quietly was natural to him.

"Come with me," he said. "Quietly. As though we were taking a walk."

His voice was entirely German, from Saxony she thought, and certainly not the voice on the radio.

"Who are you?" she said. But she followed him toward the churchyard wall. As she caught up with him she saw that he had the ghost of a limp.

"Call me August," he said. "The rest comes when we are safe."

They passed beyond the village and crossed a little plank bridge over the stream where she had waited. August's shoes were muddy. They struck out along a wood down the side of a field where there was a man on a tractor. Rooks strutted in the branches above them. "Walk more as though you knew me," said her escort. "It looks more natural." She walked close beside him. They went down a farm lane where the year's fall of beech leaves smelled of the last rain.

"Where are we going?" she said.

He took her arm. "To West Berlin," he said.

She stopped dead. "Like this?" she said.

"On the Autobahn. It is the Autobahn between West Berlin and Hamburg. That was why we asked you."

"I never thought of that," she said. "Can we really do it?"

He looked at her as though weighing whether to answer honestly. People always seemed to answer her honestly in the end, and, considering the answers they gave, she had begun to wish they wouldn't.

He said, "If no police see us get onto the Autobahn, if nobody reports us doing it, if the frontier guards do not inspect the car too carefully, then we shall be in West Berlin in two hours."

"That would be nice," she said.

He steered her toward a bank. They climbed it. At the top her shoe came loose and she bent to tie it. August gave her his arm as she straightened. There was a rough track and a small wood in which she could just see the outline of a truck. She stopped, afraid, but August pushed her on and she recognized at first a Western Volkswagen camper and then West German plates. They were close to it by then.

The door of the camper opened and a man got out and said, "I am so glad to see you here."

She recognized him, too. It was the foreigner from the café in Berlin. He still wore the same coat. It was the man on the radio as well.

She sat back. "You all know the rest," she said. She picked up a filigreed fork and cut the corner off her eclair. She said reminiscently, "Almost the worst thing about those days was something very small. I don't have a good watch. I had forgotten to check it when I left the house. I knew that when the time came to make my call I could never know if it was exactly right."

"And if it had been right," said Wop Stears, "I'd have been absolutely sure she was a decoy. She was two minutes off. It felt right for an amateur. The Comrades don't have that much imagination. Not at that level."

"What level?" said Brindle Woods. "And how could you know? You had plain damn luck." He looked at Stears, who was not forgiven, through gimlet eyes.

She had not figured Woods out. He had arrived in West Berlin from London by British Airways after them. About when, therapeutically shopping for a change of clothes in a mirrored boutique at the Europa Center, she had finally emerged from the horror of her own journey. August Herter had murmured of him to her, *"Das Frettchen"*—the ferret—without much affection.

She looked out onto the Kurfürstendamm, the great street of Berlin, her own city, which she had never seen in her life until that day. Nor had August Herter, it turned out. It was dirtier than Munich.

Brindle Woods said, "But in fact you forgot to reset the machine?"

"I was very stupid," she said. "I didn't think of it for five minutes. I had really given up by then."

Brindle Woods smiled. "I'm not surprised," he said.

Stears said, "But as it was, she just caught my last reply. I would not have sent again."

Woods snorted, but with less rancor than before, and cut a small piece of Florentine with his fork. Renate, Stears, Captain Herter, and Brindle Woods were in an alcove of the lounge of the Kempinski Hotel. It was late in the tea hour. Waiters stepped sedately with fluted teapots and trays of pastry. The armchair she sat in was of silk brocade, and a piano played diffidently in the corner where it also entertained early drinkers in the bar. It was the grandest room she had ever been in, far surpassing even Krel's restaurant in Munich. Whatever the disadvantages of espionage as a profession, a lack of ready cash never seemed to be one of them.

She had already discovered that it was almost impossible to tell whether Woods was interested or not. He was absorbed, but he was also looking at the piano as though he was trying to think of the name of the tune.

Brindle Woods said, "Well, we do know how you got here. You had a terrible time. Terrible. I have to ask you one more thing. We need several days to talk to you. Krel, Sucher as you knew him, what you saw in Berlin—there's a lot to tie down. We have no way of making you do this, but it would waste all the bad part if you didn't, wouldn't you agree?"

"Yes," she said.

His switch to this topic had been as smooth as a good dancing partner's changing steps, but she refused to follow him at once.

"What will happen to Krel?" she said.

"Fewer lunch parties," said Woods. "A different lecture circuit. Different embassies."

She flushed at his mockery, but he looked at her and said quite gently, "I was only answering your question. It doesn't alter what you did. It was very important. It was worth everything."

Which presumably included her arrival in West Berlin. She had gotten there after two hours pressed into a pitch-black cavity that stank of the inflatable boat it was designed to hide. She had known she was there when the voice of the frontier guard ceased and the door slammed and the engine started. Three minutes later they stopped again and the lid over her face was opened. They were parked on a side street in West Berlin under bright gold elm trees, and when she sat up, August Herter hugged her.

In the suite upstairs at the Kempinski, Brindle Woods said to Stears, "I will not be obvious. Give me credit for that. I will pass quickly over the facts that you went in without authorization, without authentication, without planning, without backup, that you could have created embarrassment up to cabinet level, that you could have given the East Germans an excuse to disrupt traffic to West Berlin, that you could have gotten Herter shot, that they could have debriefed you for twenty years. That you drove a goddam Volkswagen camper containing an officer of the CIA, a deserting officer of a Warsaw Pact army, and the amateur accomplice of a defector from the SSD across East Germany on some kind of picnic. Please have the grace in return to pass over the obvious yourself. You got her out. She is probably authentic. It worked. We know that. Just tell me why you did it."

Stears said, "I didn't want Herter. He insisted. He said my German is not native. He was right."

Woods waved his hand as though shooing thistledown.

But Stears did not go on at once. He felt again the empty dawn at Lauenburg, the litter of useless toys—boat, camper, radio—on the wharf, the taste in the mouth of cruelty and failure, the chill in the air pulling on fatigue. And then the radio. His anger at it first as a crass, cheap trick, for the girl he'd met in Berlin could never have survived that long.

He said slowly, "And the alternatives? Dig a tunnel to her? Send an airplane? Get another barge? But those are the old-fashioned ways, aren't they, so how about the things we do now? Get her into a delegation of French psychiatrists? Infiltrate her into the Export Bureau? Use Krel? What, Brindle? What?"

This was before dinner. Woods had found or brought with him a bottle of his malt Scotch. The Kempinski's ice bucket was elegantly black and the glasses were square crystal, not the bucolic trout flies of the chalet at Reit im Winkl. Renate's death would have made seven since then. Woods looked at him closely and silently.

Stears went on, "You're not disputing that she gave us a Soviet agent of influence who has had lunch with every member of the German cabinet except Franz-Joseph Strauss at least once in the last six months and who has probably heard more about dissent in the DDR than you have."

Woods signaled no, with his eyes alone.

"But, all right, she'd sent that already. Am I right that she increases the value of everything ELBEMAN gave us because she can confirm that he was at liberty when he made his last reports? We couldn't really have known that, could we? Also that she can help reconstruct what was really going on."

"Up to a point," said Woods. "It helps, yes."

"But not enough. All right."

" 'Enough' is a function of risk. You know that damn well."

"The risk was not very great. Herter and I had false-name passports, which I knew were not compromised. Only a small proportion of vehicles going into West Berlin these days are seriously searched by the East Germans—and only a serious search would have found that compartment. Autobahns in the East have farm roads running straight onto them, as you very well know. They're not limited-access. Not physically."

"Not physically," said Brindle Woods. "Not for the natives. Just the detail that a Western driver with a transit visa to West Berlin has committed a crime if he accidentally takes the wrong turn. He's committed a crime if he looks at a map so as not to take the wrong turn. How about turning off into the woods? What were you going to say to the Vopo—'Gee, officer, that looked like Berlin over there by the woodpile?' It's an uncontrollable risk. An uncontrollable risk is a hundred-percent risk. That is why that method has never, ever been used."

"If there had been a police car we would have abandoned the attempt," said Stears.

Drive past, just keep on going in the dapper little blue camper—so indeed they had agreed. The abandonment would have been as casual and dreamlike as the attempt. In what kind of derring-do does one drive the smuggest vehicle ever built, a vehicle that enforces on its driver the posture of a governess at a tea, over the flat country at exactly, invariably the cautious speed limit imposed by a conscientious police state, signaling carefully to pass, hour after hour, protected by one's duly obtained and paid-for transit visa, waiting for a single moment to turn off onto a gravel road, crime, rescue, peril, conceivably an act of war?

By the time the moment came, he had looked for a police car carefully. He had looked for one with longing. There had been almost no traffic at all.

He said to Brindle Woods, "We have still not taken into account a third issue. The Stasi would have gotten her sooner or later. She knew more than we realized she did when we turned her down for evacuation. Sucher was a pro, of course, and she couldn't have told them all that much, but she would have told enough to do some damage. Maybe quite a lot."

"Obviously," said Brindle Woods. "I have considered that. You could have told them even more. So could Herter."

"As a matter of interest," said Stears, "have you fired me?"

"No."

"Will you?"

"It's a complex question. Like the one I have asked you. And which you won't answer. Why did you do it?"

"I am giving you all my reasons," said Stears. "I may have miscalculated, I may have weighed things badly . . ."

"We're talking of you," said Brindle Woods. "Don't ask me to consider stupidity."

Stears went to the tray and helped himself again to Woods's whisky. He walked across the room and sat on the windowsill. The Kurfürstendamm was lighting up, the nightclub touts were passing out their leaflets, and through the crack at the bottom of the window came a lick of winter and a smell of chestnuts.

The first answer was sheer anger. Anger at the fragility of his weapons and the massiveness of theirs, anger at the almost inevitable completeness of their triumph, swelling when one realized that the voice suddenly on the radio was not theirs and was certainly doomed as well. Anger of a little boy shaking his fist at the farmer; but enough to make Stears, poring feverishly with August Herter over the map to see the thick green Autobahn, say, "Goddamm it, look!"

Anger would not have been quite enough actually to do it. Difficult to get out of it once it had been said to Herter, but he could have invoked rules and done so. He could have invoked Brindle Woods.

"No," he said. "Not stupidity. I won't say that."

One didn't know why one did something, he thought, until the moment one knew one was right. He remembered just when that had been. It came to him in the little pinewood where they had driven the camper over the needles and into the trees, almost hiding it. Just the place for the campfire, the cold swim, the hike, and any other frugal and healthy evocations of the Hitler Youth so nostalgically smiled upon by the East German authorities. He had been there an hour alone under a gray and swirling sense of futility, a premonition that yet more waste was about to be thrown on the dingy heap. This waste, of course, would include himself, and he was mundanely scared stiff. Herter had gone to the village on foot. They could see the steeple of the church.

Every sound brought his heart to his mouth. When he heard footsteps crunch the road he ducked behind the wheel, which would have done him as much good as a paper hat in a bomb raid. Herter and the woman whose photograph he had carried for a week, whom he had seen at the café in Berlin, came through the pines. As she came up onto the road she stopped, looked once behind her, stooped, and retied her shoe. Since the ground was rough, she took August Herter's arm as she rose.

And at that the veil of the secret country was rent in two and out of the murderous shabbiness of the operation, like a live canary out of a stale pie, suddenly appeared something with a life and value undeniably its own, that needed no excuse at all.

He said, "There'd have been nothing left otherwise. They'd have taken it all."

But that, when he said it, was not all of it either, for those were exactly the images of Ursula Hecht dying legless under the fence, of the Mays family trussed and delivered to the KGB, of ELBEMAN sold for a toy, of Herter himself manipulated and bargained down as he lay drugged and in pain on a bed in a strange country. And in counterpoint to all of these was always Stears himself, not malicious, with justifications up his sleeve, ironic, controlling, safe. It had begun to rot him. It had only lifted briefly after his prank on Salisbury Plain. It was exactly why his only response to Marie-Sophie's wise, unjust misery had been to go and drink four martinis at his club.

"Self-preservation," he said. "An Act of Contrition. That and all the reasons I gave you before."

Brindle Woods, who had followed Stears to the window with his eye, now nodded quietly. "I thought we'd come to that," he said. He said it with satisfaction. He added, "But it's treason, isn't it? It's betrayal." He waved the obvious away with his hand. "Not to your country, I suppose—I imagine you could get a medal for it, it's the sort of thing they give them for. But it's treason to your service. We are the only service that does not compete for honor, that does

342

not parade in front of its conscience waving flags. We are the only service that understands sacrifice and courage in terms different from those of a lion tamer at a circus. We have the courage of intellect. If you don't understand that, I shall be profoundly depressed. We have the other kinds of courage too, but that's the first one—the courage of an immunologist in front of bacilli. We don't cry during the experiment. We don't look at ourselves for spots. We don't do things because they feel good."

"I understand," said Stears."Is that how Sucher was trashed for a gadget that doesn't work?"

"Sometimes the artillery hits the wrong target," said Woods. "That is a mistake. But the artillery does not shoot Roman candles because then it would not be artillery."

"It is a good analogy," said Stears. He crossed the room and poured another drink.

"Our duty is the harder one," said Woods. "The other is rather easy. At least it is rather common."

"I consider myself reprimanded," said Stears. "I have no counter-argument. Truly, I do not."

Woods nodded and sipped his drink. He softly cupped his hands to indicate a summing-up. "It is a much harder, a much braver, thing," he said, "to hold your conscience over a flame than your hand."

"I wouldn't count on it," said Stears. "I wouldn't count on that at all."

But Woods, playing uncle very well, was in a festive mood that evening. He made them go to a tiny place, far down the Kurfürstendamm, past Bleibtreustrasse, from which Stears averted his eyes, and up a side street into a rich Levantine steam of lamb and baking bread. For a dinner of spies *en famille* it was as jolly as it could be. Woods seemed to know the owner, a Greek or Turk with Chicago phrases, and talked to him intricately of the past. Renate swapped food, all of which was wonderful, with August Herter and corrected his impressions of West Germany. Stears reflected that it was all far from over.

Afterward Woods walked beside him under the lamplit trees toward the car.

"There are loose ends," said Woods.

"Yes," said Stears.

"There are strategic questions surrounding Sucher's preparations. Those are beyond us, but they evolve into operational ones, which are not. You may be with this, one way or another, for a long time.

Apart from your little lapse you've done very well. Your first operation has given you a capital in the Company that you can spin out for years. Many people have to wait decades for that."

"That's wonderful," said Stears.

"And even before any of that," said Woods, "there's Krel."

26

Heinrich Nadermann, bureau chief of Tass in Bonn, stood in the hall of Krel's house. Krel's Slovene servant shut the door behind him, pushing it the last inch against the wind.

The servant said, "Your coat, my colonel?" and reached toward Nadermann's shoulders, which glistened with rain.

Nadermann looked at his watch and shook him off. "There is not much time," he said. "The arrangements are made for a little after midnight. I had a bad drive from Bonn, especially after dark. Where is he?" He pointed to three suitcases at the bottom of the stairs. "He has much too much baggage. I said one small bag. Did you not tell him?"

"I told him, my colonel. He says he will not leave as a thief in the night. He is in his library now, still reading papers."

"Take the coat then," said Nadermann. "What is his condition, Mikhail?"

"I know he does not sleep, my colonel. He flinches at the telephone. I think he is secretly glad that I let him have no contact with the world. He does not comment on it. He has obstinacy and pride but no longer much strength."

"Then he would not have enough for tomorrow. I was right to come for him tonight."

The servant said, "Yes, my colonel." But Nadermann had already walked across the hall, and Mikhail said it to the coat.

Krel was in the library. The overhead lights were on, and their hard light poured fear and disarray on the shelves with gaps, the books piled on the floor, the boxes full of papers. But Krel stood by the library table sorting newspaper clippings into an attaché case. His hand was unhurried and he did not quickly raise his head. When he did so, he looked levelly at Nadermann and said, "Good evening, Heinrich. There is work to be done before our trip, as you can see."

Nadermann said, "There is no time for this, Oswolt. There is no time and there is no way to carry all this. I want you at the border long before dawn, and it is not a good night. And I do not want my car to be seen outside your house."

He realized that he had used the tone one uses to an unreasonable invalid.

Krel put papers in the case with care. He said, "For twenty years I have been a man of standing. This room is the record of real accomplishments. It has been my life, Heinrich. I do not think I care to run away from it like a boy from an apple orchard because the morning paper will carry a little girl's unsupported account of some adventures in East Germany. I count you my friend, Heinrich. I would think that you would understand this. Some of this I will take with me, most will be sent on afterward."

It's the light, thought Nadermann. *Anyone would look bad under that light. Perhaps I am wrong. Perhaps Mikhail is wrong. He doesn't seem to be falling apart. Perhaps he is still strong enough to fight back. Maybe we can use him still—the Americans cannot quite prove their case. I could still undo the arrangements.* He said, "It is not so very unsupported, Oswolt. The CIA has done its homework. They timed the release of this interview with great care. Even your friends who do not quite believe it will find it safer to abandon you." Nadermann sat down on the table's edge.

Krel said, "I am close to the most eminent public figures in Germany. It would not suit them to say that they had been taken in by a Soviet agent. You could use this to make the Americans seem to be trying to destroy a patriotic German neutralist."

Krel looked him full in the eye, but wavered and looked away. *No,* thought Nadermann, *I was right to come. It's a gambler who cannot even cover his chips complaining about the service in the casino. He'll break in two days.*

He said, "Your friends have seen her story. It has been carefully circulated for twenty-four hours. They have been given time to prepare their excuses. I thought at first that we could do just as you say. No longer. The CIA are not babes in the wood, you know. Life here will not be very nice for you in future. Reporters with crude questions. Policemen coming in and out. Certainly no friends to admire you. Perhaps no hall to lecture in. Very possibly jail."

And he saw the muscles of Krel's face suddenly acknowledge exhaustion and let go, saw the face become frail and old, saw the eyes sink to the baleful pit in the air beside him. Krel supported himself on the table with both hands.

Krel said very quietly, "So now, when I finally helped you, you hold me as a traitor."

Nadermann took his arm. "Oh, no," he said. "You are still a hero, though a somewhat different one. A German hero, and so you shall remain. Only we must move quickly now to keep you so."

———

Stears and Renate sat in the car two hundred meters from Krel's house. Intermittent rain, cold and bright, was driven past the streetlights by the wind.

"Why is he so long?" said Renate. "Do you think they are not leaving after all?"

He lowered the window a little, realizing that he did not see much better with it down and that he had done it because Renate's scent was disturbing in the car.

"God knows," he said. "No. They're leaving. Why else would Nadermann have come from Bonn all by himself?"

The rain stopped. The back of Nadermann's Mercedes was still solidly in front of the house. He would anyway have seen its lights if it had started up. He thought he saw a movement within another parked car fifty meters up the street. *And who might that be?* he thought. *West Germans, East Germans, the Comrades, the State Department of the United States?* There would be no lack of forces to protect Krel's retreat. It had taken every skill of his, every wile of Brindle Woods's, to penetrate the armor of complicity surrounding Krel—and if Krel was leaving of his own accord there was possibly nobody in all Germany but Stears who would not prefer that he left silently, unofficially, in the dark. No, two people—Stears and Renate Segla. For an hour her eye had not wavered from the house.

"Where will they take him?" said Renate.

"They'll cross at Lobenstein or Eisenach. Anything closer goes through Czechoslovakia, and they won't want that. Eisenach's farther, but it's larger and more anonymous. Probably there."

"And nobody will stop him. Because his fraud is less important than those of politicians and editors and professors."

She said it in the tone of youth enduring the cowardice of its elders, and he answered briskly, "We've been through that."

"And if I can stop him for you, you will sit down with him and make a deal. Because that is also less important than your 'intelligence.' "

"Of course it is," said Stears. Now he spoke gently. "If I can debrief Krel, I strike at his masters. I'm not an assassin. I can't shoot him down in the street. I can't give orders to the Germans. I shouldn't be able to—they're your people, not mine. A deal is all I can get. The deal will be Nadermann, his boss. He's dangerous. Krel's not."

She nodded slowly and said, "How can I call you a coward? How can I refuse you? You saved my life." And then, "Do you really think I can stop him?"

"God knows," he said. "I haven't got anything else. There's been no way I could make contact with him. He's either been in his house or with that servant. But he'll have to get out of the car at passport control, and at least he's not a prisoner then. No one can stop you from getting close to him. You're shock value. You're half a ghost. You might accomplish something. If he hesitates out there, there's just a chance I can do something. Otherwise it's finished."

"Look," she said, and he realized that her one angry glance at him had been the single time her eye had strayed from the house. "There's movement behind that window by the door."

Mikhail carried the small bag to the car. Krel said, "Look after my things, Mikhail. Be sure the police do not exceed their rights."

Mikhail said, "Certainly, Dr. Krel," and walked back into the house and shut the door.

Nadermann got in and took the wheel and sighed. "We have a long drive," he said, "and not a nice night."

The rain began again as they turned onto Ludwigstrasse. The university's Tuscan facade was reflected on the wet square, and the bottom branches of the chestnut trees were bright gold in the streetlight. Windblown leaves flew through the light like firedarts until they hit the sidewalk and went out.

"One certainly cannot deny that it is a pleasant city," said Nadermann.

Krel said nothing and looked straight ahead.

When the street turned and funneled and became the Munich-Nürnberg Autobahn, Krel said, "I shall require a teaching position of importance. Has anything been done about that?"

It was not said abrasively, and Nadermann answered gently, "Not in the last five days, I should think. You have kept us rather busy. Of course, that's what they'll find for you—we're not rich enough yet to waste you."

He was concentrating on the road and the mirror. He didn't see Krel's head move, and he almost jumped when he felt the hand on his arm. Krel said, "Heinrich, what will it be like?"

"The crossing?"

"No, Henrich. My life."

Nadermann, even though carefully passing a truck and half blind

348

from its spray, felt his attention surge as though he had looked into a watch he had made himself and seen a wheel he had never put there. "Why, Oswolt, what do you mean? You will be a great professor there as well."

"I know that. But my life itself there, at home, how will it be? Will it be very different?"

"I do not understand what are you asking me. Are you afraid of having a lumpy mattress? Do you think you will only get cabbage soup?"

"No," said Krel. "That is not what I mean." Nadermann looked at him quickly and saw the face close up again, the eyes look rigidly ahead at the rain skewering the headlights. He thought, though without much urgency, *Clumsy of me. I shouldn't have twitted him. Well, maybe he'll come back to it.*

Krel raised his head suddenly and said, "'Why are you always changing speed like that? It isn't very comfortable."

"Because someone is following us and I would like to know who."

At Nürnberg, Stears almost lost it. There was traffic, and though he hung close to the Mercedes a highway bus pushed itself in between. He mistimed the forking of the Autobahn, and when the Mercedes suddenly swung off to the left he had to turn himself under the wheels of a truck in a fanfare of horns and a queasy second of balletic tires. He heard Renate say "Ah" under her breath and saw her hand on the dash.

"Damn," he said. "Sorry." Then, "Eisenach. They're going to Eisenach. Lobenstein's due north of here. Two more goddam hours."

"Don't you think he'll have seen that?" said Renate.

"He saw us just out of Munich. He's seen us ever since. I can't stay far behind in the rain. Eisenach's logical. It's one of the big three crossings—Eisenach, Helmstedt, and Valluhn. It'll be busy even in the middle of the night. Trucks mostly."

"If he knows you're following, why doesn't he get away?"

"How?" said Stears. "This isn't television. For the same reason I haven't gotten away from whoever's followed us since Krel's street. Anyway, he probably thinks we're the police. To protect him."

"Then who's following us?"

"Probably the police, to protect him. He'll think that's who we are. He can't see back behind us." He looked at her sharply. "You're not thinking of stopping him in any peculiar way, are you?"

"Yes," she said. "But I won't."

"Good," said Stears. "You've destroyed him already, you know that."

"I destroyed him only a little," she said.

North of Würzburg, the hills began and the Autobahn dipped and twisted. Nadermann looked at the clock and decided he could not slow down. Krel's posturing at the house had delayed them, and what had to be done at the border had to be done before the next shift of guards came on. *Damn Krel,* he thought, *he's going to get me in a wreck.* The rain was a little better, but on the bridges the car shuddered in the wind. He hoped he would remember the country roads. He had scouted the place at the border two days ago, but that had been in daylight.

Krel did not seem impressed by the speed. For the last hour he had asked only about their pursuers. "Only the police," Nadermann had said. "They are not dangerous tonight. After tomorrow they might have had to stop you." Krel had nodded.

Now Krel said, "Humor me, Heinrich. You are my only real friend. Let us talk."

Nadermann's curiosity leaped again. "My friend," he said, "do you think you need to ask? I was not being facetious before. I did not know what you meant."

"I have lived for an ideal," said Krel. "Not for myself."

He seemed to wait. Nadermann said piously, "That is what every serious life must be." *Where is this going?* he thought.

"I would never deny it," said Nadermann.

"But it was you who taught me. One cannot belong to the ideal without committing actions that would be unforgivable without it, because it is by those actions that one destroys whatever in oneself is not part of the ideal. That is the true courage."

"Very true," said Nadermann.

"You taught me the last lesson not long ago, in the Black Forest." He turned to Nadermann and looked him in the eye, like a curate rehearsing a four-letter word. "The story of yourself in the Lubyanka, when you pissed in the old general's face.

"I was not ready for that story then. I have thought about it since. I know now that it was a way of saying that only he who knows beyond doubt that he will do anything for the ideal possesses the ideal in full."

He paused and then went on.

"I had almost become such a man, Henrich. I rose above myself a last rung with this Renate Segla. I resisted giving her to you, but I

350

did it at last with joy. You made me see." Krel went on softly, reciting, " 'In a far country, by our feet unapproachable, there stands a fortress whose name is Montsalvat.' "

There is not long to go, thought Nadermann, *and I am glad of that. What the hell is he talking about, anyway?* He said briskly, "That is very praiseworthy, Oswolt." *Not long,* he thought, *an hour to the border.* He pictured the crossing place in his mind. *It will serve well.*

Krel heard his tone and did not reply.

At the Autobahn junction north of Fulda, the Mercedes turned east. Stears said, "Okay, Eisenach it is." The rain had nearly stopped and he had let the Mercedes lead by a quarter kilometer. Soon a sign: *Grenzübergang 43Km.* Frontier crossing. A third car still followed well behind.

It was possible to sense the hills around them. Renate opened her window. On top of the Autobahn smell was a smell of wet forest. "We're running right along the frontier now," said Stears.

Then he said, "They separate the cars and trucks at the Western frontier post. There'll be a long line of trucks, mostly Eastern. There couldn't be many cars at midnight, so you'll have a fairly open field. Krel has a Bundesrepublik passport. Nadermann's is Soviet nondiplomatic, and I'm sure he'll be using his own. It will take a couple of minutes to get it stamped, and during that time he'll be away from Krel. That's your moment. Don't get out of the car until then—it's all quite brightly lighted. The Eastern post is about two hundred meters farther on. It's much more elaborate. Obviously."

"All right," she said.

"It's important that you get the layout in your head. The passport control office is on your left. The trucks are on your right. They make a fair amount of noise. There will be activity. Can you picture it?"

She frowned. "Yes," she said. "I think I have it. Men around the trucks with papers. A line of trucks. Some bright lights. One or two cars only. An office. People will push past each other in the office door. This time of night, people are busy and tired. Krel will be having some sort of great thoughts, I am sure. Am I getting it?"

"Yes," he said. "What sort of great thoughts?"

"How should I know?"

"It could be the key," said Stears.

"I will try and think," she said. "Though it is not a pleasant task."

"About fifteen more minutes," said Stears. Then, "Damn! What's this?"

Ahead, the Mercedes dove abruptly off the Autobahn onto a rural exit. There were no lights in the countryside around. Stears braked hard and followed. The Mercedes pulled away fast onto an undulating road, full of the smell of wet woods and fall.

"Shit," said Stears. "What the fuck is this?"

From now on their progress seemed illicit, furtive, rash. They swept from dark lanes into half-timbered villages deserted by night and ominously picturesque. As far as Stears could see they were hugging the line of the frontier, which here extended as a bay twenty kilometers into the East. A moon showed through patches in ragged clouds. They were in wooded valleys, sprinkled with meadows and streams. Nadermann drove fast, but flares of his brake lights at obscure crossings suggested uncertainty. It was just conceivable that they were still making for Eisenach by some wayward route for some elaborate purpose, but Stears could not see the point in it. When Renate said, "What are they doing?" he shook his head irritably. Wherever Nadermann was going, Stears suspected he was late.

Renate said, "He would never think someone could be more clever than himself."

"What?" said Stears.

"Krel. He thinks himself very wise."

"Well?" said Stears.

"I was just thinking. You asked me to."

They came to another dim village. Nadermann braked suddenly to a stop under a sign in front of lighted windows. Stears braked hard but stopped closer than he would have wished. The Mercedes had stopped outside the village inn, Der Schwarzer Schwann. Nadermann jumped out and crossed the sidewalk. *Contact! Reinforcements!* thought Stears. *Or just directions!* The blush of the third car's lights was still somewhere behind them, and in this still, cloudswept village in the mold of gables and black cats he was almost glad of it. Krel stayed in the car. The inn sign, black wings outstretched, flapped above him. Stears said to Renate, "The map! Give me the map!" But before he could open it Nadermann returned in haste, alone, and hurried into the car. *Just directions then*, thought Stears.

Now Nadermann drove confidently. They left the village by a

lane through farms, vaulted a humpbacked bridge, and drove into beech wood. The road curved and climbed. The third lights followed them to the lane but never crossed the bridge; either they were satisfied, or unwilling to see more, or some unknown arrangement was in force. Stears took his cue and dropped well back. He kept the headlights dimmed.

Two signs by the road, supporting brambles. *Achtung! Grenzgebiet.* Another, old and with a battered star: *Soviet Zone 2m. U.S. Forces proceed no further without authorization.*

Stears said, "So that's it, Jesus, that is really it. An illicit crossing. But, God almighty, why?"

Renate said, "So even Dr. Krel comes to that."

"He's come to it before," said Stears. "This is the return trip."

The Mercedes came out of the beech wood into a narrow valley of stony meadow. There was a stream beside the road. The clouds were running; the edge of one turned silver and then moonlight poured down. Straight across the valley, the fence rose up in the light, jet black but with rows of tiny jewels where the searchlights pierced it from behind. A guard tower stood to one side.

"Almost safe, Oswolt," said Nadermann. The pavement ran out, and they drove on the stony remnant of the road. "Do not worry, the police left us at the village. There is no one here but friends." A dim light showed in the guard tower. Nadermann said, "We are expected. We have been seen."

The track grew rougher. A hundred meters away, the frontier markers came into view, like toothpicks under the fence. Between the markers and the fence, the ground was bushy but not overgrown. Where the road had run, there was a gate in the fence sewn with barbed wire and with a searchlight focused on it.

Nadermann stopped the car. "Now it is yours, Oswolt," he said. From the bottom of the guard tower three black figures emerged and walked toward the gate. Rifle muzzles stuck up above the heads of two. The fence cut them from sight.

Nadermann said, "Follow the track straight to the gate. Don't wander. Stay away from any kind of wire. You will be let in at the gate. Don't touch the fence."

"I know all about the frontier," said Krel. "I am an expert in it."

"Of course," said Nadermann. But Krel did not move. He looked down at the dash into the glowing clock as a diver into a pool, then raised his eyes to the track undulating through the bushes toward the fence.

He said, "The police would not stop me tonight. You said that."

"That has been my guess," said Nadermann.

"Then why not a crossing in the ordinary way? Why a dark path through the mines?"

Nadermann said, "I could be wrong. If you were stopped by one officious functionary it might be the end." But Krel's face did not move, and he threw in, "The Americans have some residual authority at the frontier. The Four-Power Agreement."

Krel's face did not flicker. He gazed as into a microscope with the absorbed and incredulous look of a scientist with one short, mad surmise. He shook it off with the force of common sense.

He turned and took Nadermann's hand. "Thank you, Heinrich," he said.

"For nothing," said Nadermann. "Goodbye."

Krel got out of the car and carefully shut the door. Nadermann watched him recede down the path and saw the glow of the parking lights die on his back. He noted that his step was firm. He sighed with relief and began to watch the gate. They were not late. These were still the special guards.

When Stears saw the end of the wood and the road going straight ahead, he cut off the lights. The little valley with its fields and brook stretched a half kilometer before it was guillotined by the frontier. They could see the Mercedes in the middle of the track. Beyond it a square of light bloomed in the fence. They could see no one outside the car.

"That must be a gate," said Stears. "There aren't many." He drove quietly, hoping for surprise.

"Where's Dr. Krel?" said Renate.

"Probably still in the car. They've been here a couple of minutes at most."

They had not yet been seen.

When they were a hundred meters behind the Mercedes they saw Krel. The border markers were on a little ridge, and he came up out of the dark. He was carrying a small suitcase, and he stumbled now and then. It made him look weary, like an immigrant seeking lodging. The fence was still a hundred meters from him, over rougher ground.

Stears said, "Now or never. Get ready. Just try to stop him, even for a minute. Whatever you do, don't go past the markers." He coasted toward the Mercedes.

Krel reached the markers, and the crest of the little ridge. He walked through them without pausing, but after a few meters he set his suitcase on the ground and bowed his head. He looked ahead of him to where the track sank again into darkness. He slowly bent to pick the suitcase up.

Stears's car was not seen until Renate opened the door. A searchlight flared upon the car, but she was already out of it, running through the dark toward the markers. Nadermann started to open the door of his car and then reversed himself and sank down more deeply into the seat. Stears got out of the car and crouched outside the door.

Renate called as she ran, "Dr. Krel, don't do it. Come back." If her voice was convincing, she thought, it was only because she was out of breath.

Krel stood still and seemed to turn his head toward her voice. He stayed looking at the gate and then took a step backward toward the West.

From the fence came a voice, low but metallic, like a confidential insect's, a voice whispering through a bullhorn. "You are on the territory of the Democratic Republic. You need not fear interference. You are under our protection. Please come forward and be identified."

Krel turned and lifted his eyes to the Mercedes. It was dark and no sign came from it. Renate called again. "Dr. Krel, believe me. Come back."

Krel took a step toward the West.

The searchlight found Renate and settled on her face. She opened her mouth again, but Krel froze and stared at her and put his hands in front of his eyes. The insect voice came again: "You need not fear interference."

Krel turned again. He opened his hands and began to run toward the fence. He looked once over his shoulder toward Renate. He did not see the suitcase, stumbled over it, and fell in the shadow.

Stears got up from beside the car and ran to Renate. She said, "It didn't exactly work, did it?"

Krel got up. He scuttled along the path. From the fence, Renate heard a new noise, a metallic slide and clack, repeated twice. She saw the soldiers move.

She understood the sound and watched with a small smile, clamping her lips shut. Triumphant vengeance flowed down her spine. She felt herself breathe deep. She looked at Stears beside her. She thought he had not understood.

The moment passed and turned sickly. Krel's treachery had been cold and abstract as himself. She looked at Krel blundering toward the gate and then at Stears, who had a real mission and had saved her life. She drew in breath and shouted in a voice that surprised her by its strength, "Come back, you old fool!"

Krel turned his head. He was still forty meters from the gate. There was a voice from the gate, peremptory, not wheedling. The guards stepped forward. Renate called again.

From the markers, the burst of rifle fire looked surprisingly like a riot of firecrackers. Krel spun around as though his arms were caught in a gale, then fell like a sack. He fell into shadow. He disappeared.

There was silence. The Mercedes started up, made an orderly turn, and retreated in a dignified way down the valley. The officer stepped forward in the gate, opened a box full of keys, and began to fumble with old and balky locks.

There was an irregular, shuddering movement on the ground before the fence. Stears saw it and froze. Krel crawled out of the shadow. He was in the dust and seemed half blinded. His mouth was working and covered with dark froth. But he crawled. He crawled toward the West.

Stears looked at the guards. From behind the gate, they did not seem to see. Krel crawled with rasping noises from his lungs. They were loud to Stears, but perhaps the grating of the keys was louder. Krel was now about sixty meters from the fence. Not an entirely easy shot from behind it in bad light. But Krel was moving like a dying crab. He made a sound, conceivably words.

The officer pushed the gate, and it moved. Then stuck. The officer cursed and pulled at a padlock. He took another key out of the box.

The searchlight from the tower circled and pounced on Krel. He seemed to feel it and froze. He was not far from Stears and some seventy meters from the fence. The officer looked up and spoke and jerked at the lock.

Stears held out his hand and called to Krel. "Come, you can do it. You are safe with us." Krel seemed to make a last effort. Stears stepped a few meters within the markers. Krel was close.

A burst of fire came wide. Krel cowered, but the encircling light seemed to pain him more than the bullets, which he might not have registered. He looked into the dark beyond the path. Stears threw himself down but still moved toward him.

And suddenly Krel's face took on a muddled look as at a half-understood instruction or a vague hope. He dragged himself from the light, from the path, into the dark brush. He moved with a sudden surge of strength. He moved toward a bush as if toward a burrow.

Stears always said that the intuition struck him before the blast. The ground under Krel turned into a flower of flame, surrounded by intense black, which unfolded and bore Krel up before it hurled him forward. Earth rattled on Stears. The searchlight pinned him. He got to his knees and dashed the fifteen meters to the markers.

Krel was there first. His body lay across the line of striped stakes. Around him was a bitter smell of burning. His face was seared and looked behind him from a broken neck.

Stears picked himself up off the ground. He stood over Krel. The searchlight from the guard tower circled over and joined him, playing on the body, which was limp and twisted as a scorched rag. A movement in the guard tower caught Stears's eyes. A figure stood on the observation platform following the searchbeam with binoculars. The figure gestured to the officer by the gate and went back inside. The officer reclosed the gate and reset all the locks with care.